£1·50

The Faber Book of Cricket

The Faber Book of
CRICKET

Edited by
Michael Davie and
Simon Davie

faber and faber
LONDON · BOSTON

First published in 1987
by Faber and Faber Limited
3 Queen Square London WC1N 3AU
This paperback edition first published in 1989

Photoset by Wilmaset Birkenhead Wirral
Printed in Great Britain by
Mackays of Chatham PLC, Chatham, Kent
British Library Cataloguing in Publication Data
The Faber book of cricket.
1. Cricket — Literary collections
2. English literature
I. Davie, Michael   II. Davie, Simon
820.8′0355   PR1111.C6/

ISBN 0–571–15049–7

Contents

Introduction

The former literary editor of the *Observer* and translator of Proust, Terence Kilmartin, once found himself on a flight from London to Berlin sitting directly behind a man with the look of 'an Aztec eagle': Samuel Beckett. Kilmartin watched closely to see what the Nobel Prizewinner would read. Beckett took out a newspaper, ignored the front page and news pages, and turned directly to the sports pages, which he examined in detail, right down to the schools cricket results, all the way to Berlin.

Beckett, as I think I may have been the first person to point out, is the only Nobel Prizewinner for Literature to appear in *Wisden*. He played for Trinity College, Dublin, on a tour of England. Another Irish writer, James Stern, became a friend of Beckett's in Paris in the 1930s. When they met, they talked only about boxing and cricket, Stern told me not long ago. Stern never saw Beckett play, but feels he knows exactly how he bowled: slow right-arm 'tweakers', with a rather contorted action. Unfortunately, Beckett in his writings made no allusion to cricket; though he came near it with a reference to croquet in his novel *Molloy*, when he included in a list of 'tranquil sounds' the 'clicking of mallet and ball'.

Cricket writing falls into three categories: cricket reporting, which gives a direct account of a game or performer; writing about cricket – words assembled, as it were, in the study, in an attempt to evoke the game; and cricket described or referred to in the course of a larger literary effort.

Personally, I like the literary associations and have included as many of them as seemed prudent in this anthology. They dignify the enterprise. I was fleetingly taught Eng.Lit. by Edmund Blunden, my first encounter with a cricketer–poet. When I read an essay to him in his rooms at

Merton College, Oxford, he would make a few oblique comments and then very often, if the weather was fine, suggest that we took a bat and ball, which he kept handy, into Merton Garden. Blunden was a wicket-keeper; agile even in his forties; and, it goes without saying, embarrassingly keen. He was not a bowler, but he knew the principles of batsmanship and sometimes applied them, hitting his off drives (Hammond was his exemplar) down the avenue of limes towards the mulberry tree allegedly planted when Charles I made Merton his headquarters during the Civil War. I formed the impression that cricket for Blunden provided some sort of escape from his ever-present and haunting memories of the trenches in the First World War. Like almswomen, or a pike in a pool, it had been part of his Sussex village life before, aged seventeen, he went to the war. It represented a time of peace, which is why, I think, he was moved to produce his cricket book, *Cricket Country*, during the Second World War. While he was writing it I had a letter from him, when I was abroad and he was in charge of the Merton fire-watchers, in which he said he planned to visit Siegfried Sassoon at Heytesbury, and expected they would get a bat out, with the old roller acting as wicket and a horse at square leg. His passion survived the second war as well as the first. I recall a lunch at the *Times Literary Supplement* when the poet was observed to be acting strangely. He kept putting his head under the table. Eventually it became clear that he was listening, as often as he dared (he was a jumpy man), to a Test Match commentary being broadcast on the pocket radio he had brought to the lunch. For some reason Blunden never wrote a successful poem about cricket. He had, in my undergraduate eyes, too roseate a view of the game. On his mantelpiece he kept a torn-out newspaper photograph of Bradman shaking hands with Hutton at the Oval in 1938, when Hutton passed Bradman's highest individual test innings. Blunden regarded the photograph as proof that chivalry had survived. Hutton might have demurred, when Bradman unleashed Miller and Lindwall at him in 1948. Still, it was Blunden who silently implanted in me the governing principle of this anthology, which was summarized and made explicit years later in my hearing by Michael Melford of the *Daily Telegraph*: 'Cricket isn't a game,' said Melford, 'it's a way of life.' Blunden imagined that cricket had its origins in a boy swishing at cow-parsley with a stick, or a countryman throwing a turnip at a rat. Stick and turnip came together and cricket was born.

I blame the poet Blunden for the biases revealed in this anthology. For some reason connected with my recollection of him I am always pleased and surprised when a writer reveals a taste for the game. Alec Waugh, living in Tangier towards the end of his life, financed by his best-seller, *An Island in the Sun*, which was published fifty years after his other best-seller, *The Loom of Youth*, regretted only one circumstance of his life in Morocco: he missed his collection of *Wisden*s. P.G. Wodehouse on his ninetieth birthday, spent at his home on Long Island, interrupted work on his umpteenth novel, *Sunset at Blandings*, to confirm that Bertie Wooster's valet, Jeeves, was indeed named after P. Jeeves of Warwickshire, who helped the Players to beat the Gentlemen at the Oval in 1914 by taking four for 44 off 15 overs in the Gentlemen's second innings. Dr Wodehouse kept up with cricket by subscribing to *The Times* (regarding it as a symptom of American decline that the *New York Times* no longer printed the county cricket scores) and revealed that his favourite cricketer was Knott, the Kent and England wicket-keeper.

Wodehouse was in the Dulwich XI of 1899 and 1900. Unfortunately, no extended description of him on the field survives. This is a general gap in cricket literature: there are almost no descriptions of the writers in action. Wodehouse and Conan Doyle played in the same match at Lord's in 1910; but neither wrote an account of the other's play. How good was Neville Cardus? He was a professional at Shrewsbury, but we have to take his word for it that he was a useful bowler; and writers are unreliable witnesses to their own performances. Byron, for instance, exaggerated his scores against Eton, as Byron scholars represented here have shown. Tennyson may never have played at all, judging by his ill-informed description of a boys' knock-up in *The Princess*. James Joyce was clearly a fanatical follower of the game, at least as a youth: he implies as much in *A Portrait of the Artist as a Young Man*; and only a fanatic would have included the disguised names of thirty or so cricketers in a single passage, as Joyce did in *Finnegans Wake*. Besides, we have his brother's account of bowling to him. Stanislaus says 'Jim' was a useful bat; but that is all we know, despite the massive classic biography by Professor Ellmann (an American). I have heard that Harold Pinter, though he goes to nets in the winter and is always well-equipped, has trouble with his timing. Does anyone know anything about Charles Cowden Clarke as a player, or the Rev. John Mitford? Did Mary Russell Mitford play? Who would not swap half the literary criticism of the past two hundred years for a paragraph or two by contemporaries solving these conundrums?

If the first bias of this anthology is literary, the second is technical. Sir Donald Bradman's long analysis of how to play the pull shot – he played it 'to perfection', Sir Leonard Hutton has written – is so precise that he makes the reader feel he will, next time, perform the stroke almost as well as Bradman. Top-class cricketers possess an understanding of techniques that lesser cricketers can never attain, no matter how much cricket they watch. Ian Peebles's account of Barnes demonstrating his methods could not have been written by anyone below at least county standard. There is another regrettable gap in the literature about techniques. How exactly did the old bowlers manage to bowl so fast? Nothing that survives explains the phenomenon. The word 'catapultists' applied to the old fast bowlers explains nothing. We are told by Nyren that David Harris, the greatest Hambledon bowler, who was by all accounts very fast as well as accurate, forced the ball away from the level of his armpit; but again, no plausible image of the method emerges. Yet there can be no question about the speed of the old-timers. Squire Osbaldeston bowled so fast that he needed two longstops as well as a wicketkeeper.

I have another bias, which is against ghost-writers. We have included nothing that to our knowledge was written in someone else's name by a ghost-writer, though this rule is not as easy to apply as it sounds, since ghost-writers have been invisibly at large in cricket writing since the earliest days. How much of Nyren's masterpiece *The Cricketers of My Time* was Nyren, and how much was Charles Cowden Clarke, we shall never know. If it was mainly Cowden Clarke, then this is a rare instance of the presence of a ghost-writer being beneficent. Usually it is pernicious, stifling much more interesting cricket writing than it has produced.

I can prove this statement by an eminent example. I remember the first time I saw a ghost-writer at work. It was in the press box at Brisbane during the England tour of Australia by P.B.H. May's side of 1958–9. In front of me sat two figures, the first Sir Leonard Hutton, who was covering the tour for the London *Evening News*, and the second his ghost, an *Evening News* staff member named Julian Holland. Sir Leonard, like, I suppose, other great players, can watch a game through the back of his head. Even if he had his back turned when a wicket fell, he knew what had happened. Holland's interest in the cricket was variable. On this, my first sight of the pair, Holland was reading a book about T.S. Eliot which, like all books about Eliot, surely failed to provide any information about Eliot's cricketing experiences when he was a schoolmaster at Highgate School in north London. It is known that he tried to teach the boys baseball, which creates the presumption that he thought it a reasonable alternative to cricket. At stumps, Holland shut his book, inserted a sheet of carbon paper between two sheets of typing paper, and rolled the three sheets into his portable typewriter. Then he turned expectantly to Sir Leonard. Sir Leonard, a thoughtful man, would finally break his silence with a single comment. Bang went Holland's fingers on the keyboard and away he rattled for an entire page. Then he would roll the paper out of the machine and hand the sheets to Sir Leonard, who would separate them carefully, hand the carbon paper back to Holland, and place the two other sheets in separate piles. Holland would look sideways for another comment, and off would go the machine gun again, while Sir Leonard read through the page Holland had typed. So it went on until the piece was finished.

Later on the tour I found myself standing next to Sir Leonard, having a cup of tea during an interval. To my alarm and pride, he spoke to me, established my place of work (the *Observer*), and, after a pause, said: 'It's easy for you chaps.' What was the great man talking about, I wondered. 'I'm used to having a bat in my hands, you see.' My anxiety about being unable to follow his train of thought increased, 'You've got your typewriters. I haven't got anything.' At last I understood. Who, except Gibbon, can write in his head?

Next summer, in England, the *Observer* suggested to Sir Leonard that he should become a contributor, but on one condition: he must write every word of his own copy. We would make it easy for him: we would supply him with paper and pencil. He never looked back.

That experience makes me regret Arthur Porritt. He describes in this book what it was like to be ghost-writer to W.G. Grace. But suppose Grace had been given pencil and paper and inveigled or bribed into writing his own book? When Sir Donald Bradman covered the Australian tour of England for the *Daily Mail* in 1953, he was always the last to leave the press box – a perfectionist as usual. Reading him on the pull shot, one knows he wrote every word of it himself. It conveys, unconsciously, his whole attitude to the game. Books about cricket have poured out in recent decades. One of them, by a hard-pressed former Australian test player, was called *Perchance to Bowl*. Most of these books are intolerably dull because they are written by ghost-writers. Lillee was an exciting bowler; and, to judge by published interviews, an exciting talker. His book, *Lillee on Lillee*, was the dullest and least informative cricket book of the century.

Looking back over the literature, one has to say that a higher proportion of the old stuff than of the modern stuff has lasting value. The prose before the First World War was more robust, and the enthusiasm — an essential ingredient — more marked. People in the old days, I suppose, wrote cricket books because they could not help themselves. Reading the output of the late 1920s and early 1930s, the present-day browser in libraries begins to sense ambitious publishers behind the scenes, thinking up books aimed at a mass market. But most of the memorable writing is inspired by a love of the game, not a desire for profit. The snippets that make the hairs at the back of the neck stand on end, such as H.S. Altham's description of Bradman coming out to bat with the destiny of a Test Match in his hands, were not written with an eye to the cheque that would follow.

Themes recur. Complaints about falling standards, declining crowds, or too much cricket ebb and flow. Disputes of one sort or another have rent the game since early times. Nostalgia is pervasive; and between the wars often tipped over into mere sentimentality — as in many of the self-congratulatory fictional stories of the 1930s designed to show how gentle the game was, and how quintessentially English. Discussion of character has been part of cricket writing from the start, never better done than by Nyren. During the later nineteenth century for some reason this preoccupation rather faded away; it was revived most conspicuously by Cardus. Sheer invention played a part. Cardus imagined conversations with his heroes and, when challenged, replied that his cricketers might not have said the things he made them say, but they wished they had. This admission was not made while C.P. Scott was his editor. But Cardus used invention to enhance the character of the players he wrote about; a novelty of recent cricket writing is that it is more often used for purposes of denigration. Nowadays, few professional cricket writers have heroes.

Our principles of selection are reasonably straightforward. We have included the favourite texts that must form, and often have formed, the foundation of a cricket anthology: Mary Russell Mitford's village cricket match, Nyren, Mr Jingle's account of cricket in the West Indies, Francis Thompson's Hornby and Barlow poem, Cardus on the Old Trafford Test Match of 1902.

We have also included references to the principal landmarks of cricket history: the first code of laws in 1744; the introduction of round arm bowling; the coming of W.G. Grace; the 1932–3 bodyline series; the 1935 lbw laws; the Packer revolution; and – an event that will surely not prove ephemeral – the abrupt expulsion in November 1986 of Vivian Richards and Joel Garner from the Somerset county team.

We have made due obeisance to great cricketers: Old Clarke, David Harris, Grace, Ranjitsinhji, Bradman and others, including Botham.

We have applied one criterion to every extract: does it possess some special quality – a phrase, a joke, a surprise, a fact, the re-creation of an event – that makes it worth reading more than once? We have not included extracts from books, however well-known, or from authors, however famous, merely to protect ourselves from complaints. The book contains less poetry than we had originally expected. Much cricket poetry has been written, and almost all of it is disappointing. The couplet by John Masefield is included, it should be explained, because it is, in our opinion, the worst couplet ever written about cricket, even by a Poet Laureate.

One surprise about cricket literature is that although there are innumerable cricket anthologies, there are astonishingly few general anthologies: books that range over the whole history of cricket and contain both poetry and prose, short pieces and long, descriptions of matches as well as of players, and include overseas as well as domestic prose. Eric Parker's *Between the Wickets*, published in 1926, and Gerald Brodribb's more recent anthology are, we think, the best of our predecessors. (Alan Ross's justly popular *Cricket Companion* is a collection of long pieces, rather than a general anthology as defined above.) One marked difference between this book and others is that, perhaps because of the times we live in, it contains more violence. Cricket has never been a particularly gentle game, although one might think so to read some cricket writers. We have tried accordingly to reflect not only the disputes but also the broken heads. Nostalgia can turn to sadness. Gavin Ewart's striking recent poem – *The Sadness of Cricket* – is not merely sad but profoundly depressing.

One satisfactory coup is to have discovered the only sustained piece of prose ever written about cricket by Evelyn Waugh: an anonymous essay contributed to the *Cherwell* in 1923 when he was an undergraduate at Hertford College, Oxford. It has not been republished since then, though it has some significance for Waugh's biography. Both his father, the publisher Arthur Waugh, and his elder brother, Alec, were enthusiastic cricketers. They regarded the game as an important part of Englishness. This piece shows Evelyn in the act of turning against the whole world they stood for: the world symbolized by J.C. Squire, the leader of the literary establishment known as the 'Squirearchy', which was opposed in the 1920s to and by the Sitwells, T.S. Eliot and the cosmopolitan new friends that Evelyn had met at Oxford. Squire ran his own cricket team, the Invalids. Sometimes it contained Alec Waugh and Blunden; it is the side described in A.G. Macdonnell's *England, Their England*. The match in the Evelyn Waugh article may or may not have been an Invalids match; Evelyn certainly once played for Squire, since he mentions the fact in his diaries; he was caught second ball and dropped a catch, which may or may not have affected his development. At all events, his last anonymous paragraphs reflect exactly what he had come to dislike not only about his brother's cricketing outings but about Alec and Arthur Waugh's attitudes to life and art.

Having made our selections, we have had to decide how to present them to readers. Four methods are possible: chronological; alphabetical; cricketing categories ('great bowlers'); or abstract categories that relate as much to life in general as to cricket. Alphabetical is too arbitrary. Chronological is pedagogical and dull. Cricketing categories are too restricting for our purposes. We wanted to make plain cricket's connection with the rest of life. So we settled on mainly abstract categories. One advantage of this arrangement is that it produces and allows surprising conjunctions between different periods of cricket history.

MICHAEL DAVIE
February 1987

1300   The first probable reference to cricket in the wardrobe accounts of King Edward I. The locality was Newenden in Kent.

1598   Earliest definite reference to cricket. Manuscript preserved and in the possession of the Mayor and corporation of Guildford.
Giovanni Florio's Italian–English dictionary mentions cricket.

1653   Sir Thomas Urquhart, translating Rabelais, describes Gargantua as playing cricket.

1676   Henry Teonge makes the first reference to cricket abroad; he witnessed English residents playing at Aleppo in the Levant.

1706   Earliest description of a cricket match: by William Godwin, of Eton and King's College, Cambridge, in a Latin poem entitled 'In Certamen Pilae'.

1729   Date of earliest surviving bat. It belonged to John Chitty.

1744   First full description of a cricket match, Kent v. All England at the Artillery Ground by James Love in 'Cricket: an heroic poem'.
Members of the London Club draw up the first known Code of Laws.

1750–60 The Hambledon Club is founded.

1776   Third stump added to prevent the ball passing through the wicket.

1787	Thomas Lord opens his first ground on Dorset Fields and the MCC is formed by members of the White Conduit Club.
1805	First recorded Eton v. Harrow match. Byron was in the Harrovian team.
1806	First Gentlemen v. Players game, played at Lord's.
1814	Lord's moves to present site.
1833	*The Young Cricketer's Tutor* by Nyren published and dedicated to William Wordsworth.
1851	*The Cricket Field* by the Rev. James Pycroft published.
1859	Twelve professional cricketers embark for America on the first overseas tour of an English cricket eleven.
1862	The first four volumes of Arthur Haygarth's *Scores and Biographies* published, recording the full scores of matches from 1744 onwards.
1864	*Wisden Cricketers' Almanack* first published. W.G. Grace plays in his first first-class game and scores 170 and 56 not out. 'Overhand' bowling authorized.
1868	Australian Aboriginals tour England, the first overseas cricketers to visit England.
1882	The first Australian victory in a Test Match in England, by seven runs at the Oval. The 'Ashes' tradition created by a mock obituary in the *Sporting Times*.
1890	The Lancashire League formed.
1895	W.G. Grace scores his 100th century.

1917   Neville Cardus, aged 28, joins the *Manchester Guardian* as a reporter.

1921   *The Cricketer* founded by Pelham Warner.

1926   *A History of Cricket* by H.S. Altham published.

1927   Don Bradman's first Sheffield Shield game for NSW in which he scores 118.

1932–3 'Bodyline' tour of MCC to Australia.

1935   First 'ball-by-ball' commentary of a cricket match on the wireless.

1938   First television coverage of a cricket match: 2nd Test, England v. Australia at Lord's.

1938–9 The 'Timeless Test' between England and South Africa at Durban. Lasts ten days and remains unfinished because the English team have to leave to catch their boat home. Twelve new balls used.

1960–1 First tied Test Match: Australia v. West Indies in Brisbane.

1961   South Africa ceases to be a member of the Imperial Cricket Conference.

1963   Abolition of distinction between amateur and professional status.

1966   *World of Cricket* (general editor, E.W. Swanton) published.

1977   Formation of World Series Cricket by Kerry Packer.

1977–8 Australia v. West Indies; Graham Yallop wears the first helmet ever seen in a Test Match.

1978   The first WSC match to be played under floodlights at the Sydney Cricket Ground.

1986   Second tied Test Match in cricket history: Australia v. India in Madras.

THEORY

The instinct to throw and to hit is the basis of man's primitive armoury. Nature, of her bounty, has supplied him with an endless variety of missiles, of means of striking, and of marks, and, in her wisdom, has provided that what the man must do for life, the boy should attempt for fun. That is the genesis of cricket.

From time immemorial a ball has exercised an irresistible attraction on man. Five thousand years ago the Egyptian played ninepins; Nausicaa and her maidens were having fielding practice when Odysseus discovered himself to them; the Athenian boys, in the famous relief, are obviously 'bullying off' at hockey, and, if an ingenious textual conjecture is correct, Isocrates, the orator, played it too. Only pinkeye stayed Horace and indigestion Virgil from joining Maecenas in a ball game on the famous journey to Brundisium, and hurley was popular in Ireland before St Patrick came.

But though ball games have ever been pandemic, specialization seems to have set in from a very early date. The Eastern peoples took to hitting the ball with their familiar mall, or mallet, and it was from the East, and following on the Crusades, that polo reached Europe; from the Roman 'fives' (*pila palmaris*) developed all the varieties of racquet games with royal tennis, *jeu de paume*, at their head. But the northern branch of the Nordic family had a way of their own, and preferred to hit with that which it was second nature for them to carry, a staff or club, be it straight or 'crooked'.

This pastime of 'club-ball' was no doubt the generic ancestor of most of our English ball games. From that parent tree sprang, in different branches, the hockey group, in which the ball is driven to and fro; the golf group, in which it is hit towards a mark; and lastly, the cricket group, in which it, or

3

its equivalent, is driven away from the mark when in motion. This last category again subdivides according as the missile is set in motion by the striker himself, as in tip-cat, and trap-ball, or by the hand of a second player, as in cat and dog, stool-ball, and in cricket.

H.S. ALTHAM
A History of Cricket
(1926)

A Liberal Education

Mr Daft has requested me to write an introduction to the volume of his *Kings of Cricket*. It is an old saying that 'Good wine needs no bush', and I scarcely see how the remarks of one who is a living disproof of a maxim of Mr Daft's can help the cause of the game. 'Anyone ought to make himself into a fair player by perserverance', observed this authority. Alas! a long and bitter experience has taught me that there was one exception, at least, to a rule which observation convinces me is far from general. A cricketer is born, not made. A good eye and stout muscles are necessary: and though Mr Daft thinks highly of the intellectual element in cricket, it remains true that 'muscles make the man, not mind, nor that confounded intellect'.

As to intellect, it is not so very hard to invent 'head-balls'. After weeks of reflection, I once invented a 'head-ball' myself. First, you send your man a ball tossed rather high, but really pitched rather short. The batsman detects this, or if he does not and goes in to drive it, so much the better. If he does detect it, you follow it up by a ball really pitched up, but of the same height in curve as the former. The batsman plays back again, thinking it is the same ball, and usually makes a mistake. Such studies in the subjectivity of the batsman are easily elaborated in the closet, but when it comes to practice he usually hits across the hop of the first ball and drives the second over the pavilion. In consequence of these failures to make the means attain the end, I have never taken part in really first-class cricket – not beyond playing once for my college eleven. But one beauty of cricket is that, if you cannot play at it, you can at least look on and talk very learnedly, and find fault with the captain, showing how you would order matters if you were consulted. This is the recreation of middle age, and is permitted to an incapacity for actual performance which the audience never heard of or have had time to forget.

About Mr Daft's own play it is not possible, were it desirable, for me to offer criticism, as I never saw him save on one occasion. I had gone to Nottingham to view Gloucester-shire play Notts, as two Clifton boys, friends of mine, were playing for the western county. One of them was bowling, and it is not ungracious to say that he was far from being a colossus. As Mr Daft came in, one of the crowd observed: 'I would like to see the little 'un bowl Daft!' which surely was a chivalrous expression of an Englishman's preference for the weaker side. However, the prayer was scattered to the winds. The ball, too, visited the boundaries of the Trent Bridge ground, and Notts made over five hundred.

Though one did not see very much first-class cricket before 1874, the memories of what one has seen and read about abide among our most pleasant reminiscences. Cricket is among the few institutions in England which Time has not spoiled, nay, has rather improved. The wickets are better, immeasurably better than of old. The bowling is better, the fielding is as good as ever; probably the wicket-keeping is improved, and the general temper of players and spectators leaves nothing to be desired. A fine day at the Oval makes us all akin, and a pleasant sight it is to see the vast assembly, every man with his eyes riveted on the wicket, every man able to appreciate the most delicate strokes in the game, and anxious to applaud friend or adversary. An English cricketing crowd is as fair and as generous as any assembly of mortals may be. When the Australians defeat us, though we do not like it, we applaud them till these bronzed Colonists almost blush. It is not so in all countries, nor in all countries is there the ready acceptance of the umpire's verdict, without which cricket degenerates into a wrangle.

Mr Daft is not inclined to believe that the veterans of a middle-aged man's youth were inferior to the heroes of our later day. With Dr W.G. Grace, indeed, no man competes or has competed. The hardness and the subtlety of his hitting and placing of the ball, his reach and certainty at such a field as point, and the sagacious perseverance which he displays as a bowler, combine to make him unique – 'W.G.' – a name to resound for ages.

There is something monumental in his stance at the wicket, wholly free from a false refinement, without extraneous elegancies. His is a nervous, sinewy, English style, like that of Fielding. Better graced cricketers we may have seen, such as Mr Edward Lyttelton, Mr Charles Studd, Mr A.G. Steel, all of them, in their day, models of classical dexterity and refinement. But it is always, or almost always, Dr W.G. Grace's day: his play is unhasting, unresting like the action of some great natural law. With him, then, nobody can compare; and we who have seen may report to the age unbred that ere they were born the flower of cricket had blossomed. Nevertheless, methinks that even before Fuller Pilch and Clarke, there had been very great cricketers, who, could they return in their prime, after a few weeks' practice might match our best.

Aylward, of Hampshire, must have been a truly sterling batsman. Lambert may also be reckoned among the immortals, and it is highly probable that David Harris, on those wickets which he knew how to prepare, would puzzle even men like Shrewsbury.

In those days the bowler laid out his wicket to suit himself. None of us now living can equal the old underhand bowling, which, in some mysterious way, was delivered high, from under the armpit, got up very fast and erect from the pitch, and was capable of many changes of curve and pitch. Brown, of Brighton, and others, appear to have bowled underhand as fast, or faster, than Tarrant, or Jackson, or Mr Cecil Boyle.

This seems quite probable. Perhaps the swiftest bowling I ever saw was the underhand of a fast roundhand bowler, now in Canada, and at no time known to fame. He is a clergyman of the Scottish church, the 'Jointer', so styled of yore. 'He says he's a meenister, he says he's a beginner; I think he's a leear,' observed the caddie, when asked, at golf, who this gentleman might be. Hail, Jointer, across the wide seas and the many years, I salute thee. *Bayete!* as the Zulu says.

Now, allowing for odd wickets, and for the peculiarities of very fast underhand with a high delivery, it seems likely, that, on an old Hampshire wicket, Nyren's team might have tackled as good an eleven as we moderns could send to meet them. In the fields of asphodel (which, of course, would need returfing), some such game may be played by heroes dead and gone.

But in this world one can never thus measure strength any more than we can judge of old actors, and compare Molière to Garrick, and Garrick to Monsieur Poquelin. The cricketer, unlike the actor, leaves something permanent – his scores; but we cannot discover the true equation, as the different conditions cannot be estimated. Thus in golf, a round of 94, on St Andrews Links, in 1761, with feather balls, and unkempt putting greens, and whins all over the links, is surely, at least as good as Hugh Kirkcaldy's round of 73 today, now that the iron age has come in, and the baffy spoon exists only as venerable relic. Men's thews and skill have ever been much on a level.

It is the conditions that alter, and all old cricketers will believe in the old heroes of the past. To do so is pleasant, pious, and provides a creed not to be shaken by criticism. We who remember Carpenter and Hayward, Caffyn and H.H. Stephenson, are not to be divorced from these idols. They wore 'billy-cock' hats (the true word is 'bully-cock') and oddly-coloured shirts, and blue belts with snake clasps, and collars and neckties, as their great-grandfathers had worn jockey caps and knee-breeches, and their fathers tall hats. But these were unessential details.

The style in bowling of that age – Caffyn's age – with a level arm, was peculiarly graceful. The command of the ball was less than at present. Peate's delivery was level, or nearly level; yet his dexterity was unsurpassed. The most favourable admirers can hardly call Mr Spofforth's style a model of grace. It has withal a something truculent and overbearing. Yet, on the modern wickets, bowling needs every fair advantage that it can obtain, and throwing has gone distinctly out of favour. I remember an excellent cricketer and most successful bowler, concerning whom I chanced to remark to a friend that I thought him quite fair. 'I think him a capital man to have on our side', was the furthest to which my companion's lenity of judgement would stretch. Probably no bowler throws consciously, but it was certainly high time that umpires should bring some fast bowlers to the test of an objective standard.

When roundhand bowling came in, the veteran Nyren declared that all was over with the game; that it would become a mere struggle of physical force. But, for this once, pessimism was mistaken, and prophecy was unfulfilled. Still there was the grace of a day that is dead in the old level deliveries, while some slinging bowlers, of whom Mr Powys, I think, was the last, could be extremely dangerous, if occasionally erratic. The regrets of him who praises times past are natural, but are tempered.

As for the present day, we are all tired – Mr Daft is tired – of the Fabian policy which leaves balls to the off alone, in a scientific cowardice. Once Mr Ernest Steel, then by no means a big boy, playing for Marlborough, at Lord's, taught a

Rugby boy the unwisdom of this course. He bowled two balls to the off which were left alone; the third looked like them, but broke viciously, was left alone, and down went the off stump. This was not in first-class cricket, but it was a pleasant thing to see and remember. Many such pleasant memories recur to an old spectator.

There was Ulyett's catch, at Lord's, when the gigantic Mr Bonnor drove a ball to the off, invisible for its speed, and the public looked to see where the ring would divide. But the ball was in Ulyett's hands. There was Mr A.J. Webbe's catch of Mr Edward Lyttelton, who had hit a ball, low and swift as a half-topped golf ball, to the ropes. Running along the ropes, Mr Webbe caught it, low down, at full speed, a beautiful exhibition of graceful activity. Pindar would have commemorated it in an ode, and Dioscorides in a gem. Mr G.F. Grace's catch, under the pavilion at the Oval, I had not the fortune to witness, but Mr Gale has described it in impassioned prose.

Then there was Mr Steel's bowling, in his youthful prime, a sad sight for Oxford eyes, when the ball seemed alive and unplayable.

Mr Berkeley's bowling at Lord's, in 1891, at the end of the second Cambridge innings, was also a thing to dream upon, when for a moment it seemed as if the glories of Mr Cobden were to be repeated; but Mr Woods was there! As to Mr V.T. Hill's innings, in 1892, I cannot speak of it in prose.

Mr Daft has not dwelt much on University cricket, the most powerfully exciting to the spectator whose heart is in the right place (not unfrequently 'in his mouth') when we wait for a catch to come to hand.

The memories of old players in these affairs – Mr Mitchell, Mr Ottaway, Mr Yardley, Mr Steel, Mr Kemp (who won matches by sheer pluck and force of character), are fragrant and immortal. There is no talk, none so witty and brilliant, that is so good as cricket talk, when memory sharpens memory, and the dead live again – the regretted, the unforgotten – and the old happy days of burned out Junes revive. We shall not see them again. We lament that lost lightness of heart, 'for no man under the sun lives twice, outliving his day', and the day of the cricketer is brief. It is not every one who can go on playing, 'once you come to forty years', like Mr Daft and Dr W.G. Grace; the eye loses its quickness. An old man at point must be a very courageous old man; the hand loses its cunning, the ball from the veteran fingers has no work nor spin, and the idea of throwing in 'from the country' is painfully distasteful. Dr E.M. Grace, of course, is not old; he reckons not by years. Fortunately, golf exists as a solace of old age, and trout can always be angled for; and to lose a trout is only loss, not 'infinite dishonour', like missing a catch.

Cricket is a very humanizing game. It appeals to the emotions of local patriotism and pride. It is eminently unselfish; the love of it never leaves us, and binds all the brethren together, whatever their politics and rank may be. There is nothing like it in the sports of mankind. Everyone, however young, can try himself at it, though excellence be for the few, or perhaps not entirely for the few. At Nottingham, during the practice hour, how many wonderfully good bowlers you see, throwing off their coats and playing without even cricket shoes. How much good cricket there is in the world!

If a brief and desultory sermon may end with a collection, as is customary, I would fain ask cricketers to remember the London Playing Fields Committee, and send their mites to provide the grounds for those eager young players who draw their wickets with chalk on the wall, or bowl at a piled heap of jackets. Their hearts are in the right place, if their wickets are not, and we can help to get them better grounds. Many good cricketers are on the Committee of the Playing Fields. I believe a cheque to Mr Theodore Hall, Oxford and Cambridge Club, Pall Mall, will go to the right place also. So pay up, that young town-bred boys may play up, ye merry men of England.

Cricket ought to be to English boys what Habeas Corpus is to Englishmen, as Mr Hughes says in *Tom Brown*.

At no ruinous expense, the village cricket might also be kept alive and improved; for cricket is a liberal education in itself, and demands temper and justice and perseverance. There is more teaching in the playground than in school-rooms, and a lesson better worth learning very often. For there can be no good or enjoyable cricket without enthusiasm – without sentiment, one may almost say: a quality that enriches life and refines it; gives it, what life more and more is apt to lose, zest.

Though he who writes was ever a cricketing failure, he must acknowledge that no art has added so much to his pleasures as this English one, and that he has had happier hours at Lord's, or even on a rough country wicket, than at the Louvre or in the Uffizi. If this be true of one, it is probably true of the many whose pleasures are scant, and can seldom come from what is called culture.

Cricket is simply the most catholic and diffused, the most innocent, kindly, and manly of popular pleasures, while it has been the delight of statesmen and the relaxation of learning. There was an old Covenanting minister of the straitest sect, who had so high an opinion of curling that he said if he were to die in the afternoon, he could imagine no better way than curling of passing the morning. Surely we may say as much for cricket. Heaven (as the bishop said of the strawberry) might doubtless have devised a better diversion, but as certainly no better has been invented than that which grew up on the village greens of England.

ANDREW LANG
Introduction to Richard Daft's *Kings of Cricket*
(1893)

The Influence of Lunch

Volumes might be written on the cricket lunch and the influence it has on the run of the game; how it undoes one man, and sends another back to the fray like a giant refreshed; how it turns the brilliant fast bowler into the sluggish medium, and the nervous bat into the masterful smiter.

On Mike its effect was magical. He lunched wisely and well, chewing his food with the concentration of a thirty-three-bites a mouthful crank, and drinking dry ginger-ale. As he walked out with Joe after the interval he knew that a change had taken place in him. His nerve had come back, and with it his form.

P.G. WODEHOUSE
Psmith in the City
(1910)

Barnes the Pioneer

I am willing to bet if you made a census of competent opinion on who is the greatest bowler of the last century, over 90 per cent would unhesitatingly reply, 'Barnes'. As late as 1929, when he had reached the age of fifty-seven, the South African team, having suffered enjoyably at his hands, were agreed he was still the best in England.

Barnes was a pioneer, just as W.G. and Bosanquet, with the difference that, although he must have attracted many imitators, he has not yet found a successor. He started his career as a fast bowler of beautiful action if no other outstanding merit, but characteristically he very soon discovered exactly what he wanted to achieve and started working towards it.

With what curiosity must he regard the modern school,

whose almost universal tendency is to make the ball come *in* to the batsman. For him the wheel must have turned full circle. When he started, as a fast bowler for Warwickshire, all were aware that the most dangerous ball was that which went away from the bat, yet the prevailing cult was the break-back, erroneously called 'body spin', in the case of the fast bowler and the off-break in the medium-paced classes. The left-hander and the slow leg-break bowler alone made the ball break away, and, the outswinger being a very occasional phenomenon, no bowler of pace made the ball run towards the slips.

Barnes, having pondered these factors, came to the conclusion that this could only be achieved at any real speed by bowling the leg-break in the same manner as the off-break; that is without the rotation of the bent wrist. Endowed with every physical requirement, he set about delivering the leg-break at quick-medium pace with the wrist straight and the palm of the hand towards the batsman. The advantages of this mode are obvious, but Barnes spent some years experimenting before, as he says, it came to him quite suddenly. It was rather as though he had penetrated the sound barrier, as from then on he encountered no further difficulties, the question then resolving itself into one of refinement and application.

This technique must not be confused with that of the modern cutter, which is to flip the fingers over the surface of the ball and impart enough spin to give the ball a little bias in advantageous conditions. Barnes gripped the ball firmly between first and third fingers and *spun* it. Possibly cutters have produced as good a delivery on occasions, but for consistent effect on all surfaces his method has never been equalled. The leg-break was the keystone of the attack, but it was, of course, combined with every refinement of flight, change of pace, life, and accuracy.

There came at a later date the swerver, who in given conditions could produce somewhat similar results. The swerver should never be underrated, as in his greatness, exemplified by Maurice Tate, he could produce the unplayable ball and that with disconcerting frequency. In the 1930s there were many very capable exponents, but now it seems that the outswerver has largely disappeared, and the inswing and off-break bowlers are all-powerful.

Even the best swerver, however, is dependent on a number of elements beyond his control, such as the state of the ball, the humidity of the atmosphere, and the greenness of the pitch. He cannot therefore produce his effects so consistently as the man who achieves them purely by his own manipulations. Barnes's spin was equally potent with an old ball in any weather.

It is natural that one who could achieve such power from a theoretical start would exploit it with an unusual intelligence. Aubrey Faulkner, who presented as sound a defence as any batsman, had an illustrative tale of the craft and resource that lay behind those superb mechanics. Like his team mates Aubrey had a pretty rough passage with Barnes on the wet wickets of 1912, but at the Oval Test Match he became entrenched. At the end of an hour he had made no more than 10 but, as the Army says, 'time spent in reconnaissance is seldom wasted', and he reckoned he had seen the whole bag of tricks. Great was his astonishment when he received a rank long-hop. Greater was his consternation when he picked up the bat to give full rein to his favourite hook and saw his middle stump shoot out of the ground. It had been a long-hop all right, but just about twice as quick as anything before it.

It was apropos of this period of Barnes's career that I heard the sincerest compliment a rival genius could accord him. Many years ago a dinner party took place at Oxford. The hosts were Pat Kingsley, who captained the Varsity side that year, the Nawab of Pataudi, and myself. The guests were Charlie Macartney, Bert Oldfield, and Clarrie Grimmett. In that company it could hardly have been otherwise than an enthralling evening, and as it wore on the talk, surprisingly enough, turned to cricket and thence to Syd Barnes. He was at that time, to me, a legendary figure whom I had never seen nor met, and I asked Charlie Macartney just how good he was. The 'Governor General' wrinkled his brow and paused in careful thought before replying without trace of affectation.

He said, 'I'll tell you how good he was. In 1912 as I went out to bat I told the chaps I was going to hit this Barnes for six.' He paused again to give full weight to the point before adding, 'I had to wait until I was 68 before I did.'

IAN PEEBLES
Talking of Cricket
(1953)

Herby Taylor Masters Barnes

'Barnes [Herby Taylor said] was a marvellous bowler. He bowled leg-breaks and off-spinners at about the same medium pace as Bill O'Reilly did for Australia years later. He could also roll one for a top-spinner that was very difficult to detect. In fact, in 1912 we just never saw it. In addition Syd often opened the bowling and he used to swing the new ball away from the right-handed batsmen at more or less the same speed as Eddie Barlow does these days.

'On English wickets he was a real terror but I had a lot of experience batting against googly bowlers and I'd learnt to watch a bowler's finger movements as he delivered the ball. This made me quite confident that I would be able to handle Barnes under South African conditions.

'I made no secret of the fact that I was looking forward to batting against him on matting wickets, but I doubt very much if anybody took me seriously. In those days you only had to mention Barnes's name to have batsmen scurrying for cover.

'Overemphasis on forward play and poor footwork contributed to many a batsman's downfall against Barnes, but he was nevertheless the finest bowler I ever saw.'

15

In the 1913–14 season, J.W.H.T. Douglas brought an MCC side to South Africa. After missing the first two matches because of illness, Barnes began a personal reign of terror. Against admittedly minor opposition he produced match figures like 7 for 11 in 10 overs, 9 for 57 and 13 for 48 and by the time the first Test rolled along in Durban he had the Springboks fearing the worst.

Not without reason either. He had them mesmerized from the start – except for small, slightly-built, hawk-faced Herby Taylor.

He was absolutely determined to show that Barnes was not unplayable after all and this he proved in what must rate with the great innings of all time.

'I played Barnes the way I did those magnificent googly bowlers Vogler, Schwartz, Faulkner, and White when I first came into first-class cricket,' he remembers. 'I kept my eyes glued to the ball in his hand as he ran up to the wicket. And just before he delivered it I would switch my eyes to about a yard above his head to catch any finger movement as the ball left his hand. It was no use picking up the ball after it has left the hand of a bowler like Barnes because you would have no idea of what it would do off the pitch.

'Once I knew what sort of delivery it was going to be it was a case of forward to the ball you can meet and back to the ball you can't. Of course, you have to be quick with your footwork but what I have told you now is the really very simple secret of batting.'

It certainly worked against Barnes on that humid December day in Durban, fifty-eight years ago.

Springbok wickets were tumbling with nerve-shattering regularity, but Taylor never faltered. With machine-like precision, he reduced Barnes to the ranks of the mere mortals. Finally, the Springboks were all out for 182, of which 109 came from Taylor's bat. What is more, Barnes did not even have the satisfaction of taking his wicket. He was out caught Strudwick off Douglas.

An indication of how completely Taylor dominated the South African innings is the fact that Dave Nourse, with 19, was second top-scorer and Baumgartner, with 16, was the only other Springbok to get double figures.

In spite of Taylor's brilliance, it was still Barnes who wrecked the South African innings. He took 5 for 57 in 19.4 overs and when England went on to score 450 runs it was obvious that they would win. In the second innings, it was Barnes's turn to win the duel against Taylor and the Springboks folded for only 111 runs. Barnes again took 5 wickets, this time for 48 runs.

LOUIS DUFFUS
Giants of South African Cricket
(1971)

Challenge to Bowlers

You have all heard about the mythical bowler who could pitch the ball on a sixpenny piece. Well, I ask how many of you imagine you could drop the ball on an unfolded newspaper laid on the wicket where a good length pitches? 'Pooh!', I can hear you saying, 'that is child's play.' Well, try and do it. Take any newspaper – the bigger the better – and open the first sheet (first and last pages) and spread it lengthwise down the wicket.

You will tear your hair when you find out how many times you can miss it. I challenge all bowlers – Woolley, Rhodes, Parkin, Cook, Kennedy, the more the merrier – I challenge 'em all to hit the paper. But bowling at a mark on the wicket – even if it is only imaginary – improves the length wonderfully. Never bowl without an objective.

CECIL PARKIN
Cricket Reminiscences
(1923)

17

'It was no joke', said the old man, 'to play without pads and gloves on a bumpy down against quick bowling. We had first to look after our wickets, for many men would bowl (which word he pronounces as "owl") thirty-nine balls out of forty straight to the wicket; and then you must remember that there were as many kinds of underhand bowling as there are now of round. One man would turn his wrist with his thumb right out; another would do precisely the reverse. One would run with his right hand up in the air and bring it down with a swing, like the fan of a windmill; and another – Lambert, the little farmer, for instance – would send them in with his hand almost on the ground, and yet pitch a good length. Some bowlers turned the elbow out, like old Clarke, of Nottingham, and bowled four balls of a different pitch and spin all pretty lengths, one just out of your reach, another a regular tice.

'Then, sir, you must remember the rough ground which made the long hops so difficult. First you had to mind the shooter, and if the ball pitched short and rose she would be on your knuckles, and if you played her back, point had a rare chance of taking her almost off the bat, if she popped up. And what was a man to do with a ball full pitch, all the way straight from the bowler's hand to the bails? One did not like to block it, and if you hit her you could only do it with a cross bat, and the chances were that she went up, and if she did, it wasn't often that she would be missed; for don't you see, sir, men practised catching then as much as they do batting now, and when a match was over they stood round and tried how far they could throw and catch.

'We used to get our runs mostly by draws, little tips in the slips, and hard driving on or off.

'If the ground was hard and the ball not likely to shoot, every over-pitched ball was hit right away – a ball which might or might not take the inner stump, if only half-wicket high, would be met with a straight bat, with the pod slanted a little from the wicket and drawn behind, or if to the off, dropped in the slips; and with a good partner backing up either of those hits would generally be worth one run – as the watches were placed deep – and if not within the fieldman's reach they might be worth four or five; for, remember, sir, we played mostly on large unenclosed grounds.'

Bowyer says, as a rule, there was not much cutting or hitting to cover point in the days of underhand bowling, though he bears witness to the hard cutting of Beldham, Lord Frederick Beauclerk, and Tom Shearman. Mr Ward and Mr E.H. Budd were tremendous hard hitters, and used to knock Lord Frederick Beauclerk's slows to pieces, which made him very angry. Lord Frederick, he says, liked everything his own way, and was very cross with the players if anything went wrong; but he was a fine cricketer, and a good judge of the game.

FREDERICK GALE
Echoes from Old Cricket Fields
(1871)

Old-fashioned Underhand Bowling

Among batsmen who played against all the old bowlers there was and is a consensus of opinion that 'Old Clarke', who made as many wise saws as John Franklin of pious memory was the best underhand bowler they ever met, and that Mr V.E. Walker came next to him – and by no means *longo intervallo*. Clarke's great points were extreme accuracy of pitch, which has been described as irritating; a subtle variation of pace, and a profound knowledge of human nature, which was never better shown than by his custom of preying upon the terrors of his victims by making caustic and cocksure remarks about what he would do with them when he had them in front of him. His great failing was that he could not field his own bowling very well.

When the performances of Mr Walker and Old Clarke have been compared a most important consideration seems to have been always overlooked. But Thoms, who as a member of Clarke's All-England Eleven had as many opportunities of studying his methods as he had afterwards of studying those of Mr Walker, did not fail to notice this consideration, which was that when Clarke's reputation was at its highest the conditions were very different from those which obtained when Mr Walker was in his prime. 'Clarke had an immense advantage over Mr Walker,' said Thoms to me, 'for when he was enjoying his summer-time he had to bowl to fast-footed batsmen. It was considered *infra dig.* to go out to him, although many men knew well enough that it would be the best way to play him. I remember that Joe Guy said to me, "I could do the jump right enough, but they don't like you to do it." Whereas when Mr Walker was at his best all this had been altered. Just think what a vast difference this means to a bowler! What took the stuffing out of Old Clarke was the way in which Julius Cæsar and one or two others stepped out to him, and knocked him all over the place.'

W.A. BETTESWORTH
The Walkers of Southgate
(1900)

Theorists

Cricket is full of theorists who can ruin your game in no time.

IAN BOTHAM
Ian Botham on Cricket
(1980)

The First Code of the Laws (1744)

Several transcripts exist of this code, which was drawn up by and for the London Club, which played at the Artillery Ground, and issued as a pamphlet in 1755. The version below is taken from *Lillywhite's Scores and Biographies*, vol. 1 (1862).

'THE GAME OF CRICKET AS SETTLED BY Y^e
CRICKET CLUB
AT Y^e STAR AND GARTER IN PALL MALL

'The pitching ye first Wicket is to be determined by ye cast of a piece of Money   When ye first Wicket is pitched and ye popping Crease Cut which must be exactly 3 Foot 10 Inches from ye Wicket ye Other Wicket is to be pitched directly opposite at 22 yards distance and ye other popping crease cut 3 Foot 10 Inches before it   The Bowling Creases must be cut in a direct line from each stump   The Stumps must be 22 Inches long and ye Bail 6 Inches   The Ball must weigh between 5 and 6 Ounces   When ye Wickets are both pitched and all ye Creases Cut The party that wins the toss up may order which side shall go in first at his Option

'LAWS FOR Y^e BOWLERS 4 BALLS AND OVER.
'The Bowler must deliver ye Ball with one foot behind ye Crease even with ye Wicket and When he has Bowled one Ball or more shall Bowl to ye number 4 before he Changes Wickets and he Shall Change but once in ye Same Innings. He may order ye Player that is in at his wicket to Stand on which side of it he Pleases at a reasonable distance   If he delivers ye Ball with his hinder foot over ye Bowling crease ye Umpire Shall Call no Ball though she be Struck or ye Player is Bowled out Which he shall do without being asked and no Person shall have any right to ask him

21

'If ye Wicket is bowled down its out   If he Strikes or treads down or falls himself upon ye wicket in Striking [but not in over running] its out   A Stroke or Nip over or under his Batt or upon his hands [but not arms] if ye Ball be held before She touches ye Ground though She be hugged to the Body its out   If in Striking both his feet are over ye popping Crease and his Wicket put down except his Batt is down within its out   If he runs out of his Ground to hinder a Catch its out   If a Ball is nipped up and he Strikes her again Wilfully before she comes to ye Wicket its out.   If ye Players have crossed each other he that runs for ye Wicket that is put down is out   If they are not Crossed he that returns is out   If in running a Notch ye Wicket is struck down by a Throw before his Foot Hand or Batt is over ye Popping crease or a Stump hit by ye Ball though ye Bail was down its out But if ye Bail is down before he that catches ye Ball must strike a Stump out of ye Ground Ball in Hand then its out   If ye Striker touches or takes up ye Ball before she is lain quite still unless asked by ye Bowler or Wicket-keeper its out.

'BATT FOOT OR HAND OVER Y^e CREASE.

'When ye Ball has been in Hand by one of ye Keepers or Stopers and ye Player has been at home He may go where he pleases till ye next Ball is bowled   If Either of ye Strikers is crossed in his running Ground designedly, which design must be determined by the Umpires   NB The Umpires may order that notch to be Scored   When ye Ball is hit up either of ye strikers may hinder ye catch in his running Ground or if She is hit directly across ye Wickets ye Other Player may place his Body any where within ye Swing of his Batt so as to hinder ye Bowler from catching her, but he must neither Strike at her nor touch her with his hands   If a striker nips a Ball up just before him he may fall before his Wicket, or pop down his Batt before Shee comes to it to Save it   The Bail hanging on one stump though ye Ball hit ye Wicket its not out.

'LAWS FOR WICKET KEEPERS.

'The Wicket Keepers shall stand at a reasonable distance behind ye Wicket and shall not move till ye Ball is out of ye Bowler's Hands and shall not by any noise incommode ye Striker and if his hands knees foot or head be over or before his Wicket though the Ball hit it, it shall not be out.

'LAWS FOR Y^e UMPIRES.

'To allow 2 Minutes for each man to come in when one is out, and 10 Minutes between Each Hand   To mark ye Ball that it may not be changed   They are sole judges of all outs and ins, of all fair and unfair Play of frivolous delays, of all hurts whether real or pretended and are discretionally to allow what time they think Proper before ye Game goes on again   In case of a real hurt to a Striker they are to allow another to come in and the Person hurt to come in again But are not to allow a fresh Man to Play on either side on any Account   They are sole judges of all hindrances, crossing ye Players in running and Standing unfair to Strike and in case of hindrance may order a Notch to be Scored   They are not to order any man out unless appealed to by one of ye Players   These Laws are to ye Umpires Jointly   Each Umpire is ye Sole Judge of all Nips and Catches Ins and outs good or bad runs at his own Wicket and his determination shall be absolute and he shall not be changed for another Umpire without ye Consent of both Sides   When ye 4 Balls are Bowled he is to call over   These Laws are Separately   When both Umpires shall call Play 3 Times 'tis at ye Peril of giving ye Game from them that refuse Play.'

23

A Notion of Happiness

The omnibus driver informed us that he had backed the Surrey Eleven last year, owing to the report of a gentleman bowler, who had done things in the way of tumbling wickets to tickle the ears of cricketers. Gentleman batters were common: gentleman bowlers were quite another dish. Saddlebank was the gentleman's name.

'Old Nandrew Saddle?' Temple called to me, and we smiled at the supposition of Saddlebank's fame, neither of us, from what we had known of his bowling, doubting that he deserved it.

'Acquainted with him, gentlemen?' the driver inquired, touching his hat. 'Well, and I asks why don't more gentlemen take to cricket? 'stead of horses all round the year! Now, there's my notion of happiness,' said the man condemned to inactivity, in the perpetual act of motion; 'cricket in cricket season! It comprises – count: lot's o' running, and that's good; just enough o' taking it easy, that's good; an appetite for your dinner, and your ale or your port, as may be the case, good number three. Add on a tired pipe after dark, and a sound sleep to follow, and you say good morning to the doctor and the parson; for you're in health body and soul, and ne'er a parson'll make a better Christian o' ye, that I'll swear.'

As if anxious not to pervert us, he concluded: 'That's what *I* think, gentlemen.'

Temple and I talked of the ancient raptures of a first of May cricketing day on a sunny green meadow, with an ocean of a day before us, and well-braced spirits for the match.

GEORGE MEREDITH
The Adventures of Harry Richmond
(1871)

The Pull Shot

When I was very young and just beginning to learn the rudiments of the game, I was compelled by circumstances to play most of my cricket on concrete pitches covered with coir matting.

As anyone with experience on them knows, these pitches give rise to a more uniform but much higher bounce than turf.

I was very short and consequently found great difficulty in playing with a straight bat the ball pitched short of a length on the stumps. It came too high for comfort. Remember, I was a schoolboy and often faced the bowling of grown men.

To overcome this predicament, I developed the pull shot to a marked degree.

It simply consisted of going back and across with the right foot and pulling the ball with a horizontal bat somewhere between mid-on and square leg.

Because of my grip I was able to roll the wrists over as the stroke was played and keep the ball on the ground. Keen eyesight was needed, and one had to be careful the ball did not keep low, but this seldom happened on the coir mats.

After arriving in Sydney and commencing my career on turf, I began exploiting the same shot.

Now turf is much more uncertain than concrete and I began to lose my wicket occasionally because the greater speed and lower bounce of the ball off turf sometimes caused me to hit over the ball and be bowled or lbw. When that happened the shot looked a real haymaker and I am sure this, above anything else, gave rise to the story that I played with a cross bat.

Actually, there is no other way to play the pull shot than with a cross bat, but on turf greater judgement is required and the stroke must be used more sparingly.

I was counselled by many older players to give it up. They said it was too risky. But I was loath to do so because I felt sure it would bring me lots of runs, providing it was used with discretion.

A medium-pace bowler quite often operates without a fieldsman between mid-on and square leg, and this huge unprotected area is most inviting. Even if a man is stationed there, one has plenty of room on either side.

Slow bowlers usually have a man or two on the fence, but a pull shot can be played with very great power and it can be placed with precision so that there may still be a reasonable hope of getting four runs.

No batsman should attempt to pull a ball which is over-pitched or of good length. This is courting disaster.

However, assuming the ball to be the right sort, the method is very similar to the hook shot.

Go back and across with the right foot so that the right toe is pointing almost straight down the pitch towards the bowler. Then as the ball comes along (normally knee to stomach high) pull it hard to mid-wicket – at the same time pivoting the body and rolling the wrists over to keep the ball on the ground. In many respects the movement is similar to a square cut, but instead of cutting against the line of flight, you pull with it.

In order to control the shot and to have the best chance of combating any uneven bounce, it is essential to pivot the body and to get the legs fairly well apart...

If my batting was known for any one particular shot, this was it, mainly because of (a) the frequency with which I employed it, and (b) because I was able to keep the ball on the ground.

The great majority of players who attempt the stroke hit the ball in the air because they hit up and under it, and in their grip they keep the left wrist more in front of the handle than I do.

When pulling with the left wrist in this position, the blade of the bat is slightly open. The ball can be struck satisfactorily but it will automatically go in the air and the slightest mis-hit will cause it to fly off the top edge of the bat.

That is one reason why so few first-class players (especially

Englishmen) try the shot at all. For them it isn't worth the risk. But they are missing a grand scoring medium.

The stroke is particularly effective against a slow leg-break bowler should he stray in his length. It then becomes a natural, even though it means hitting against the break and thereby flaunting one of cricket's so-called sacred principles.

Also it is tremendously valuable against the off-spinner with a close leg field. There is nothing like a full-blooded pull shot right into the teeth of the short-leg fieldsmen to disturb their confidence and shift them back a yard or two. That in itself is a big contribution in minimizing their danger.

If there is no outfield at all the ball can deliberately be lofted over the men close in, but the shot is such a powerful one and it is so seldom used, except with full power, that I found it satisfactory to hit the ball mainly on to the ground and be content with trying to place it between the fieldsmen.

At the finish of the shot the batsman will find himself facing square leg, providing he has pivoted correctly and has swung right through the ball.

In addition to rolling his wrists the striker should, if possible, always keep the blade of the bat not quite horizontal and pointing slightly downwards. This is of further assistance in keeping the ball on the ground.

A batsman need not hesitate to pull a ball from outside the off stump. The risk of pulling it on to the stumps from the underside of the bat is negligible, and in any case the legs are positioned so that they would stand a good chance of intercepting such a mis-hit.

I advocate concentrated net practice to perfect the technique, and repeat my warning not to try to pull the ball unless it is pitched well short of a length. Even then the great danger is the irregularity of the height of bounce after it pitches.

In addition to pulling the ball by the method outlined, I frequently employed a slightly different technique. The difference between the two pull shots is this.

Instead of putting the right foot back and across to the off side, just put the right foot straight back. Then, as the ball is hit between mid-on and square leg, pull your body away from the line of flight as the left foot is swung round to the leg side whilst you pivot on the right foot.

In this way tremendous power can be generated, even more than with the other method, because there seems to be scope for greater leverage. The whole mechanism of the wrists, arms and body can be harnessed to give the ball a tremendous crack.

Should the ball be missed, it will pass on the off side of the body, often with fatal results, because the ideal ball to pull in this way is one delivered on the stumps.

With the orthodox pull one has to finish within the crease area and must be careful, in swinging the body round, not to hit the stumps. But this way there is virtually no limit to the pivotal action which ends with the weight on the left leg...

If a fast bowler is trying to engineer a catch on the leg side off a hook shot, this alternative type of pull shot offers a counter because it holds better prospects of pulling a ball which is bouncing quite high and still keeping it down. In fact, it is the easiest of the lot to keep down with those rolling wrists.

But it has its risks, especially when the ball is coming in towards the body.

I tried it against Bill Bowes at Bramall Lane and had my cap tilted sideways when the ball hit the peak, but then who wants to play cricket at all if not prepared to take a chance occasionally?

Just one caution. Don't try the pull shot on a greasy pitch after a shower of rain. Or if you do, have a spare set of teeth ready.

SIR DONALD BRADMAN
The Art of Cricket
(1958)

Definition

Cricket. A sport at which contenders drive a ball with sticks or bats in opposition to each other.

SAMUEL JOHNSON
A Dictionary of the English Language
(1755)

The Story of Spedegue's Dropper

The name of Walter Scougall needs no introduction to the cricketing public. In the 1890s he played for his University. Early in the century he began that long career in the county team which carried him up to the War. That great tragedy broke his heart for games, but he still served on his county club committee and was reckoned one of the best judges of the game in the United Kingdom.

Scougall, after his abandonment of active sport, was wont to take his exercise by long walks through the New Forest, upon the borders of which he was living. Like all wise men, he walked very silently through that wonderful waste, and in that way he was often privileged to see sights which are lost to the average heavy-stepping wayfarer. Once, late in the evening, it was a badger blundering towards its hole under a hollow bank. Often a little group of deer would be glimpsed in the open rides. Occasionally a fox would steal across the path and then dart off at the sight of the noiseless wayfarer. Then one day he saw a human sight which was more strange than any in the animal world.

In a narrow glade there stood two great oaks. They were thirty or forty feet apart, and the glade was spanned by a cord which connected them up. This cord was at least fifty feet above the ground, and it must have entailed no small effort to get it there. At each side of the cord a cricket stump had been

29

placed at the usual distance from each other. A tall, thin young man in spectacles was lobbing balls, of which he seemed to have a good supply, from one end, while at the other end a lad of sixteen, wearing wicket-keeper's gloves, was catching those which missed the wicket. 'Catching' is the right word, for no ball struck the ground. Each was projected high up into the air and passed over the cord, descending at a very sharp angle on to the stumps.

Scougall stood for some minutes behind a holly bush watching this curious performance. At first it seemed pure lunacy, and then gradually he began to perceive a method in it. It was no easy matter to hurl a ball up over that cord and bring it down near the wicket. It needed a very correct trajectory. And yet this singular young man, using what the observer's practised eye recognized as a leg-break action which would entail a swerve in the air, lobbed up ball after ball either right on to the bails or into the wicket-keeper's hands just beyond them. Great practice was surely needed before he had attained such a degree of accuracy as this.

Finally his curiosity became so great that Scougall moved out into the glade, to the obvious surprise and embarrassment of the two performers. Had they been caught in some guilty action they could not have looked more unhappy. However, Scougall was a man of the world with a pleasant manner, and he soon put them at their ease.

'Excuse my butting in,' said he. 'I happened to be passing and I could not help being interested. I am an old cricketer, you see, and it appealed to me. Might I ask what you were trying to do?'

'Oh, I am just tossing up a few balls,' said the elder, modestly. 'You see, there is no decent ground about here, so my brother and I come out into the Forest.'

'Are you a bowler, then?'

'Well, of sorts.'

'What club do you play for?'

'It is only Wednesday and Saturday cricket. Bishops Bramley is our village.'

30

'But do you always bowl like that?'

'Oh, no. This is a new idea that I have been trying out.'

'Well, you seem to get it pretty accurately.'

'I am improving. I was all over the place at first. I didn't know what parish they would drop in. But now they are usually there or about it.'

'So I observe.'

'You said you were an old cricketer. May I ask your name?'

'Walter Scougall.'

The young man looked at him as a young pupil looks at the world-famed master.

'You remember the name, I see.'

'Walter Scougall. Oxford and Hampshire. Last played in 1913. Batting average for that season, 27.5. Bowling average, 16 for 72 wickets.'

'Good Lord!'

'The younger man, who had come across, burst out laughing.

'Tom is like that,' said he. 'He is Wisden and Lillywhite rolled into one. He could tell you anyone's record, and every county's record for this century.'

'Well, well! What a memory you must have!'

'Well, my heart is in the game,' said the young man, becoming amazingly confidential, as shy men will when they find a really sympathetic listener. 'But it's my heart that won't let me play it as I should wish to do. You see, I get asthma if I do too much – and palpitations. But they play me at Bishops Bramley for my slow bowling, and so long as I field slip I don't have too much running to do.'

'You say you have not tried these lobs, or whatever you may call them, in a match?'

'No, not yet. I want to get them perfect first. You see, it was my ambition to invent an entirely new ball. I am sure it can be done. Look at Bosanquet and the googly. Just by using his brain he thought of and worked out the idea of concealed screw on the ball. I said to myself that Nature had handicapped me with a weak heart, but not with a weak brain, and that I might think out some new thing which was within the compass of my strength. Droppers, I call them. Spedegue's droppers – that's the name they may have some day.'

Scougall laughed. 'I don't want to discourage you, but I wouldn't bank on it too much,' said he. 'A quick-eyed batsman would simply treat them as he would any other full toss and every ball would be a boundary.'

Spedegue's face fell. The words of Scougall were to him as the verdict of the High Court judge. Never had he spoken before with a first-class cricketer, and he had hardly the nerve to defend his own theory. It was the younger one who spoke.

'Perhaps, Mr Scougall, you have hardly thought it all out yet,' said he. 'Tom has given it a lot of consideration. You see, if the ball is tossed high enough it has a great pace as it falls. It's really like having a fast bowler from above.'

SIR ARTHUR CONAN DOYLE
The Maracot Deep and Other Stories
(1929)

Spedegue, coached by Scougall, went on to win a famous victory for England against Australia.

PERFORMANCE

The Prowess of Lambert

The only incident of my residence in Notts worth mention is the match I made between gentlemen who hunted with me against any two of the County Club, my side to be allowed a fieldsman. Dennis and Hopkins were selected by the Club, and I secured for my fieldsman Lambert, who was by far the best cricketer in England in a double match, and the most wonderful man that ever existed at catching a ball. Perhaps I may be allowed to mention two facts in support of my statement. I could bowl faster than anybody at that time, and to give my readers an idea of the pace I could put on the ball, two stops were required behind the wicket-keeper to stop it. I could bowl across Lord's cricket ground, from one end to the other, and sometimes when I bowled a man out the bails were found fifteen or sixteen yards from the stumps. Lambert frequently caught the ball behind the wicket, and stumped men out when I was bowling.

Now for the issue of the match against Dennis and Hopkins, who were both first-rate performers. I won the toss and went in first. I had scored 70 runs and was not out when they asked me to let them go in against that number; to which I assented. I was careless at first, as I knew no four or five men, to say nothing of only two, could get 70 runs; after they had made five or six Lambert came and whispered to me, 'Don't let them get twenty, as I have betted they don't!' I then commenced in earnest, and they got only about four or five more in their four innings, not having been out once up to the moment of Lambert's request.

I could beat anyone at single wicket, even my friend Lambert, and nobody ever attempted to play against me singly. As wicket-keeper, fieldsman, bowler and batter, no man ever equalled Lambert. Apropos batting and catching, Mr Budd was the hardest hitter I ever saw; several times he hit the ball over the palings without touching them. In one match

35

Lambert was bowling and Mr Budd caught the ball a half-volley, hitting it as hard as he did when he sent it over the palings, and Lambert caught it with one hand, throwing it up as if he had taken it out of his pocket. The eye could only follow the ball for half a second and then it was out of sight.

When I first appeared in the character of a cricketer at Lord's I was about twenty-two or twenty-three years old. Lambert was the first to discover I was so fast a bowler. Lord Frederick Beauclerk, a first-rate player, very long-headed and a great judge of the game, was not then aware that I could bowl so great a pace, and by the advice of Lambert I made a match [in 1810] to play against Lord Frederick and Howard; the latter not so fast a bowler as I was, but steadier. Some time before the match came off I was taken very ill and was confined to my room. I wrote to Lord Frederick, informing him of my situation and saying how obliged I should be to him if he would consent to postpone the match. He wrote a very laconic answer back, declining my request, and I thought nothing then remained to be settled but a forfeit. I named this to Lambert, who came to see me. He said, 'I think if I could be allowed a fieldsman I could beat them both.' I told him I thought such an issue never could occur, but if he liked to try the experiment he should have the stakes if he won.

I applied for a fieldsman, but with the same result as attended my suggestion of postponement. Lambert then said that if I could only hit a ball and get a run he could *claim* a fieldsman. I told him I was so weak and reduced I could never accomplish it; but at his earnest desire I consented and went to Lord's in my carriage. Fully half the match was over and Lambert being just then out, I went in; but from the quantity of medicine I had taken, and being shockingly weak from long confinement to my room, I felt quite dizzy and faint. Lord Frederick bowled to me; luckily he was a slow bowler, and I could manage to get out of harm's way if necessary, but it did not so happen. I hit one of his balls so hard I had time to *walk* a run. He then became vexed and desired Howard to bowl; but I gave up my bat and claimed a fieldsman. This claim was not admitted. When I walked the run many of the spectators cheered, all the cricketers knowing the circumstances. The match was not over that day as Lord Frederick had to go in against Lambert's score. I attended and saw the issue, and was never more gratified in my life than I was when Lambert bowled his lordship out and won the match [by 15 runs].

Lord Frederick had a trick of raising his left shoulder higher than the other to make spectators who did not know better believe that he was deformed; to add to the deception he used to put his pocket-handkerchief under his cricketing waistcoat to increase the pretended deformity. When Lambert bowled him out there was a general cheer; and his demeanour returning to the pavilion put me in mind of crooked-backed Richard.

GEORGE OSBALDESTON
Squire Osbaldeston: His Autobiography
(first published 1926)

The First West Indian Tour (1900)

It has been decided to include black men in the coming team, and there is little doubt that a fairly strong side can be got together. Without these black men it would have been quite absurd to attempt to play the first-class counties, and no possible benefit would have been derived from playing those of the second class only.

The fielding will certainly be of a high class. The black men will, I fear, suffer from the weather if the summer turns out cold and damp, as their strength lies in the fact that their muscles are extremely loose, owing to the warm weather to which they are accustomed. Woods takes only two steps and bowls as fast as Mold!

Englishmen will be very much struck with the throwing powers of these black men, nearly all of them being able to throw well over a hundred yards. On the whole, I feel pretty confident that the team will attract favourable attention all round, and my view is, I know, shared by many sound judges of the game. The visit of any new team to England is always an experiment, attended with more or less possibilities of failure; but that they will be a failure I do not for a moment think, and in any case West Indian cricket will be greatly improved.

P.F. WARNER
Cricket in Many Climes
(1900)

Constantine in the Lancashire League

McDonald in 1932 had retired from Lancashire County. That means only that he cannot stand the grind of three-day county matches day after day. In a half-day match he is still a formidable bowler. Mac has never lost his machine-like run and his perfect action. Today he is at his best, good pace, a slight but late swing from the off side and periodically one that straightens. All this is on the basis of an impeccable length – Constantine has this effect on most bowlers. Constantine in his turn knows that he cannot afford to get out cheaply; still more, for the sake of the morale of his side, as a professional, he cannot afford to let the opposing professional get him out cheaply. This is a big match, with far more spectators and more tension than two-thirds of the first-class county matches played in a season. For an over or two this sparring continues. The crowd is silent but patient. It knows from long experience that sooner or later Constantine will explode. A length ball straightens, pops and lobs into the slips off the shoulder of Constantine's bat, a catch that eight-year-old Bobby would scorn and ask please to be thrown a real one. First slip all season has been beside himself with anxiety to drop as few as possible of the balls that fly towards him. This lob takes him by surprise and he muffs it. Constantine jumps with joy like an eight-year-old and settles down to take the rest of the over. All the *habitués* know now that the spell has been broken and things will happen soon. Mac too knows. But what? When it does happen no mortal could have foretold it. Constantine takes a long stride with his left foot across the wicket and, leaning well forward, glances McDonald from outside the off stump to long leg for four. Pandemonium. Mac stands startled, as well he might, if only for one fleeting fraction of a second. He is too experienced a campaigner to attempt to translate his surprise into anything immediate and rash. He does not attempt to bowl any faster; he does not budge an inch from his length. A few balls later Constantine leans forward and puts him away again to fine leg from outside the off stump. That breaks it. Next over the field is rearranged and Constantine begins to play a normal game, normal for him.

In these two strokes there was not the slightest recklessness or chanciness. The unorthodoxy was carried out with a precision and care fully equal to the orthodoxy of Mac's classical action and perfect length. They were almost as unpredictable, in fact more so, as the strokes against Hammond in 1926. Yet where those were adventures these were strictly business. As far as I remember, the field being opened up, he did not make the stroke again that afternoon. I used to drop in to Lancashire and see league cricket whenever I could. I do not remember ever seeing that stroke again.

These strokes were characteristic of Constantine's batting in the league. That is the way he transferred the liabilities of one-day cricket into assets. Assets for cricket of all days, one as well as five, if that last-named monstrosity continues. It is along that road that the present deadlock in Test cricket will be broken. It is a West Indian heritage. George Challenor in his early days in the West Indies was known for it. Whatever the match, he looked upon a maiden over as a personal affront. For All West Indies in British Guiana he hit inswinger Root for six over cover point's head in the first over.

C.L.R. JAMES
Beyond a Boundary
(1963)

Young Malcolm Hilton (1948)

Bradford on the one side of the Pennine Hills and Manchester on the other each helped the Australians to add to their limited store of wet wicket experience.

When Cranston won the toss from Bradman he asked the Australians to take first use of the rain-sodden pitch, but on taking the field the Lancashire captain proceeded to conduct the game as though the pitch was a batsman's paradise. He set his field deep and kept his fast-medium and medium-paced bowlers at work for more than an hour before he decided to try out his spin attack. It was quite obvious from the first over that the new-ball bowlers were not likely to cause an Australian upset. Dick Pollard got an occasional ball to rise fairly high but the pitch was so dreadfully slow that neither of the openers, Barnes and Morris, showed the slightest concern. When nineteen-year-old left-hander Hilton was asked to bowl he was given a typical defensive field with one man deep in the covers on the boundary and only one slips-fieldsman. This field placing was either arrant nonsense or a categorical admission that the skipper's decision to send the opposition in to bat was a fatal error.

Pollard effected the separation of the opening partnership when he had Morris caught, and Bradman came in to receive a hearty smack in the chest from the third ball he received from Pollard. Hilton soon won world-wide fame; he had Bradman tickle a leg-break into his stumps and the lad tasted his first dose of stardom. I can imagine the feelings of the Lancashire boy as he realized the full purport of his success. No one could ask for a better start in first-class cricket than to take Bradman's wicket for little cost. Within a few hours young Hilton became a national figure. He had walked on to the field that morning unnoticed and unknown. He could not have dreamed that by the time he was to walk off the field again he would be surrounded by Pressmen eager to get the story of his life. But such is fame. It was no less a splendid tribute to Bradman than to the boy's bowling feat that Hilton suddenly found himself the most discussed young cricketer in England. He was immediately regarded as a Test possibility.

The Lancashire selection committee did a solid job for English cricket when they refused to be stampeded by the sudden heat of publicity which was turned upon their colt. They refused to hurl him into the full county programme and they quite wisely nursed him along. Hilton was at a dangerous age for stardom to be thrust upon him in the twinkling of an eye. It could have meant the end of his cricket career had the Lancashire selectors considered that he was a heaven-sent gift instead of a promising boy feeling his way up the ladder of cricket fame.

Public opinion and esteem is a fickle jade. Whilst one produces the goods life can be delightfully rosy, but a few even mediocre performances can quickly dampen the public's ardour and once they have found their newly fledged hero to be a false alarm he is worse off than when he started. It is part of the important training of a young cricketer to know how to cope with the applause and the catcalls of the general public which wax and wane like the moon. When a chap is doing well there are hosts of people who want to shake him by the hand and slap him on the back. But loneliness sets in when the going becomes hard. Good luck to you, Lancashire, over your refusal to be yarded in by the glamour which momentarily surrounded your very promising colt.

Hilton has lots of ability. He spins the ball nicely from the leg and he is not afraid to keep the ball well up to the batsman, even to the spot where a venturesome batsman can give him a whacking. But he needs the experience which will come to him as he plays his county cricket. He is inclined to bowl mechanically just now. When he obtains some mastery over the subtlety of 'change of pace' he will be a greater force in the game.

Young Hilton repeated his first innings' performance when he accounted for Bradman in the second innings; but the second event was such a convincing dismissal that the spectators were overcome with joy. In the second innings the young left-hander virtually accounted for Bradman three times all told. When the Australian captain walked to the wicket it seemed to be written all over him that he intended to make the boy pay dearly for his first innings' presumptuousness. His method of dealing with Hilton left nothing to doubt about this course. Bradman made a crude agricultural swipe of the rusty-gate variety at a leg-break which eluded the bat, hit his pads and was fielded in the slips; then he played forward in defence with meticulous care at one which missed his bat and his stumps by the proverbial coat of varnish. The breathtaking show finished with Bradman flat on his back, legs pointing towards heaven and arms in knots, with the keeper quietly removing the bails. Another mighty haymaker had gone haywire. Bradman's efforts to square his account with the boy were as undignified as they were unsuccessful.

Hilton's performance, together with the bowling of Walsh at Leicester and Smailes at Bradford, must surely have suggested to the English selectors that spin bowling was a feature which should not be neglected in choosing the national team.

W.J. O'REILLY
Cricket Conquest
(1949)

Tom Emmett's Wides

'Can you give an explanation of the extraordinary number of wides you used to bowl?'

'Oh, yes – a perfectly simple one. In the first place, I don't believe I used to bowl half as wide as people say I did, and I should very much doubt if I ever sent one down much wider than point. In the second place, I used to try to get the ball as nearly as possible just out of a man's ordinary reach, and yet just within the distance which he could reach if he tried, and, fortunately for me, he often *did* try. But as men vary ever so much in the distance which they can cover, I sometimes used to make mistakes, which the umpires described as wides. I used to find that it put a man off a good deal to have several balls pitched in unexpected places, with an extra good one put in now and then. I remember Lord Hawke saying to me in a match, "I say, Tom, do you know you have bowled 44 wides this year?" "Have I, my lord?" I asked. "Then just give me the ball and I'll soon bring them up to 50, and earn talent money."'

'How was it that you sometimes would put every man on the off side, and then bowl three or four balls to leg?'

'Ah! I expect that was bad bowling, you know. I couldn't get my arm into position, or something of that sort. Besides, nobody used to hit them very often, and they sometimes put a batsman off a bit. But it has always struck me that I was libelled about those leg balls.'

W.A. BETTESWORTH
Chats on the Cricket Field
(1910)

The Demon

On the occasion of Grace's first visit to Australia I only played in one match against him and, when we met in

England six years later, he said: 'I only remember this Demon as a long, thin fellow standing in the deep field and throwing in terribly hard.' In those days I practised long shying, and could generally bung in a ball a hundred and twenty-eight yards. I had a lark with the Old Man at the nets. In those days, though I stood six feet three, I only weighed ten stone six. But I could bowl faster than any man in the world. 'W.G.' was at the nets at Melbourne, and I lolled up two or three balls in a funny slow way. Two or three of those round asked, 'What's the matter with you, Spoff?' I replied, 'I am going to have a rise out of that "W.G."' Suddenly I sent him down one of my very fastest. He lifted his bat half up in his characteristic way, but down went his off stump, and he called out in his quick fashion when not liking anything, 'Where did that come from? Who bowled that?' But I slipped away, having done my job.

F.R. SPOFFORTH
The Memorial Biography of W.G. Grace
(1919)

A National Hero

When Boycott, deputizing for the injured Brearley, brought the 1977–8 team to tour, New Zealand rejoiced, nationwide, at its greatest cricket triumph. The defeat of Australia four years earlier had been a splendid success, but the major goal, a victory over England, had been awaited for almost fifty years. There was erratic bounce at the Basin Reserve, Wellington, and New Zealand made only 228. Despite Boycott staying in 442 minutes for 77, England trailed by 13 runs, with Richard Hadlee giving a spirited display of fast bowling. England's powerful fast attack had New Zealand out for 123 and England needed only 137. But the tall left-hander Collinge whipped away 3 batsmen, including

Boycott, and Richard Hadlee then struck swiftly. The bowlers were supported by catching of a standard rarely achieved by a New Zealand team, and by vigorous encouragement from ecstatic spectators. Life stood still, throughout the country, as the nation listened, or watched this spectacular collapse on television. Even the hotel trade came to a standstill in New Zealand, a remarkable happening. At the end of the fourth day England were an incredible 53 for 8. Rain delayed play for 40 minutes on the last morning but Hadlee soon had the last 2 wickets, the final one through an athletic gully catch by Howarth. Hadlee took 6 wickets, 10 in the match, and became a national hero.

R.T. BRITTENDEN
Barclay's World of Cricket
(1980)

Hammond and the Ashes (1938)

But 1938 is more than a year of county vagaries. It is of course the year of Munich too and that will not fail to affect Hammond's and everybody else's story; but it is primarily, in the narrative of this one man's career, the season of the signal honour which when he first turned amateur can hardly have been far from his mind, at least as a strong possibility – the captaincy of England against Australia, offered for the first time to a player who had been a professional; the thin end of a valuable and effective wedge, demonstrating its strength in the light of history when among his eleven for the first Test would be found the man who in years to come would be chosen for this same responsibility without having to turn amateur at all. He did not ease into his position without immense qualms and what he felt to be a severe struggle in the Test Trial at Lord's, where he captained England against The Rest and on his own confession was a mass of nerves from the moment he went in to the very end of an innings which he determined to make a good one and which by virtue of that very determination was as laborious and painful a century as he ever made. He did not pass his own test, but the Selection Committee were not as stringent in their standards as he. He captained England in all the Tests; he captained the Gentlemen against the Players at Lord's, a happy switch from last year's game when he had captained the Players against the Gentlemen, a comic little sequence that is a vest-pocket record of his own; he established himself quite incontrovertibly during that season as England's premier cricketer by right and prerogative and choice. During those strange and long-drawn out matches of the 1938 series, none of them quite sane or real, none of them ringing quite true in the ears of posterity, all having something exaggerated about them, something unsymmetrical, something strained – during those last lurid days of the eighteen months or so before the war snuffed out all easy joys and careless arts together, Hammond was the central authoritarian figure in English cricket. English cricket, for that short heightened term or two, was Hammond if it was anybody at all.

He led England, with his customary air of impassive and controlled detachment, match by match through a gruelling and indecisive series. Four Tests were played, and the notorious fixture at Manchester was washed catastrophically down the gutter without a ball being bowled. Of the four practicable games, the first one at Nottingham was capsized with an overload of runs; the second, at Lord's, which might have gone the same way, faltered in uncertain weather and lost direction at the end; the Leeds game looks splendid on paper but suffered throughout from tentative and unworthy bats-manship, Australia with fewer blots on her copybook winning by a rather short head; and the Oval monstrosity passed into history before it was half over, presented to the world the longest innings then played by a batsman in first-class cricket and the highest total compiled by one side in a Test, built by the third afternoon the foundations of what looked like the most colossal construction of a cricket match in civilized history and ironically, by twisting Bradman's ankle, brought the whole thing down in ruin within twenty- four hours, to the relief of everyone without exception. The series was left drawn, the powerful and resourceful batting at nearly every point outfacing the bowling, as it was bound to do in a hard-wicket season with such talents as Bradman, Hammond, McCabe, Brown and Paynter were known to command; not to speak of the welcome new blood and transcendent potentialities introduced in the more than promising persons of Hutton and Compton. I cannot help feeling that the groundsmen at Nottingham and the Oval had done their work too well for cricket, as one would wish to see it, to be feasible. When a bowler of O'Reilly's calibre is reduced to analyses of 3 for 164 and 3 for 178, when Fleetwood-Smith rates 4 for 153 or 1 for 298, there is something other than mere pride of batsmanship against them. It was a defensive cast of mind, affecting everyone alike who had to do with England's policy, that arose directly from the shocking mauling administered to our several attacks by Bradman over a whole crowded decade. This tactic of negotiation from strength meant that England (on being given the advantage of first innings, with which Hammond coolly endowed her by winning the toss all four times) played all along to make sufficient runs to avoid defeat even if Bradman could not be wholly contained. This I am convinced was in Hammond's mind when he sharply ticked off Denis Compton, returning to the pavilion after being dismissed for 102 in his first Test against Australia, with the scoreboard reading 487 for 5; he had told him to play himself in again on reaching the century, and be blowed to pleasure and excitement and fulfilment of a life's ambition as they are no excuse for getting out when you have been told to stay in. I am certain that Hutton at the Oval batted under specific instructions, that in this timeless Test Hammond was determined to beat Bradman at his own colossal game, that it was under his orders that Hardstaff, over 100 not out with

England 770 for 6, played back to half-volleys and played a maiden to Bradman. There is a tale that McCabe, bowling the first ball of this fabulous match to Hutton, had observed with some insight to the umpire as it was played firmly back to him, 'They'll make a thousand.' I think this intention was in Hammond's mind, and that he marshalled his forces to that end right up to the unhappy moment when Bradman caught his foot in the rut. What would have been the shape of this phenomenal encounter had the accident not occurred, and Australia been able to bat all eleven, hardly bears thinking of. Bowes and Farnes were a better attacking proposition than Waite and McCabe, and it is possible that the odds might have remained slightly with England ... but I do not know. It is sufficient to note that Hammond's policy throughout these Tests appears to have been largely dictated by a healthy and rational respect for Bradman's powers. It is difficult to find any other comments to make about it. His leadership would seem to have been sensible but uninspired; combined with other factors, weather, talents, groundsmanship, it made the series a dull one enough. 'A new game has been invented,' said Cardus in an apathetic moment with the score between 700 and 800, 'which employs the implements of cricket.'

RONALD MASON
Walter Hammond
(1962)

As They Stood A-blocking

As they stood a-blocking, a-blocking, a-blocking,
Wearily I yawned while I sat and watched the play:
     The bowling was all right,
     But they did not try to smite,
     Though many balls they might
       Have put away:
As they stood a-blocking, I sat yawning at the play.

Yes, I sat a-yawning, a-yawning, a-yawning,
And several persons yawned who turned and looked
    at *me*:
        A lady sitting nigh
        Who chanced to catch my eye,
        In the middle of a sigh
           Yawned at *me*,
As I sat a-yawning; it was comical to see.

As I sat a-yawning, a-yawning, a-yawning,
The people started each one yawning who sat near;
        First one and then another,
        My cousin, then her brother,
        Her sister and her mother
           So severe;
As I sat a-yawning: it was ludicrously queer.

As I sat a-yawning, a-yawning, a-yawning,
The pack'd spectators were all yawning far and nigh;
        They yawned the innings through,
        It was more than they could do
        To prevent it; nor could you
           If you try
Keep from yawning if you fix on me your eye.

                DOUGLAS MOFFAT
                Crickety Cricket
                (1897)

True Praise

My dear John,
    Thank you for writing. It was very good to hear from you.
Though I hear your voice every day: from Trent Bridge, at the
moment. You're not only the best cricket commentator — far

and away that; but the best sports commentator I've heard, ever; exact, enthusiastic, prejudiced, amazingly visual, authoritative, and friendly. A great pleasure to listen to you: I do look forward to it. Here, in the hills above Florence, I lead the quietest life I ever remember leading: it is sizzling hot, the hill to the nearest village is a spinebreaker...

DYLAN THOMAS
Letter to John Arlott
(11 June 1947)

Tom and Harry Walker

And now for those anointed clod-stompers, the Walkers, Tom and Harry. Never sure came two such unadulterated rustics into a civilized community. How strongly are the figures of the men (of Tom's in particular) brought to my mind when they first presented themselves to the club upon Windmill-down. Tom's hard, ungain, scrag-of-mutton frame; wilted, apple-john face (he always looked twenty years older than he really was), his long spider legs, as thick at the ankles as at the hips, and perfectly straight all the way down – for the embellishment of a calf in Tom's leg Dame Nature had considered would be but a wanton superfluity. Tom was the driest and most rigid-limbed chap I ever knew; his skin was like the rind of an old oak, and as sapless. I have seen his knuckles handsomely knocked about from Harris's bowling; but never saw any blood upon his hands – you might just as well attempt to phlebotomize a mummy. This rigidity of muscle (or rather I should say of tendon, for muscle was another ingredient economized in the process of Tom's configuration) – this rigidity, I say, was carried into every motion. He moved like the rude machinery of a steam-engine in the infancy of construction, and when he ran, every member seemed ready to fly to the four winds. He toiled like a tar on horseback. The uncouth actions of these men furnished us, who prided ourselves upon a certain grace in movement and finished air, with an everlasting fund of amusement, and for some time they took no great fancy to me, because I used to worry, and tell them they could not play. They were, however, good hands when they first came among us, and had evidently received most excellent instruction; but after they had derived the advantage of first-rate practice, they became most admirable batters, and were the trustiest fellows (particularly Tom) in cases of emergency or difficulty. They were devilish troublesome customers to get out. I have very frequently known Tom to go in first, and remain to the very last man. He was the coolest, the most imperturbable fellow in existence: it used to be said of him that he had no nerves at all. Whether he was only practising, or whether he knew that the game was in a critical state, and that much depended upon his play, he was the same phlegmatic, unmoved man – he was the Washington of cricketers. Neither he nor his brother were active, yet both were effective fieldsmen. Upon one occasion, on the Mary-le-bone grounds, I remember Tom going in first, and Lord Frederick Beauclerk giving him the first four balls, all of an excellent length. First four or last four made no difference to Tom – he was always the same cool, collected fellow. Every ball he dropped down just before his bat. Off went his lordship's white hat – dash upon the ground (his constant action when disappointed) – calling him at the same time 'a confounded old beast'. – 'I doan't care what ee zays', said Tom, when one close by asked if he had heard Lord Frederick call him 'an old beast'.

JOHN NYREN
The Young Cricketer's Tutor
(1833)

An Oxford Freshman

As he had fully equipped himself for archery, so also Mr Verdant Green (on the authority of Mr Bouncer) got himself up for cricket regardless of expense; and he made his first appearance in the field in a straw hat with blue ribbon, and 'flannels', and spiked shoes of perfect propriety. As Mr Bouncer had told him that, in cricket, attitude was everything, Verdant, as soon as he went in for his innings, took up what he considered to be a very good position at the wicket. Little Mr Bouncer, who was bowling, delivered the ball with a swiftness that seemed rather astonishing in such a small gentleman. The first ball was 'wide'; nevertheless, Verdant (after it had passed) struck at it, raising his bat high in the air, and bringing it straight down to the ground as though it were an executioner's axe. The second ball was nearer to the mark, but it came in with such a swiftness, that, as Mr Verdant Green was quite new to round bowling, it was rather too quick for him, and hit him severely on the —, well never mind – on the trousers.

'Hallo, Gig-lamps!' shouted the delighted Mr Bouncer, 'nothing like backing up; but it's no use assuming a stern appearance; you'll get your hand in soon, old feller!'

But Verdant found that before he could get his hand in, the ball was got into his wicket; and that while he was preparing for the strike, the ball shot by; and, as Mr Stumps, the wicket-keeper, kindly informed him, 'there was a row in his timber-yard'. Thus Verdant's score was always on the *lucus a non lucendo* principle of derivation, for not even to a quarter of a score did it ever reach; and he felt that he should never rival a Mynn or be a Parr with any one of the 'All England' players.

CUTHBERT BEDE

The Adventures of Mr Verdant Green (An Oxford Freshman)
(1911)

James Joyce: 'A Useful Bat'

He disliked football but liked cricket, and though too young
to be even in the junior eleven, he promised to be a useful bat.
He still took an interest in the game when he was at
Belvedere, and eagerly studied the feats of Ranji and Fry,
Trumper and Spofforth. I remember having to bowl for him
for perhaps an hour at a time in our back garden in
Richmond Street. I did so out of pure goodness of heart since,
for my part, I loathed the silly, tedious, inconclusive game,
and would not walk across the road to see a match.

PROFESSOR JOHN STANISLAUS JOYCE
My Brother's Keeper
(1958)

A Poet's Average

The Blue Mantles averages in my old scrap-book show that in
the years 1910 and 1911 I had 51 innings, with 10 not-outs,
and an average of 19. This I consider quite a creditable record
for a poet.

SIEGFRIED SASSOON
The Weald of Youth
(1942)

A Wicket-keeping Trick

Before I forget it I must record a story of a wicket-keeping
'ramp' which Pooley, the famous Surrey wicket-keeper, used
to bring off with great success. The story was told me by the
late T.F. Fowler, who played for Cambridge in the 1860s.
Pooley would take a ball on the leg side and turn round as if

he had missed it altogether: off would go short leg and short slip running hell-for-leather to save the four byes. The batsman would look round, see them tearing after the ball and run: Pooley, with eyes at the back of his head and the ball in his hand would swing round and stump him. He got quite a lot of wickets that way. Fowler was taken in by this trick. It was, however, a wet wicket and Fowler, starting to run, slipped and fell, not leaving his crease. Down went the wicket and up went the confident appeal. Fowler told me that Pooley laughed like anything. 'Nearly 'ad you that time, sir: nearly 'ad you that time,' he said, and was not a whit ashamed.

F.B. WILSON
Sporting Pie
(1922)

CHARACTER

Mr John Small

The whole of the Hambledon Club have now been bowled down by death; Mr John Small, sen., of Petersfield, Hants., who was the *last* survivor of the original members, having terminated his mortal career on the 31st of December, 1826, aged nearly ninety.

The *great* have their historians, and why should not the *small*? Nay, since every one in the present day exercises his right of publishing his 'reminiscences', if he can but find a bookseller who is bold enough to venture on the speculation, we trust we shall stand excused for preserving a few stray notices of this venerable cricketer, whose exploits were once the theme of universal praise, and whose life was as amiable as his station was humble.

John Small, sen., the celebrated cricketer, was born at Empshott, on the 19th of April, 1737, and went to Petersfield when about six years of age, where he afterwards followed the trade of a shoemaker for several years; but being remarkably fond of cricket, and excelling most of his contemporaries in that manly amusement, he relinquished his former trade, and practised the making of bats and balls, in the art of which he became equally proficient as in the use of them; and, accordingly, we find that these articles of his manufacture were, in the course of a short time, in request wherever the game of cricket was known.

Mr Small was considered the surest batsman of his day, and as a fieldsman, he was decidedly without an equal. On one occasion, in a match made either by the Duke of Dorset, or Sir Horace Mann (for we cannot exactly call to mind which), England against the Hambledon Club, Mr Small was *in* three whole days, though opposed to some of the best players in the kingdom — nor did he at last lose his wicket, his ten mates having all had their wickets put down. At another time, in a five-of-a-side match, played in the Artillery ground, he got 75 runs at his first innings, and went in the last mate for seven runs, which it is hardly necessary to say, were soon scored. On this occasion, the Duke of Dorset being desirous of complimenting him for his skill, and knowing that Small was as passionately fond of music as he was of cricket, he made him a present of a fine violin, which he played upon many years, and which is now made use of by his grandson.

We shall not, however, enter into a detail of the numerous proofs he gave of his skill as a cricketer, nor of the flattering testimonies of approbation he at various times received from the patrons of the game: suffice it to state, that the first *County* match he played in was in the year 1755, and that he continued playing in all the grand matches till after he was seventy.

Mr Small was also an excellent sportsman, and capital shot. He held the deputation of the Manor of Greatham and Foley for many years, as game-keeper under Madame Beckford, and retained it under her son and successor, till the property was parted with, which did not happen till Small was nearly seventy years of age; yet, such was his strength and activity at that time of life, that, before he began his day's amusement, he regularly took his tour of seven miles, frequently doing execution with his gun, which to relate would appear almost incredible.

We ought also to mention that among other active exercises for which Mr Small was famed, was that of skating – those who have witnessed his evolutions on Petersfield Heath Pond (a fine sheet of water, a mile in circumference), have no hesitation in pronouncing him equal to any who have figured away on the Serpentine, how much soever they may have 'astonished the natives'.

But we turn from Mr Small's athletic amusements to notice his taste for music; and, though we cannot say that his excellence as a musician was equal to his excellence as a cricketer, still, among his compeers he was pre-eminent; and, we have no doubt, that to the soothing power of music he was not a little indebted for the equanimity of temper he possessed, and the tranquil delight he felt in the company of his friends – for those who knew him can conscientiously declare that no man was more remarkable for playful wit, cheerful conversation, or inoffensive manners.

So early did he display his taste for music, that at fourteen years of age he played the bass at Petersfield choir, of which choir he continued a member about *seventy-five years*, having performed on the tenor violin there within the last twelve months, and that too without the aid of spectacles. After what has been said it will not be a matter of surprise to hear that Mr Small was highly respected by all the gentlemen who patronized cricket; and, as they knew nothing could gratify him more, they frequently joined in a concert with his musical friends after cricket was over for the day.

His two surviving sons, John and Eli, not only inherit his love for the game, but the first mentioned particularly excels in it, and both are equally celebrated for their musical attainments; indeed, during their father's life this musical trio ranked high among the performers at all the amateur concerts in the neighbourhood.

O, that our readers would but tolerate our 'fond garrulity', for much could we yet inform them concerning John Small! We should delight in telling them that he was not merely a *player* on the violincello and violin, but that he was both a *maker* and a *mender* of them! With pleasure should we descant on his mechanical, as well as his musical skill, and show that his proficiency in each was the result of his own untutored ingenuity, proving that he had a natural genius for fiddle-making, as well as for bat and ball-making. We should bring proof that he once made a violincello, aye, and a right good one too, which he sold for two guineas – nay, we should further prove, that the old instrument which his son, the present John Small, plays on at church every Sunday (made by Andria Weber, Genoa, 1713), was thoroughly repaired by him, and an entire new belly put thereto, and that since it has been so repaired, an eminent professor has pronounced it to be worth as many guineas as would reach from one end of it to the other. We should ... but we have not forgotten the old proverb, which says, 'too much of a good thing is good for nothing'; and we desist, fearing that too much *may* be said even of our old friend John Small. But, notwithstanding our deference to the proverb, and our wish to be as taciturn as possible, there is *one* more musical anecdote which we must be allowed to narrate, inasmuch as it not only shows that our praises of his skill are by no means exaggerated, but because it cannot fail to be regarded as a corroboration of a most important fact – the influence of music upon the brute creation – or to speak in the language of the poet, an additional proof that 'Music hath charms to soothe the savage *beast*!'

In his younger days, Mr Small was in the habit of attending balls and concerts; sometimes contributing to the delight of the gay votaries of Terpsichore – at others forming one of the instrumental band, which met for the gratification of himself and his amateur friends. Returning one evening with a musical companion from a concert in the neighbourhood, they were rather suddenly saluted, when in the middle of a large field, by a *bull*, who, in no very gentle mood, gave them reason to believe that, to insure their safety, they must either hit upon some expedient to allay his rage, or make a hasty retreat. Mr Small's companion adopted the latter plan; but our hero, like a true believer in the miraculous power of Orpheus, and confiding in his own ability to produce such tones as should charm the infuriate animal into lamb-like docility, boldly faced him, and began to play a lively tune. Scarcely had the catgut vibrated, when the bull suddenly stopped, and listened with evident signs of pleasure and attention. The skilful master of the bow, felt a secret satisfaction on discovering so unquestionable a proof of the influence of sweet sounds; and, continuing to play, while he gradually retreated towards the gate, quietly followed by the bull, he there gave his quadruped auditor an example of his agility by leaping over it, and unceremoniously left him to bewail the loss of so agreeable a concert.

Having thus given such *memorabilia*, in the life of Mr John Small, as we conceive ought to be handed down to posterity, and (with humility be it spoken) hoping to obtain some distinction for ourselves in this necrological, autobiographical, and reminiscent age, we shall close our remarks by observing that so great a *degree* of health and vigour did Mr Small uninterruptedly enjoy, that even during the last three or four years of his life he took the most active exercise as a sportsman, and frequently followed the hounds on *foot!*

Thus it will be seen, that by an attention to temperance and exercise, and by encouraging cheerfulness and equanimity of temper, a man may still attain the age of a patriarch, enjoying to the last, health of body, peace of mind, and the rational amusements of life.

Were we to write his epitaph, it should be an unlaboured composition of quaint simplicity, just such a one as the parish clerk himself would indite – something, for example, after the following fashion:

> Here lies, bowl'd out by DEATH's unerring ball,
> A CRICKETER renowned, by name JOHN SMALL;
> But though his name was *small*, yet *great* his fame,
> For nobly did he play the 'noble game'.
> His *life* was like his *innings* – long and good;
> Full ninety summers he had DEATH withstood,
> At length the *ninetieth* winter came – when (Fate
> Not leaving him one solitary *mate*)
> This last of *Hambledonians*, old JOHN SMALL,
> *Gave up* his BAT and BALL – his LEATHER, *wax* and *all*.

> *Pierce Egan's Book of Sports*
> (1832)

Stout Players

I retain a wistful regard for – among other matters – the county cricket I used to watch when I was young. The players all looked so unlike one another then; and there was an air of alfresco intimacy about their exploits which lent them a fuller flavour than seems perceptible now. For one thing, a fair number of obviously fat men were still taking plenty of wickets with slow medium-pace bowling. Quite comfortably corpulent some of them were, with impressive untrimmed moustaches which might sometimes be seen emerging from a tankard of beer in the pavilion. One of the stoutest bowlers I ever saw on the field was Baldwin of Hampshire. For some reason it gave me peculiar pleasure when I was told that in everyday life he was a wheelwright. It was nice to think of him making honest farm-waggons all the winter; and there was something about the way he hitched up his large loose trousers at the end of an over which made me see him standing outside an old workshop door daubed with the trial smearings of red, blue, and yellow paint that he'd used these many years on the wheels. But perhaps Baldwin wasn't a wheelwright after all, in which case I owe his rotund memory a respectful apology. Old Walter Humphreys, the Sussex lob-bowler, used to appear in a pale pink flannel shirt – made for him, I hope, by his wife – with an artfully flapping sleeve which deceived the batsman's anticipation of the break of the ball. It seemed more like home-made cricket in those days, and the people who played it really went home after the game, instead of – as one imagines now – being incorporated into the machinery of the popular Press. I have always maintained that the proper place for a first-class cricketer to achieve perpetuity is in *Wisden's Almanack*. Once there, he is academically preserved for future reference. If he chooses to be a wheelwright when away from the public eye it is nobody's business but his own, though the fact enriches his personality when divulged with decorum. And the stouter he is when nearing the age of retirement the better I like him. Even the slim, silk-shirted Ranjitsinhji had put on weight when he reappeared in his later years. The willowy magician had become an almost ponderous potentate. As for W.G. Grace, the last time I beheld him he was trotting doggedly along behind a pack of foot-beagles; and while he pushed his way through a gap in a hedge I reverently computed that he must turn the scale at somewhere near fifteen stone.

SIEGFRIED SASSOON
The Weald of Youth
(1942)

Yorkshire v. The Australians (1938)

I shape up for the first ball from the bespectacled Bowes. He lumbers along and, ah! in that moment, the agony of mind of the opening batsman who takes strike on a sticky wicket, a wicket whose extent of nastiness waits to be probed!

The ball from Bowes hits the sodden turf, takes a seamful of it, and, evidently disliking the taste of it, rears violently. A nasty wicket, a cranky wicket obviously full of moods!

Bowes comes again and the ball pitches on the off. It does not rear this time, but, like a rabbit streaking for its burrow, it darts viciously in and hits me on the pad.

Bedlam breaks loose. Bowes shows his teeth, he curls one leg behind the other, looks in agony to the heavens and, with both hands apart, wails 'Owzat' with a venom which sends Duckworth pale with jealousy as he hears it in the next county.

What does a batsman think in that pregnant moment between the appeal and the decision? His eyes dart to the umpire's face and try to interpret there a ray of hope; his courage sinks to his sprigs if he thinks the umpire must justly give him out, or, if he thinks he has right on his side, his courage flutters like a spiralling dove.

English umpires cannot be hastened into a decision. A Chester remains mute for the eternity of a second and none can read his face. Then he either turns his head away from the bowler if it is not out (giving him the bleakness of an entire back if the appeal is a frivolous one) or raises one solitary finger to the batsman with the finality of a judge sentencing a murderer. That prolonged in-between period gives a batsman more agony of mind, but the English method of calm deliberation is preferable to the general Australian one of answering an appeal almost before it has fallen from the bowler's lips.

None of these thoughts crossed my mind with the Bowes appeal. A hazy thought did occur to me that a man who wore spectacles should bear himself with more dignity and respect for his lenses, but any other thoughts I had on the subject were frightened out of me by a blood-curdling yell in my rear. The 'Owzat' of the rotund, red-faced wicket-keeper Woods split the heavens and threatened the same to my back, but it was only by a short breath that he beat nine Yorkshire fieldsmen, who faced in all directions and demanded 'Owzat'; they, for their part, barely beating 15,000 Yorkshire men and women, who frenziedly wanted to know of each other if this wasn't indeed 'Owzat'. And high in the factories surrounding the ground wee Yorkshire lassies turned from their windows and hurled 'Owzat' at their foremen.

A self-respecting batsman would not have dared to await a verdict. To such an appeal he would have dismissed himself and gone his way, but Test experience dulls such chivalries. I stood my ground, and the umpire, who has played all his cricket with Lancashire, and knew the ins and outs of Yorkshire cricket, answered with a spirit possible only to a Lancastrian. He roared 'Naht oot', matching the Yorkshireman look for look.

This, you might be pardoned for thinking had you known not Bramall Lane, might easily have led to a crisis. Such an appeal and dismissed so contemptuously! One might have had visions of eleven outraged Yorkshiremen walking stiffly off the field to the plaudits of a sympathetic crowd, but there was none of that. The Yorkshiremen accept the decision as if nothing untoward has happened. They hitch their trousers and settle down again, thrilled in the experience that the very second ball of the day has given them the chance to show their fire and oil, as it were, their larynx...

The Pudsey products, Sutcliffe and Hutton, are now together. They are master and pupil, so it is said, but their methods and stroke play are entirely dissimilar. Sutcliffe's nostrils are dilated with the recurring sniff of battles of other days. He is loving every minute of this, more so when he sees O'Reilly afar off in street clothes in the pavilion. He feels himself master of the situation and positively purrs. His eyes are not as keen as they were, but his supreme confidence is unchanged.

'Wait thar', he calls. He plays the ball, peers at it, runs three yards up the wicket, crosses the bat across his chest, comes to rigid attention and then holds up a traffic-police arm to the man at the other end. 'Wait thar', says Sutcliffe, bristling with polished dignity from sleek hair to immaculate boots.

I think whimsically of Sutcliffe as I cross to and fro between the overs. I notice his emphatic smack, smack on his block with the bat as the bowler runs up and then his shuffle, shuffle across with his feet before the bowler delivers. No cricketer has more mannerisms; no batsman has possessed a better fighting temperament.

I like most the spit and polish of Sutcliffe when he is master of the situation and knows it. I see him in his element at Lord's, where none can match the outraged indignities he suffers when, with Lord's packed, somebody has the misfortune to move in the Members' Pavilion as the bowler runs to deliver the ball. Up shoots Sutcliffe's traffic arm, his planked palm daring anything to move between his end and Buckingham

Palace. He draws away from the wicket, makes vigorous sweeps with his bat to the pavilion, and all eyes follow it to discover some hapless wretch (possibly a Baronet) who had dared to move in his seat at such a moment in British history.

Sutcliffe and his dignity then return stiffly to the wickets. He plays the next ball meticulously and slowly back to the bowler in a pretentious manner which calls up to the Members' Stand, 'Had you not moved in your seat, sir, and momentarily distracted me, I should have swept that ball to the boundary.'

And everybody looks again at the Baronet, who slinks in his seat and creeps from the ground at the first opportunity, possibly never again to go to Lord's or his club.

Who could match the cool calm of Sutcliffe in Sydney in 1932 when he chopped a ball from O'Reilly hard on to his stumps? For some unknown reason the bails did not fall off and the surrounding Australians almost swooned in agony. But not so Sutcliffe. He looked at the Australians with arched brows as if to say, 'Pray, please, what is all this fuss and ado about?' Sutcliffe was 43 then; he made 194 and not a flicker of his steely black eyes suggested that anything untoward had happened, let alone the greatest piece of good fortune ever to befall a batsman.

> J.H. FINGLETON
> *Cricket Crisis*
> (1946)

Physical Presence

Not since W.G. Grace can a cricketer, by his physical presence, have so caught the attention of the sporting world. Bradman's feats were, of course, more phenomenal, Sobers's more effortlessly versatile; but off the field they maintained a lower profile than Botham. Bernard Darwin, in a vintage profile of W.G., wrote of his 'schoolboy love for elementary and boisterous jokes ... his desperate and undisguised keenness, his occasional pettishness and pettiness, his endless power of recovering his spirits' – all of which could equally apply to Botham.

No one has ever sent the ball huge distances so frequently as Botham did last summer. His 80 sixes, most of them hit with the full face of the bat, often over extra cover, were a record for an English first-class season. He scored at something like a run a ball for Somerset, yet still averaged 100 for them, and in the six Test matches he took 31 Australian wickets and held 8 catches, some of them quite breathtaking. Wherever he played he added substantially to the gate, and when the winter came he tested a recent operation on a knee by walking from John O'Groats to Land's End and raising over £600,000 for charity, an astonishing achievement. There was much else, not all of it quite so admirable. There are times when Botham needs to be saved from his unrestraint, as well perhaps as from those who would exploit him.

JOHN WOODCOCK
Notes by the Editor,
Wisden Cricketers' Almanack
(1986)

Ian Botham

As a Pom, he'd make a great Aussie.

JEFF THOMSON
Thommo Declares
(1986)

Short leg. This place should be filled by a cheerful man. His responsibilities are not so great as those of any other situation; he should be ready with a cheerful remark, and so generally to keep the game alive. In other words. Put your comic man here.

He must be always ready to back up. Don't let him talk to the umpire; but don't let him shrink from knocking that individual down should it be necessary to do so in order to make a catch. Short leg should be careful how he throws; he should have no private animosity or misunderstanding with the wicket-keeper, for he is in a position to inflict upon that gentleman grievous bodily harm.

He should be a man of observation, for no two men play the same at a leg-ball; and he should be ready even to anticipate any wish of the bowler, by watching the batsman's play on the leg side, as many a run is saved by paying attention to the first few overs to each batsman.

Wicket-keeper. Have you got one? Yes – then you are in luck. No – then what are you to do? We confess it is a difficult question to answer. Perhaps the best course is to consult the field generally whether they, or any of their relations, ever filled the situation. Talent sometimes is hereditary. We remember a case where a gentleman was desired to fill the post, from his stating that he had once heard his father say that he had put the gloves on, but he wasn't sure whether it was in the cricket-field or the P.R. [prize ring]. Many men have risen to eminence with no better recommendation than this. We are inclined to think that, except with slow bowling – where even an apology is better than none – the wickets had better not be kept at all. Your flashy and funky keeper is a terrible worry to the long stop and slips. It is impossible to estimate too highly the qualities that make up a good wicket-keeper. It demands the quickest of eye, the staunchest of nerve, the steadiest of purpose, the most unflinching of resolution. But to the eye and nerve that makes the post pre-eminent, must be added the judgement and art of directing, that will keep all the other posts alive to their work...

The hand, not the voice, must be ready to signify the change required by the batsman's play, and as from his position he is the best judge, so should he be the first to recommend any change in the bowling; strictly speaking, he is the only man in the field entitled to make a remark at all. If he is not, he should be the captain. He should endeavour to inculcate a good style of throwing in, but he should not be above taking a half-volley or a one-hander high to the right or left. As he for the most part tries, and gets his fingers ends repeatedly warmed in so trying, more allowance should be made for him than for any other man; and as we have hinted above, an unnecessary hard throw at him is wanton cruelty.

The Plodding Cricketer. To our mind this type is the most painful and most mysterious of all. He plays in more matches than all the other types collected. His name is always found in the penultimate order of going in. He is very seldom a bowler, and is at best a long stop. Yet he hammers on, like the fabulous horse, on the 'ard 'ard road to honour and glory. He is the best-tempered fellow in the world, and his name appears weekly in some facetious contribution to the sporting prints, under some new *nom de guerre.* You may catch him any afternoon at practice; and when he isn't oiling his bat, he is reading Lillywhite's *Guide and Advice to Cricketers.*

Now, in *what* lies the secret of his attachment to the game? Can it be a thirst for success? Surely such a prospect can be but a mirage. Cricket has much of the will-o'-the-wisp delusion about it; it holds out to the plodding cricketer a sufficient glimmer of momentary success to light him on his path; it has so many funny turns and slices of luck, that the

69

most erratic must sometimes fall into the right groove, and the most hungry come in for an unexpected innings at its board.

The Plodder is after all a very useful man in the field. He will always field out when you are a man 'short' (and when are you *not?*) and will, if properly appealed to, for the sake of cricket, go so far as to carry your bag to the railway station; and we hope cricket will never be without many representatives of this little appreciated but valuable type.

R.A. FITZGERALD
Jerks in from Short Leg
(1866)

Why Don't They Learn?

Having, the other day, once again spent an afternoon in watching a village cricket match, I am again perplexed by the passion for that game which is displayed by those who cannot shine at it. They cannot bat, they cannot bowl, they leave their place in the field, they miss catches, they fumble returns; and yet, every Saturday, there they are, often in perfect flannels, ready to fail once more. What is this lure, this attraction, that cricket exercises, and why is it that so few village elevens can ever muster more than two or three players who know anything? No wonder it is so hard for first-class teams to be brought together. As, the other day, I saw this lack of any kind of skilled resistance to the bowler, I meditated afresh on the difficulties of those observant pilgrims from green to green whose duty it is to build up the county's nursery; and as one defeated batsman after another, with a nought to his name and no sense of humiliation, sank into his deck-chair, I deplored anew the absence of national pride. Why on earth, I wondered, don't they watch better men and learn something? Why do they think they can hit before they have tried to defend? Why do they want to make four off the first ball? But so it is, and so it will be until September, when football again comes in, and if they make mistakes they will hear about it.

But the passion for cricket is in our blood. Small boys have it, youths have it, grown men have it, old men have it; and no amount of disappointment, no ducks, can change it. Even that scholarly cleric, the Rev. John Mitford, rector of Benhall, in Suffolk, collector, connoisseur and dilettante – he whom Lamb called 'a pleasant layman spoiled' – had it. In a man of letters so cultured you would not expect to see the spell of this unlettered game thus active; but it was there. Even as late in Mitford's life as 1827, when he was forty-six, we find Bernard Barton writing to Lamb a letter, now first published in a book, with these words in it:

'Mitford is gone crazy about cricket – he has, I am told, organized a cricket club in his Parish, and enters into its advancement and success with all the interest of an amateur. The Benhall Club (Benhall is Mitford's Parish) sent a challenge the other day to the Saxmundham Club – and the approaching contest was a matter of as much discussion in the vicinity as the Battle of Waterloo was some few years bygone among politicians. The Benhallites were beaten, and Mitford, so far as I hear, has [kept] house ever since. I fancy he has had a knock or two with the balls, for his letter talks of a disjointed thumb, a contusion on the hip, and a sightless eye; in another letter he describes himself as bandaged from head to foot, and as full of sores as Lazarus.

'In despite of all this he is a perfect enthusiast on the subject of bat and ball, wickets and bye slows. What is the Laurel, he asks, compared to the Willow? For that Tree alone makes good cricket bats; or the Myrtle to the Ashen? – of which the wicket, it seems, is fashioned. He

71

apostrophizeth, anon, certain Cricket Players, just as he was wont to speak of Homer, Virgil, Dante, or Tasso. Poor M – I am sorry for his case: 'tis lucky we have a Lunatic Asylum erecting in the neighbourhood: but he may receive his quietus from bat or ball, and die ere his wits are wholly gone – and have this epitaph on his headstone:

> Mitford! mighty once at cricket,
> Head erect, and heart elate,
> Now, alas! he heeds no wicket
> Save John Bunyan's wicket gate.'

E.V. LUCAS
Only the Other Day
(1936)

A Country Cricket Match

For the last three weeks our village has been in a state of great excitement, occasioned by a challenge from our north-western neighbours, the men of B., to contend with us at cricket. Now, we have not been much in the habit of playing matches. Three or four years ago, indeed, we encountered the men of S., our neighbours south-by-east, with a sort of doubtful success, beating them on our own ground, whilst they in the second match returned the compliment on theirs. This discouraged us. Then an unnatural coalition between a high-church curate and an evangelical gentleman farmer drove our lads from the Sunday-evening practice, which, as it did not begin before both services were concluded, and as it tended to keep the young men from the ale-house, our magistrates had winked at, if not encouraged. The sport, therefore, had languished until the present season, when under another change of circumstances the spirit began to revive. Half-a-dozen fine active lads, of influence amongst their comrades, grew into men and yearned for cricket; an enterprising publican gave a set of ribands: his rival, mine host of the Rose, an outdoer by profession, gave two; and the clergyman and his lay ally, both well-disposed and good-natured men, gratified by the submission to their authority, and finding, perhaps, that no great good resulted from the substitution of public houses for out-of-door diversions, relaxed. In short, the practice recommenced, and the hill was again alive with men and boys, and innocent merriment; but farther than the riband matches amongst ourselves nobody dreamed of going, till this challenge – we were modest, and doubted our own strength. The B. people, on the other hand, must have been braggers born, a whole parish of gasconaders. Never was such boasting! such crowing! such ostentatious display of practice! such mutual compliments from man to man – bowler to batter, batter to bowler! It was a wonder they did not challenge all England. It must be confessed that we were a little astounded; yet we firmly resolved not to decline the combat; and one of the most spirited of the new growth, William Grey by name, took up the glove in a style of manly courtesy, that would have done honour to a knight in the days of chivalry. 'We were not professed players,' he said, 'being little better than schoolboys, and scarcely older; but, since they had done us the honour to challenge us, we would try our strength. It would be no discredit to be beaten by such a field.'

Having accepted the wager of battle, our champion began forthwith to collect his forces. William Grey is himself one of the finest youths that one shall see – tall, active, slender and yet strong, with a piercing eye full of sagacity, and a smile full of good humour – a farmer's son by station, and used to hard work as farmers' sons are now, liked by everybody, and admitted to be an excellent cricketer. He immediately set forth to muster his men, remembering with great complacency that Samuel Long, a bowler *comme il y en a peu*, the very man who had knocked down nine wickets, had beaten us, bowled us out at the fatal return match some years ago at S., had luckily, in a remove of a quarter of a mile last Ladyday, crossed the boundaries of his old parish, and actually belonged to us. Here was a stroke of good fortune! Our captain applied to him instantly; and he agreed at a word. Indeed, Samuel Long is a very civilized person. He is a middle-aged man, who looks rather old amongst our young lads, and whose thickness and breadth give no token of remarkable activity; but he is very active, and so steady a player! so safe! We had half gained the match when we had secured him. He is a man of substance, too, in every way; owns one cow, two donkeys, six pigs, and geese and ducks beyond count – dresses like a farmer, and owes no man a shilling – and all this from pure industry, sheer day-labour. Note that your good cricketer is commonly the most industrious man in the parish; the habits that make him such are precisely those which make a good workman – steadiness, sobriety, and activity – Samuel Long might pass for the *beau idéal* of the two characters. Happy were we to possess him! Then we had another piece of good luck. James Brown, a journeyman blacksmith and a native, who, being of a rambling disposition, had roamed from place to place for half-a-dozen years, had just returned to settle with his brother at another corner of our village, bringing with him a prodigious reputation in cricket and in gallantry – the gay Lothario of the neighbourhood. He is said to have made more conquests in love and in cricket than any blacksmith in the county. ...

That Sunday evening's practice (for Monday was the important day) was a period of great anxiety, and, to say the truth, of great pleasure. There is something strangely

74

delightful in the innocent spirit of party. To be one of a numerous body, to be authorized to say *we*, to have a rightful interest in triumph or defeat, is gratifying at once to social feeling and to personal pride. There was not a ten-year-old urchin, or a septuagenary woman in the parish, who did not feel an additional importance, a reflected consequence, in speaking of 'our side'. An election interests in the same way; but that feeling is less pure. Money is there, and hatred, and politics, and lies. Oh, to be a voter, or a voter's wife, comes nothing near the genuine and hearty sympathy of belonging to a parish, breathing the same air, looking on the same trees, listening to the same nightin-gales! Talk of a patriotic elector! Give me a parochial patriot, a man who loves his parish! Even we, the female partisans, may partake the common ardour. I am sure I did. I never, though tolerably eager and enthusiastic at all times, remember being in a more delicious state of excitement than on the eve of that battle. Our hopes waxed stronger and stronger. Those of our players who were present were excellent. ...

On calling over our roll, Brown was missing ... Charles Groven – the universal scout and messenger of the village, a man who will run half-a-dozen miles for a pint of beer, who does errands for the very love of the trade, who, if he had been a lord, would have been an ambassador – was instantly despatched to summon the truant. His report spread general consternation. Brown had set off at four o'clock in the morning to play in a cricket match at M., a little town twelve miles off, which had been his last residence. Here was desertion! Here was treachery! Here was treachery against that goodly state, our parish! To send James Brown to Coventry was the immediate resolution; but even that seemed too light a punishment for such delinquency. Then how we cried him down! At ten on Sunday night (for the rascal had actually practised with us, and never said a word of his intended disloyalty) he was our faithful mate, and the best player (take him for all in all) of the eleven. At ten in the morning he had run away, and we were well rid of him. ... But I have since learned the secret history of the offence (if we could know the secret histories of all offences, how much better the world would seem than it does now!) and really my wrath is much abated. It was a piece of gallantry, of devotion to the sex, or rather a chivalrous obedience to one chosen fair. I must tell my readers the story. Mary Allen, the prettiest girl of M., had, it seems, revenged upon our blacksmith the numberless inconsistencies of which he stood accused. He was in love over head and ears, but the nymph was cruel. She said no, and no, and no, and poor Brown, three times rejected, at last resolved to leave the place, partly in despair, and partly in that hope which often mingles strangely with a lover's despair, the hope that when he was gone he should be missed. He came home to his brother's accordingly; but for five weeks he heard nothing from or of the inexorable Mary, and was glad to beguile his own 'vexing thoughts' by endeavouring to create in his mind an artificial and factitious interest in our cricket-match – all unimportant as such a trifle must have seemed to a man in love. Poor James, however, is a social and warm-hearted person, not likely to resist a contagious sympathy. As the time for the play advanced, the interest which he had at first affected became genuine and sincere: and he was really, when he left the ground on Sunday night, almost as enthusiastically absorbed in the event of the next day as Joel Brent himself. He little foresaw the new and delightful interest which awaited him at home, where, on the moment of his arrival, his sister-in-law and confidante presented him with a billet from the lady of his heart. It had, with the usual delay of letters sent by private hands in that rank of life, loitered on the road, in a degree inconceivable to those who are

76

accustomed to the punctual speed of the post, and had taken ten days for its twelve miles' journey. Have my readers any wish to see this *billet-doux*? I can show them (but in strict confidence) a literal copy. It was addressed,

> 'For mistur jem browne
>   'blaxmith by
>   'S.'

The inside ran thus: 'Mistur browne this is to Inform you that oure parish plays bramley men next monday is a week, i think we shall lose without yew. from your humbell servant to command

> Mary Allen.'

Was there ever a prettier relenting? a summons more flattering, more delicate, more irresistible? The precious epistle was undated; but, having ascertained who brought it, and found, by cross-examining the messenger, that the Monday in question was the very next day, we were not surprised to find that *Mistur browne* forgot his engagement to us, forgot all but Mary and Mary's letter, and set off at four o'clock the next morning to walk twelve miles, and play for her parish, and in her sight. Really we must not send James Brown to Coventry – must we? Though if, as his sister-in-law tells our damsel Harriet he hopes to do, he should bring the fair Mary home as his bride, he will not greatly care how little we say to him. But he must not be sent to Coventry – True-love forbid!

At last we were all assembled, and marched down to H. common, the appointed ground, which, though in our dominions according to the maps, was the constant practising place of our opponents, and *terra incognita* to us. We found our adversaries on the ground as we expected, for our various delays had hindered us from taking the field so early as we wished; and, as soon as we had settled all preliminaries, the match began.

But alas! I have been so long settling my preliminaries, that I have left myself no room for the detail of our victory, and must squeeze the account of our grand achievements into as little compass as Cowley, when he crammed the names of eleven of his mistresses into the narrow space of four eight-syllable lines. *They* began the warfare – those boastful men of B. And what think you, gentle reader, was the amount of their innings! These challengers – the famous eleven – how many did they get? Think! imagine! guess! – You cannot? – Well! – they got twenty-two, or, rather, they got twenty; for two of theirs were short notches, and would never have been allowed, only that, seeing what they were made of, we and our umpires were not particular. – They should have had twenty more if they had chosen to claim them. Oh, how well we fielded! and how well we bowled! our good play had quite as much to do with their miserable failure as their bad. Samuel Long is a slow bowler, George Simmons a fast one, and the change from Long's lobbing to Simmons's fast balls posed them completely. Poor simpletons! they were always wrong, expecting the slow for the quick and the quick for the slow. Well, we went in. And what were our innings? Guess again! – guess! A hundred and sixty-nine! in spite of soaking showers, and wretched ground, where the ball would not run a yard, we headed them by a hundred and forty-seven; and then they gave in, as well they might. William Grey pressed them much to try another innings. 'There was so much chance', as he courteously observed, 'in cricket, that advantageous as our position seemed, we might, very possibly, be overtaken. The B. men had better try.' But they were beaten sulky, and would not move – to my great disappointment; I wanted to prolong the pleasure of success. What a glorious sensation it is to be for five hours together – winning – winning! always feeling what a whist-player feels when he takes up four honours, seven trumps! Who would think that a little bit of leather, and two pieces of wood, had such a delightful and delighting power!

MARY RUSSELL MITFORD
Our Village
(1824)

Maidan Cricket

The maidan is, probably, the most evocative place in Indian urban life. It has been called the equivalent of an English park but this is grossly misleading. The only similarity it has with a park is that it is a vast, open area, very often at the centre of cities. But beyond that there are no similarities. It is not merely that the grass in an English park is much greener and finer than that of the maidan, but that, whereas an English park is an oasis of calm, a shelter from the hustle and bustle of city life, the maidan reproduces Indian city life with all its noise and clamour. The grass is matted, raggy, struggling to stay alive amidst the dirt and rubble. Flowing through the maidan are little canals, the surface is pock-marked with ditches, even what looks like small ravines and the whole area is filled with people from every walk of life. It is amidst such confusion and noise that Indians learn to play their cricket ... But just as the lotus, that great Hindu flower, springs from the dirtiest and most inhospitable of surroundings, so does Indian cricket arise, grow and blossom on these maidans dotted all over the urban landscape.

Nowhere can maidan cricket be better appreciated than Bombay, particularly south Bombay, where I grew up. That area is dominated by three great maidans: Azad, Cross and the Oval. Azad, meaning free, had the distinction of being the home of the club to which Vijay Merchant, one of India's great batsmen, belonged. Opposite is the Cross, so called because at one end of it there is a huge cross bearing the inscribed legend INRI. Azad is a regular venue for many of the matches played in the inter-schools tournaments of the city. Cross often attracts large crowds to watch famous Tests, or ex-Test players playing in the inter-office *Times* shield tournament. This competition, organized by the leading local daily, *The Times of India*, is very well reported and, at times, an even better draw than the Ranji trophy. It costs nothing to watch and it is not unusual for a few thousand people to gather along the boundary edges, sometimes spilling over onto the adjoining roads, to watch the stars of today and yesteryear do fierce competitive battle. This is what may be called *mali*-dominated cricket.

Malis generally live in the shacks that dot the edge of a maidan and efficiently police the pitches on the maidans. These pitches are distinguished from the rest of the field not merely in the normal cricket sense, but by special arrangements. No sooner is a cricket match over than the mali comes trundling in with wooden staves and ropes and encloses the whole area of the pitch. It would not take much to remove the wooden staves and dismantle the ropes but such is the aura possessed by these illiterate, but shrewd guardians of the pitches of the maidan, that nobody dares. Also playing on these pitches is part of a package that you have to earn. Along with pitch comes a tent, specially erected for the match, and acting as a pavilion and changing rooms. A tent that comes with a little cubicle attached to it and serving as a lavatory. It is when the malis start erecting the tents that the people on the maidan know that a proper cricket match, on a proper pitch is about to be played.

The maidan pitches are also used for net practice – mostly on weekday afternoons. The Azad maidan lay between school and home, and on my way back from school I would occasionally pause to watch these cricket nets and find nothing surprising in the fact that the batsmen, with their boxes happily attached outside their trousers, practised at the nets. Today when I revisit Bombay, and occasionally visit Azad maidan, the sight of hundreds of batsmen in full cricket regalia proudly displaying their boxes as they practise the forward defensive stroke seems odd, even faintly obscene. Then it was part of normal mali-maidan-cricket.

Most of my maidan cricket and, for that matter, most people's, was played on dirt tracks with some grass on it which formed the space between the pitches. This wasn't the only impromptu part of our cricket. There was the problem of equipment. I had been generously provided with full cricket gear, some of it from my father, and some of it gifts from friends and relations. But most of the members of my team were not quite so happily placed, and in most of our matches we had at best two pairs of pads, and very often just three pads. I mean not three *pairs* of pads, but one pair of pads and another solitary pad! So for much of the time, since most of us were right handed, we wore a pad on the left leg, leaving the right unprotected. Gloves were a scarcity and, though I had a set of stumps, only very rarely did we play in matches where we had two sets of stumps. Generally we had four stumps which imposed its own constraint. Three stumps would constitute the wicket at one end, the solitary stump the bowler's wicket at the other end. This meant that at the end of overs the batsmen would cross over, not the wicket-keeper or the fielders. Again the bat which had been a gift of a friend of my father was our prize bat, and very often the non-striker would have to do with a broken bat, or a wooden plank. At the end of an over, or when it was his turn to bat, he would exchange his bat, or plank, for a proper one. These are, of course, personal recollections but they mirror cricket as it was played then and now.

Not surprisingly maidan cricket gave rise to a new vocabulary. Thus maidan cricket uses the expression 'runner' in a totally different way from the common cricketing meaning of the term. In cricket a runner is one who runs for a batsman who has been injured during the game and cannot run for himself. In maidan cricket the number one batsman is called the 'opener', his partner is called the 'runner'. Very often in this class of cricket there are only three stumps and the stumps at the bowler's end are indicated by a pile of *chappals* – Indian slippers – heaped at the spot where the proper stumps would be. The runner is the one who immediately takes up his position at the chappal end.

There is also 'twoodie'. In maidan cricket boundaries have to be laboriously fixed. There are often very serious arguments about where the boundaries of the ground are. This is not surprising since the ground is not marked out, there are very many matches taking place all at the same time and the square leg of one match is the cover point of another match. Often there are objects on a maidan which conveniently indicate a boundary: a roller, a tree, perhaps the spot where a pitch has been protected by the mali's wooden staves and ropes. But very often there are insurmountable objects on the ground too near the wicket to classify as a four and a hit to the object is denoted as twoodie, meaning two runs.

But perhaps the most major innovation of maidan cricket is the reinterpretation of the two-fingered salute. Now, normally in cricket the index finger of the right hand raised upward into the heavens is seen as the traditional mark of the umpire's decision in favour of the fielding side. This is all very well when the umpire is giving a decision in favour of the fielding side. But what if he is signifying not out? How does he do it? He could say 'Not out', but in maidan cricket this is considered not enough. So an innovation has been introduced whereby one finger raised to the heavens is out and two fingers raised to the heavens is not out. In maidan cricket, the umpire wishing to turn down an appeal doesn't say 'not out' or shake his head – a gesture which in India has a very different meaning – but raises two fingers of his right hand.

MIHIR BOSE
A Maidan View
(1986)

James Aylward

The next player I shall name is James Aylward. His father was a farmer. After he had played with the club for a few years, Sir Horace got him away from us, and made him his bailiff, I think, or some such officer; I remember, however, he was but ill qualified for his post. Aylward was a left-handed batter, and one of the safest hitters I ever knew in the club. He once stayed in two whole days, and upon that occasion got the highest number of runs that had ever been gained by any member – *one hundred and sixty-seven!* Jemmy was not a good fieldsman, neither was he remarkably active. After he had left us, to go down to live with Sir Horace, he played against us, but never, to my recollection, with any advantage to his new associates – the Hambledonians were almost always too strong for their opponents. He was introduced to the club by Tom Taylor, and Tom's anxiety upon the occasion, that his friend should do credit to his recommendation, was curiously conspicuous. Aylward was a stout, well-made man, standing about five feet nine inches; not very light about the limbs, indeed he was rather clumsy. He would sometimes affect a little grandeur of manner, and once got laughed at by the whole ground for calling for a lemon to be brought to him when he had been in but a little while. It was thought a piece of finnikiness by those simple and homely yeomen.

JOHN NYREN
The Young Cricketer's Tutor
(1833)

Failure (1932)

Constantine still had his mind set on becoming a lawyer. To enter an Inn he would require a Senior Cambridge Certificate and I began to give him lessons. He wanted these lessons and I was anxious to give them. (That I forced them upon him is a slander.) What with one thing and another, and the disruptive presence of a strange personality in the house, I believe, for the first and only time in all his long years in league cricket, Learie began the season badly and for many weeks could not score. It was a horrible business. He would come back home on Saturday evening, cheerful and taking his failure in good part, too good a part. Norma watched him anxiously. The friends came around that evening or the next day to talk it over. Jack, a municipal worker, was a real comfort. He did not commiserate; neither did he go into whether the ball had kept low or jumped high. 'Nelson needs a new professional,' he would announce on entering the house. Shaking his head from side to side, he would pontificate, 'Norma, your old man is getting down,' all the kindness in the world beaming behind the solemnity of his face. Constantine would perk up at once and the chaff would begin to fly. After half an hour Jack would leave, he and everyone else in wonderful good humour. But, as weeks passed with no change, you could see that Learie was faking it. On Saturday he would leave home full of confidence, by Saturday night it was the same old story. It seemed as if all Nelson and half of Lancashire had nothing else on their minds but Learie's batting failures. He knew that every person he passed in the street thought of it as soon as they saw him. 'Well, it happens to the best!' 'That's cricket, you know' can wear pretty thin in time. I came in for my share of the condolences. Early one week Learie took leave and went off to spend a few days with friends in Nottingham. No use. The lessons discontinued and never began again. Constantine, of course, was worth his place for bowling and fielding and strategy alone. But the carefree batsman of the Trinidad years was no more. He came out of it in the end and I shall always remember Norma's smiling face and shining eyes when he began to score as usual. Jack was his usual contrary self. 'Not a bad innings,' he would say, 'though I have seen better.' And the match would be lived over again. Jack specialized in stories of who had said what and when, around the ropes and in the pavilion or the pub afterwards. The whole episode opened a window into the life of a professional cricketer, especially a league professional. There can be raw pain and bleeding where so many thousands see the inevitable ups and downs of only a game. Learie maintained on the whole an equable front, but I saw him inside. I knew what it did to me.

C.L.R. JAMES
Beyond a Boundary
(1963)

Dr Beech Rolls About

On Tuesday, in July 1828, on Clapham Common, a match took place between eleven blacksmiths, of Clapham, and a similar number of Wandsworth Vulcans, for a supper. The parties wore white leather aprons, brand new for the occasion; and after a well-contested match the Clapham men won with three wickets to go down. Dr Beech, one of the Clapham heroes, happened to get quite full of half-and-half, and, being upwards of twenty stone in weight, he was placed for a long stop, but, in pursuing the ball, he frequently tumbled, and rolled about like a sick elephant.

Pierce Egan's Book of Sports
(1832)

Taunton

Perhaps there are other English county grounds as completely central in their towns as Taunton. Portsmouth, Scarborough, Eastbourne, and Hastings come readily to mind, but none ever seems so much at its urban heart as Taunton. No transport is needed to stroll from the Castle or the County Hotel to the ground enclosed between St James's Street, the River Tone, Priory Bridge Road, the Cattle Market and the Coal Market.

Once there, the tall new pavilion, its Edwardian predecessor, and the old Stragglers pavilion on the corner near the Coal Market; the school, and the main entrance through the J.C. White Gates emphasize the almost domestic intimacy of the place. Above all, the red sandstone tower of St James's occupying as it were one corner of the site and echoed, with subtle difference, by St Mary's, sets the cricket field in the very core of Taunton.

For many years at least one commentator used often to be late for the start of play there, delayed by the purchase of second-hand books, glass, china or, on occasions, even furniture, from Chapman's rambling old shop and warehouse almost immediately opposite the gates.

There is still much along the way to beguile the casual playgoer on his morning saunter. The idea of a picnic at the cricket has persuaded many to the County Stores who have emerged laden with something nearer an open-air banquet. Antique dealers, bookshops, restaurants, grocers, camera shops, off-licences tug at the sleeve. Lately, too, most conveniently close at hand for the spectator's lunch, Dennis Noble has decorated the walls of the Ring of Bells with cricket photographs and souvenirs, and provides palatable lunch – hot or cold – and wine or beer to taste.

An early memory of the ground is of the lowing cows in the Cattle Market punctuating the applause from the crowd. It is the most companionable and pervasive of county grounds and, within its gregarious climate, men from origins as diverse as Sammy Woods, Len Braund, Bill Alley, Arthur Wellard, Viv Richards, Johnny Lawrence, Ian Botham, Frank Lee have become as much part of the Taunton scene as the Somerset-born Harold Gimblett, Horace Hazell, Jack White, Mervyn Kitchen, Peter Denning, Colin Dredge, and Bertie Buse.

It is as if they had all been drawn into the same atmosphere, like the people converging on the market from the countryside for miles around. On a July Saturday market day, cricket and the weekly visitors and shoppers all merge together into a unique yet typically West Country warm, busy, relished – purely Taunton – summer's day.

JOHN ARLOTT
Somerset CCC Yearbook
(1982)

GENIUS

Amongst the eminent Victorians was W.G. Grace; he enjoyed the proper authority. The nation called him the G.O.M., and, like another monument called the same, he looked the part. There is a lot in 'appearance' if the crowd is to give full respect and worship. W.G. Grace possessed physical size – and he was bewhiskered. I have seen faded photographs taken of Grace when he was under twenty years of age; the beard is already profuse and impressive. To catch the popular sense of dramatic fitness, Grace simply *had* to be big, for he stood for so much in the history of cricket at a time when hardly any other game challenged it as the national out-of-door sport and spectacle. Also there is another point which was to Grace's advantage in his character of a G.O.M.: he lived in a period which not only believed in great men but actually insisted on them and went about looking for them. And because there was no idea then of the trick of exploitation called nowadays publicity, a politician, actor, jockey, or a cricketer could remain at a romantic distance from the eyesight of the multitude: he did not get too familiar. Grace was a household possession, true, but only by reason of the performances he achieved day by day. Advertisement did not give him a spurious reputation and wear out belief in him by damnable iteration. Off the cricket field he was concealed in suggestive anonymity, and if people saw him in the streets, they turned round and gazed and gaped, and were pleased if they could feel that no mistake had been made.

Astonishing that by means of a game of bat and ball, a man should have been able to stamp his shape and spirit on the imagination of thousands. As I say, no rhetorical Press pointed out his prowess incessantly. Not long ago I had cause to look through the files of an old newspaper in search of some bygone fact of cricket. I found a match at Lord's in which W.G. scored 152 not out; the game was reported in very small type with no headlines but this – in tiny print:

ANOTHER GOOD SCORE BY DR GRACE

Grace got his renown during the years that did not know the literary persuasions of cricket writers who describe an innings by Hobbs in the rhetoric of a Macaulay; alone he conquered – with his bat and (this is certain) by his beard.

When I was a boy I lived in a family that did not interest itself in games. Yet often at breakfast W.G. Grace's name was mentioned. Everybody understood exactly who he was and what he signified in the diet of the day's news. From time to time, *Punch* used him as the subject for a cartoon; the Royal Family occasionally inquired after his health. When he was reported not out at Lord's at lunch, the London clubs emptied, and the road to St John's Wood all afternoon was tinkling with the old happy noise of the hansom cab. Sometimes he would play, at the height of his fame, in a country cricket match in some village in the West of England. And from far and wide the folk would come, on foot, in carriages, and homely gigs. On one of these occasions Grace had made a score of twenty or so when he played out at a ball and missed it. The local wicket-keeper snapped up the ball in his gloves triumphantly, and swept off the bails and – seeing visions of immortality – he screamed to the umpire: 'H'zat!'

The umpire said: 'Not out; and look 'ee 'ere, young fellow, the crowd has come to see Doctor Grace and not any of your monkey-tricks.'

I have always been amused that W.G. Grace became famous while the Victorians were endowing cricket with moral unction, changing the lusty game that Squire Osbaldeston knew into the most priggish of the lot, and stealing rigour, temper, and character from it. Cricket was approved at the private schools for the sons of gentlemen; the detestable phrase, 'It isn't cricket', was heard in the land. The game acquired a cant of its own, and you might well have asked why two umpires were necessary at all, and why the bowler ever appealed for leg before wicket. W.G. could not have contained his large humanity in any genteel pursuit; he was of more than ordinary human bulk, and therefore he had more than ordinary frailty. He exercised his wits, went about the job of winning matches with gusto.

'Did the old man ever cheat?' I once asked an honest Gloucestershire cricketer, who worshipped Grace.

'Bless you, sir, never on your life,' was the quite indignant answer. 'Cheat? No, sir, don't you ever believe it — he were too clever for that.'

When Grace and Gloucestershire met Hornby and Lancashire, there was sport indeed. Grace had a habit of moving a fieldsman surreptitiously from the slips to fine leg, while the batsman was concentrating his vision on the next ball. Once on a time at Old Trafford, A.N. Hornby decided to hoist Grace with his own petard. So, even as Grace was standing with his left toe up from the ground, getting ready for a stroke while the bowler was running to the wicket — at that very moment A.N. Hornby quietly signalled to first slip, who on tiptoe moved towards the leg side behind Grace's back. But he was not half-way there before W.G.'s high-pitched voice cried out: 'I can see what you're doin'; I can see what you're at!'

If a man is going to give his whole life to a game, let him play it like a *full* man, with no half-measures and no repressions. Cricket was a battle of wits with Grace, first and last. His enormous technique was saved from mechanical chilliness because he never practised it without some artful end in view; he larded the green earth wherever he played; he dropped juicy flavours of sport; he loved an advantage, and hated to be beaten.

In his long career, which lasted from 1863 to 1908, he scored more than 54,000 runs and took 2,664 wickets. I write down these statistics here to give some slight idea of his mastery over the two main technical departments of cricket.

But one of the purposes of my essay has really no use for records, which mean nothing to folk who are not cricketers. I am trying to get Grace into the Victorian scene, to see him as a Representative Man, and also to see him in relation to the crowd that invented his legend. 'Was he a fraud?' a young man at Oxford asked me not long ago. 'I fancy there is a bit of the fraud in all the Victorians.'

The question was, on the face of it, senseless: no charlatan can be a master and forge a lasting technique. There would have been no Hobbs if Grace had not extended the machinery of batsmanship and achieved a revolution in bowling, by his great synthesis of offensive and defensive stroke play.

The hint of the triumphant charlatan which comes to us when we read of Grace (just as the same hint comes to us when we read of Gladstone and Irving) arises from a habit of mind supposed to be peculiar to the Victorians. They rather lacked flippancy, and for that reason they appear to this flippant generation to have blown out fulsomely all the objects of their admiration; they seized on the day's heroes, and invested them with the significance of a whole tradition. In an epoch of prosperity, when the idea of material expansion was worshipped for its own sake, even the vast runs made on a cricket field by W.G. Grace seemed symbolical; his perpetual increase of authority and perform-ance suited a current love and respect for size and prosperity. W.G. became an institution in a day of institutions, all of which, like the Albert Memorial, had to be impressive by sheer bulk. W.G. himself, of course, did not know what he stood for in the national consciousness: he was content to be a cricketer. He shared none of the contemporary modern habit of self-exposition.

Today, even though we pretend to possess a humorous sense of proportion, all sorts of small persons regard themselves much too seriously, and are ready to submit to an 'interpretation', psychological or scientific. I expect any moment a treatise by Bradman on 'The Theory and Economy

94

of Batsmanship'. And I would not be surprised to hear, any Sunday evening, an address broadcast from St Martin's by Jack Hobbs on 'The Cricketer as an Ethical Influence', with some moving metaphors about 'The Great Umpire' and 'Playing the Game'. W.G. Grace never lapsed into solemnity about himself. Once he was asked to explain the best way to stop an off-break. He did not let loose a cartload of theory, or drag in the blessed word 'psychology'. He simply said: 'You must put your bat to the ball.' Frequently I wonder whether the 'Victorian age' has not been a consequence of the modern tendency to write 'studies' of everything; and to turn irony against itself by too close a search for significant overtones. Grace, I am sure, would be the last person in the world to regard himself a theme for such a 'study' as I am attempting now; I can see his great ghost stroking the immortal beard, and saying: 'Get on with the game.' ...

When Grace began to stamp his personality on English sport, cricket was scarcely established, save as a rough-and-ready pastime on the village green. The technical elements of the game had yet to be gathered together; the counties had to be organized. A spectacular interest was wanting to attract the crowds; and the money was required to make a national game. W.G. came forward, at the ripe moment; the technique of cricket stood ready for expansion and masterly summary; the period was also ready for a game which everybody could watch, the gentry as well as the increasing population of town workers. Grace's skill as a batsman may be said to have orchestrated the simple folk-song of the game; his personality placed it on the country's stage.

He came from out of the West Country, and though in time his empire stretched from Lord's to Melbourne, never did he forget the open air of Gloucestershire, and the flavours of his birthplace. In an orchard at the dawning of June days, he learned his cricket; yet in his prime, at the age of forty-seven, he was still waking every summer morning fresh as a lad, eager for a match. If he knew that the other side were about to give a trial to a new bowler of awe-inspiring reputation, Grace would get up all the earlier, make haste to the field, and take a glance at the latest demon.

Once it happened that the Australians brought to England a bowler of unknown witchery; Grace straightway went to their captain, W.L. Murdoch, and he said: 'And so you've found a good bowler, eh? What does he do with the ball? Is he a fast 'un, or slow?'

'Ah,' was the sinister reply, 'he mixes 'em.'

'Very well, then,' answered W.G., 'I'll have a look at him this afternoon; I'll have a look at him.' And that afternoon he went in first with some old professional, whom we'll call Harry.

W.G. played a few overs from the new bowler most warily; the devil might have been in every ball, so carefully did Grace keep his bat down, and so suspiciously did his eyes sharpen. After a short time he hit the new bowler for two fours and a three off successive balls. And while the two batsmen were passing one another up and down the pitch, Grace's voice cried out, in immense glee: 'Run up, Harry, run up! We'll mix 'em for him; we'll mix 'em!' Is it any wonder that the man's vital character made cricket seem part of the English way of life in summertime, lusty and manly, yet artful and humorous? A great company of 'originals' grew around the Old Man: Tom Emmett, A.N. Hornby, Crossland, Barlow, Johnny Briggs – scores of them, all men of ripe comedy, home-spun and fresh, each of them as vivid as characters on a page of Dickens or Surtees.

Cricket is not the best game *as* a game. There is more excitement in Rugby football; as much style and skill in tennis at Wimbledon; a swifter and more certain decision in a cup tie. But cricket is without a rival amongst open-air pastimes for the exhibition of native characteristics in Englishmen. It is a leisurely game on the whole, and its slow movement enables the cricketers to display themselves. A lot of nonsense is talked about the 'team spirit' in cricket; but as a fact the greatest batsmen and bowlers and fieldsmen have been those who have stood out from the ruck and have taken charge of a situation in ways entirely their own. You could not merge into a drilled efficient mass the Johnsonian bulk of Grace, or the Figaro alacrity of a Macartney. In no other game than cricket does the result mean so little to true lovers of it. ...

At the present time, nearly all the performances of W.G. Grace have been surpassed by cricketers here and there – some of whom will not be remembered a year after they have ceased playing the game. Hendren of Middlesex has scored more hundreds than W.G. Grace scored in his long career. Yet the fact of Grace's posterity remains to this moment: he is still the most widely known of all cricketers amongst folk who have seldom, if ever, seen a match. After all, he really did transcend the game; I have tried in this article not to treat him with less proportion than he would have treated himself. But I cannot, and nobody possibly could, contain the stature of the man within the scope of bat and ball. Nobody thinks of Grace in terms of the statistics recorded of his skill; like Dr Johnson, he endures not by reason of his works but by reason of his circumferential humanity. I always think of him as the great enjoyer of life who, after he had batted and bowled and fielded throughout the whole three days of a match between Gloucestershire and Yorkshire, was at the end of the third afternoon seen running uphill from the ground, carrying his bag, in haste for the train to London – running with a crowd of cheering little boys after him, and his whiskers blowing out sideways in the breeze.

NEVILLE CARDUS
'William Gilbert Grace'
The Great Victorians
(1932)

Warwick Armstrong

Surely no one has ever paid the just tribute of prose or rhyme to Warwick Armstrong. His practical irony has eclipsed his technical greatness. We read of him as one who pointed out to England, at a moment when we were apprehending no such set back, the laws of the game, overlooked by umpires of endless age. We see him posting himself – a stately landmark – at the greatest distance from the wickets, enjoying a fragment of the home edition blown to him by a gust of wind as dry as his own humour; all to express, in laconic sort, his opinion on the right and wrong way to play cricket, even if it were Test Match cricket. But, that day in Somerset, I departed with the enduring impression that W.W. Armstrong was one of the supreme executants of his game. He made a bat look like a teaspoon, and the bowling weak tea; he turned it about idly, jovially, musingly. Still, he had but to wield the bat – a little wristwork – and the field paced after the ball in vain. It was almost too easy. W.W. Armstrong sat down while they fetched the ball.

EDMUND BLUNDEN
Cricket Country
(1944)

Great Bowlers

While waiting, I inspected the famous pavilion. It was antiquated, and, despite periodic renovations, the authorities evidently found it unusable. There was little to show it had been requisitioned, for tables and chairs had accumulated much dust, and faded photographs still lined the walls.

Examining these, I recognized many celebrated cricketers, while two individual portraits hung apart. One was of F.R. Spofforth, the other of Sydney Barnes.

I was peering at them in the uncertain light, when I heard someone sniff and turned to discover an old gentleman at my elbow. He had white hair, side-whiskers, and sunken cheeks, and wore a frock coat over tight-fitting trousers. He seemed to have emerged from the Committee Room, whose door stood ajar.

I wished him good morning, and explained that I was just having a look round. 'I'm waiting for a friend,' I added, 'but he can't see me for another half-hour.'

The old fellow gave an asthmatic chuckle, while his brown, bird-like eyes flitted from me to the photographs and back again. He shook his head smilingly, and I wondered whether he was deaf.

'Great bowlers,' I remarked, nodding at Spofforth and Barnes. 'I suppose nobody will ever know who was the greater.'

He shook his head and smiled again before answering in precise tones:

'Very fine in their way no doubt. Able enough. But not to be compared with David Harris.'

David Harris! This was going back to antiquity. Had he said Alfred Shaw or Tom Emmett, I would not have been surprised. But the eighteenth century seemed rather too remote.

'An underarm bowler', I protested, 'could hardly challenge comparison with modern speed and swing.'

'My dear young man,' came the amused voice, 'forgive my bluntness, but your logic will not bear an instant's examination. By similar reasoning, present-day military commanders are superior to Bonaparte, because they have the advantage in weapons. A man's genius must surely be judged by the manner in which he employs the powers actually at his disposal.'

He paused to indulge in the wheezing chuckle and head-shake which regularly punctuated his remarks.

'I have watched cricket from this pavilion for many years. Much longer than you suspect' — he gave a cryptic smile — 'and, in my judgement, the fact that Harris bowled underarm, and in his earlier days at two stumps, is an added proof of his superiority.'

Obviously he was riding a pet hobby-horse, and it was only charitable to humour him.

'That's an interesting point of view,' I observed politely.

The brown eyes twinkled. 'Of course,' he mused, 'he had frequently the advantage of choosing where the wickets should be pitched. But that again was a test of skill, judgement, and character. Compare him with his contemporaries – Lumpy, for instance, who ignored the needs of his fellow-bowlers – and you see the difference. Harris never forgot his partner at the other end, though his own delivery was best suited by an upward slope, to help the rise of the ball.'

'It must have come awkwardly off the pitch,' I hazarded.

'Awkwardly! Heh! Why, Harris *invented* the real length-ball that got batsmen caught! It came from just under his arm, pitched near the bat, spun away – and rose. But his action was superb, sir. He would raise his right arm, draw back the right foot, and then advance with the left – no stooping or side-stepping – before he let loose that ball which beat the batsman by its sharp lift.'

'This would be about 1780, wouldn't it?'

I felt rather proud of knowing this, but an amused head-shake quelled my complacence.

'1778, sir, was Harris's first big match. He didn't only show bowlers how to bowl. He compelled batsmen to *go forward in defence*. There was nothing like it before.'

'How do you suppose he acquired his art? Wasn't he a potter or something?'

'By practice, sir. That's what modern bowlers don't understand – the need for practice. Why, David Harris practised during his dinnertime – aye, and in a barn all the winter. He'd wear away a patch of grass by his accuracy – you could see it turning brown!'

'Did anyone ever master him?'

'Beldham was the nearest. There was a lad called Crawte too. But they couldn't be sure. No, sir, David Harris was the greatest bowler ever known, and *nobody* really mastered him.'

I became somewhat exasperated with this ancient's extremism. Every age has its champions, but after all he was eulogizing someone he had only read about, for, despite his years, he could hardly even have met anyone who had seen David Harris.

'All this is hearsay,' I commented firmly. 'There's nothing to show that Harris, however successful in the eighteenth century, would have triumphed in the twentieth. Consider the strain of modern Test Matches...'

That asthmatic chuckle interrupted me.

'Strain!' he scoffed. 'Yes, I've watched your moderns strain themselves – come off the field with hurt muscles! Why, David Harris was afflicted with gout – crippled, sir! D'ye think he gave in? Not he! When he couldn't stand up, they brought an armchair on to the field, and, as soon as he'd delivered a ball, he sat down in it! Strain of modern matches! Tell me another, young man!'

I was so irritated by his derisive chuckle and headshaking that I turned away in annoyance, and, when I looked round again, he had gone – back to the Committee Room, I imagined, to brood over the dim past.

G.D. MARTINEAU
The Field is Full of Shades
(1946)

A Prince of India on the Prince of Games

This Jubilee year [1897] is the apogee of the British Empire; it may also fairly be considered as the apogee of cricket. The art of preparing consummate wickets – wickets which make batting an ease and a delight, bowling a game of patience and

101

endurance – has reached its height. A brilliantly sunny summer has done such wickets full justice; and a wonderful fertility of consummate batsmen has taken full advantage of the wickets and the weather. Yet – extraordinary to relate – it has also been a year in which a race of bowlers has arisen capable of coping with these conditions. It might be supposed that they would be slow or at least medium-paced bowlers. But not so. Three of the most successful bowlers of the season have been Richardson, Mold, and Kortright – all three fast bowlers. What it means, in the way of endurance, for a fast bowler to keep up pace and length through these enormous innings on wickets enough to numb the pluck of any bowler, only a thorough cricketer can understand. Yet another consideration completes the appropriateness of the title. The peculiar feature of the Jubilee has been the way in which it has drawn attention to the bonds between England and its dependencies: and the batsman of the day who is acknowledged to be the most consummate in style and all- round power (though he may not be at the head of the averages) is an Indian prince.

This batsman, Prince Ranjitsinhji (perhaps the finest who has appeared in England, except Grace), is the author of this *Jubilee Book of Cricket*. A native of India teaches Englishmen their own national game; and all, with one accord, hasten to sit at his feet. He is not only a practical master in the game, but he has analysed it as a critic analyses the laws of literature. Training and outfit, fielding in all its branches, bowling, batting, captaincy, and umpiring are the principal divisions of his work. He even instructs the batsman how to choose his bat and batting-gloves and leg-guards. He has subjected everything, in fielding, bowling, and batting, to an unprecedented process of analysis, which provides us with a textbook at all points corresponding to modern needs. The older books were in effect based on the laws handed down from the times of underhand bowling. But the methods of modern good-length bowling, with off- and leg-break, a crowded off-field, and few chances for leg-hitting, you will seek in vain in them. The 'pull' is mentioned by them only to be reprobated. Prince Ranjitsinhji discards tradition, and the 'pull' and the 'hook' figure largely in his instructions. Nevertheless, there was real reason for the proscription of these strokes by the old players. He himself recognizes that they are dangerous off a fast bowler, even on a true wicket, and that on a wicket rendered slippery by rain which has affected the surface, or a 'sticky' wicket, they must be eschewed.

Prince Ranjitsinhji has done well to place fielding foremost, in the hope that by so doing he may stimulate attention to the most neglected, yet very important, branch of the cricketer's art. Fine fielding is very largely the work of a captain who is himself a fine fielder. Many a match has been won rather in the field than at the wicket. And, if only a boy will set himself really to study its niceties, it is a most fascinating branch of cricket. Prince Ranjitsinhji remarks on the splendid opportunities of cover point, and cites the Rev. Vernon Royle as the cover point to whom all cricketers give the palm during the last thirty years. 'From what one hears,' he says, 'he must have been a magnificent fielder.' He was. And I notice the fact, because Vernon Royle may be regarded as a concrete example of the typical fielder, and the typical fielder's value. He was a pretty and stylish bat; but it was for his wonderful fielding that he was played. A ball for which hardly another cover point would think of trying he flashed upon, and with a single action stopped it and returned it to the wicket. So placed that only a single stump was visible to him, he would throw that down with unfailing accuracy, and without the slightest pause for aim. One of the members of the Australian team in Royle's era, playing against Lancashire, shaped to start for a hit wide of cover point. 'No, no!' cried his partner, 'the policeman is there!' There were no short runs anywhere in the neighbourhood of Royle. He simply terrorized the batsmen; nor was there any necessity for an extra cover –

now so constantly employed. In addition to his sureness and swiftness, his style was a miracle of grace. Slender and symmetrical, he moved with the lightness of a young roe, the flexuous elegance of a leopard – it was a sight for an artist or a poet to see him field. Briggs, at his best, fell not far short in efficiency; but there was no comparison between the two in style and elegance. To be a fielder like Vernon Royle is as much worth any youth's endeavours as to be a batsman like Ranjitsinhji, or a bowler like Richardson.

In the chapter on bowling Prince Ranjitsinhji shows that he has studied this art as closely as his own art of batting. He is full of wise counsel with regard to all the styles of bowling, and their relation to the various kinds of wickets and batsmen. Nothing in his book is more useful than his analysis of a typical game on a good wicket (from the bowler's standpoint) between two first-class sides. The batting side, under thinly disguised names, is easily to be recognized as Surrey; the bowling side, from the absence of names, is harder to be recognized. It is evidently an actual match which the writer had the chance of observing; therefore, it is possible that the other side may be Sussex. I am glad to see that Prince Ranjitsinhji does not think it beneath him to recognize the possible value of lob-bowling, to expound its principles, and recommend its cultivation by cricketers who are that way inclined. He even goes so far as to surmise that other kinds of underarm bowling might prove baffling to present-day batsmen if they were revived. I am of opinion that this would certainly be the case. On one point I think that the author does not quite bring out the peculiarities of underarm. Namely, that 'good-length bowling' is not as continuously necessary to underarm as to overarm bowling. Now, I think that the underarm bowler can afford to pitch his balls well up, more than the overarm bowler can; and that it often pays to do so – at least, against the present race of batsmen, who are unaccustomed to underarm. For two reasons. In the first place, the overarm bowler shrinks from pitching his balls up on account of the extra exertion involved. He does so only occasionally, as Prince Ranjitsinhji states, on account of this exertion. The underarm bowler, on the contrary, because of the ease and naturalness of his action, can pitch his balls well up without any difficulty. In the second place, because of the difference of trajectory between the two methods of bowling. An overarm ball describes approximately a parabola, and when it is well pitched up comes therefore thoroughly on to the bat. But the drop of an underarm ball, particularly if it be slow, is so much more sudden that it may comparatively and roughly be considered a straight drop. Even if fast or quick-medium, it is much more abrupt in descent than a like overarm ball. Consequently a batsman who attempts to clout a well-pitched-up underarm as he would a like overarm ball stands a fair chance of playing over it, especially when he is unaccustomed to this kind of bowling. If, on the other hand, he plays back, it is difficult to get the ball away. So that he may be deceived, and if he adopts caution is not likely to score off the ball. Yorkers, again, are perfectly easy to an underarm bowler; they put no great strain on the weakest arm. Admirable are all the author's lessons on bowling, had we space to follow them; and admirable his concluding declaration that it is headwork, and the study of the batsman's peculiarities, which puts the crown on a bowler. 'There are bowlers', he says, 'who, for some reason or other, seem to fascinate the batsman, and make him do what they want in spite of himself ... The batsman has to fight not only against the particular ball bowled, but against a mysterious unseen influence. There are "demon" bowlers in more senses than one. They are few and far between; but when they come, they win matches by their own individual might.' In other words, genius tells in cricket as in all else.

In batting, Prince Ranjitsinhji is on his own ground, and he dwells on forward play in a manner not to be met in the older treatises, though he confesses that his own predilections (as

105

might be expected from a player so quick of eye and supple of wrist) are towards back play. His minute and perfect instructions must be sought in the book. Only one point I will comment on, because it is not borne out in the illustrations, though the author seems to imagine it is. He says, quite truly, that the position of the left (that is, the upper) hand should be changed in the forward stroke. That is, the left hand should be shifted round the bat, so that the fingertips are presented towards the bowler, instead of the back of the hand, as in the ordinary position of holding the bat. Some players, he allows, do not so twist the upper hand round the bat in playing forward. He refers to the illustrations to exemplify the action. But, unless my eyes are deceived, all the batsmen here photographed in the act of playing forward have the left hand unchanged. If so, it is a singular chance; for there can be no doubt of its advantage. The position of the hand may be understood by reference to the portrait of Prince Ranjitsinhji playing back; for here he has the left hand shifted round as it should be in forward play. It is advisable, above all, in forward defensive play. And this because it guards against the two chief dangers in such play. These are, that the bat may not be kept straight, so as to cover the stump from top to bottom; and that the tip of the blade may be pushed forward in advance of the upper portion of the blade, so as to put the ball up and give a catch. If the left hand be not shifted round, it exercises by its position a natural drag upon the handle of the bat, so as to deflect the upper portion of the blade to the left, and leave the superior portion of the stump exposed. Moreover, besides this lateral deflection of the handle, and consequently of the upper part of the blade, it also exercises a backward drag upon them, so as to leave the tip of the blade dangerously advanced, with the likelihood of a catch. Careful practice may overcome both these tendencies; but in a moment of excitement and inattention they are liable to assert themselves with ruinous results. Whereas the twisting of the left hand round the handle mechanically keeps the bat straight, and the upper portion of the blade well advanced over the lower. A single experiment and comparison will convince any player of this. Another point which may be learned by studying the various photographs of Prince Ranjitsinhji batting given in this book is, that a batsman will do well to alter the relative position of his hands in varying kinds of play. Thus, the Prince's ordinary position at the wicket is with the two hands together at the top of the handle; but in back play his right hand is slid down towards the blade. In glance play back and forward, his right hand is apparently about two inches above the blade, but well separated from the left hand. Some batsmen, who go in for steady play, ordinarily keep the right hand a little above the blade, and apart from the left. Such a batsman, if he lunges forward to drive a ball, where an inch or two of reach makes all the difference, will do well to slide the right hand up to the left at the top of the handle, in order to get the full length of the bat in reaching out at the ball. In fact, any adaptable batsman will find the use of not keeping his hands in one uniform stiff position for all kinds of strokes. Here is part of the value of the instantaneous photographs in this book. It may be doubtful whether Prince Ranjitsinhji himself was conscious of this feaure in his play – at least, he never mentions it; and so the photographs supply hints sometimes not given by the author.

Upon back play, and the methods of making it available for offensive purposes, the author is excellent. The subtlest and newest refinements of stroke all round the wicket are expounded with beautiful clearness: the drive to cover point or extra cover, the peculiar stroke with a horizontal bat between a forward cut and a drive, leg-glances and forcing-strokes on the on side; and, above all, those once-condemned strokes made possible by the perfection of modern wickets. There is one very significant omission. The draw, that most stylish stroke of the older batsman, is never once described. The conditions of modern bowling have, indeed, rendered it obsolete. The last time I saw it used was by A.P. Lucas in a match between England and Australia. On wrist play he is very strong, as might be supposed from the most beautiful wrist player in England.

Talk of modern enthusiasm for cricket! It is nothing to that of the ancients of the game. Witness this of the Rev. John Mitford, describing a visit he paid to Beldham's cottage, when that veteran of Hambledon and Surrey was in his last years: 'in his kitchen, black with age, ... hangs the trophy of his victories, the delight of his youth, the exercise of his manhood, and the glory of his age – his BAT. Reader! believe me when I tell you I trembled when I touched it; it seemed an act of profaneness, of violation. I pressed it to my lips, and returned it to its sanctuary.'

Let that fine bit of rhodomontade put you in tune for approaching the best analysis of cricket yet produced by a magnificent cricketer.

FRANCIS THOMPSON
Selected Essays
(1927)

God on Concrete

He [R.C. Robertson-Glasgow] was, in his day, a vigorous fast bowler but met with very moderate success. Once, when he had spent an exhausting and unprofitable morning against Hobbs and Sandham at the Oval, he paused on his way up the pavilion steps to issue his brief confidential report: 'It's like trying to bowl to God on concrete.'

BEN TRAVERS
94 Declared
(1981)

Sobers Gets Out

It is easy to give one's wicket away, but it takes an artist to do this as well as Gary did to me in a Benefit game in the 1960s. He decided he had provided sufficient entertainment and had scored enough runs, so he got out. Nothing unusual about that. It was the way he did it which typified both the man and his craft. He waited until I sent down a ball of good length which pitched on his leg stump and hit the middle as he played a full forward defensive stroke, deliberately and fractionally down the wrong line. He made it look a very good delivery – it wasn't a bad one! But he played his shot so well that the wicket-keeper and first slip – though both county professionals – came up to congratulate me. I knew instinctively what Gary had done. But no spectator realized it was an act of charity; only Gary and myself.

TREVOR BAILEY
Sir Gary
(1976)

F.E. Woolley

Frank Woolley was easy to watch, difficult to bowl to, and impossible to write about. When you bowled to him there weren't enough fielders; when you wrote about him there weren't enough words. In describing a great innings by Woolley, and few of them were not great in artistry, you had to go careful with your adjectives and stack them in little rows, like pats of butter or razor-blades. In the first over of his innings, perhaps, there had been an exquisite off-drive, followed by a perfect cut, then an effortless leg-glide. In the second over the same sort of thing happened; and your superlatives had already gone. The best thing to do was to presume that your readers knew how Frank Woolley batted and use no adjectives at all.

I have never met a bowler who 'fancied himself' against Woolley, nor heard one who said, with conviction,' 'Woolley doesn't like an off-break on the middle stump or a fast bumper on the leg stump.' I never heard Woolley confess that he preferred or disliked any bowler whatsoever. But then he is a very quiet man. I have a belief that he was particularly fond of them fast and short. They went that much more quickly to the boundary.

It has been said that he was not a good starter. Like other great batsmen, he would sometimes miss in the first minutes. But equally he could kill two bowlers in the first six overs of any match. His own innings might be only about 50 or so, but he had fathered the centuries that followed. Only a few years ago, when he was some forty-seven years old, I saw him 'murder' Voce and Butler, the Nottinghamshire bowlers, in the first overs of a match at Canterbury. They were pitching a little, only a little, too short, and they extracted an exhibition of cutting and hooking which was ... but we have refused the use of adjectives.

Merely from a personal aspect, I never knew so difficult a target as Woolley. His great reach, and the power of his pendulum, made a fool of length. Balls that you felt had a right to tax him he would hit airily over your head. He was immensely discouraging. The only policy was to keep pitching the ball up, and hope. He could never be properly described as being 'set', since he did not go through the habitual process of becoming set. There was no visible growth of confidence or evident strengthening of stroke. He jumped to his meridian. He might hit the first ball of the match, a good ball too, if left to itself, crack to the boundary over mid-on; then, when he had made 60 or more, he might snick a short one past slip in a sudden freak of fallibility, a whim of humanity.

Sometimes he is compared with other famous left-handers, such as the late F.G.J. Ford. But these comparisons seem to be

110

concerned only with attack. It is often forgotten, I think, that Woolley's defence was as sure and correct as that of Mead or Bardsley. Of its kind it was just as wonderful to see, on a sticky wicket, as was his attack. It had a corresponding ease and grace, without toil or trouble. For this reason I think that Woolley will rank as the greatest of all left-handers so far seen in the game. None has made so many runs while giving so much delight.

For many years Woolley was a great part of the Canterbury Festival. Myself, I preferred to watch him or play against him on some ground not in Kent. Praise and pride in home-grown skill are natural and right; but at Canterbury, in the later years, these had degenerated into a blind adulation that applauded his strokes with a very tiresome lack of discrimination. They had made a 'raree' show of a great batsman.

No one, when County cricket is resumed, will fill the place of Frank Woolley. I have tried to avoid metaphor and rhapsody; but there was all summer in a stroke by Woolley, and he batted as it is sometimes shown in dreams.

R.C. ROBERTSON-GLASGOW
Cricket Prints
(1943)

Doing Honour to J.T. Tyldesley

The batsman who is an artist before he is a cricketer has a fastidiousness which is set all on edge, so to say, at the very sight of a stroke 'off the carpet'. Tyldesley had no such compunction. Nor is his lofty on-driving to be taken as evidence that after all he was more than the canny utilitarian, that he liked now and then to live dangerously for the good of his spirit. No; when Tyldesley sent the ball into the air he knew exactly what he was doing; he was not snapping fingers

111

at Providence, nor indulging in quixotry. It is doubtful whether Tyldesley ever hit in the air during a big match out of sheer high spirits. Perhaps the field was set inconveniently for ground hits; very well then, they must go over the heads of the scouts. He could place the ball almost to a nicety. So with his famous cut from the middle stump. Surely, you might object, this stroke was a piece of coxcombry – a display of skill for skill's sake, or, at any rate, a display of skill intended to astound us. Why should it have been? The cut was Tyldesley's master-stroke; he had it under perfect control. 'But', you may still object, 'why from the middle stump? – nothing canny about an adventure like that.' You may be sure Tyldesley did not cut from the middle stump without a good workmanlike reason. Bowlers knew that he would cut to ribbons anything on the off side at all short, and they would in consequence keep on or near Tyldesley's wicket. Was Tyldesley then going to let his cut go into disuse? Was his most productive hit to run to waste? Why should he not cut a short ball on the middle stump? Let him only get into position for it – his foot-play was quicker than the eye could follow – and it was much the same as a ball on the off side, made for cutting. Of course if he missed it the chances were that he would be out. Well, he weighed the chances against his marvellous ability at the cut, and the risk was not palpably greater than the risk a cricketer takes in playing any straight ball – either defensively or offensively.

Macartney used to cut from the middle stump – but for a reason different from Tyldesley's. Macartney would exploit the hit even when it was in his power to make another and safer and even more profitable stroke. For Macartney, though a good antagonist, was a better artist; the spoils of war became in time cheap and tawdry to him. Often did one see disillusion on his face at the end of an opulent innings. Then would he find the challenge of the best bowler irksome: he would throw discretion to the winds in a way that a sound tactician like Tyldesley never did. To refresh his spirit, to save himself from the stale and the flat, Macartney was ready to risk the profitable – to indulge in some impossibly fanciful play of the bat. In this hot quixotic mood his wicket would go to the simplest ball. 'Macartney gets himself out', was a common saying. How seldom one heard that much said of Tyldesley. A bowler had to work for the wicket of Tyldesley. You might baffle him by skill, inveigle him into a false step; never could you hope that he would give himself away. He wore the happy-go-lucky colours of the carefree soldier of fortune, but they were as borrowed plumes: in the flesh Tyldesley was a stern Ironside, with a Cause – the cause of Lancashire – so sacred that it demanded that a man cast the vanities of art and self-glorification to the wind. This most dazzling of all Lancashire batsmen was, forsooth, a Puritan – a conscript of conscience even, trusting in Lancashire but keeping his powder dry!

There lived not a bowler in his time that did not suffer the scourge intolerable from Tyldesley's bat. Rarely was he to be found not 'ware and waking – on a sticky wicket he was as formidable as on a dry one. At the Oval, or at Edgbaston, his happy hunting-ground, the bowler all too soon would behold Tyldesley's wicket as a wicket a long way distant, his bat a sword of fire guarding it. 'Heaven help me!' the sweaty toiler would appeal to the sky. 'If only he would let one go! I don't ask for his wicket – I've been flogged out of vanity like that – but merciful power can surely grant me a maiden over now and then.' Maiden over, indeed, with Tyldesley in form! He would plunder the six most virgin deliveries you ever saw. It was hard even to pitch a decent length to him. For he knew, unlike the modern batsman, that length is not absolute, but relative to a batsman's reach. And though Tyldesley was a little man, his feet had the dancing master's lightness and rapidity of motion. He covered a larger floor space as he made his hits than any batsman playing today – not even excepting Hobbs. What a disdain he must have in these times for the excuse of timid batsmen that they must needs practise

113

patience till bad bowling comes to them! How long would Tyldesley have required to wait for half-volleys from J.T. Hearne, Trumble, Blythe, Noble, and the rest? He turned the well-pitched bowling of these masters into the length a punishing hit asks for by swift footplay. He would jump a yard out of his ground to make a half-volley; he would dart back to the wicket's base to make a long-hop. Two old cricketers once discussed an innings by Tyldesley after the day's cricket was over in something like this language: 'Tha's a reight bowler, Tom. What's thi analysis today – after Johnny'd done wi' thi?' 'Nay, Bill, be fair – tha can't deny I bowl'd well. It wer' t' wicket were too good; I couldn't get any spin on t' ball.' 'Spin, eh? I likes that. Spin on t' ball? Why, I never saw thi hit t' floor all t' afternoon.'

He was in possession of all known strokes, and, as we have seen, he improvised strokes of his own when circumstances challenged him to do so. His square cut was powerful, and the action of it has been vividly described by C.B. Fry: 'He threw the bat at the ball without letting go of the handle.' Many a day-dreaming point – they needed a point, very deep, to Tyldesley – has been seen hopping agitatedly after the advent of the Tyldesley cut. Sometimes he went on his toe-points to make this stroke. His driving was accomplished by a vehement swing of the bat and a most gallant follow-through. There was no saying whether forward or back play was the mark of his style, he combined the two so thoroughly. He was perhaps the best batsman of all time on a bad wicket. P.F. Warner is never tired of singing the praises of Tyldesley's innings of 62 made on a 'glue-pot' at Melbourne in 1904. England's total was then 103, and Relf was the only other batsman to get double figures.

A great batsman is to be estimated, of course, not merely by his scores, or even by his technique, but also by taking into account the quality of the bowling he had to tackle in his day, and the quality of the grounds he mainly played on. When Tyldesley came to greatness English bowling was in a classic period; he had to face men like Lohmann, Richardson, Peel, J.T. Hearne, Noble, Jones. But not only did he take his whack out of some of the best of our classical bowlers; he was also one of the first batsmen to master the new googly bowling. He passed, in fact, through all the manifold changes in fashion which came over bowling between 1903 and 1919. And whether it was J.T. Hearne or R.O. Schwarz, Rhodes or D.W. Carr, Tyldesley was always the same brilliant and punitive Tyldesley. Then let us bear in mind as we do honour to his genius that half of Tyldesley's cricket was played at Old Trafford, where in his time wickets were not above suspicion.

NEVILLE CARDUS
Days in the Sun
(1924)

Ramadhin and Valentine

Sonny Ramadhin, only 5 ft 4 in, wears a Chaplin-style moustache and a smile like a toothpaste advertisement in a Bombay newspaper. To one grandfather, who went from India to work on a cocoa estate, he owes his small bones, glistening wavy hair and, no doubt, an infusion of the mysticism of the East with the witch-doctor type of magic he inherits from the other side of the family. Whisked from a South Trinidad oilfield into his country's team at nineteen, Ramadhin knows no first name except Sonny.

Alfred Lewis Valentine is 6 ft tall and every inch a Negro, with crinkly hair and full lips. Before taking the field this lean Jamaican has rubbed his dark face and hands with an eau-de-Cologne lotion to prevent sunburn. As he bowls in the sunshine, some hidden power is suggested by flashes from his spectacles, from a gold chain bracelet on his right wrist and from his teeth, bared in an expectant grimace.

Valentine comes around the wicket with four long, bent-kneed strides, like Groucho Marx getting into a lift before the door closes. On the way to the crease Valentine passes the ball from his bangle hand into his business hand, jamming it between the first two fingers. He coils the wrist inward and straightens it with a flick that imparts more leg-spin to the ball than any left-hander since Victoria's renowned Ironmonger between the wars. As the ball leaves, his forefinger pokes after it – pointing the bone at the batsman.

Ramadhin forks his first two fingers, small, lean and damp, over the ball's seam. He flits across the crease with six lively paces. The ball shoots at the batsman from a one-two-three flutter of black and white, because he flaps his right and left sleeves over before his right hand delivers in its next circle. As this hand comes up behind his head, something mysterious happens too quickly for the eye to take in – a half-hint that his elbow bows and straightens. That is Ramadhin's secret, an essential part of his voodoo rite. The bewitched ball darts from the pitch, mostly whipping back from the off. Occasionally Ramadhin releases a slower ball which looks as if it will be a full toss but dips late in its flight. Sometimes this slower ball is the sly leg-break which batsmen have trouble in detecting from his hand, or it may be a retarded version of his off-break. Lynx-eyed opponents take a slightly higher ball as a sign that a leg-break is coming.

Australia's top batsmen, proven masters of Englishmen's bowling, rational and civilized, were spellbound when they first came up against the Caribbean conjurations of Ramadhin and Valentine. The inky illusionists humbled the finest batsmen in a manner not seen on a good wicket since the bodyline ordeal nearly twenty years before. The last man, Bill Johnston, was in before Ian Johnson put Australia ahead amid howls of excitement.

Though Valentine's left-hand turn and quicker straight balls took five wickets in the first innings to his partner's one, Ramadhin's original flight and spin beat the bat more and upset the batsmen most. Ramadhin reminded me of a

116

kerbside salesman holding the people's attention while his accomplice picked their pockets. Not all the resource of Morris and Hassett, men of calm purpose, or the dash of Harvey, daringly brilliant, could break the spell, though it was partly lifted by the death-or-glory hitting of Miller and Lindwall and the spirited strokes of Hole who, at twenty, was too old to believe in fairies yet not old enough for cares and superstitions.

Among those outside the teams who underestimated the potency of the voodoo was Sir Donald Bradman. On the last morning, when the Australians needed only 128 runs and had eight wickets to get them, Sir Donald laughed aside a friend's suggestion that they were still in peril. In little more than half an hour three of the best wickets went for 31, half the side was out and the game had swung against Australia. Gripped by the Australians' struggle for survival, the thousands were so silent you could have heard a bail drop. We did. It was Harvey's, dislodged by a swerving yorker from Ramadhin.

After an hour's unchanged bowling, the captain took a new ball, long overdue, but, fearful of interrupting Ramadhin and Valentine and relaxing the pressure, he did not call on his new-ball bowlers. Instead, the shiny, red ball was rubbed against the pitch before the same pair carried on. We presumed that this was done to roughen its surface for their finger grip but, looking at the match in perspective, I have since wondered whether the West Indians were rubbing the ball, Aladdin-like, to summon up some genie. If so, Hole, Lindwall and Ring were not conscious of his presence, and Australia scraped home. Ramadhin and Valentine bowled 647 consecutive balls in the last innings (after 392 in the first innings before a rest) and they equally shared 12 of the 16 Australian wickets taken by bowlers.

RAY ROBINSON
The Glad Season
(1955)

117

Silver Billy

We must hasten on, for we are at length arrived at the tent of *Achilles* himself. Stop, reader, and look, if thou art a cricketer, with reverence and awe on that venerable and aged form! These are the remains of the once great, glorious, and unrivalled William Beldham, called for love and respect, and for his flaxen locks and his fair complexion, 'Silver Billy'. Beldham was a close-set, active man, about five feet eight inches. Never was such a player! so safe, so brilliant, so quick, so circumspect; so able in counsel, so active in the field; in deliberation so judicious, in execution so tremendous. It mattered not to him who bowled, or how he bowled, fast or slow, high or low, straight or bias; away flew the ball from his bat, like an eagle on the wing. It was a study for Phidias to see Beldham rise to strike; the grandeur of the attitude, the settled composure of the look, the piercing lightning of the eye, the rapid glance of the bat, were electrical. Men's hearts throbbed within them, their cheeks turned pale and red. Michelangelo should have painted him. Beldham was great in every hit, but his peculiar glory was the *cut*. Here he stood with no man beside him, the laurel was all his own; it was like the cut of a *racket*. His wrist seemed to turn on springs of the finest steel. He took the ball, as Burke did the House of Commons, between wind and water; not a moment too soon or late. Beldham still survives. He lives near Farnham; and in his kitchen, black with age, but, like himself, still untouched with worms, hangs the trophy of his victories, the delight of his youth, the exercise of his manhood, and the glory of his age – his BAT. Reader! believe me, when I tell you I trembled when I touched it; it seemed an act of profaneness, of violation. I pressed it to my lips, and returned it to its sanctuary.

THE REV. JOHN MITFORD
The Gentleman's Magazine
(July–September 1833)

Ghost-writer to W.G. Grace

My happiest days in journalism, I think, were the cricket seasons of 1890 and 1891, when I was writing descriptive reports of cricket in London for the *Manchester Examiner*, and following the Lancashire team on its southern tours. A day in the Press box at a first-class county match is still a long-drawn-out ecstasy to me. For a time I was thrown among cricketers, amateur and professional, and found them sterling, healthy-minded, large-hearted men with scarcely an exception. For George Lohmann I had a great affection. But the cricketer with whom I was brought into closest contact was the incomparable W.G. Grace.

I spent all the leisure of twelve months, some years later, working in collaboration with Dr Grace on his well-known book, *W.G.: Cricketing Reminiscences*. It is not a breach of faith now to say that I wrote the book. Grace was chock-full of cricketing history, experience and reminiscences, but he was a singularly inarticulate man, and had he been left to write his own cricketing biography it would never have seen the light. My friend Mr James Bowden (through Mr Coulson Kernahan) sought my co-operation with Grace, who had entered into an agreement with him to produce a volume of reminiscences for publication in his jubilee year. It had seemed as if the contract would expire without a line of the book having been written. Grace accepted me as his collaborator with the utmost heartiness, and, although the task of getting the material from him was almost heartbreaking, I enjoyed the work immensely. My plan was to spend three half days a week with W.G. in his own study – he was living at Sydenham then – and by every conceivable artifice that an experienced interviewer could bring into operation, lure him into a flow of reminiscence. Many days I drew a blank and came away with scarcely sufficient material for a paragraph. On other days I managed to inveigle him into a reminiscent vein, and he would send me off with data enough for one or two chapters.

W.G. Grace's mind functioned oddly. He never stuck to any train of recollection, but would jump from an event in the 1860s to something that happened in, say, the last Test Match. Often I left his house in absolute despair. Once, at least, I asked leave to abandon the enterprise; but I was urged to persist. I remember very distinctly one age-long afternoon when I was trying to get out of W.G. something of the psychology of a batsman making a big score in a great match. All that he wanted to say in recording some dazzling batting feat of his own was, 'Then I went in and made 284.' 'Yes,' I would reply, 'but that is not good enough. People want to know what W.G. Grace felt like when he was doing it; what thoughts he had and what the whole mental experience of a big innings means to a batsman.' 'I did not feel anything; I had too much to do to watch the bowling and see how the fieldsmen were moved about to think of anything.' The very best that I could get out of him was that 'some days a batsman's eye is *in* and other days it is not. When his eye is *in*, the cricket ball seems the size of a football and he can't miss it. When his eye isn't *in* then he isn't in long, because he's soon bowled out.'

I failed utterly, I confess, to draw from W.G. anything adequate in the way of a chapter on the art of cricket captaincy. He had the generalship of the game by instinct, and, in his autocratic fashion, was a sound captain with every artifice at his fingertips. But he had no consciousness of what he did know in that department of cricket strategy – which, it must be remembered, was an empirical matter and not the exact science to which Australian captaincy has reduced it. So his advice to captains in his reminiscences is poor stuff. I could get nothing out of him that was in the slightest degree illuminating or helpful.

Conscious of his own inarticulateness, Grace was fearfully apprehensive lest I should put into his reminiscences any

120

words that were not in his accustomed vocabulary. One day in running through a chapter I had written and which we were revising together, he pulled up at the word 'inimical'. 'No,' he said firmly, 'that word can't go in. Why, if that went into the book I should have the fellows at Lord's coming to me in the pavilion and saying, "Look here, W.G., where did you get that word from?"'

About Dr W.G. Grace there was something indefinable – like the simple faith of a child – which arrested and fascinated me. He was a big grown-up boy, just what a man who only lived when he was in the open air might be expected to be. A wonderful kindliness ran through his nature, mingling strangely with the arbitrary temper of a man who had been accustomed to be dominant over other men.

His temper was very fiery – perhaps gusty is a better word – and his prejudices ran away with him. He detested Radicals in politics, and disliked umpires who had ever given him out lbw. I asked him one day what he thought of a once-famous Lancashire bowler, at that time ranking as a first-class umpire. 'I don't want to say much about *him* in this book,' he replied. 'He gave me out lbw to a ball that broke four inches when I was just "getting my eye in" at the Gentlemen v. Players match at the Oval in——'. He could not forget that crowning offence. Of other men he made idols – they could do no wrong. 'Ranji' was one of them. So were Charles B. Fry, F.S. Jackson and Archie MacLaren. We had warm arguments and all the little differences that collaboration almost necessarily involves; but never a moment of anger disturbed our relations, and we were good friends to the end of the partnership, and afterwards.

W.G. Grace would have made an excellent subject for a modern psychoanalyst who might, from W.G.'s subconscious stores of forgotten cricket lore, have extracted for us a classic of cricket literature. Reverting to W.G.'s choleric temperament, I think I once did make him really cross. It was when I flatly refused to believe his statement that he had only one lung, and had, in fact, had only one lung since his childhood. 'Now who', I asked him incredulously, 'is going to believe that?' I simply could not credit it. Grace was, for the moment, nettled, and then he said rather testily, 'I'm not going to have you doubting what I say; I'll call my wife, and she'll confirm what I have told you.' He called Mrs Grace, who corroborated W.G.'s story. Then I apologized and we made peace.

ARTHUR PORRITT
The Best I Remember
(1922)

Don Bradman

In the many pictures that I have stored in my mind from the 'burnt-out Junes' of forty years, there is none more dramatic or compelling than that of Bradman's small, serenely moving figure in its big-peaked green cap coming out of the pavilion shadows into the sunshine, with the concentration, ardour and apprehension of surrounding thousands centred upon him, and the destiny of a Test Match in his hands.

H.S. ALTHAM
The Cricketer's Spring Annual
(1941)

One Great Landmark

An underarm bowler could only bowl a certain number of different balls, and when roundarm bowling was legalized there were added to the game all those balls which roundarm bowlers could deliver but underarm bowlers could not: similarly, when overarm bowling came in, the sum total of bowlable balls was again increased. An underarm bowler can make the ball twist – that is, curl off the ground – but he cannot make it break or bump; a roundarm can make the ball twist from leg and break somewhat from the off and also cause it to swing across the wicket; an overarm can do all these things and also make the ball bump. All three kinds differ in the flight of the ball in the air and in its manner of coming from the pitch.

Naturally a batsman had to know more strokes as the number of balls to be played increased; so the development of batting must have gone hand in hand with that of bowling. The change from under- to roundarm was begun by Mr John Willes in 1822, and the style became general about 1827. F.W. Lillywhite was the great exponent of the innovation. He and a bowler named Broadbridge were so good that Sussex was able to play All England on level terms. Those must have been good days! But, apart from its gradual adaptation to the requirements of changes in bowling style, there is one great landmark that separates the old batting from the new – the appearance of Dr W.G. Grace in the cricket world. In 1865 W.G. came fully before the public that has admired and loved him ever since. He revolutionized batting. He turned it from an accomplishment into a science. All I know of old-time batting is, of course, gathered from books and older players, but the impression left on my mind is this: Before W.G. batsmen were of two kinds – a batsman played a forward game or he played a back game. Each player, too, seems to have made a specialty of some particular stroke. The criterion of style was, as it were, a certain mixed method of play. It was bad cricket to hit a straight ball; as for pulling a slow long-hop, it was regarded as immoral. What W.G. did was to unite in his mighty self all the good points of all the good players, and to make utility the criterion of style. He founded the modern theory of batting by making forward and back play of equal importance, relying neither on the one nor on the other, but on both. Any cricketer who thinks for a moment can see the enormous change W.G. introduced into the game. I hold him to be, not only the finest player born or unborn, but the maker of modern batting. He turned the old one-stringed instrument into a many-chorded lyre. And, in addition, he made his execution equal his invention. All of us now have the instrument, but we lack his execution. It is not that we do not know, but that we cannot perform. Before W.G. batsmen did not know what could be made of batting. The development of bowling has been natural and gradual; each great bowler has added his quota. W.G. discovered batting; he turned its many narrow straight channels into one great winding river.

PRINCE RANJITSINHJI
The Jubilee Book of Cricket
(1897)

Game Old Merrimynn

Kickakick. She had to kick a laugh. At her old stick-in-the-block. The way he was slogging his paunch about, elbiduu-bled, meet oft mate on, like hale King Willow, the robberer. Cainmaker's mace and waxened capapee. But the tarrant's brand on his hottoweyt brow. At half past quick in the morning. And her lamp was all askew and a trumbly wick-in-her, ringeysingey. She had to spofforth, she had to kicker, too thick of the wick of her pixy's loomph, wide lickering jessup the smooky shiminey. And her duffed coverpoint of a wickedy batter, whenever she druv gehind her stumps for a tyddlesly wink through his tunnil-clefft bagslops after the rising bounder's yorkers, as he studd and stoddard and trutted and trumpered, to see had lordherry's blackham's red bobby abbels, it tickled her innings to consort pitch at kicksolock in the morm. Tipatonguing him on in her pigeony linguish, with a flick at the bails for lubrication, to scorch her faster, faster. Ye hek, ye hok, ye hucky hiremonger! Magrath he's my pegger, he is, for bricking up all my old kent road. He'll win your toss, flog your old tom's bowling and I darr

124

ye, barrackybuller, to break his duck! He's posh. I lob him. We're parring all Oogster till the empsyseas run googlie. Declare to ashes and teste his metch! Three for two will do for me and he for thee and she for you. Goeasyosey, for the grace of the fields, or hooley pooley, cuppy, we'll both be bye and by caught in the slips for fear he'd tyre and burst his dunlops and waken her bornybarnies making his booby-babies. The game old merrimynn, square to leg, with his lolleywide towelhat and his hobbsy socks and his wisden's bosse and his norsery pinafore and his gentleman's grip and his playaboy's plunge and his flannelly feelyfooling, treading her hump and hambledown like a maiden wellheld, ovalled over, with her crease where the pads of her punishments ought to be by womanish rights when, keek, the hen in the doran's shantyqueer began in a kikkery key to laugh it off, yeigh, yeigh, neigh, neigh, the way she was wuck to doodledoo by her gallows bird (how's that? Noball, he carries his bat!) nine hundred and dirty too not out, at all times long past conquering cock of the morgans.

JAMES JOYCE
Finnegans Wake
(1939)

The following cricketing names seem to appear in this extract:
S.A. Block, Charles Stewart Caine, F.A. Tarrant (or George Tarrant), A.B. Quick, Hugh Trumble, K.S. Ranjitsinhji, F.R. Spofforth, G.L. Jessop, R.A. Duff, J.T. Tyldesley, J. Tunnicliffe, C.T. Studd (or Sir Kynaston or G.B. Studd), A.E. Stoddart, A.E. Trott (or G.H.S. Trott), Victor Trumper, Lord Harris, J.M. Blackham, Robert Abel, J. Iremonger (or Albert Iremonger), Tom Richardson, A.G. Daer, C.F. Buller, George Parr, W.G. Grace, Ted Pooley, Alfred Mynn, James Lillywhite (or some member of this family), Sir Jack Hobbs, John Wisden, Dave Nourse (or Dudley Nourse) and J.T. Morgan.

125

COMMENT

Advice to a Literary Aspirant

With a thorough knowledge of the Bible, Shakespeare and *Wisden* you cannot go far wrong.

ARTHUR WAUGH
quoted by his son Evelyn Waugh in
A Little Learning
(1964)

Temptation as Bowler

'Life is simply a cricket match – with Temptation as Bowler. He's the fellow who takes nearly every boy's wicket some time or other. But perhaps you can't stand this, Baxter. I'll stop it.'

'No,' said Baxter, 'I'm as right as a trivet. Please go on. I know you won't preach.'

'Well,' continued the Captain, 'stop me if I bore you. You see every boy has three wickets to defend. The first is Truth, the second Honour, the third Purity.'

ANON
Baxter's Second Innings
(1892)

Raffles

Old Raffles may or may not have been an exceptional criminal, but as a cricketer I dare swear he was unique. Himself a dangerous bat, a brilliant field, and perhaps the very finest slow bowler of his decade, he took incredibly little interest in the game at large. He never went up to Lord's without his cricket-bag, or showed the slightest interest in the result of a match in which he was not himself engaged. Nor was this mere hateful egotism on his part. He professed to have lost all enthusiasm for the game, and to keep it up only from the very lowest motives.

'Cricket,' said Raffles, 'like everything else, is good enough sport until you discover a better. As a source of excitement it isn't in it with other things you wot of, Bunny, and the involuntary comparison becomes a bore. What's the satisfaction of taking a man's wicket when you want his spoons? Still, if you can bowl a bit your low cunning won't get rusty, and always looking for the weak spot's just the kind of mental exercise one wants. Yes, perhaps there's some affinity between the two things after all. But I'd chuck up cricket tomorrow, Bunny, if it wasn't for the glorious protection it affords a person of my proclivities.'

'How so?' said I. 'It brings you before the public, I should have thought, far more than is either safe or wise.'

'My dear Bunny, that's exactly where you make a mistake. To follow crime with reasonable impunity you simply must have a parallel ostensible career – the more public the better. The principle is obvious. Mr Peace, of pious memory, disarmed suspicion by acquiring a local reputation for playing the fiddle and taming animals, and it's my profound conviction that Jack the Ripper was a really eminent public man, whose speeches were very likely reported alongside his atrocities. Fill the bill in some prominent part, and you'll never be suspected of doubling it with another of equal prominence. That's why I want you to cultivate journalism, my boy, and sign all you can. And it's the one and only reason why I don't burn my bats for firewood.'

Nevertheless, when he did play there was no keener performer on the field, nor one more anxious to do well for his side. I remember how he went to the nets, before the first match of the season, with his pocket full of sovereigns, which he put on the stumps instead of bails. It was a sight to see the professionals bowling like demons for the hard cash, for whenever a stump was hit a pound was tossed to the bowler and another balanced in its stead, while one man took £3 with a ball that spreadeagled the wicket. Raffles's practice cost him either eight or nine sovereigns; but he had absolutely first-class bowling all the time, and he made 57 runs next day.

It became my pleasure to accompany him to all his matches, to watch every ball he bowled, or played, or fielded, and to sit chatting with him in the pavilion when he was doing none of these three things. You might have seen us there, side by side, during the greater part of the Gentlemen's first innings against the Players (who had lost the toss) on the second Monday in July. We were to be seen, but not heard, for Raffles had failed to score, and was uncommonly cross for a player who cared so little for the game. Merely taciturn with me, he was positively rude to more than one member who wanted to know how it had happened, or who ventured to commiserate him on his luck; there he sat, with a straw hat tilted over his nose and a cigarette stuck between lips that curled disagreeably at every advance.

E. W. HORNUNG
The Amateur Cracksman
(1899)

Raffles and Morality

Raffles, of course, is good at all games, but it is peculiarly fitting that his chosen game should be cricket. This allows not only of endless analogies between his cunning as a slow bowler and his cunning as a burglar, but also helps to define the exact nature of his crime. Cricket is not in reality a very popular game in England – it is nowhere near so popular as football, for instance – but it gives expression to a well-marked trait in the English character, the tendency to value 'form' or 'style' more highly than success. In the eyes of any true cricket-lover it is possible for an innings of ten runs to be 'better' (i.e., more elegant) than an innings of a hundred runs:

cricket is also one of the very few games in which the amateur can excel the professional. It is a game full of forlorn hopes and sudden dramatic changes of fortune, and its rules are so ill-defined that their interpretation is partly an ethical business. When Larwood, for instance, left a trail of broken bones up and down Australia, he was not actually breaking any rule: he was merely doing something that was 'not cricket'. Since cricket takes up a lot of time and is rather expensive to play, it is predominantly an upper-class game, but for the whole nation it is bound up with such concepts as 'good form', 'playing the game', etc., and it has declined in popularity just as the tradition of 'don't hit a man when he's down' has declined. It is not a twentieth-century game, and nearly all modern-minded people dislike it. The Nazis, for instance, were at pains to discourage cricket, which had gained a certain footing in Germany before and after the last war. In making Raffles a cricketer as well as a burglar, Hornung was not merely providing him with a plausible disguise; he was also drawing the sharpest moral contrast that he was able to imagine.

GEORGE ORWELL
Raffles and Miss Blandish
(1944)

The Curse of Gentility

Pray, are you a cricketer? We are very great ones – I mean our parish, of which we, the feminine members, act audience, and 'though we do not play, o'erlook' the balls. When I wrote to you last I was just going to see a grand match in a fine old park near us, Bramshill, between Hampshire, with Mr Budd, and All England. I anticipated great pleasure from so grand an exhibition, and thought, like a simpleton, the better the play the more the enjoyment. Oh, what a mistake! There they were – a set of ugly old men, whiteheaded and baldheaded

132

(for half of Lord's was engaged in the combat, players and gentlemen, Mr Ward and Lord Frederick, the veterans of the green) dressed in tight white jackets (the Apollo Belvedere could not bear the hideous disguise of a cricketing jacket), with neckcloths primly tied round their throats, fine japanned shoes, silk stockings and gloves, instead of our fine village lads, with their unbuttoned collars, their loose waistcoats, and the large shirt-sleeves which give an air so picturesque and Italian to their glowing, bounding youthfulness: there they stood, railed in by themselves, silent, solemn, slow – playing for money, making a business of the thing, grave as judges, taciturn as chess players – a sort of dancers without music, instead of the glee, the fun, the shouts, the laughter, the glorious confusion of the country game. And there were we, the lookers-on, in tents and marquees, fine and freezing, dull as the players, cold as this hard summer weather, shivering and yawning and trying to seem pleased, the curse of gentility on all our doings, as stupid as we could have been in a ball-room. I never was so disappointed in my life. But everything is spoilt when money puts its ugly nose in. To think of playing cricket for hard cash! Money and gentility would ruin any pastime under the sun. Much to my comfort (for the degrading my favourite sport into a 'science', as they were pleased to call it, had made me quite spiteful) the game ended unsatisfactorily to all parties, winners and losers. Old Lord Frederick, on some real or imaginary affront, took himself off in the middle of the second innings, so that the two last were played without him, by which means his side lost, and the other could scarcely be said to win. So be it always when men make the noble game of cricket an affair of bettings and hedgings, and, maybe, of cheatings.

MARY RUSSELL MITFORD
Letter to R.B. Haydon
(24 August 1823)

The Deserted Parks (Oxford)

Solitudinem faciunt: Parcum appelant

Amidst thy bowers the tyrant's hand is seen,
The rude pavilions sadden all thy green;
One selfish pastime grasps the whole domain,
And half a faction swallows up the plain;
Adown thy glades, all sacrificed to cricket,
The hollow-sounding bat now guards the wicket;
Sunk are thy mounds in shapeless level all,
Lest aught impede the swiftly rolling ball;
And trembling, shrinking from the fatal blow,
Far, far away thy hapless children go.

The man of wealth and pride
Takes up space that many poor supplied:
Space for the game, and all its instruments,
Space for pavilions and for scorers' tents;
The ball, that raps his shins in padding cased,
Has wore the verdure to an arid waste;
His Park, where these exclusive sports are seen,
Indignant spurns the rustic from the green;
While through the plain, consigned to silence all,
In barren splendour flits the russet ball.

LEWIS CARROLL
'Notes by an Oxford Chiel' (1865–74)
from *The Complete Works* (1939)

Harold Pinter: Cricketer

'At the age of forty I am a batsman who has never fulfilled his promise. What's more,' added Harold Pinter, 'I've never made 50. My highest score is 49.'

134

Pinter – poet, playwright, actor, director, screenwriter, even writer – is the least oblique man you could ever hope to meet. He's as straight as a gun-barrel – a man who, if he put his mind to it, might carry off the Queen's Prize at Bisley.

I've never seen him play cricket, only seen him in plays. A pity. You can't help thinking that his enthusiasm and love of the game might outshine his natural cricketing ability. But then there's his knowledge of the game. In 1969 he wrote an article 'Memories of Cricket' for the *Daily Telegraph* Magazine. After initial resistance to the style, you concede the knowledge – and so acknowledge the style.

Pinter is superb on defining cricketers in terms of what they did and who they were. Hardstaff, Simpson, Sims, Worrell, Weekes, Compton, Hutton, Bradman ... And supreme at what it was like at the time.

Take the great 1948 Test at Lord's when Bradman came back to town. 'After lunch, the Australians, arrogant, jocular, muscular, larking down the pavilion steps. They waited, hurling the ball about, eight feet tall.' There you are. That's what it was all about. I was there. A very hard, precise objective judgement. And he's very good on the field placings, knows the game inside out, spares the adjectives, knows a hawk from a handsaw.

The boy Pinter got up early in the morning and played cricket with his friends against a tree in the local field. 'But there was no coaching at school and the wickets were bad. Had I started in my teens with proper coaching – well, I might not have been too bad.'

Pinter's son Daniel (thirteen) obviously had little chance in the shadow of his father's obsession. Father and son went through the mill at Alf Gover's cricket school. The man who put the Pinters through their paces was Fred Paolozzi.

Now it's Arthur Wellard at the Middlesex School. Wellard's views on the Pinters (father and son) are not known to me. But Pinter says: 'You might say that Daniel is a better man than his father.'

A note about Wellard: Pinter recalls a game in 1929. Notts v. Somerset. He's right, it's in *Wisden*: H. Larwood b Wellard 0. A.W. Wellard b Larwood 0. Another bowler called Voce 'dismissed three batsmen in 4 overs without a run being registered off him.'

The last quote is *Wisden*, not Pinter.

But as Pinter says: 'It's different in the nets.' When he gets down to play he finds himself a bit rooted in the crease, a bit flashy outside the off-stump, a bit more out than in. But he fields at silly mid-off. (Remember what happened to Sid Barnes at Old Trafford?)

Pinter's actual cricket is played with Gaieties, a cricket club that plays on Sundays, captained by Laurie Lupino-Lane. The cricket is not solemn but it's dead serious. Pinter has no time for those matches where the first ball is a cricket ball and the second a grapefruit. 'Gaieties,' he says, 'make a great difference to my life. Simply, the rest of the world ceases to exist. I want our side to win.'

And now hear this. 'In my mind, what I'm doing most of the time is playing forward. At my best I'm a front-foot player. When I write, direct, or see my own plays I'm playing cricket shots in my mind, I'm always going through these motions, the feet perfectly in position, the perfect shot.'

In Losey's film *Accident* (screenplay by Pinter) there's a cricket match — or rather a bit of one. Pinter admitted that he'd shoved in this scene because of his love of the game. Actually it fits neatly into the plot and pushes the people a little nearer to their end. But the cricket bit doesn't quite come off. It just isn't good and sharp enough. In fact it's not cricket.

But there's another cricket match in the film of L.P. Hartley's *The Go-Between* (screenplay by Pinter). Pinter says: 'One of the principal reasons that the cricket match in *The Go-Between* is superior to that of *Accident* is that Fred Paolozzi was cricket adviser and coach on *The Go-Between*.'

So back to a Grand Master. Pinter confirmed what he'd written in 1969 about Hutton. Pinter said this. 'Hutton . . . he was never dull. His bat was part of his nervous system ... The handle of his bat seemed electric. Always, for me, a sense of his vulnerability, of a very uncommon sensibility.' That's our Sir Len right enough. Had Pinter ever met him? No. Would he like to? Yes. What about cricketing dialogue between Pinter and Hutton? Perhaps.

What a Test match that would be. Certainly Pinter would need a special session in his mental nets before that one. It's difficult, almost impossible, to catch out Sir Len when he starts talking: 'Yes, you see in Australia even the stumps seem to be made of harder wood ... yes, those chaps Lindwall, Miller and Johnston gave me a bit of trouble ... and that chap Bradman was another player who...'

Pinter is a dark, spare, tough-looking fit man without a touch of intensity. His mind is certainly not elsewhere. Cricket apart, he plays squash and table tennis. Robert Shaw (another writing, acting and competitive demon) stretches Pinter a bit on these occasions.

I left Pinter and saw a cricket bat, battered and relaxed like an old umbrella, in a corner of the hall. A big chunk was knocked out of it. A thick edge in fact. 'What I like most,' he said, 'is a well-pitched ball outside the off-stump.'

Ideal. And waiting behind the wicket, Hammond, Bailey, Cowdrey, Evans, Tallon....

But Pinter's last words were: 'I intend to get my head down and score some runs.'

CLIFFORD MAKINS
The Observer
(3 January 1971)

Tour Reporters

Apart, perhaps, from the odd Cuban revolutionary, one or two lighthouse-keepers and the hibernating complex of

Britain, the whole world seems to be playing cricket at the moment. It is manifestly unfair.

Sports pages have been decorated during the past month with cricket datelines from Brazil, Australia, the West Indies and South Africa, not to mention various watering holes in India. But more than that: the evidence is mounting that, away from head office, our golf writers are also trying to get their hands on cricket.

Henry Longhurst of the *Sunday Times*, writing from the shade of a coconut tree in Tobago, described how he had spent a 'largely hilarious afternoon' watching Colin Cowdrey and Kent play the Island team. 'Here was the sort of game that would fill the cricket grounds of England again overnight,' he wrote. 'With the game fairly well in hand, Cowdrey elected to give himself an over or two and almost at once scattered a West Indian's stumps, which seemed to give rise to unseemly merriment. The incoming batsman, however, hit the next ball over the crowd, over the main road, over the beach and into the Atlantic.'

Meantime, the *Sunday Telegraph*'s golf man, Donald Steel, was filing a cricket story from Rio de Janeiro: an inside story, no less, because Steel was writing as a member of the Twenty Club's party (Bob Gale, Stuart Surridge and company). 'Noel Coward would never believe it and Lord's would never stand for it,' wrote Steel, 'but a side of English cricketers have won what they were pleased to call a Test match against Brazil ... but since no Brazilian (cricket) side has ever been known to contain a single Brazilian, it was not surprising that the proceedings caused little stir.' ...

[The men out in India and Pakistan] have been writing in Technicolor. Clive Taylor of the *Sun* offered us this introduction: 'In a moment of drama that burst like a phial of acid over another day of hateful heat, England preserved for themselves just a droplet of hope.'

And Peter Laker of the *Daily Mirror*, after Tony Lewis had followed his resignation as Glamorgan's captain with a century in the fourth Test, had this to say: 'Tony Lewis, an ardent devotee of classical music, composed his own symphony here today.' Who said the *Mirror* had no culture?

My very favourite introduction, however, was built by Robin Marlar in the *Sunday Times*. He wrote: 'The vultures sit, 16 to a tree, the big brown kites whirl and dive, hundreds of thousands of bicycles are pedalled through Kanpur's crowded streets, the cars hoot and are ignored, and not so far from the bridge over the Ganges where the massacred bodies were disposed during the mutiny of a century and more ago, in the new Modi Stadium in Green Park, England are trying to square up a series watched by 14,000 cheerful but potentially dangerous students and most of the police force of Uttar Pradesh.'

Ornithology, local custom, high adventure, colonial history, international sport and social comment all in a sentence. Not bad.

BRYON BUTLER
in *The Cricketer*
(March 1973)

Arlott's Voice

I hear John Arlott's voice every weekend, describing cricket matches. He sounds like Uncle Tom Cobleigh reading Neville Cardus to the Indians...

DYLAN THOMAS
Letter to Margaret Taylor
(11 July 1947)

The Cow-shot

It was in 1904 that John Buttery, who was then Sporting Editor of the *Daily Mail*, got a very good idea from the circulation point of view. It was, as many may remember, to get the County Captains to write about 150 words – a small message anyway – on the day's cricket and wire it down to the *Daily Mail*, signed by their own names. Bertie Evans and I were asked to send along our contributions also, and did so. ...

Of course it was impossible to take the thing too seriously, especially at Oxford and Cambridge, where one could not praise up a man too much, unless he was already in the side, without more or less hinting that he would play at Lord's. At the same time, being paid, one had to do something honest to merit the 'beer money' as we called it. Following such people as Gerald Winter, Rockley Wilson, and Dowson, and with the pride of knowing Laurence Grossmith, the master of comic phrases, I naturally dashed off some Cambridgese which was appreciated by John Buttery. It was in those days that the 'cow-shot' was first printed. I wired – it was all done by wire of course in those days – one day that 'K.R.B. Fry played the cow-shot magnificently off' some bowler whose name I have forgotten. It did not appear in print, but I got a letter next day which I well remember. Buttery wrote, 'You use the expression the "cow-shot" in your wire, but I think it must be a Post Office error. Jessop says he has never heard the expression, though he knows the donkey-waggle. If it is a new Cambridge expression please repeat in your next report.' Jessop, it should be mentioned, was a newspaper man, or writer would be the better term, for some years and was on the *Daily Mail* for some time. ...

'The donkey-waggle' was a new expression to me and I expect that Jessop coined it himself. The cow-shot could not be repeated for about a week, because nobody happened to play it: but it appeared as soon as possible, 'made discussion', and has since developed into a classic. The invention of the term is very generally put down to me but, unfortunately, incorrectly. I always thought that Rockley Wilson originated it, but have been told since that the real author was Gerald

Winter. Gerald, in a different way, was as great a humorist as Rockley was himself. At any rate you will now find the 'cowshot' printed as a recognized term of cricket in *The Times*, even as is the googly: both are now unquestioned terms in cricket, though they will not yet allow the easy catch to be described as a 'percher', an older expression than either.

F.B. WILSON
Sporting Pie
(1922)

The Googly and Lewis Carroll

Sir,

The word 'googly' was first used in a newspaper article in New Zealand in 1903 to describe Bosanquet's new ball. The word means uncanny, weird, ghostly, and is supposed to be of Maori origin. There are many words with the ō or oo vowel sound associated especially with k, j or g, which express the same quality of fear and wonder. Bogey, boogey-woogey, spook, etc., and Lewis Carroll must have been aware of this when he coined the word Boojum.

A more apt word to describe a leg-break from the off could not be imagined, and we remain indebted to an unknown New Zealand journalist.

R.W. COCKSHUT
Letter to *The Times*
(10 May 1963)

... and Hegel

Sir,

Do you want to be torn to pieces by nettled Bosanquets? That family claims two major innovations: (1) the introduc-

141

tion into Oxford of Hegel and 'German idealism', (2) the introduction into cricket of the googly. It is obvious that (2) was merely the sporting consequence of (1): but just as Bradley must be granted to have helped with the philosophical juggle, so must my dear mother (née Louise Bosanquet) be allowed her share in the bowling one.

As a little girl she hero-worshipped her cousin, 'BJT', and paid for it in the 1890s by being made to stand at one end of a lawn for hours, retrieving his experimental googlies. A tennis ball was always used – 'Not a *billiard* ball, a *tennis* ball' were among my mother's last words to me. As she knew nothing about German idealism, I must append the following highly significant dates off my own bat:

1886. Publication of B. Bosanquet's *The Introduction to Hegel's Philosophy of Fine Art*.

1890. The googly ideal conceived by B.J.T. Bosanquet.

1893. Publication of Bradley's *Appearance & Reality*.

1893–1900. Intensive work, helped by my mother, to hide the reality behind the googly's appearance.

1903. The Ashes regained by the googly – German idealism's first and last sporting victory.

NIGEL DENNIS
Letter to *The Times*
(13 May 1963)

... and Andrew Lang

Sir,

Mr Nigel Dennis rightly points out the connexion between Hegelian Idealism and the philosophy of cricket at the turn of the century. It was well understood that the game was a necessary incident in the evolution of the Absolute Idea, in which all differences are reconciled, and that in every cricket match the Absolute was achieving self-realization. You will recall the lines of Andrew Lang, which indicate the ultimate reality behind the invention of the googly:

> 'If the wild bowler thinks he bowls
>   Or if the batsman think he's bowled,
> They know not, poor misguided souls,
>   They too shall perish unconsoled.
> *I* am the batsman and the bat,
>   *I* am the bowler and the ball,
> The umpire, the pavilion cat,
>   The roller, pitch, and stumps and all.'

ALAN RICHARDSON
Letter to *The Times*
(18 May 1963)

Chinaman

A cricketing term (not to be confused with GOOGLY) denoting an off-break bowled from the back or side of the hand by a left-handed bowler. It is said that the name derives from the Chinese bowler Ellis Achong, who played for the West Indies, and who practised this kind of bowling, although he was not the first to do so.

Brewer's Dictionary of Phrase and Fable
(1970)

A Bit of a Bleat

This is going to be a bit of a bleat, I am afraid.

It is not that I think that English cricket is in irreversible decline. Far from it. We are losing more Test matches than we used to because, with the singular exception of Australia, the opposition is so much better than it was.

Most days and on most county grounds, there is something pretty good to be seen from our home-bred cricketers. But there is a growing cancer, too, and I shall come to that.

Several young English batsmen of the highest promise are establishing themselves. Whitaker, of Leicestershire, has had the sort of season that would have satisfied Denis Compton in his prime. Half a dozen others, all under twenty-five, have done wonderfully well in what has become a fiercely, often hazardously competitive game. Every county would now have at least one batsman they believe to be destined for great things. I expect they always did, but at least they are still there.

The fielding, too, is quite extraordinarily keen and generally of a high standard. Runs are saved, especially on the boundary, that would have been written off not many years ago. At the end of a typical one-day match, few trousers are unstained from where the players have been throwing themselves around. You would never have found the old county pros doing that, though some of the amateurs might.

But it is bowlers that make the most successful sides, and the shortage of these with English qualifications is a cause of real concern.

County cricket has allowed itself to become dominated by West Indian fast bowlers. That is what is eating away at the English game.

Ten years ago, only two of the seventeen first-class counties engaged a West Indian to bowl fast for them; now ten do. Next year it will be at least eleven, possibly twelve, Warwickshire having just signed a little-known Antiguan express, and Nottinghamshire have an eye on another should Richard Hadlee leave them. The more there are, the more fingers get broken and the less need there is for Englishmen to take wickets or to learn how to.

A breed of English bowlers is developing who spend their time either concentrating on containment in one-day cricket or aiming to shut up an end in the championship while the hired assassin is resting between forays.

It is no coincidence that Neil Foster, the only Englishman to have taken over 100 wickets this season, plays for Essex or that Essex have sent out three of their bowlers to play for England this summer. It has been allowed to happen by the absence from their side of a Marshall or a Walsh, a Clarke or a Holding.

No doubt Ellison, being broadly of the same bowling type, learnt from the Australian Alderman when they first played together for Kent. This season, though, Alderman's presence has reduced Ellison's opportunities of bowling himself back into form.

It is a vicious circle. Counties import fast bowlers to boost their championship chances (and hence their finances), but at a high cost to the success of the England team. This is not the march of progress or the inevitable process of evolution; it is short-sighted and unfortunate.

To me, the damage that is being done to cricket generally by the violence that has crept into it matters much more than England's failure to win Test matches. Quite apart from anything else, it restricts the art and beauty of batsmanship. Neville Cardus used to write that cricket mirrors the customs and conventions and, I suppose, the vulgarities of the times. We live now in a permissive society, and cricket reflects it.

On the television recently, in a delightful interview, Pat Pocock drew a contrast between batting in his first Test match against Wes Hall and Charlie Griffith at Bridgetown in 1968, and playing sixteen years later against the bowling of Malcolm Marshall at the Oval. Hall and Griffith tried to bowl him out, and Marshall to knock him out or frighten him out.

Dennis Amiss, now with 100 first-class hundreds to his name, refers to the rapid growth of short-pitched fast bowling. If England could field four fast bowlers of the best West Indian calibre, they would win a lot of Test matches and lose very few. But that would not restore the balance, and especially the charm, of the English game.

The combination of weak umpiring, the virtual abdication by the International Cricket Conference of its responsibilities of guardianship, the introduction of the helmet and the ethic which considers the batsman himself to be as fair a target as the wicket he defends, is malignly influential.

The extension of the rule which limits short-pitched bowling in one-day cricket, or some modification of it, should be a priority.

At the end of a day's play in early August, in which Marshall had been a central figure, one of the umpires said it had frightened him just to stand and watch.

For as long as anyone can possibly remember, there have been those who say that there is too much first-class cricket in an English season.

For the leading players, too, there are no free winters any more. Three weeks ago Gower found it all too much. Since the last Test match, Gatting has dropped himself down the Middlesex order. We have one too many one-day competitions, which involve so much extra travelling and nervous stress, and one too many Test matches which, while underwriting the counties, undermines their premier competition, the championship.

But the stumps have been drawn on another English season. Although the Meteorological Office said at different times that the weather was 'about average', I can hardly remember a summer when so few early mornings have had about them the certain scent of warmth and sunshine, or when one has become so bored reading about one man, albeit a remarkable cricketer.

Botham's appeal against his suspension for having smoked cannabis cost the TCCB a five-figure sum in legal fees, and his more recent public utterances on the Somerset 'affair' have been unhelpful. He is right, of course, to be sad that Garner and Richards are having to go, but to imply that the Somerset committee know nothing about loyalty, after the way they have protected him in the past, was not fair. But 'Who can be

146

wise, amazed, temperate and furious, loyal and neutral in a moment? No man.' Has the bard done it again?

We have much to be grateful for: good county champions, willing sponsors, an Australian tour to look forward to.

I hope, at the same time, that the Test and County Cricket Board will heed the warning implicit in the unprecedented number of broken bones there have been in the summer of 1986, and address themselves to the constant interruptions caused by the comings and goings of batsmen and fielders as helmets and gumshields and shin guards and boxes and breastplates and all the other paraphernalia are swapped and shuffled around.

'I love cricket, you know,' Sir Pelham Warner said to me once, as though the matter might be in doubt. If he were to come back, would he feel the same today about a game he would find so changed? I expect so, but it is a question that the administrators at Lord's should ask themselves every now and again.

JOHN WOODCOCK
The Times
(17 September 1986)

The Welfare State of Mind

What exactly is wrong? It seems to me that most of the commentators and analysts do not pay sufficient attention to a very important aspect of the game, the way in which at any particular period it reflects tendencies in the national life. It is admitted that the Golden Age lasted from about 1890 to the beginning of the First World War. It produced men who to this day are names to conjure with: C.B. Fry, Ranjitsinhji, G.L. Jessop, Victor Trumper, Frank Woolley. They and their contemporaries were not only men of exceptional skill, they were what the modern audience finds so lacking in contemporary players, men of dazzling personality, creative, original, daring, adventurous. I have never seen it stated anywhere that these men displayed on the cricket field the same characteristics that distinguished their contemporaries in other fields. 1890–1914 was the age of Joseph Chamberlain, F.E. Smith and David Lloyd George; of Northcliffe and Beaverbrook, the creators of modern journalism; of Cecil Rhodes and Lord Lugard; of personalities like Bernard Shaw and G.K. Chesterton; even in crime it produced the unique figure of Horatio Bottomley...

The prevailing attitude of the players of 1890–1914 was daring, adventure, creation. The prevailing attitude of 1957 can be summed up in one word – security. Bowlers and batsmen are dominated by it. The long forward-defensive push, the negative bowling, are the techniques of specialized performers (professional or amateur) in a security-minded age. As a corollary, we find much fast bowling and brilliant and daring close fielding and wicket-keeping – they are the only spheres where the spirit of adventure can express itself. The cricketers of today play the cricket of a specialized stratum, that of functionaries in the Welfare State. When many millions of people all over the world demand security and a state that must guarantee it, that's one thing. But when bowlers or batsmen, responsible for an activity essentially artistic and therefore individual, are dominated by the same principles, then the result is what we have.

And it is clear that those who support the Welfare State idea in politics and social life do not want it on the cricket field. They will not come to look at it.

C.L.R. JAMES
The Cricketer
(22 June 1957)

Manchester

I have not heard that John Bright or W.E. Gladstone ever
played cricket, but, if they did, they should never have played
away from Old Trafford, which, on a rainy day, is the nearest
thing I know to an academic speech on Free Trade. It must
have taught many a cricketer its own philosophy, batsmanship such as that of Harry Makepeace or, in his stubborn
days, Charles Hallows, which seldom deviated into brilliance, but flowed on with a staid majesty like the lines of
Milton or a leader of the great C.P. Scott, with scarcely the
easement of a paragraph, without ever the hope of an
anacoluthon! Indeed, I always consider that it was almost a
rebuff to Nature that Lancashire permitted, I will not say
encouraged, such batsmen as A.C. MacLaren, who refused to
unlearn what Harrow and youth had taught him; R.H.
Spooner, whose grace was of no one County or time; such
masters of bowling and clowning as Johnny Briggs and Cecil
Parkin. In more modern years Old Trafford has seen the
'mutiny' of Ernest Tyldesley, whose wickets were visible
when you bowled, and who might use the pull-drive in the
first over; of Eddie Paynter, who sometimes plays a stroke
with neither foot on the ground; great heretics all.

R.C. ROBERTSON-GLASGOW
Cricket Prints
(1943)

An Earnest Protest

Max Beerbohm subscribed to W.G. Grace's testimonial 'not
in support of cricket but as an earnest protest against golf'.

Carr's Dictionary of Extraordinary English Cricketers
(1977)

All His Life

Last Munday youre Father was at Mr Payns and plaid at Cricket and came home please anuf for he struck the best Ball in the Game and wishd he had not anny thing else to do he would play at Cricket all his Life.

MARY TURNER of East Hoathly, Sussex
Letter to her son
(September 1739)

A Choice of Lawns

I have a cricket bat & a hard ball and a choice of lawns.

DYLAN THOMAS
Letter to Daniel Jones
(24 June 1946)

MATCHES I

THE ARGUMENT
of the
THIRD BOOK

The Game.   Five on the Side of the COUNTIES *are out for
three Notches.   The Odds run high on the side of* KENT.
*Bryan and Newland go in; they help the Game greatly.
Bryan is unfortunately put out by Kips.* KENT, *the first
Innings, is thirteen ahead.   The* COUNTIES *go in again, and
get fifty-seven ahead.* KENT, *in the Second Innings is very
near losing, the two last Men being in.   Weymark unhappily
misses a catch, and by that means* KENT *is victorious.*

BOOK III.

With wary Judgment, scatter'd o'er the Green,
Th' ambitious Chiefs of fruitful *Kent* are seen.
Some, at a distance, for the *Long Ball* wait,
Some, nearer planted, seize it from the *Bat.*
5   *H——l* [Hodswell] and *M——s* [Mills] behind the
      Wickets stand,
And each by Turns, the flying Ball command;
Four times from *H——l's* arm it skims the grass;
Then *M——'s* succeeds.   The *Seekers-out* change
      Place.
Observe, cries *H——l* to the wond'ring Throng,
10   Be Judges now, whose Arms are better strong!
He said—then pois'd, and rising as he threw,
Swift from his Arm the fatal Missive flew.
Not with more Force the Death-conveying Ball,
Springs from the Cannon to the batter'd Wall;
15   Nor swifter yet the pointed Arrows go
Launch'd from the Vigour of the *Parthian* Bow.
It whizz'd along, with unimagined'd Force,
And bore down all, resistless in its Course.
To such impetuous Might compell'd to yield

153

20　The *Bail*, and mangled *Stumps* bestrew the Field.
　　Now glows with ardent Heat th' unequal Fray,
　　While *Kent* usurps the Honours of the Day;
　　Loud from the *Ring* resounds the piercing Shout,
　　Three *Notches* only gain'd, five *Leaders* out,
25　But while the drooping *Play'r* invoked the Gods,
　　The busy *Better* calculates his *Odds*.
　　Swift round the Plain, in buzzing Murmurs run,
　　I'll hold you Ten to Four, Kent.—*Done* Sir.—*Done*.
　　　　What Numbers can with equal Force, describe
30　Th' increasing Terrors of the losing Tribe!
　　When, vainly striving 'gainst the conq'ring Ball,
　　They see their boasted Chiefs, dejected fall!
　　Now the two mightiest of the fainting Host
　　Pant to redeem the Fame their Fellows lost.
35　Eager for Glory;—For the Worst prepar'd;
　　With pow'rful Skill, their threat'ned *Wickets* guard.
　　B——*n* [Bryan] collected for the deadly Stroke
　　First cast to *Heav'n* a supplicating Look,
　　Then pray'd—*Propitious Pow'rs! Assist my Blow*
40　*And grant the flying Orb may shock the Foe!*
　　This said; he wav'd his *Bat* with sourceful Swing,
　　And drove the batter'd Pellet o'er the Ring.
　　Then rapid *five Times* cross'd the shining Plain,
　　E'er the departed Ball return'd again.
45　　Nor was thy Prowess valiant *N*——*d* [Newland]
　　　　mean,
　　Whose strenuous Arm increased the Game *eighteen;*
　　While from thy Stroke, the Ball retiring hies,
　　Uninterrupted Clamours rend the Skies.
　　But oh, what horrid Changes oft' are seen,
50　When faithless Fortune seems the most serene!
　　Beware, unhappy *B*——*n*! oh beware!
　　Too heedless Swain, when such a Foe is near.
　　Fir'd with Success, elated with his Luck,
　　He glow'd with Rage, regardless how he struck;

154

55 But, forc'd the fatal Negligence to mourn,
   K——s [Kips] crush'd his *Stumps*, before the Youth
      could turn.
   The rest their unavailing Vigour try.
   And by the Pow'r of *Kent*, demolish'd die.
   Awakened *Eccho* speaks the *Innings* o'er,
60 And forty *Notches* deep indent the *Score*.
      Now *Kent* prepares her better Skill to shew;
   Loud rings the Ground, at each tremendous Blow.
   With nervous Arm, performing God-like Deeds,
   Another, and another Chief succeeds;
65 'Till, tired with Fame, the conq'ring Host give Way;
   And lead by *thirteen* Strokes, the toilsome Fray.
      Fresh rous'd to Arms, each Labour-loving Swain
   Swells with new Strength, and dares the Field
      again.
   Again to *Heav'n* aspires the cheerful Sound;
70 The *Strokes* re-eccho o'er the spacious Ground.
   The *Champion* strikes.   When, scarce arriving fair,
   The glancing Ball mounts upwards in the Air!
   The *Batsman* sees it; and with mournful Eyes,
   Fix'd on th' ascending *Pellet* as it flies,
75 Thus suppliant claims the Favour of the Skies.
   O mighty *Jove*! and all ye Pow'rs above!
   Let my regarded Pray'r your Pity move!
   Grant me but this.   Whatever Youth shall dare
   Snatch at the Prize, descending thro' the Air;
80 Lay him extended on the Grassy Plain,
   And make his bold, ambitious Effort vain.
      He said.   The Powers, attending his Request
   Granted one Part, to Winds consign'd the rest.
      And now Illustrious *S*——*e* [Sackville: Lord John
         Sackville, son of the Duke of Dorset], where he
         stood,
85 Th' approaching Ball with cautious Pleasure
      view'd;

155

At once he sees the Chief's impending Doom,
And pants for mighty Honours yet to come:
Swift as the *Falcon*, darting on its Prey,
He springs elastic o'er the verdant Way;
90 Sure of Success, flies upward with a Bound,
Derides the slow Approach, and spurns the Ground.
Prone slips to Youth; yet glorious in his Fall,
With Arm extended shows the captive Ball.
Loud Acclamations ev'ry Mouth employ,
95 And Eccho rings the undulating Joy.
     The *Counties* now the Game triumphant lead,
And vaunt their Numbers fifty-seven *a Head*.
     To end th' immortal Honours of the Day
The *Chiefs* of *Kent*, once more, their Might essay;
100 No trifling Toil ev'n yet remains untry'd,
Nor mean the Numbers of the adverse *Side*,
With doubled Skill each dang'rous Ball they shun,
Strike with observing Eye, with Caution run.
At length they know the wish'd for Number near,
105 Yet wildly pant, and *almost own* they fear.
The two last *Champions* even now are in,
And but three Notches yet remain to win.
When, almost ready to recant its Boast,
Ambitious *Kent* within an Ace had lost;
110 The mounting Ball, again obliquely driven,
Cuts the pure *Aether*, soaring up to Heav'n.
W——*k* [Weymark] was ready: W——*k* all must
     own,
As sure a Swain to catch as e'er was known;
Yet, whether *Jove*, and all-compelling Fate,
115 In their high Will determin'd *Kent* should beat;
Or the lamented Youth too much rely'd
On sure Success, and Fortune often try'd.
The erring Ball, amazing to be told!
Slip'd thro' his out-stretch'd Hand, and mock'd his
     Hold.

156

And now the Sons of *Kent* compleat the Game,
And firmly fix their everlasting Fame.

JAMES LOVE
Cricket: An Heroic Poem
(1744)

Byron Plays at Lord's (1805)

PLAYED AT LORD'S, AUGUST 2, 1805

Eton won by an innings and 2 runs

HARROW

Lord Ipswich, b Carter	10	—b Heaton.....	21
T. Farrer, b Carter	7	—c Bradley	3
T. Dury, b Carter	0	—st Heaton.....	6
– Boulton, run out	2	—b Heaton.....	0
J. A. Lloyd, b Carter	0	—b Carter.......	0
A. Shakespear, st Heaton	8	—run out........	5
Lord Byron, c Barnard	7	—b Carter.......	2
Hon. T. Erskine, b Carter	4	—b Heaton	8
W. Brockman, b Heaton	9	—b Heaton	10
E. Stanley, not out	3	—c Canning	7
W. Assheton, b Carter	3	—not out........	0
B	2	B	3
Total	55	Total....	65

ETON

J. Heaton, b Lloyd	0
J. Slingsby, b Shakespear	29
W. Carter, b Shakespear	3
G. C. Farhill, c Lloyd	6
S. Canning, c Farrer	12
G. Camplin, b Ipswich	42
F. Bradley b Lloyd	16
C. T. Barnard, b Shakespear	0
H. W. Barnard, not out	3
J. H. Kaye, b Byron	7
H. Dover, c Boulton	4
B	0
Total	122

Played on Lord's first ground, where Dorset Square now is. The players wore knee-breeches and silk stockings, as continued to be the case for the next twenty-five years or so.

'The late Lord Stratford de Redcliffe remembered seeing him (Lord Byron) playing in the match against Eton with another boy to run for him.' – *Dictionary of National Biography*, viii. 133. Lord Byron, afterwards the famous poet, had a club foot.

Arthur Shakespear, in his reminiscences ... wrote: 'In a match of cricket played at Lord's ground, Lord Byron insisted upon playing, and was allowed a person to run for him, his lameness impeding him so much. 1804 We beat the Etonians.'

T. Dury, playing for Harrow, was grandfather of T.S. Dury of the Harrow Eleven of 1870, and great-grandfather of G.A.I. Dury of the Harrow Elevens of 1913 and 1914.

The above is the first fully-recorded game between Eton and Harrow, but several matches (besides that of 1804) are known to have been played even earlier between the two schools. None of these, however, is to be found in Epps', Britcher's, or Bentley's printed books of scores.

Francis Bradley, afterwards Bradley-Dyne, was great-uncle of Lord Harris of the Eton Elevens 1868–70.

Harrow men object strongly to this match being counted as one of the regular series of games between the two sides. It was, in all probability, a holiday fixture arranged between Lord Byron, acting for Harrow, and Kaye, for Eton. John Arthur Lloyd, who captained the Harrovians and was Head of the School this year, stated to Dean Merivale, who has repeated it in his *Recollections*, that: 'Byron played in that match and very badly too. He should never have been in the Eleven if my counsel had been taken.'

Edward Stanley, playing for Harow, was only thirteen years of age.

Referring to the above match, Byron wrote from Burgage Manor, Southwell, Notts, on 4th August 1805, to Charles O. Gordon: '...We have played the Eton and were most confoundedly beat; however, it was some comfort to me that I got 11 notches the 1st Innings and 7 the 2nd, which was more than any of our side except Brockman & Ipswich could contrive to hit. After the match we dined together, and were extremely friendly, not a single discordant word was uttered by either party. To be sure, we were most of us rather drunk and went together to the Haymarket Theatre, where we kicked up a row, as you may suppose, when so many Harrovians and Etonians met at one place; I was one of seven in a single hackney, 4 Eton and 3 Harrow, and then we all got into the same box,' etc., etc. – See *The Works of Lord Byron*. Edited by R.E. Prothero, vol. i, pp. 70–71. It will be seen that

Byron states that his scores were 11 and 7, but according to the printed and generally accepted account he made only 7 and 2. The poet's version, however, may well be correct, for the score which is inserted in *Scores and Biographies* was taken from a half-sheet of paper sent anonymously through Frederick Lillywhite to the Hon. Robert Grimston, who forwarded it to the editor of *Bell's Life*, for what it was worth, and from that paper it was copied in *Scores and Biographies*.

According to *The Tyro* magazine, the Etonians, after their success, sent the following lines to their opponents:

> Adventurous *boys* of Harrow School,
>   Of cricket you've no knowledge.
> You play not cricket, but the fool,
>   With *men* of Eton College.

The reply, attributed to Byron, was:

> Ye Eton wits, to play the fool
> Is not the boast of Harrow School;
> No wonder, then, at our defeat –
> Folly like yours could ne'er be beat.

In *Eton of Old* (p. 112) it is suggested strongly that no match took place between Eton and Harrow between 1805 and 1818. 'The renewal used to be talked of every year; but there were difficulties in the arrangement. It could not be played in school time, since neither of the Headmasters was sufficiently educated to give leave to the Eleven of Eton to go to Harrow, or that of Harrow to step across to Eton: and the obstacles to bringing them to any neutral ground seemed for a long time to be too numerous and too heavy for accomplishment. It was at length determined in 1818, almost at the last moment, to have the match in the beginning of Holidays at Lord's.'

F.S. ASHLEY-COOPER
Eton and Harrow at the Wicket
(1922)

Cobden's Match (1870)

In a short time the innings was over, and Oxford had to face a total of 179 to win the match. In these days on a hard wicket this is regarded as a comparatively easy feat; but runs were not so easy to accumulate eighteen years ago, and the betting was now even, Cambridge for choice. One Oxford wicket was soon got, and then a long stand was made by Messrs Fortescue and Ottaway, both of whom played excellent cricket. The total was brought up to 72 for only one wicket, the betting veered round to 2 to 1 on Oxford, and Mr Ward was put on to bowl. This change was the turning point of the game. Mr Fortescue was soon bowled, so was Mr Pauncefote, and with the total at 86 the betting was again evens, Oxford for choice. Mr Ward had found his spot and was bowling with deadly precision when Mr Tylecote came in. Both Ottaway and Tylecote now batted cautiously and well, and Mr Ward went off for a time. Mr Tylecote was a very good bat, but compared to Ottaway only mortal; how on earth Ottaway was to be got out was a problem that seemed well-nigh insoluble. The total went up to 153, or only 26 runs to win and seven wickets to go down; the betting 6 to 1 on Oxford. A yell was heard, and Mr Tylecote was bowled by Mr Ward, and Mr Townshend came in.

Mr Ward, from the pavilion end, was at this stage bowling to Ottaway, who made a characteristic hit, low and not hard, to short leg. Mr Fryer was not a good field, and Cambridge generally were fielding badly, but he rose to the occasion and made a good catch close to the ground, so close that Ottaway appealed, but in vain, and the score stood at 160 for 5 wickets down – 19 runs wanted to win. Mr Hill now came in, and began to play a free, confident game at once. A bye was run and a sharp run was made by Townshend by a hit to third man, but Townshend was then caught off Ward, and Francis came in, and after making a single was lbw to the

160

same bowler. During Hill's partnership with Townshend and Francis he knocked up 11 runs by good bustling play, and he now stood at the nursery end to receive the last ball of an over from Ward, 5 runs being wanted to win, and Butler in the other end. Hill hit the ball fairly hard to sharp short leg, and Bourne measured his length on the ground, stopped the ball, and converted the hit from a fourer to a single. Hill got to the other end, an over was called and the ball tossed to Cobden, who was faced by Hill, 4 runs being wanted to win and 3 to tie.

We say with confidence that never can one over bowled by any bowler at any future time surpass the over that Cobden was about to deliver then, and it deserves a minute description. Cobden took a long run and bowled very fast, and was for his pace a straight bowler. But he bowled with little or no break, had not got a puzzling delivery, and though effective against inferior bats, would never have succeeded in bowling out a man like Mr Ottaway if he had sent a thousand balls to him. However, on the present occasion Ottaway was out, those he had to bowl to were not first-rate batsmen, and Cobden could bowl a good yorker.

You might almost have heard a pin drop as Cobden began his run and the ball whizzed from his hand. Mr Hill played the ball slowly to cover point, and rather a sharp run was made. As the match stood, Oxford wanted 2 to tie and 3 to win, and three wickets to go down: Mr Butler to receive the ball. The second ball that Cobden bowled was very similar to the first, straight and well up on the off stump. Mr Butler did what anybody else except Louis Hall or Shrewsbury would have done, namely, let drive vigorously. Unfortunately he did not keep the ball down, and it went straight and hard a catch to Mr Bourne, to whom everlasting credit is due, for he held it, and away went Mr Butler – amidst Cambridge shouts this time. The position was getting serious, for neither Mr Stewart nor Mr Belcher was renowned as a batsman. Rather pale, but with a jaunty air that cricketers are well aware frequently conceals a sickly feeling of nervousness, Mr Belcher walked to the wicket and took his guard. He felt that if only he could stop one ball and be bowled out the next, still Mr Hill would get another chance of a knock and the match would probably be won. Cobden had bowled two balls, and two more wickets had to be got; if therefore a wicket was got each ball the match would be won by Cambridge, and Mr Hill would have no further opportunity of distinguishing himself. In a dead silence Cobden again took the ball and bowled a fast ball well up on the batsman's legs. A vision of the winning hit flashed across Mr Belcher's brain, and he raised his bat preparatory to performing great things, hit at the ball and missed it, and he was bowled off his legs. There was still one more ball to complete the over, and Mr Belcher, a sad man, walked away amid an uproarious storm of cheers.

Matters were becoming distinctly grave, and very irritating must it have been to Mr Hill, who was like a billiard player watching his rival in the middle of a big break; he could say a good deal and think a lot, but he could do nothing. Mr Stewart, *spes ultima* of Oxford, with feelings that are utterly impossible to describe, padded and gloved, nervously took off his coat in the pavilion. If ever a man deserved pity, Mr Stewart deserved it on that occasion. He did not profess to be a good bat, and his friends did not claim so much for him; he was an excellent wicket-keeper, but he had to go in at a crisis that the best bat in England would not like to face. Mr Pauncefote, the Oxford captain, was seen addressing a few words of earnest exhortation to him, and with a rather sick feeling Mr Stewart went to the wicket. Mr Hill looked at him cheerfully, but very earnestly did Mr Stewart wish the next ball well over. He took his guard and held his hands low on the bat handle, which was fixed fast as a tree on the block-hole; for Mr Pauncefote had earnestly entreated Mr Stewart to put the bat straight in the block-hole and keep it there without moving it. This was not by any means bad advice, for the bat covers a great deal of the wicket, and though it is a piece of counsel not likely to be offered to W.G. Grace or Stoddart, it might not have been inexpedient to offer it to Mr Stewart. Here, then, was the situation – Mr Stewart standing manfully up to the wicket, Mr Cobden beginning his run, and a perfectly dead silence in the crowd. Whiz went the ball; but alas! – as many other people, cricketers and politicians alike, have done – the good advice is neglected, and Stewart, instead of following his captain's exhortation to keep his bat still and upright in the block-hole, just lifted it: fly went the bails, and Cambridge had won the match by two runs! The situation was bewildering. Nobody could quite realize what had happened for a second or so, but then – up went Mr Absalom's hat, down the pavilion steps with miraculous rapidity flew the Rev. A.R. Ward, and smash went Mr Charles Marsham's umbrella against the pavilion brickwork.[1]

[1] The difficulty of getting accurate facts about this unique over has been immense. The author has before him the written statement of Mr Hill, a copy of the *Illustrated Sporting and Dramatic News* containing a letter of Mr Yardley, who was keeping wicket and was therefore in a position to judge, and a letter from Mr Cobden and Mr Belcher. In the first edition of this book Mr Stewart is said to have been bowled off his legs; this is inaccurate, and the author apologizes for the blunder. Mr Cobden complains of the account generally, and says that all three balls were of a good length, and that he never bowled better balls in all his life. The author in the above has written what he believes to be accurate, relying chiefly on the written evidence of Messrs Hill, Yardley, and Belcher, and in a less degree from what he has heard from some spectators. It was not Stewart that was bowled off his legs, but Belcher; and in order that the public may form their own judgement, the written statements of Messrs Hill, Yardley, and Belcher are here inserted. Mr Hill writes: 'Belcher was bowled with a yorker (half-volley?) and Stewart with a half-volley, but whether off his leg or not I do not remember.' Mr Hill also writes that on meeting Cobden some years later, Cobden repeated that they were three of the best balls he ever bowled, to which Mr Hill replied that they were all half-volleys, and that he believed that if he had had any one of them he could have won the match with a fourer. Now Mr Yardley, in allusion to the author's statement that the ball that Butler was caught off was straight and well up on the off stump, writes: 'As a matter of fact the ball in question was a very

long hop, extremely wide on the off, so much so that I have no hesitation in stating that if Mr Butler had made no attempt to strike at it the umpire would have called a wide. The batsman, however, was possessed of an exceptionally long reach, and just managed to strike the ball with the extreme end of his bat to cover-point, where it was beautifully caught by Mr Bourne.'

Now as to Belcher's ball, Mr Yardley says: 'The ball in question was the most delicious half-volley on the legs, which Mr Belcher did his utmost to hit out of Lord's ground. Fortunately for Cambridge his deeds were not so good as his intentions, for he hit too hard at the ball, which he missed, and which, striking him on the left leg, cannoned on to his right leg, and from thence on to his wicket.'

On the point of Mr Stewart's ball Mr Yardley writes: 'This fourth and last ball was the only straight one of that celebrated over. It was an exceedingly long hop, scarcely pitching half-way, and coming along surprisingly slow off the pitch. Had it not been for that circumstance Mr Stewart would probably have not lost his wicket as he did, for it was only at the very last moment that he neglected his captain's instructions and removed his bat from the block-hole, thereby allowing the ball to strike his off stump about three-quarters of the way up.' Mr Yardley also writes that the scene appears to him as vivid after a lapse of twenty years as it did then.

Mr Belcher writes: 'I am *quite certain* that I was bowled off my legs; the ball to the best of my recollection hit me just below the knee of the right leg and went into the wicket. At any rate I am quite clear as to my leg being hit, and my impression is that it was a very good-length ball, and not a half-volley. I don't think I hit it at all. Of course at such a distance of time my recollections are somewhat vague, *but the one point I am quite sure of is that I was bowled off my leg.'*

With these extracts before them, the matter is now left to posterity.

THE HON. R.H. LYTTELTON
Cricket: The Badminton Library
(1901)

How Spofforth Became Famous (1878)

When Mr Warner asked me to write an article for him, he said he wanted something about the Test match at the Oval in 1882. It is a long time ago; yet I can recall almost every incident in that famous game as well as if it had been played last week.

164

The first great match that an Australian team played in England was against the MCC eleven in 1878 at Lord's. This has not been counted as a Test match, but it really was; for in those days cricket was almost solely managed by the Marylebone Club, and they had the call of any cricketer they wanted. It was a fine eleven, and when we arrived at Lord's, fresh from our first defeat at Nottingham, we were not very confident. Dr W.G. Grace and Mr A.N. Hornby started the batting, and our bowlers were Messrs Boyle and Allan. Now, although the latter got Grace caught at short leg, off a shocking bad stroke, he was changed and I was deputed to bowl. The fun then commenced, and the strong MCC team were out for 33 runs, I myself taking 6 wickets for 4 runs, and Boyle 3 for 14 runs. But more was to happen. Australia only made 41. MCC commenced again with 'W.G.' and A.N. Hornby. I began the bowling to 'W.G.', and Mr Murdoch, behind the wickets, missed him off my first ball, much to my sorrow; but the next ball knocked his leg bail thirty yards, and I screamed out 'Bowled'.

My third ball clean bowled A.J. Webbe, Boyle quickly disposed of C. Booth and A.W. Ridley, and A.N. Hornby had the misfortune to be 'cut over' and had to retire. Mr Boyle then bowled Wild and Flowers, and G.G. Hearne and Mr Vernon fell to me. A.N. Hornby then resumed, but could only just stand, and Boyle bowled him.

Boyle's analysis read 6 for 3 runs, and mine 4 for 16, total 19. We had 12 runs to get, and lost C. Bannerman in getting them. Thus four innings, including luncheon and intervals, occupied only five and a half hours.

The news spread like wildfire, and created a sensation in London and throughout England, and our hotel was almost besieged. The next day I read the following in a paper:

'The progress of the Australian eleven is dramatic. Their tame début at Nottingham was in the nature of an unpretending overture; but the curtain fell to the first act at Lord's to rounds of applause when Grace, the far-famed batsman, went out for four and nought, and the wickets went flying right and left, so that the last fell for a ridiculously small score. It is evident that they will more than hold their own in this country. Their fielding is the admiration of all. Left-handed Mr Allan is known as the "Bowler of a Century", Mr Boyle is described as the "Very Devil", but Mr Spofforth as the "Demon Bowler" carries off the palm. His delivery is quite appalling, the balls thunder in like cannon shot, and yet he has the guile, when seemingly about to bowl his fastest, to drop a slow which is generally fatal to the batsman.

'Mr Spofforth is a Yorkshireman by extraction. His father was well known as a sportsman, and rode as straight as the best with the York and Ainsty and other packs.'

I found myself famous almost at once, and always regarded this match as one of the most interesting I ever played in. I think the most exciting game, however, was the Test match at the Oval in 1882. They were two splendid teams, and both thought they would win. Mr Murdoch won the toss, and sent in H.H. Massie and A.C. Bannerman, but we made a sorry show, being all out for 63, and were most disappointed. I might speak for myself, and say I was disgusted, and thought we should have made at least 250; but when England went in they did very little better, only making 101. Australia's second innings started well enough, Massie and A.C. Bannerman putting on 66 before the former was bowled by A.G. Steel for 55. On returning to the pavilion Massie, disappointed, told me he was very sick, because he had no right to hit at the ball; but he said Steel was commencing to bowl well, and he thought another four would cause him to be taken off.

The second wicket fell at 70, and with the exception of our captain, run out 29, no one did anything, and we were all out for 122, leaving England 85 to win.

An unfortunate incident occurred in this match, namely, the running out of S.P. Jones, but so much has been written on the event that I merely mention it. Anyway, it seemed to put fire into the Australians, and I do not suppose a team ever worked harder to win. With only 85 to make to win, W.G. Grace and A.N. Hornby commenced England's second innings. I bowled Hornby at 15, and Barlow at the same total, but then W.G. Grace, who had been missed by A.C. Bannerman, fielding very close in at silly mid-on, and Ulyett made a stand, and reached 51 before another wicket fell, Ulyett being caught at the wicket by Blackham. I had before asked Murdoch to let me change ends, as I was having no luck, and Boyle then got 'W.G.' caught by Bannerman.

Then came the most exciting cricket I ever witnessed. Four wickets were down, and only 32 runs required; but I must confess I never thought they would be got. A. Lyttelton and A.P. Lucas then came together, and at one time Boyle bowled no less than 9 overs for 1 run, and I 10 overs for 2 runs. Then we agreed to let Lyttelton get a run, so as to change ends. Bannerman was to allow one to pass at mid-off, which he did, and Lyttelton faced me, when I bowled him. This was the real turning-point, as Lucas, getting opposite to me again, turned the first ball into his wicket, and 6 wickets were down for 63, and we all felt we were on top.

With 7 more runs added I bowled M. Read, and Boyle got Barnes caught. A.G. Steel then came in. I pitched a ball about four inches outside his off stump, he started to play forward to it, before he had touched the ball I was off in the direction of silly mid-on, and Steel quietly played the ball right into my hands. C.T. Studd and Peate then came together, and Boyle bowled Peate for 2, and Australia had won by 7 runs.

F.R. SPOFFORTH
in *The Cricketer*
(May 1921)

The Oval (1882)

Boyle took the ball; he turned; he ran; he bowled,
All England's watching heart was stricken cold.

Peate's whirling bat met nothing in its sweep.
The ball put all his wickets in a heap ...

JOHN MASEFIELD (Poet Laureate)
The Bluebells, and Other Verse
(1961)

The Ashes: Old Trafford (1902)

The most thrilling finish of all the Test matches ever fought at
Old Trafford happened on the Saturday afternoon of July
26th, 1902. It was the decisive game of the rubber, and
Australia won it by three runs, snatching the spoils from the
lion's mouth. The match at the end seemed to get right out of
the control of the men that were making it; it seemed to take
on a being of its own, a volition of its own, and the mightiest
cricketers in the land looked as though they were in the grip
of a power of which they could feel the presence but whose
ends they could not understand. As events rushed them to
crisis even MacLaren, Ranjitsinhji, Trumper, Noble, and
Darling – most regal of cricketers – could only utter: 'Here
we do but as we may; no further dare.' The game, in Kipling's
term, was more than the player of the game.

The match was designed, surely, by the gods for their
sport. Even the victors were abominably scourged. On the
second day, when the issue was anybody's, Darling played an
innings which, as things turned out, must be said to have won
Australia's laurels as much as anything else. Australia in their
second innings had lost 3 wickets – those of Trumper, Duff,
and Hill – for 10 runs and now possessed an advantage

worth no more than 47. Under a sky of rags, the fitful and sinister sunlight coming through, Darling let all his superb might go at the English attack. His hitting had not the joyfulness of mastership in it; its note was desperation. He plainly felt the coils of circumstance about him; he plainly was aware of the demon of conflict that had the game in grip. And the defiant action of his bat was like a fist shaken at the unfriendly heavens. It was in this innings of Darling's that the gods played their first cruel trick. For with Darling's score only 17 he was impelled to sky a ball to the deep field – a high but easy catch. And who was the wight that the ironic powers had decreed should shoulder the responsibility of taking that crucial catch? His name was Tate – Tate of Sussex, a kindly fellow who never did harm to a soul. The humour of the gods really began when this cricketer was asked to play for England instead of George Hirst. Tate was a capital bowler, but as soon as he was seen in the company of the great the question went out: 'What is he doing in this galley?' Tate had not the stern fibre of character that can survive in an air of high tragedy; his bent was for pastoral comedy down at Horsham. Tate missed the catch, and never looked like holding it. As he stood under the ball, which hung for a while in the air – an eternity to Tate – and then dropped like a stone, his face turned white. Darling survived to make 37 out of a total of 86. Had Tate held the catch Australia could hardly have got a score of more than 50, for Lockwood and Rhodes, that Friday afternoon, bowled magnificently. Yet when Tate laid himself down to rest in the evening, can he not be imagined as saying to himself: 'Well, it's nearly all over now, and as far as Tate of Sussex is concerned, the worst must have happened. I never *asked* to play for England – they thrust greatness on me – and I'll be well out of it this time tomorrow, back to Brighton, and who'll remember my missed catch after a week? What's a muff in the field in a cricketer's career – everybody makes them.' If Tate did console his spirit in this way the poor man did not know he was born. The gods had not finished with him; the next day he was to be put on the rack and have coals of fire heaped on his head.

On the Saturday England were left with 124 to get for victory. A tiny score – with the cream of batsmanship at hand. But there had been five hours of rain in the night, and Trumble and Saunders were bowling for Australia. Still, England seemed nicely placed at lunch; the total 36 for none and MacLaren and Palairet undefeated. The crowd took its sustenance light-heartedly; everybody lived at ease in a fool's paradise as rosily lighted as Tate's. Here, again, was the humorous touch of the gods: men that are taken suddenly out of contentment are the more likely to writhe in Gehenna. After lunch the sun got to work on the wicket, and straightway Palairet was bowled by an intolerable break from Saunders. Tyldesley came in, and, with MacLaren, the game was forced. The play of these two batsmen gave the crowd the first hint that all was not yet settled in England's favour, for it was the play of cricketers driven to desperate remedies. The runs, they seemed to say, can only be got if we hurry; there's the sun as well as Trumble and Saunders to frustrate. Tyldesley jumped to the bowling; he hit 16 runs in quick time before he was caught in the slips. England 68 for 2 – 56 wanted now. And, said the crowd, not yet sniffing the evil in the wind, *only* 56, with Ranji, Abel, Jackson, Braund, and Lilley to come, to say nothing of Rhodes and Lockwood. Why, the game is England's! Four runs after Tyldesley's downfall MacLaren was caught by Duff in the long field. An indiscreet stroke, yet whose was the right to blame the man for making it? It had come off time after time during his priceless innings of 35, and England could not afford to throw a single possible run away. MacLaren had played like a gambler at a table – not looking as though he were making runs, but rather as one who had ample boundaries at his bat's end to bank on every throw of the dice.

Abel and Ranji were in when at last the multitude unmistakably saw the evil day face to face. For what sort of a Ranji was

170

this? Palsy was on him. You could have sworn that he shook at the knees. It looked like Ranji; his shirt rippled in the wind even as it did on that day at Old Trafford six years earlier than this, the day on which he conjured 154 runs out of the Australians. Yes, it looked like Ranji – the same slight body, the same inscrutable, bland face. Alas! the spirit had gone – here was a deserted shrine. Thousands of eyes turned away from Ranji and looked to Abel for succour. Ah, this is better – the pertness of little Abel lightened the soul. He made gallant runs – a boundary over Hill's head. 'Cheeky' work this – batsmanship with *gaminerie*. 'Bravo, Bobby!' shouted the Old Trafford crowd. At 92 Ranji was out, leg before wicket to Trumble. Well, the sophist crowd told itself, that was bound to happen; he never looked good for any at all. But 5 runs more and Trumble bowled Abel. England 97 for 5 – 27 needed. 'It's quite all right,' said a parson on the half-crown stand; 'there's really no cause for anxiety. To doubt the ability of Jackson, Braund, Lilley, Lockwood, and Rhodes to get a paltry 27 runs would be scandalous. Besides, I do believe that fellow Tate is a batsman – he has an average of 16 for Sussex.' The century went up with cheers to herald it – the crowd made as much of joyful noise as it could, presumably in the hope that cheering would put a better face on the scoring-board. Jackson, who made a century in the first innings, scored seven in his best 'parliamentary' manner – neat, politic runs. Then he was caught by Gregory, and now the cat was indeed out of the bag; sophistry passed away from the heaped-up ranks. 'Who'd 'a' thowt it?' said a man on the sixpenny side. Who, indeed? At that very moment of agony at Old Trafford, people far away in the city read in the latest editions, 'England 92 for 3', and agreed that it wasn't worth the journey to Old Trafford, that it had been a good match, that the Australians were fine sportsmen, and jolly good losers.

Sixteen runs – four good boundaries or four bad ones – would bring the game into England's keeping when Lilley reached the wicket.

He was frankly and unashamedly in some slight panic. He hit out impetuously, as who should say: 'For the Lord's sake let it be settled and done with quickly.' Braund was overthrown at 109, and Lockwood made not a run. Lilley lashed his bat about like a man distraught. Rhodes is his companion now, and stands on guard ever so cool. Eight runs will do it, and 'There goes four of them!' affirms the red-hot crowd as Lilley accomplishes a grand drive into the deep. 'Well hit, sir!' shouts our parson. 'Nothing like taking your courage in both hands against these Australian fellows. Well hit, sir!' Clem Hill is seen running along the boundary's edge as though the fiend were after him. Trying to save the four, is he? – even from as certain a boundary hit as this! Extraordinary men, Australians; never give anything away. Hill, in fact, saved the boundary in the most decisive manner in the world by holding the ball one-handed before it pitched. The impetus of his run carried him twenty yards beyond the place where he made the catch – a catch which put incredulity into the face of every man and woman at Old Trafford that day. 'A sinful catch,' said the parson. Tate, the last man in, watched Rhodes ward off three balls from Trumble, and then rain stopped play. Yes, rain stopped play for forty minutes – and England eight runs short of triumph with the last men in. But though it was heavy rain there was always a bright sky not far away – another piece of subtle torture by the gods, for nobody could think that the weather was going to put an end to the afternoon. It would clear up all right in time; the agony had to be gone through. The crowd sat around the empty field, waiting, but hardly daring to hope. The tension was severe. Yet surely there were calm minds here and there. Why, under a covered stand sat two old gentlemen who were obviously *quite* indifferent to the issue. One was actually reading to the other the leading article from one of the morning papers. Moreover, he was reading it in a controlled and deliberately articulated voice. 'Sir M. Hicks-Beach argued yesterday,' he read, 'that even if

172

Ireland was overtaxed in 1894, its grievance was less today, because taxation had not increased quite so rapidly in Ireland as in the United Kingdom.' And the other old gentleman, so far was he from troubling his head needlessly over a mere cricket match, promptly took up the points in the argument, and he too spoke in a perfectly controlled and deliberately articulated voice. 'Two wrongs', he commented, 'do not make a right.' Excited about England and Australia? Not a bit of it, sir! We trust we are old and sensible enough to put a correct valuation on a game of cricket.

In the pavilion Tate was dying a thousand deaths. All depended on him – Rhodes was safe enough. In his head, maybe, notions went round and round like a wheel. 'You've only to keep your bat straight,' he might well have said to himself time after time. 'Don't even move it from the block-hole. I've heard tell if you keep your bat quite still it's a thousand to one against any ball hitting the wicket.' . . . At six minutes to five the Australians went into action again. Saunders bowled at Tate – a fast one. Tate saw something hit the ground and he made a reflex action at it. Click! Tate looked wildly around him. What had happened? A noise came to him over the wet grass, sounding like a distant sea. The crowd was cheering; he had snicked a boundary. Another snick like that and the game is England's and Tate safe for posterity! The ball was returned from the ring, and Darling slightly but impressively rearranged his field, the while Saunders bent down to a sawdust heap. Bloodless, calculating Australians they were. Tate got himself down on his bat once more, and the wheel in his poor head went round faster and faster. '. . . Bat straight . . . don't move . . . can't hit wicket . . . block-hole . . . don't move. . . . Bat straight . . . can't hit wicket. . . .' And the gods fooled him to the top of his bent – to the last. Saunders's fourth ball was not only good enough for Tate's frail bat; it was good enough for the best bat in England. It was fast through the air and – it was a shooter. It broke Tate's wicket, and, no doubt, broke Tate's heart and the heart of the crowd.

In twenty minutes Old Trafford was deserted save for one or two groundsmen who tended to the battlefield. The figures on the scoreboard had revolved, obliterating all records of the match from the face of it, which now looked vacantly over the grass. The gods had finished their sport – finished even with Tate. Yet not quite. A week later, on the Saturday afternoon following this, Tate met the Australians again in his beloved Sussex, and he was graciously permitted to play an innings of 22 not out against them – and a capital innings at that.

NEVILLE CARDUS
Days in the Sun
(1924)

Jessop's Match (1902)

Now, after almost eighty years, Jessop's Match still seems to retain a special sort of fabulous and glamorous reputation of its own. When I mentioned it in that commentators' eyrie the immediate response was, 'That match – Jessop's match – you saw that?' Primed with John Arlott's Moët I told them a bit about it. But what bit? Simply the finish and some of the details of the never-to-be-forgotten last day's play leading up to that finish. And now that I come to write about it I find myself faced with the fact that the first two days' play contained some incidents which tickle the memory but few to haunt it.

I am glad now that I watched Trumper starting off the match with a characteristic 42, for it was the only time I ever saw Trumper make double figures. But the latter end of the first day's play produced in me a good deal of lingering resentment and muffled snorting as Trumble persisted in a long and stubborn tail-ender's innings of 64 not out ('pottering about' in my view) and, along with Hopkins and

174

Kelly, put on about 150 for the eighth and ninth wickets. The second morning belonged to Trumble too, as bowler this time, unchanged throughout England's first knock and taking 8 for 65. As a result England were left 141 behind, which was all pretty depressing, but we had a great stroke of luck when Australia batted again. Trumper had only made 2 when he went for a quick run, stumbled, fell flat halfway down the pitch and was run out. Then Lockwood put in a great spell of bowling and Australia were all out soon after the start of the third morning for 121 (Lockwood 5 for 45). So the second day was a great deal more eventful than the tedious first and I am sure I watched every ball with those hopes and fears which only the cricket lover can appreciate. But it is no good pretending that I can still give an eye-witness account of all that happened. Some of those for-no-particular-reason incidents survive. I remember one immaculate cover drive of Palairet's better than I remember any individual cover drive of Hammond's or Hutton's. Above all, two first-slip catches by MacLaren. They were not difficult catches; they came straight into his hands. It was the manner with which he accepted them. He took the ball and tossed it, not over his head to recatch it, but away into outer space with a flick of the wrist in the most disdainful fashion. 'Take it away: it stinks.' Oh, yes, yes; the name of A.C. MacLaren will always honour that 'and' – at any rate on *my* cricket poster.

Trumble and Lockwood must in turn have demonstrated that, ever since the first day, the wicket had got worse and worse. After England's first innings total of 183 and Australia's second innings total of 121, how could we possibly be expected to make 263 to win? We couldn't, of course, but the impossibility needn't have been rubbed in to me so cruelly. That hateful Saunders immediately came sailing in at the Vauxhall end, slinging destruction. MacLaren b. Saunders 2, Palairet b. Saunders 6, Tyldesley b. Saunders 0, Hayward c. Kelly b. Saunders 7. Jackson, at number five, was not out at lunchtime. Braund had joined him, but only for a very short time (c. Kelly b. Trumble 2).

During the lunch interval I noticed quite a number of disgruntled elderly members gathering up their belongings in the pavilion and departing home, unable to face the indignity of witnessing England's abasement. And I wonder what MacLaren had to say about what was served up to him for his mid-day meal.

So then – Braund out but with Jackson still there and appearing remarkably unruffled. And in came Jessop.

Jessop was a favourite subject for Craig's contemporary rivals as cricket poets. I recall two pleasing lines from an unidentified bard:

> At one end stocky Jessop crouched,
> The human catapult –

Crouched was an obvious description: 'the croucher' was a familiar nickname for Jessop owing to his stance at the wicket. 'Stocky' was descriptive of him too, though I think 'jaunty' would be nearer the mark. I knew, of course, all about his reputation as the biggest hitter in the game, but he had disappointed us in England's first innings (b. Trumble 13). Oh, well – perhaps he might treat us to a good slog or two before the inevitable and dismal defeat.

Again I must stick to my genuine and lasting recollections and impressions. It is obviously impossible to recall that Jessop innings in detail but there are certain features of it, and of its effect upon the crowd, that remain as clearly in my mind as though it all happened yesterday. To begin with, I was struck by Jessop's undaunted, almost it seemed heedless, approach – no 'desperate situation' about it. Jaunty. He was his own aggressive self from the start. Before long he took the triumphant Saunders in hand, to my especial delight, and hit him for two fours off successive balls to the long-on boundary. Darling immediately posted two fielders out there but Jessop ignored them and hit Saunders' next two deliveries between them or round them or through them as well. However despondent the crowd must have been during the morning, Jessop aroused them now to a state of wild exhilaration and Jackson must have been scoring steadily on his own. But I confess that the only thing I can remember about Jackson's invaluable innings is his getting caught and bowled by Trumble when he had made 49 and Jackson's exasperated thump with his bat on his pad as he turned to go.

Oh, damn and blast. Any faint gleam of hope of our getting those 263 runs vanished with Jackson into the pavilion. But the Australians had still another Yorkshireman to deal with. Confidence was the last thing that Jessop seemed to require but, had he needed it, George Hirst was the man to supply it – sturdy, defiant and the best all-rounder in the country in his day. (No one else had ever taken 200 wickets and made 2,000 runs in one season and they never will.) Sure enough, Hirst settled down while Jessop continued as before. Trumble was still on at the pavilion end. Still on? He was never off throughout the whole of England's two innings. Jessop hit him for six on to a canvas awning above part of the members' enclosure. The ball came back only to land on almost exactly the same spot immediately afterwards.

On they went, Hirst unmoveable, Jessop irrepressible. Presently the roars of the crowd subsided and gave way to an awesome, aspiring hush. They had roared Jessop to the verge of his century.

How well all cricket lovers know that tremulous moment and, goodness me, how often have I experienced it myself, but never, never in my whole life has it meant to me what it meant then.

Hush. Jessop crouched. The bowler started his run. It was just as well for me that my heart was only fifteen years old. The bowler bowled. Bang. Uproar.

The conventional Londoner wore a hat in those days and the conventional hat he wore was a straw boater. As Jessop made that stroke dozens of straw boaters were sent sailing from the crowd like boomerangs. Unlike boomerangs they failed to return to the owners, but who cared?

Like all cricket devotees I have many, many times shared with all around me that infectious 'breathless hush' tension as a batsman, however well-set, however self-possessed, has to face up to the obligation of scoring that hundredth run. He brings it off and, amid the general enthusiasm, one feels a spasm of pleasurable secret relief and a glow of fraternal satisfaction in the case of a batsman one is particularly fond of. I know I was young and almost foolishly impressionable at the time but I have always treasured and still treasure that century of Jessop's above and apart from all the rest.

The frenzy gradually subsided; boaters were or were not recovered; the crowd settled down. England still had a long way to go; but so long as Jessop and Hirst were there ... Then, oh no, Jessop mistimed a hook-shot and was caught at fine leg. What a tragedy. But that seemed to settle it; that stupendous effort of 104 was sacrificed. We couldn't hope to win now, could we? Hirst was still battling away and scoring steadily but Lockwood didn't last long. Lilley did though. Beyond all expectation Lilley stuck there with Hirst. The score crept up – 230, 240 – the whole Oval became almost as intent and intimidated as I was, hesitating to applaud too loudly for fear of inciting Hirst and Lilley to rashness.

Lilley got caught for 16 when the total had reached 248. Fifteen wanted and Rhodes came in to join his fellow Yorkshireman for a last-wicket partnership which was to become a sort of historic addendum to Jessop's hundred: though the legend that Hirst greeted Rhodes with the pronouncement: 'We'll get 'em in singles,' was later refuted by Rhodes himself. They got 'em steadily, a single here a couple there, until they'd levelled up the match at 262.

That is the moment – or rather the marathon minute – which remains clearest of all in my memory. Duff was fielding at deep long on to Trumble, who was bowling, as ever, from the pavilion end. An Australian from his seat in the stand a few rows behind me shouted, 'Never mind, Duff; you've won the Ashes.' I saw Duff turn his head with a quick resigned grin and return at once to attention. He of all the Australians in the field was required to be at attention. Trumble, as crafty a bowler as ever existed, presented Rhodes with a slow half-volley on the leg stump. How could any human batsman resist such a heaven-sent gift? 'Hurrah, here it is and here it goes' – wallop. And the ball would sail high into the outfield and, well within the range of possibility, into the safe hands of Duff. Not Rhodes. Not Yorkshire. Rhodes tapped the ball gently past square leg, ran the safe single and the match was won.

When by some means long forgotten I managed to arrive back home that evening, there was my father waiting to welcome me in the open doorway, his arms outstretched in mutual rejoicing. I felt a bit of a hero at having actually been there on Jessop's Day. I still do.

In the world of sport of those days cricket was held in a privileged regard of its own. During the summer seasons cricket was a logical, routine opening topic of conversation at City luncheons, West End clubs and barbers' shops. It was only to be expected that England's victory caused a sudden tidal wave of public jubilation. In sentiment if not in actual demonstration it was a modest echo of the recent unprecedented exultations of Mafeking Night. This almost miraculous restoration of our prestige was hailed with panegyrics which overlooked the fact that the prestige had been in dire and ignominious need of restoration. Who cared about the Ashes now? Boaters in the air.

The newspaper versifiers had the time of their lives:

A Croucher at the wicket took his stand
And thrashed the Cornstalk trundlers to the ropes.

AUSTRALIA

Batsman	First innings		Second innings	
V.T. Trumper	b Hirst	42	run out	2
R.A. Duff	c Lilley b Hirst	23	b Lockwood	6
C. Hill	b Hirst	11	c MacLaren b Hirst	34
J. Darling	c Lilley b Hirst	3	c MacLaren b Lockwood	15
M.A. Noble	c & b Jackson	52	b Braund	13
S.E. Gregory	b Hirst	23	b Braund	9
W.W. Armstrong	b Jackson	17	b Lockwood	21
A.J. Hopkins	c MacLaren b Lockwood	40	c Lilley b Lockwood	3
H. Trumble	not out	64	not out	7
J.J. Kelly	c Rhodes b Braund	39	lbw b Lockwood	0
J.V. Saunders	lbw b Braund	0	c Tyldesley b Rhodes	2
Extras	(B 5, LB 3, NB 2)	10	(B 7, LB 2)	9
Total		**324**		**121**

ENGLAND

Batsman	First innings		Second innings	
A.C. MacLaren	c Armstrong b Trumble	10	b Saunders	2
L.C.H. Palairet	b Trumble	20	b Saunders	6
J.T. Tyldesley	b Trumble	33	b Saunders	0
T. Hayward	b Trumble	0	c Kelly b Saunders	7
F.S. Jackson	c Armstrong b Saunders	2	c & b Trumble	49
L.C. Braund	c Hill b Trumble	22	c Kelly b Trumble	2
G.L. Jessop	b Trumble	13	c Noble b Armstrong	104
G.H. Hirst	c & b Trumble	43	not out	58
W.H. Lockwood	c Noble b Saunders	25	lbw b Trumble	2
A.A. Lilley	c Trumper b Trumble	0	c Darling b Trumble	16
W. Rhodes	not out	0	not out	6
Extras	(B 13, LB 2)	15	(B5, LB 6)	11
Total		**183**	(9 wkts.)	**263**

ENGLAND

	O.	M.	R.	W.	O.	M.	R.	W.	FALL OF WICKETS			
										Aust.	*Eng.*	*Aust.*	*Eng.*
Lockwood	24	2	85	1	20	6	45	5	*Wkt.*	1*st*	1*st*	2*nd*	2*nd*
Rhodes ..| 28	9	46	0	22	7	38	1	1st	47	31	6	5
Hirst ....| 29	5	77	5	5	1	7	1	2nd	63	36	9	5
Braund ..| 16.5	5	29	2	9	1	15	2	3rd	69	62	31	10
Jackson ..| 20	4	66	2	4	3	7	0	4th	82	67	71	31
Jessop ....| 6	2	11	0					5th	126	67	75	48
AUSTRALIA									6th	174	83	91	157
Trumble ..| 31	13	65	8	33.5	4	108	4	7th	175	137	99	187
Saunders .| 23	7	79	2	24	3	105	4	8th	256	179	114	214
Noble ...	7	3	24	0	5	0	11	0	9th	324	183	115	248
Armstrong					4	0	28	1					

BEN TRAVERS
94 Declared
(1981)

The Tie in Brisbane (1961)

Six runs were wanted by Australia when Hall began what had to be the final over. The first ball hit Grout high on the leg, dropped at his feet, and he and Benaud scampered a single. Now the odds were heavily on Australia for Benaud was 52 and batting in match-winning vein. But immediately the odds were levelled. The next ball was a bouncer and Benaud aimed to hook it, as Davidson a few minutes earlier had superbly hooked a similar ball. He merely nicked it, and every West Indian leapt for joy as Alexander took the catch. So Meckiff arrived to play his first ball quietly back to Hall, and Australia needed a run off each ball.

A bye was run, and Grout skied the fifth ball just out on the leg side. Fielders converged from all directions, but Hall was the tallest and most determined, and he alone put his hands to it as the batsmen were running a single. It bounced out, and the fielders drooped in despair. The next delivery almost completed their despair, for Meckiff courageously clouted it loftily away to leg. He and Grout ran one, then another, and staked all on a third to win the match as Hunte was preparing to throw from the square-leg boundary. It was a glorious low throw, fast and true, and though Grout hurled himself at the line and skidded home on severely grazed forearms he could not counter the speed of the ball.

Umpire Hoy flung his right arm high to announce the decision immediately to everyone anxiously looking towards him, and again the West Indies leapt and flung their arms in triumph. A minute or so later umpire and fielders repeated their actions, only more so. At the fall of the last wicket the joy of the West Indies was so expressed in leaps and bounds and running about that the scene might have served for a ballet of ultramodern abandon. The man who sent them into transports of delight and tied the match was little Solomon when Kline smoothly played the seventh ball of that fateful last over towards square leg. Meckiff at the other end was well launched on a run, but he never made it. With little more than one stump's width to aim at, Solomon threw the wicket down, as he had done some dozen minutes earlier from farther away to run out Davidson and give his side the chance to save themselves.

E.M. WELLINGS
Wisden Cricketers' Almanack
(1961)

England v. West Indies (1963)

The First Day

At Waterloo and Trafalgar Square the Underground train begins to fill. Young men in tweed jackets, carrying mackintoshes and holdalls. Older men in City black, carrying umbrellas. At every station the crowd grows. Whole families now, equipped as for a rainy camping weekend. And more than a sprinkling of West Indians. At Baker Street we are like a rush-hour train. It is eleven o'clock on a Thursday morning and we are travelling north. The train empties at St John's Wood. Buy your return ticket now, the boards say. We will regret that we didn't. Later. Now we are in too much of a hurry. We pass the souvenir sellers, the man selling the West Indian newspaper, the white-coated newspaper vendors. The newspaper posters. What billing these cricket writers get!

Then inside. It is wet. Play has not begun. A Barbadian in a blue suit, a tall man standing behind the sightscreen, has lost his brother in the crowd, and is worried. He has been in London for four years and a half. He has the bearing of a student. But: 'I works. In transport.' The groundsmen in vivid green lounge against the wicket-covers. Someone rushes out to them with a plate of what looks like cakes. There is applause. Few people have eaten before such a large appreciative audience. Presently, though, there is action. The covers are removed, the groundsmen retreat into obscurity, and the rites begin.

Trueman bowling to Conrad Hunte. Four, through the slips. Four, to mid-wicket. Four, past gully. Never has a Test opened like this. A Jamaican whispers: 'I think Worrell made the right decision.' A little later: 'It's all right now. I feel we getting on top.' The bowling tightens. The batsmen are on the defensive, often in trouble.

'I think Conrad Hunte taking this Moral Rearmament a little too seriously. He don't want to hit the ball because the leather come from an animal.'

A chance.

The Jamaican says: 'If England have to win, they can't win now.'

I puzzle over this. Then he leans back and whispers again: 'England can't win now. *If* they have to win.'

Lunch. In front of the Tavern the middle-class West Indians. For them too this is a reunion.

'... and, boy, I had to leave Grenada because politics were making it too hot for me.'

183

'What, they have politics in Grenada?'

Laughter.

'You are lucky to be seeing me here today, let me tell you. The only thing in which I remain West Indian is cricket. Only thing.'

'... and when they come here, they don't even change.'

'Change? Them?'

Elsewhere:

'I hear the economic situation not too good in Trinidad these days.'

'All those damn strikes. You know our West Indian labour. Money, money. And if you say "work", they strike.'

But the cricket ever returns.

'I don't know why they pick McMorris in place of Carew. You can't have two sheet-anchors as opening batsmen. Carew would have made 16. Sixteen and out. But he wouldn't have let the bowling get on top as it is now. I feel it have a lil politics in McMorris pick, you know.'

After lunch, McMorris leg before to Trueman.

'Man, I can't say I sorry. Poke, poke.'

Hunte goes. And, 65 runs later, Sobers.

'It isn't a healthy score, is it?'

'My dear girl, I didn't know you followed cricket.'

'Man, how you could help it at home? In Barbados. And with all my brothers. It didn't look like this, though, this morning. Thirteen in the first over.'

'But that's cricket.'

A cracking drive, picked up almost on the boundary.

'Two runs only for that. So near and so far.'

'But that's life.'

'Man, you're a philosopher. It must be that advanced age of yours you've been telling me about.'

'Come, come, my dear. It isn't polite to agree with me. But seriously, what you doing up here?'

'Studying, as they say. Interior decorating. It's a hard country, boy. I came here to make money.' Chuckle.

184

'You should have gone somewhere else.'

In a doorway of the Tavern:

'If Collie Smith didn't dead, that boy Solomon wouldn'ta get pick, you know.'

'If Collie Smith didn't dead.'

'He used to jump out and hit Statham for six and thing, you know.'

'I not so sure that Worrell make the right decision.'

'Boy, I don't know. I had a look through binoculars. It breaking up already, you know. You didn't see the umpire stop Dexter running across the pitch?'

'Which one is Solomon? They look like twins.'

'Solomon have the cap. And Kanhai a lil fatter.'

'But how a man could get fat, eh, playing all this cricket?'

'Not getting *fat*. Just putting on a lil *weight*.'

'O Christ! He out! Kanhai.'

Afterwards, Mrs Worrell in a party at the back of the pavilion:

'Did you enjoy the cricket, Mrs Worrell?'

'All except Frank's duck.'

'A captain's privilege.'

The Second Day

McMorris, the West Indian opening batsman whose failure yesterday was so widely discussed by his compatriots around the ground, was this morning practising at the nets. To him, bowling, Sobers and Valentine. Beyond the stands, the match proper continues, Solomon and Murray batting, according to the transistors. But around the nets there is this group that prefers nearness to cricketers. McMorris is struck on the pads. 'How's that?' Sobers calls. 'Out! Out!' the West Indians behind the nets shout, and raise their fingers. McMorris turns. 'You don't out down the line in England.' Two Jamaicans, wearing the brimless porkpie hats recently come into fashion among West Indian workers in England, lean on

185

each other's shoulders and stand, swaying, directly behind the stumps.

'Mac, boy,' one says, 'I cyan't tell you how I feel it yesterday when they out you. I feel it, man. Tell me, you sleep well last night? I couldn't sleep, boy.'

McMorris snicks one into the slips from Valentine. Then he hooks one from Sobers. It is his favourite shot.

'I wait for those,' he tells us.

A Jamaican sucks his teeth. 'Tcha! Him didn't bat like that yesterday.' And walks away.

The West Indian wickets in the meantime fall. Enter Wesley Hall. Trueman and he are old antagonists, and the West Indians buzz good-humouredly. During this encounter the larger interest of the match recedes. Hall drives Trueman straight back for four, the final humiliation of the fast bowler. Trueman gets his own back by hitting Hall on the ankle, and Hall clowningly exaggerates his distress. The middle-class West Indians in the Tavern are not so impressed.

'It's too un-hostile, man, to coin a word. You don't win Test matches with that attitude.'

West Indies all out for 301.

And England immediately in trouble. At ten past one Dexter comes in to face a score of 2 for 1. Twenty for one, lunch nearly due, and Griffith gets another wicket. A Jamaican, drunk on more than the bitter he is holding, talks of divine justice: Griffith's previous ball had been no-balled.

'You know, we going to see the West Indies bat again today.'

'But I want them to make some runs, though, I don't want it to be a walk-over.'

'Yes, man. I want to see some cricket on Monday.'

But then Dexter. Tall, commanding, incapable of error or gracelessness. Every shot, whatever its result, finished, decisive. Dexter hooking: the ball seeming momentarily *arrested* by the bat before being redirected. Dexter simplifying: an illusion of time, even against these very fast bowlers.

'If they going to make runs, I want to see Dexter make them.'

'It would be nice. But I don't want him to stay too long. Barrington could stay there till kingdom come. But Dexter does score too damn fast. He could demoralize any side in half an hour. Look, they scoring now at the rate of six runs an over.'

'How you would captain the side? Take off Griffith?'

Sobers comes on. And Dexter, unbelievably, goes. West Indian interest subsides.

'I trying to sell a lil insurance these days, boy. You could sell to Barbadians. Once they over here and they start putting aside the couple of pounds every week, you could sell to them. But don't talk to the Jamaicans.'

'I know. They pay three weeks' premiums, and they want to borrow three hundred pounds.'

In the Tavern:

'You know what's wrong with our West Indians? No damn discipline. Look at this business this morning. That Hall and Trueman nonsense. Kya-kya, very funny. But that is not the way the Aussies win Tests. I tell you, what we need is *conscription*. Put every one of the idlers in the army. Give them discipline.'

The score mounts. Worrell puts himself on. He wants to destroy this partnership between Parks and Titmus before the end of play. There is determination in his run, his delivery. It transmits itself to the West Indian crowd, the West Indian team. And, sad for Parks, who had shown some strokes, Worrell gets his wicket. Trueman enters. But Hall is damaged. There can be no revenge for the morning's humiliation. And matters are now too serious for clowning anyway.

West Indies 301. England 244 for 7.

Afterwards, Mrs Worrell in her party.

'You can still bowl, then, Mrs Worrell. You can still bowl.'

'Frank willed that, didn't he, Mrs Worrell?'

'Both of us willed it.'

'So, Mrs Worrell, the old man can still bowl.'

'Old man? You are referring to my father or my husband?'

The Third Day

Lord's Ground Full, the boards said at St John's Wood station, and there was two-way traffic on Wellington Road. No one practising at the nets today. And Trueman and Titmus still batting. Hall, recovered this morning, wins his duel with Trueman by clean bowling him. But England is by no means finished. Shackleton is correct and unnervous against Hall and Griffith, Titmus regularly steals a run at the end of the over.

Titmus won't get 50; England won't make 300, won't make 301. These are the bets being made in the free seats, West Indian against West Indian. Lord's has restrained them: in the West Indies they will gamble on who will field the next ball, how many runs will be scored in the over. For them a cricket match is an unceasing drama.

Titmus gets his 50. All over the free stands money changes hands. Then England are all out for 297. More money changes hands. It has worked out fairly. Those who backed Titmus for 50 backed England for 300.

Anxiety now, as the West Indians come out for the second innings. With the scores so even, the match is beginning all over again. 'I feel we losing a wicket before lunch. And I feel that it not going to be McMorris, but Hunte. I don't know, I just have this feeling.' Hunte hits a six off a bad ball from Trueman, and alarms the West Indians. 'Trueman vex too bad now.' What opens so brightly can't end well. So it turns out. Hunte is caught by Cowdrey off Shackleton. And in comes Kanhai, at twenty past one, with ten minutes to lunch, and the score 15 for 1. How does a batsman feel at such a time?

I inquire. And, as there are few self-respecting West Indians who are not in touch with someone who is in touch with the cricketers, I am rewarded. I hear that Kanhai, before he goes in to bat, sits silent and moody, 'tensing himself up'. As soon as the first West Indian wicket falls he puts on his gloves and, without a word, goes out.

Now, however, as he appears running down the pavilion steps, bat in one hand, the other hand lifted and slightly crooked, all his tenseness, if tenseness there ever was, has disappeared. There is nothing in that elegant figure to suggest nervousness. And when he does bat he gives an impression of instant confidence.

The crowd stirs just before the luncheon break. There is movement in the stands. Trueman is bowling his last over. McMorris is out! Caught Cowdrey again. McMorris has made his last effective appearance in this match. He goes in, they all go in. Lunch.

For West Indians it is an anxious interval. Will Worrell send in Sobers after lunch? Or Butcher? or Solomon, the steady? It is Butcher; the batting order remains unchanged. Butcher and Kanhai take the score to 50. Thereafter there is a slowing up. Kanhai is subdued, unnatural, over-cautious. It isn't the West Indians' day. Kanhai is caught in the slips, by Cowdrey again. Just as no one runs down the pavilion steps more jauntily, no one walks back more sadly. His bat is a useless implement; he peels off his gloves as though stripping himself of an undeserved badge. Gloves flapping, he walks back, head bowed. This is not the manner of Sobers. Sobers never walks so fast as when he is dismissed. It is part of his personality, almost part of the grace of his play. And this walk back is something we will soon see.

84 for 4.

'You hear the latest from British Guiana?'

'What, the strike still on?'

'Things really bad out there.'

'Man, go away, eh. We facing defeat, and you want to talk politics.'

It looks like defeat. Some West Indians in the free seats withdraw from the game altogether and sit on the grass near the nets, talking over private problems, pints of bitter between their feet. No need to ask, from the shouts immediately after tea, what has happened. Applause; no hands thrown up in the air; the West Indians standing still. Silence. Fresh applause, polite, English. This has only one meaning: another wicket.

The English turn slightly partisan. A green-coated Lord's employee, a cushion-seller, says to a West Indian: 'Things not going well now?' The West Indian shrugs, and concentrates on Solomon, small, red-capped, brisk, walking back to the pavilion.

'I can sell you a good seat,' the man says, 'I am quite comfortable, thank you,' the West Indian says. He isn't. Soon he moves and joins a group of other West Indians standing just behind the sightscreen.

Enter Worrell.

'If only we make 150 we back in the game. Only 150.'

And, incredibly, in the slow hour after tea, this happens. Butcher and Worrell remain, and, remaining, grow more aggressive.

The latest of the Worrell late cuts.

'The old man still sweet to watch, you know.'

The old man is Worrell, nearly thirty-nine.

The 50 partnership.

'How much more for the old lady?' The old lady is Butcher's century, due soon. And it comes, with two fours. A West Indian jumps on some eminence behind the sightscreen and dances, holding aloft a pint of bitter. Mackintoshes are thrown up in the air; arms are raised and held in massive V-signs. Two men do an impromptu jive.

'Wait until they get 200. Then you going to hear noise.'

The noise comes. It comes again, to mark the 100 partnership. Butcher, elegant, watchful, becomes attacking, even wild.

'That is Mr Butcher! That is Mr Basil Fitzpatrick Butcher!'

And in the end the score is 214 for 5.

'Boy, things was bad. Real bad. 104 for 5.'

'I didn't say nothing, but, boy, I nearly faint when Solomon out.'

In the Tavern:

'This is historic. This is the first time a West Indian team has fought back. The first time.'

'But, man, where did you get to, man? I was looking for a shoulder to lean on, and when I look for you, you gone.'

Many had in fact sought comfort in privacy. Many had joined the plebeian West Indians, to draw comfort from their shouting. But now assurance returns.

'I know that Frank has got everything staked on winning this match, let me tell you. And you know what's going to happen afterwards? At Edgbaston they are going to beat Trueman into the ground. Finish him off for the season.'

Behind the pavilion, the autograph hunters, and some West Indians.

'That girl only want to see Butcher. She would die for Butcher tonight.'

'I just want to see the great Gary and the great Rohan.'

Gary is Sobers, Rohan is Kanhai. These batsmen failed today. But they remain great. West Indies 301 and 214 for 5. England 297.

The Fourth Day

After the weekend tension, farce. We are scarcely settled when the five remaining West Indian wickets fall, for 15 runs. England, as if infected, quickly lose their two opening batsmen. Hall is bowling from the pavilion end, and his long run is accompanied by a sighing cheer which reaches its climax at the moment of delivery. Pity the English batsmen. Even at Lord's, where they might have thought they were safest, they now have to face an audience which is hostile.

And Dexter is out! Dexter, of the mighty strokes, out before lunch! Three for 31.

Outside the Tavern:

'I just meet Harold. Lance Gibbs send a message.'

How often, in the West Indian matches, conspiratorial word is sent straight from the players to their friends!

'Lance say', the messenger whispers, 'the wicket taking spin. He say it going to be all over by teatime.'

Odd, too, how the West Indians have influenced the English spectators. There, on one of the Tavern benches, something like a shouting match has gone on all morning between an English supporter and a West Indian.

'The only man who could save all-you is Graveney. And all-you ain't even pick him. You didn't see him there Thursday, standing up just next to the tea-stand in jacket and tie, with a mackintosh thrown over his arm? Why they don't pick the man? You know what? They must think Graveney is a black man.'

Simultaneously: 'Well, if Macmillan resigns I vote Socialist next election. And – I am a Tory.' The speaker is English (such distinctions are now necessary), thin, very young, with spectacles and tweed jacket. 'And,' he repeats, as though with self-awe, 'I am a Tory.'

In spite of that message from Lance Gibbs, Barrington and Cowdrey appear to be in no trouble.

'This is just what I was afraid of. You saw how Cowdrey played that ball? If they let him get set, the match is lost.'

When Cowdrey is struck on the arm by a fast rising ball from Hall, the ground is stilled. Cowdrey retires. Hall is chastened. So too are the West Indian spectators. Close comes in. And almost immediately Barrington carts Lance Gibbs for two sixes.

'Who was the man who brought that message from Lance Gibbs?'

'Rohan Kanhai did send a message, too, remember? He was going to get a century on Saturday.'

Where has Barrington got these strokes from? This aggression? And Close, why is he so stubborn? The minutes pass, the score climbs. 'These West Indian cricketers have some mighty names, eh: *Wesley* Hall. *Garfield* Sobers. *Rohan* Kanhai.'

'What about McMorris? What is his name?' A chuckle, choking speech. 'Easton.'

Nothing about McMorris, while this match lasts, can be taken seriously.

Now there are appeals for light, and the cricket stops. The Queen arrives. She is in light pink. The players reappear in blazers, the English in dark blue, the West Indians in maroon. They line up outside the pavilion gate, and hands are shaken, to a polite clapping which is as removed from the tension of the match as these courtly, bowing figures are removed from the cricketers we have been watching for four days.

With Barrington and Close settled in, and the score at the end of play 116 for 3, the match has once more swung in England's favour. Rain. The crowd waits for further play, but despairingly, and it seems that the game has been destroyed by the weather.

The Fifth Day

And so it continued to seem today. Rain held up play for more than three hours, and the crowd was small. But what a day for the 7,000 who went! Barrington, the hero of England's first innings, out at 130, when England needed 104 to win. Parks out at 138. Then Titmus, the stayer, came in, and after tea it seemed that England, needing only 31 runs with five wickets in hand, was safely home. The match was ending in anti-climax. But one shot – May's cover drive off Ramadhin at Edgbaston in 1957 – can change a match. And one ball. That ball now comes. Titmus is caught off Hall by – McMorris. And, next ball, Trueman goes. Only Close now remains for England, with 31 runs to get, and the clock advancing to six. Every ball holds drama. Every run narrows the gap. Hall bowls untiringly from the pavilion end. Will his strength never give out? Will Worrell have to bring on the slower bowlers – Sobers, himself or even Gibbs, whose message had reached us yesterday? Miraculously to some, shatteringly to others, it is Close who cracks. Seventy his personal score, an English victory only 15 runs away. Close pays for the adventuring which until then had brought him such reward. He is out, caught behind the wicket. However, the runs trickle in. And when, two balls before the end, Shackleton is run out any finish is still possible. Two fours will do the trick. Or a four and a two. Or a mighty swipe for six. Or a wicket. Cowdrey comes in, his injured left arm bandaged. And this is the ridiculous public-school heroism of cricket: a man with a bandaged arm saving his side, yet without having to face a ball. It is the peculiar *style* of cricket, and its improbable appreciation links these dissimilar people – English and West Indian.

Day after day I have left Lord's emotionally drained. What other game could have stretched hope and anxiety over six days? A slow game, but there were moments when it was torment to watch, when I joined those others, equally exhausted, sitting on the grass behind the stands. And what other game can leave so little sense of triumph or defeat? The anguish and joy of a cricket match last only while the match lasts. Close was marvellous. But it didn't seem so to me while he was in. Frustration denied generosity. But now admiration is pure. This has been a match of heroes, and there have been heroes on both sides. Close, Barrington, Titmus, Shackleton, Trueman, Dexter. Butcher, Worrell, Hall, Griffith, Kanhai, Solomon. Cricket a team game? Teams play, and one team is to be willed to victory. But it is the individual who remains in the memory, he who has purged the emotions by delight and fear.

V.S. NAIPAUL
Queen Magazine
(1963)

The Ideal Eleven

What would be your Ideal Eleven if you were sole selector and given the job of naming the type of players whom you think would represent the perfect balance under normal playing conditions?

I can't find out your answer, but here is mine.

Two recognized opening batsmen of whom one shall be a
  left-hander;
three other batsmen of whom one at least should be a left-
  hander;
one all-rounder;
one wicket-keeper who is also a good bat;
one fast bowler to open with the wind;
one fast or medium pace to open into the wind;
one right-hand off-spinner;
one left-hand orthodox first-finger spinner.

England's Test team at the Oval in 1956 went very close to it. She had a left and right-hander to open, but there was neither a left-hand batsman nor an all-rounder in the next four. Otherwise the selection was very close in principle to the combination I have set out. This was her team:

Richardson
Cowdrey
May
Compton
Sheppard
Washbrook
Evans
Statham
Tyson
Lock
Laker

The Australian team of 1921 also went very close. It was:

Collins	Armstrong
Bardsley	Gregory
Macartney	Oldfield
Andrews	McDonald
Taylor	Mailey
Pellew	

There were two recognized openers, one left-handed. Macartney was an all-rounder, right-hand bat and slow left-arm first-finger spin bowler.

There is not a left-hand batsman from two to six, but as Gregory was left-handed he partially made up for this.

Two fast bowlers opened, Gregory and McDonald. Then, instead of my theoretical right-hand off-spinner and my left-hand spinner, the team had Warwick Armstrong, a nagging, persistent type of slow leg-spinner (and a very fine batsman) with a genuine googly bowler, Arthur Mailey, to complete the side. It was by every standard a wonderful combination.

Another team which came very close to my ideal was Australia's fifth Test side at the Oval, 1948:

Barnes	Tallon
Morris	Miller
Bradman	Lindwall
Hassett	Ring
Harvey	Johnston
Loxton	

SIR DONALD BRADMAN
The Art of Cricket
(1958)

Test Match at Lord's

Bailey bowling, McLean cuts him late for one.
I walk from the Long Room into slanting sun.
Two ancients halt as Statham starts his run.
Then, elbows linked, but straight as sailors
On a tilting deck they move. One, square-shouldered as a
    tailor's
Model, leans over, whispering in the other's ear:
'Go easy. Steps here. This end bowling.'
Turning, I watch Barnes guide Rhodes into fresher air,
As if to continue an innings, though Rhodes may only play
    by ear.

ALAN ROSS
Poems 1942–67
(1968)

MATCHES II

The National Game

My brother said to me at breakfast:

'When you last played cricket, how many runs did you make?' And I answered him, truthfully, 'fifty'.

I remembered the occasion well for this was what happened. At school, oh! many years ago now, I had my sixth-form privileges taken away for some unpunctuality or other trifling delinquency and the captain of cricket in my house, a youth with whom I had scarcely ever found myself in sympathy, took advantage of my degradation to put me in charge of a game, called quite appropriately a 'Remnants' game'. I had resented this distinction grimly, but as a matter of fact the afternoon had been less oppressive than I had expected. Only twenty-one boys arrived so, there being none to oppose me, I elected to play for both while they were batting. I thus ensured my rest and for an hour or so read contentedly having gone in first and failed to survive the first over. When eventually by various means the whole of one side had been dismissed – the umpire was always the next batsman, and, eager for his innings, was usually ready to prove himself sympathetic with the most extravagant appeal – I buckled on the pair of pads which a new boy had brought, although they were hotly claimed by the wicket-keeper, and went out to bat. This other side bowled less well and after missing the ball once or twice, I suddenly and to my intense surprise hit it with great force. Delighted by this I did it again and again. The fielding was half-hearted and runs accumulated. I asked the scorer how many I had made and was told 'thirty-six'. Now and then I changed the bowlers, being still captain of the fielding side and denounced those who were ostentatiously slack in the field. Soon I saw a restiveness about both sides and much looking of watches. 'This game shall not end', I ordained, 'until I have made fifty.' Almost immediately the cry came 'Fifty' and with much clapping I allowed the stumps to be drawn.

Such is the history of my only athletic achievement. On hearing of it my brother said, 'Well, you'd better play today. Anderson has just fallen through. I'm taking a side down to a village in Hertfordshire – I've forgotten the name.'

And I thought of how much I had heard of the glories of village cricket and of that life into which I had never entered and so most adventurously, I accepted.

'Our train leaves King's Cross at 9.20. The taxi will be here in five minutes. You'd better get your things.'

At quarter past nine we were at the station and some time before eleven the last of our team arrived. We learned that the village we were to play was called Torbridge. At half-past twelve, we were assembled with many bags on the Torbridge platform. Outside two Fords were for hire and I and the man who had turned up latest succeeded in discovering the drivers in the 'Horse and Cart'; they were very largely sober; it seemed that now everything would be going well. My brother said,

'Drive us to the cricket ground.'

'There isn't no cricket ground,' brutishly, 'is there, Bill?'

'I have heard that they do play cricket on Beesley's paddock.'

'Noa, that's football they plays there.'

'Ah', very craftily, 'but that's in the winter. Mebbe they plays cricket there in the summer.'

'I have heard that he's got that field for hay this year.'

'Why, so 'e 'ave.'

'No, there ain't no cricket ground, mister.' And then I noticed a sign post. On one limb was written 'Lower Torbridge, Great Torbridge, Torbridge St Swithin', and on the other 'Torbridge Heath, South Torbridge, Torbridge Village', and on the third just 'Torbridge Station', this pointing towards me.

We tossed up and, contrary to the lot, decided to try Torbridge Village. We stopped at the public house and made enquiries. No, he had not heard of no match here. They did say there was some sort of festification at Torbridge St

Swithin, but maybe that was the flower show. We continued the pilgrimage and at each public house we each had half-a-pint. At last after three-quarters of an hour, we found at the 'Pig and Hammer', Torbridge Heath, eleven disconsolate men. They were expecting a team to play them – 'the Reverend Mr Bundles'. Would they play against us instead? Another pint all round and the thing was arranged. It was past one; we decided to lunch at once. At quarter to three, very sleepily the opposing side straddled out into the field. At quarter past four, when we paused for tea, the score was thirty-one for seven, of these my brother had made twenty in two overs and had then been caught; I had made one and that ingloriously. I had hit the ball with great force on to my toe from which it had bounced into the middle of the pitch. 'Yes, one', cried the tall man at the other end; he wanted the bowling; with great difficulty I limped across; I was glad that the next ball bowled him. One man did all the work for the other side – a short man with very brown forearms and a bristling moustache.

At quarter to five we went out to field and at seven, when very wearily we went back to the pavilion, only one wicket had fallen for 120. The brown-armed man was still in. Even on the occasion of my triumph I had not fielded; this afternoon, still with a crushed toe, I did not do myself credit. After a time it became the habit of the bowler whenever a ball was hit near me, immediately to move me away and put someone else there; and for this I was grateful.

In the shed at the end of the field there was no way of washing. We all had to change in one little room each with his heap of clothes; we all lost socks, studs and even waistcoats; it was all very like school. And finally when we were changed and feeling thoroughly sticky and weary, we learned from the cheery captain with the brown arms that there were no taxis in Torbridge Heath and no telephone to summon one with. It was three miles to Torbridge Station and the last train left at half-past eight. There would be no time for any dinner; we had heavy bags to carry.

One last sorrow came upon us when it would have seemed that all was finished, and just as we were coming into King's Cross I found that somewhere in that turmoil of changing I had lost my return ticket. My poor brother had to pay, I having no money. When he had paid he discovered that he would have no money left for a taxi. We must go back by tube and walk. To travel by tube with a heavy bag is an uneasy business. And when I returned home, I reasoned thus with myself; today I have wearied myself utterly; I have seen nothing and no one of any interest; I have suffered discomfort of every sense and in every limb; I have suffered acute pain in my great toe; I have walked several miles; I have stood about for several hours; I have drunken several pints of indifferently good beer; I have spent nearly two pounds; I might have spent that sum in dining very well and going to a theatre; I might have made that sum by spending the morning, pleasantly, in writing or drawing.

But my brother maintained that it had been a great day. Village cricket, he said, was always like that.

SCARAMEL (pseudonym of EVELYN WAUGH)
The Cherwell
(26 September 1923)

Eton and Harrow

Though short of wind and long of tooth,
Though old, and bent, and bald, forsooth!
Each summer I renew my youth
　　By basking, like a lizard,
Upon that sun-baked stand at Lord's
Where schoolboys sit in serried hordes,
Whose presence strikes familiar chords
　　Within my agèd gizzard;
Where Mem'ry helps me to recapture
My boyhood's first fine careless rapture!

Once more I keenly watch each ball,
As in those days beyond recall;
Once more, when friendly wickets fall,
    I groan and grind my molars!
Once more when breathless I behold
Opponents stumped, or caught, or bowled,
With feelings wholly uncontrolled
    I cheer the brilliant bowlers;
I thump the woodwork with my 'brolly',
And feel quite young again and jolly!

Then, later, when the innings ends
Pavilionwards my path extends,
To meet and gossip with old friends
    Of days and deeds departed!
In reminiscent style we brag
Of bygone 'beaks' we used to rag,
Of statesmen we were wont to 'fag',
    When we were all light-hearted,
Before our hair with grey was sprinkled,
Before our brows with care were wrinkled!

See, once again the game's begun!
We watch a nephew, or a son,
Between the wickets lightly run,
    Where once *we* ran as lightly!
And as we cheer those bound'ry drives,
Our boyhood's interest revives,
And in the evening of our lives
    We feel as young and sprightly
As when we sipped the springs of knowledge
At Harrow School or Eton College!

HARRY GRAHAM
in *The Observer*
(1927)

'A Curious Match'

From the novelty of the advertisement announcing a cricket-match to be played by *eleven Greenwich Pensioners with one leg against eleven with one arm,* for one thousand guineas, at the new cricket-ground, Montpelier Gardens, Walworth, in 1796, an immense concourse of people assembled. About nine o'clock the men arrived in three Greenwich stages; about ten the wickets were pitched, and the match commenced. Those with but one leg had the first innings, and got ninety-three runs. About three o'clock, while those with but one arm were having their innings, a scene of riot and confusion took place, owing to the pressure of the populace to gain admittance to the ground: the gates were forced open, and several parts of the fencing were broke down, and a great number of persons having got upon the roof of a stable, the roof broke in, and several persons falling among the horses were taken out much bruised. About six o'clock the game was renewed, and those with one arm got but forty-two runs during their innings. The one legs commenced their second innings, and six were bowled out after they got sixty runs, so that they left off one hundred and eleven more than those with one arm.

A match was played on the Wednesday following, and the men with *one leg* beat the *one arms* by one hundred and three runnings. After the match was finished, the *eleven one-legged men* ran one hundred yards for twenty guineas. The three first divided the money.

Pierce Egan's Book of Sports
(1832)

Fowler's Match

FOWLER, Capt. Robert St Leger, MC, born on April 7, 1891, died at Rahinston, Enfield, County Meath, on June 13, 1925, aged thirty-four. Owing to his profession, he was not very well-known to the general cricket public, but he was the hero of a match which may, without exaggeration, be described as the most extraordinary ever played. The story of the Eton and Harrow match in 1910 has been told over and over again, but it can never grow stale. No victory in a match of widespread interest was ever snatched in such a marvellous way. As captain of the Eton XI Fowler – it was his third year in the big match – found his side for about a day and a half overwhelmed. On the first day Harrow scored 232, and Eton, before bad light caused stumps to be drawn, lost 5 wickets for 40 runs. This was bad enough, but worse was to come. Eton's innings ended on the Saturday morning for 67, and in the follow-on 5 wickets were lost for 65. Fowler, scoring 64, played splendidly and received valuable help, but, in spite of all his efforts, the game reached a point at which the odds on Harrow could not have been named. With one wicket to fall Eton were only 4 runs ahead. But the Hon. J.N. Manners – killed in the War in 1914 – hit so fearlessly and had such a cool-headed partner in Lister-Kaye that the last wicket put on 50 runs. Honour was in a measure saved, no one imagined that Harrow would fail to get the 55 runs required. Then came the crowning sensation. Fowler bowled his off-breaks with such deadly accuracy that he took 8 wickets – 5 of them bowled down – and won the match for Eton by 9 runs. No one who was at Lord's on that eventful Saturday evening will ever forget the scene at the finish. Old Harrovians, bearing their sorrow with as much fortitude as could have been expected, said sadly that a grievous blunder had been committed in putting the heavy roller on the rather soft pitch, and there was a good deal in their contention. Still, nothing could detract from Fowler's achievement. Something heroic was demanded of him, and he rose to the height of his opportunity.

S.H. PARDON
Wisden Cricketers' Almanack
(1926)

Vitaï Lampada

There's a breathless hush in the Close to-night –
Ten to make and the match to win –
A bumping pitch and a blinding light,
An hour to play and the last man in.
And it's not for the sake of a ribboned coat,
Or the selfish hope of a season's fame,
But his Captain's hand on his shoulder smote –
'Play up! play up! and play the game!'

The sand of the desert is sodden red –
Red with the wreck of a square that broke –
The Gatling's jammed and the Colonel dead,
And the regiment blind with dust and smoke.
The river of death has brimmed his banks,
And England's far and Honour a name,
But the voice of a schoolboy rallies the ranks:
'Play up! play up! and play the game!'

This is the word that year by year,
While in her place the School is set,
Every one of her sons must hear,
And none that hears it dare forget.
This they all with a joyful mind
Bear through life like a torch in flame,

And falling, fling to the host behind –
'Play up! play up! and play the game!'

SIR HENRY NEWBOLT
Admirals All, and Other Verses
(1897)

Partners Against the World

Maurice squatted at their feet, and watched the game. It was exactly like other years. The rest of his side were servants and had gathered a dozen yards away round old Mr Ayres, who was scoring: old Mr Ayres always scored.

'The captain has put himself in first,' said a lady. 'A gentleman would never have done that. Little points interest me.'

Maurice said, 'The captain's our best man, apparently.'

She yawned and presently criticized: she'd an instinct that man was conceited. Her voice fell idly into the summer air. He was emigrating, said Mrs Durham – the more energetic did – which turned them to politics and Clive. His chin on his knees, Maurice brooded. A storm of distaste was working up inside him, and he did not know against what to direct it. Whether the ladies spoke, whether Alec blocked Mr Borenius's lobs, whether the villagers clapped or didn't clap, he felt unspeakably oppressed: he had swallowed an unknown drug: he had disturbed his life to its foundations, and couldn't tell what would crumble.

When he went out to bat, it was a new over, so that Alec received first ball. His style changed. Abandoning caution, he swiped the ball into the fern. Lifting his eyes, he met Maurice's and smiled. Lost ball. Next time he hit a boundary. He was untrained, but had the cricketing build, and the game took on some semblance of reality. Maurice played up too. His mind had cleared, and he felt that they were against the whole world, that not only Mr Borenius and the field but the audience in the shed and all England were closing round the wickets. They played for the sake of each other and of their fragile relationship – if one fell the other would follow. They intended no harm to the world, but so long as it attacked they must punish, they must stand wary, then hit with full strength, they must show that when two are gathered together majorities shall not triumph.

E.M. FORSTER
Maurice
(1914, first published 1971)

George IV and his Domestics

King George the Fourth, when riding in the Great Park, at Windsor, once came across a large party of his domestics playing the game near the Lodge. At the unexpected approach of the King the servants began to scamper in all directions, but His Majesty, much amused, sent one of the gentlemen in attendance to desire them to continue their game, and never to let his approach interrupt their sports. The King then continued his ride in another direction, observing in his attendants that cricket was a noble game, and that when he used to play cricket he enjoyed it as much as anyone.

W.A. BETTESWORTH
Chats on the Cricket Field
(1910)

Cricket in Corfu

People in search of the vanished Imperial culture of England would find very little in Corfu: and that little curious. I do not

210

speak about prevailing attitudes of mind; we have, of course, a certain number of Greeks educated abroad, who ape the English. I have inherited, for example, from my family – which once governed here under the British – a strong taste for good manners and fair dealing as a living part of my *amour propre*, not as independent virtues of character. It is the great difference between French culture and British; the British have no character – they depend upon very highly developed principles. It is convenient because they do not have to think. But apart from this Britain's legacy to Corcyra is an odd one; you have seen, have you not, in the dirty little alleys between the Hebraica and the port, a strange symbol chalked upon the walls? No? Wander into the alleys, and you will be suddenly surprised to see the wickets and bails of the slum cricketer every-where; you will suddenly think you are in Stepney. Cricket lives on as independently as the patron saint. It is a mysterious and satisfying ritual which the islanders have refused to relinquish; and every year in August when the British Fleet comes in, cricket enjoys her festival. A ripple of anticipation runs through the groups of dawdlers on the sunny esplanade; and the two cricket clubs of the town can be seen practising ferociously at the nets on the hard red earth, in the shadow of Schulemberg's statue. Groups of peasants, mysteriously drawn by their anticipation, stand in the shadow of the trees talking and observing. Meanwhile the British battleships ride squatly in the harbour and their fussy pinnaces throw up lines of ripples which, hours later, will disturb your Father Nicholas at his lobster-pots off St Stephano and cause him mightily to curse 'the cuckold British'. When the news comes that the challenge to a cricket match has been received, there is an audible sigh of relief and pleasure which runs the length of the town. At once a profound clamour of activity breaks out; a matting pitch is laid in the centre of the esplanade; a marquee is hastily run up; the Ministry of Supply in Athens receives an

211

incoherent telegram asking it to obtain from the British Legation the recipe for rock cakes, which has somehow been mislaid once again this year. The British Consul is to be seen in morning clothes. All British residents of the town gain face in a remarkable way. Some receive presents of fruit and poultry – for this is after all, not far short of a saint's day. And when the teams, eleven a side, and clad in their ceremonial white, meet on the ground for the toss, excitement and admiration reach their height. Peasants come in to town and take the afternoon off to sit under the trees on those uncomfortable café chairs, gravely applauding whenever the specialists (who sit in the marquee among the naval representatives and the consuls, and whose role is that of officiating priests) think fit to give them the cue. The British chaplain, who looks like nothing so much as a half- drowned blackbeetle rescued from a water-butt, sits in the midst of the distinguished guests, confirming by his presence the religious quality of the ritual. Everybody except St Spiridion himself appears to be present. And in the evening, by time-honoured custom, a British band in brilliant coats marches to the bandstand and delights the crowds by its martial flourishes until the last light dies away and the fireflies come flashing out in their thousands. For the benefit of Zarian I must add here that the terminology of cricketers in Corcyra has suffered with the passage of years. In some curious way the cry 'How's that?' has come to mean 'Out' while 'runs' are known as 'ronia'. The bails on the wickets are known as 'rollinia' and the drive is called 'pallia'. A yorker and a leg glide are known respectively as a 'primo salto' and a 'sotto gamba'; there are a few other small anomalies but I forget them for the moment. But while we are on the question of words I recall two English words which have been baptized into modern Greek. One is the verb 'to cost' which is used with a conventional verb-ending and pronounced very much as it is English; the other is an English draper's measure 'the peak' which has become 'pika'. When you add to all this the

212

private manufacture of apple chutney you have, I think, exhausted the subject of British cultural traces in the Ionian.

LAWRENCE DURRELL
Prospero's Cell
(1945)

An Innings and 851 Runs

It happened thirteen years ago this week, and that is the appropriate time after which to commemorate it. Dera Ismail Khan – or 'Dik' to old colonial hands – is on the west bank of the Indus, itself the westernmost of the Punjab's rivers. The muddy Indus flows softly in winter, little bigger than the Thames. But in summer, when the Karakoram snows melt, the Indus trebles its volume, filling the canals and irrigating the fields of cotton and sugar-cane.

The town of Dera Ismail Khan – or Dikhan to its inhabitants – consists of a long, dusty main street and a bazaar. It is mud-bricked, one-storeyed and poor, its pride a Plaza cinema, and baking hot so that its people are swarthier than most other Pakistanis.

But for want of anywhere else in those parts, the British made the town an administrative centre, and so it remains. The Raj lingers on in the bungalows and clubs (now Army property) of the suburb: in the two mud-brick churches, each with but a weekly service, and in the one-room municipal library stocked with biographies of Palmerston and the Earl of Derby, unread since 1947, and the complete works of Scott.

Little different therefore from any other Pakistani town in which the Raj set up shop. But Dikhan once played a first-class cricket match, exactly thirteen years ago: and they had the misfortune to lose it by the margin of an innings and 851 runs.

In the sub-continent weirder sides have slipped through the net of first-class status: the Hindustan Breweries XI and the Maharastra Small Savings Minister's XI (the savings were small, presumably, not the Savings Minister himself).

In 1964 it was reasonable by such standards for the new Ayub Zonal Tournament to be accorded first-class status. In the first round Dikhan, instead of playing another small fish like Baluchistan, were drawn against the mighty Railways, the match to be played at the Railways Stadium in Lahore.

A Dikhan team was assembled, but they had no wicket-keeper until someone visiting his brother in the town volunteered. Eight of them travelled to Lahore by train, two by bus, and Inayet, their best bowler, set off on the 250-mile journey by motorbike.

Railways won the toss, batted, overcame the loss of an early wicket, and finished the first day at 415 for 2. Ijaz Husain made 124 and Javed Baber, out early next day, chipped in with 200. But when Javed was out, the rot set in as Railways collapsed to 662 for 6. Pervez Akhtar and Muhammad Sharif, however, revived Railways and took the score to 825 for 6 at the close. They slaughtered the enemy with a mighty slaughtering, and the morning and the evening were the second day.

It had occurred to the Dikhan team that a declaration was about due. They were exhausted, and it was only on the assumption that they would be batting that they went to the ground on the third day. But, risking nothing, Railways batted on to 910 for 6 before declaring, with Pervez Akhtar, who had never made a century before, 337 not out. The declaration did not please Pervez because he had Hanif's world record 499 in sight.

The bowling figures testify to a carnage. Whereas Anwar Husain represented penetration (46 overs, 3 for 295), Inayet was accuracy (59 overs, 1 for 279). They both bowled fast-medium. At one point, while walking back to his mark, Anwar, now an Army major, was moved to continue past it and to hide behind the sightscreen.

214

Dikhan's reply was brief. They were all out for 32. Railways then gambled on a lead of 878 and enforced the follow-on. This time Dikhan were less successful, being all out for 27. Ahad Khan took 9 for 7 with mixed spin. Whereas Railways had batted for two and a quarter days, Dikhan were dismissed twice in two hours.

The cricketers of Dikhan were too tired and dejected to go home. They stayed in Lahore for several days recuperating, and then, on their return, by the waters of the Indus, they lay down and wept.

Two of the side gave up playing cricket after that match (or even during it — but that is unfair for they used no substitute fielders: they had none). And most of them left Dikhan in the course of time to find work, so that only three members still remain there.

Inayet lives in a back street of Dikhan. His full name is Inayet Ullah, but everyone knows him as Inayet Bowler. He is about six feet tall, with long strong fingers. His wife was ill. Whether it was that, or hashish, or his job in a bank, an intense sadness shrouded him. He spoke in the local tongue, save for the odd word in English and the one sentence: 'The fielding was very poor.' He estimated that eleven or twelve catches were dropped, one of them Pervez Akhtar (337) before he had made 10, off his own bowling. When he said that, he seemed near the heart of his sadness.

No one who has experienced a hard day in the field would mock these men of Dera Ismail Khan. Their endurance was more admirable than the easy records set up against them. It would not have been unusual in such cricket if they had conceded the match, or resorted to the common expedient of walking out in protest at an umpire's decision. With their performance indelible in cricket's history and records, they and their successors live under an eternal stigma. They talk of the match, and smile about it, but with an obvious sense of shame. Ever since, they have been almost ostracized by the Pakistani authorities, for suffering the most humiliating defeat in first-class cricket, in the only first-class match they ever played.

SCYLD BERRY
The Observer
(27 November 1977)

Tom Bats

Little Tom Clement is visiting at Petersfield, where he plays much Cricket: Tom bats, his grandmother bowls, and his great-grandmother watches out!!

GILBERT WHITE
Letter to Samuel Barker
(1 August 1786)

DISPUTES

At Adelaide Oval on Saturday, 14 January 1933 – the second day of the
Third Test of the 1932–3 series – the Australian captain, W.M. Woodfull,
was hit over the heart by the last ball of Larwood's second over. For
Larwood's third over, the England captain, D.R. Jardine, immediately
switched to a leg trap. This action so incensed the 50,000 crowd that it was
feared they might come over the fence at the players. The confrontation
reported below marked the point at which a dispute about cricket became a
controversy involving the pride of two nations.

On the following day, Sunday, there leaked out sensational
news – of an 'incident' in the Australian dressing-room in
which Woodfull and Mr Warner were concerned. The
English manager, hearing that Woodfull was in pain, had
gone there – as he afterwards put it – 'on an errand of
sympathy', and Woodfull, forgetting his usual diplomatic
reticence, had told him from the massage table what he
thought about our bowling. The news was going round
among Australian journalists and the following day would be
known throughout the Commonwealth, with inflammatory
results in stirring public prejudice.

That morning, I remember, I spent an hour at service at the
cathedral, within cricket-ball throw of the silent Oval. My
thoughts were elsewhere. There was no edition of the
Evening Standard on Sunday. But so grave was the news that
all my instincts rebelled against inactivity and I cancelled an
arrangement to go to an afternoon tennis party and
determined to spend the afternoon seeking Mr Warner, who
had left the team's hotel at Glenelg, Adelaide's seaside
suburb, for an unknown address.

The version of the Woodfull remarks which I had heard
from an Australian source was as follows:

I don't want to speak to you, Mr Warner. Of two teams out here one is playing cricket, the other is making no effort to play the game of cricket. It is too great a game for spoiling by the tactics your team are adopting. I don't approve of them and never will. If they are persevered with it may be better if I do not play the game. The matter is in your hands. I have nothing further to say. Good afternoon.

Mr Warner withstood any temptation towards argument. Beyond inquiring for Woodfull he made no remark and left the dressing-room, in which were several members of the Australian team and others.

Obviously I could not take the responsibility of sending the story home without probing it from the English side. I spent some hours and shillings in telephone inquiries which eventually discovered not Mr Warner, but Mr Jardine. He was diplomatically unaware of the occurrence and referred me to Mr Warner at a telephone number at Victor Harbour, by the sea, some fifty miles from Adelaide. I rang again and this time was lucky. Mr Warner naturally was unwilling to add fuel to the flames by public discussion, but was unable to deny the substantial accuracy of the quoted words. I cabled the story home to the *Daily Express*.

BRUCE HARRIS
Jardine Justified
(1933)

The Storm Bursts

It was on the fifth day of the match, Wednesday, January 18th, that the Board of Control, or at least the minority group at Adelaide, showed a regrettable inability to differ without deference. Mr Jeanes [Secretary of the Board] called a score of wondering newspaper men to his room and announced that this cablegram had been sent to London:

220

Bodyline bowling assumed such proportions as to menace best interests of game, making protection of body by batsmen the main consideration, causing intensely bitter feeling between players as well as injury. In our opinion is unsportsmanlike. Unless stopped at once likely to upset friendly relations existing between Australia and England.

Could anything be more tactless than this blunt and clumsy challenge? Accuse any Englishman of being impolite, dishonest, even immoral, and he may hold in his anger. Accuse him of being unsportsmanlike and you wound his deepest susceptibilities.

BRUCE HARRIS
Jardine Justified
(1933)

A Meaningless Term

I do not know if Mr Harris has any fresh light to throw on so-called 'bodyline bowling'. To me, I confess, the term is meaningless; what is the body line? The term was coined by a sensational Press to explain or excuse defeat, and would have died a natural and speedy death had it not been adopted by the Australian Board of Control in its lamentable wire to the MCC.

D.R. JARDINE
Foreword to *Jardine Justified* by Bruce Harris
(1933)

Barracking

A cricket tour in Australia would be a most delightful period in one's life if one was deaf.

HAROLD LARWOOD
Body-line?
(1933)

Rewards and Fairies

It is always a little disconcerting to the friends of great players of games to read obituary notices which confine themselves to the field of play. Jardine himself always regarded cricket as 'only a game'. He never wanted to talk about it. His main preoccupation, in the years when I knew him both in a City office and in my own home, was Hindu philosophy. He had a speculative mind, intent on ethical and religious problems. Kindly and high-minded, he had in those years an antipathy to Christianity, to which he always referred as 'Rewards and Fairies', equal to Gibbon's. Nor, in his manner and bearing, was there the faintest trace of the stern, aloof, decisive cricket captain. He was gentle and diffident in all his ways; slow and hesitant in speech, and, as it seemed to us, in thought; he chewed things over and came to cautious and tentative conclusions, except when attacking 'Rewards and Fairies'. Then he could be trenchant, and we realized how this mild-mannered philosopher could have been the instigator of 'bodyline' bowling.

It must be seldom that a great cricketer can have played the game so seriously and yet, on retirement from it, have put cricket so firmly in its proper place.

SIR LAWRENCE JONES
An appreciation in *The Times*
(24 June 1958)

'Supercilious Snobbery'

And here I must stop a moment to cross an angry nib with Mr Alec Waugh, who amuses himself (and others like him perhaps) at the expense of Village Cricket in a neat little essay, called 'The Village Heath', which was published in a volume *On Doing What One Likes*. It may be true of his experience, just as it may be true that he liked doing it, as the name of the book suggests (some people take their pleasures pretty grimly). But in all the dozen years or more I have played Village Cricket I have never played on a ground so bad as he describes or in a game so feeble. However, one man sees the same thing with very different eyes from another. I have met a few superior gentlemen who have deigned to turn out for some village: but I have never met anyone quite so supercilious as Mr Waugh. Listen to him:

The art of bowling is equally subject to complete reversal of existing standards. On the village heath a good bowler is not necessarily more dangerous than a poor one. 'We can understand', you may say, 'that a good batsman would be puzzled by the new conditions; that he could not in a short space of time adapt himself to the peculiar conformation of the pitch, the absence of screen and the decisions of a squint-eyed umpire. But bowling is different. If a bowler without length or swerve or spin can frustrate a good batsman, surely a decent bowler would be unplayable.' He isn't, though. He bowls too well. As I have said before, village cricket is not in a different class from club cricket. It is a different game altogether. The principle of the thing is different. The tactics of the club or school or county bowler are aggressive. He has to get the batsman out. The tactics of the village bowler might be described as passively co-operative. He helps the batsman to get himself out.

223

One would like to be able to read the essay as an ironical *tour de force*, showing into what silliness supercilious snobbery may lead a man. As though, for instance, a bowler in the finest cricket did not 'help a batsman to get himself out'. How else did Bradman dispose of Hammond in an Australian Test? But I am afraid the dreadful little exhibition of smartness must be read quite straight. It ends with a word of advice:

> Sirs, take warning: when you next take a weekend in the country and your host suggests that you should spend Saturday afternoon on the village green, be not tempted. Be you batsman, bowler or cover point, here assuredly you will meet disaster. You will not make runs, you will not take wickets, you will chase after the balls that you have missed. Your many accomplishments will be of no value to you there. This village cricket is, believe me, altogether a different game. A word of warning, sirs: remain in the pavilion.

Or still better stop at home and play with yourself – in the billiard-room. I read out this essay to Old Ben, our scorer for many years. I cannot mention what part of the writer's anatomy he suggested was in need of rubbing with a brick. A homely specific, often proposed hopefully as a cure for many disagreeable qualities. I am less hopeful, though I must own I have never actually applied a brick in the manner suggested, so I cannot speak, as I like to do, from experience. But I am inclined to think it would take more than any punishment, however simple and drastic, to get the sneer out of a man. Sneering goes so subtly deep into his make-up: an insidious poison.

HUGH DE SELINCOURT
Moreover
(1934)

Stump Orators

The first requirement for good village green cricket is that the village itself should be a *bona fide* village, not an outlying colony full of cockney villas inhabited by stuck-up people. There ought to be at least two or three old fogeys who attend every match and declare there never were such days as when Squire A or Squire B, as the case may be, was alive; there must be an inn where the cricketers have met within the memory of all the oldest inhabitants; I prefer a green where the stocks are still standing, and I would rather not play at all if there is no parish beadle. I think a village more perfect where a feud is always going on in the vestry about the roads, or a pump, or an organ (for parishioners hate one another more about a church question than anything), or some other bone of contention which draws out the eloquence of stump orators at the vestry.

FREDERICK GALE
Echoes from Old Cricket Fields
(1871)

International Cricket Conference v. Packer

At the meeting today, member countries gave long and earnest consideration to the effect of the Packer proposals on cricket at all levels and in all countries. They reaffirm the views of the Test-match playing countries, at their meeting on 14 June, that the whole structure of cricket, for which their governing bodies are responsible, could be severely damaged by the type of promotion proposed by Mr Packer and his associates.

Following the breakdown of negotiations with Mr Packer, when the Conference was unable to accede to his demand to exclusive TV rights in Australia, members of the ICC today unanimously resolved to ensure that it could honour its responsibilities to players at all levels. To do so, they are determined to continue to promote international matches between countries and to oppose to the maximum extent the series of exhibition matches arranged to take place in Australia during the forthcoming Australian summer. These matches will not rate as first-class, nor appear in official records. In order to give effect to these views the ICC passed unanimously a change in the ICC rules, relating to qualifications for Test matches: 'Notwithstanding anything herein before contained, no player who, after 1 October 1977, has played or has made himself available to play in a match previously disapproved by the Conference, shall thereafter be eligible to play in any Test match, without the express consent of the Conference, to be given only on the application of the governing body for cricket of the country for which, but for this sub-rule, the player would be eligible to play.'

In addition to this new rule, the Conference passed unanimously a resolution disapproving certain matches. This read: 'It is hereby resolved that any match arranged, or to be arranged by J.P. Sport Pty Ltd, Mr Kerry Packer, Mr Richie Benaud or associated companies or persons, to take place in Australia or elsewhere between 1 October 1977 and 31 March 1979 is disapproved.'

The Conference also passed a guidance resolution as follows: 'For future guidance, the Conference records and minutes that matches are liable to be disapproved if so arranged, whether by reference to date or otherwise, as to have the probable result that invitations to play in such matches will conflict with invitations which have been or may be received, to play in first-class matches subject to the jurisdiction of the governing bodies of foundation and full members of the Conference.

The Conference strongly recommended that each member country should pursue as soon as possible, at first-class level

and in other domestic cricket activities, the implementation
of decisions made in regard to Test matches.

INTERNATIONAL CRICKET CONFERENCE STATEMENT
(1977)

Never Argue

I want to stress again one aspect of the game which is most
important. *Never argue with an umpire.*

IAN BOTHAM
Ian Botham on Cricket
(1980)

Knaves and Fools

'If gentlemen wanted to bet,' said Beldham, 'just under the
pavilion sat men ready, with money down, to give and take
the current odds: these were by far the best men to bet with,
because, if they lost, it was all in the way of business; they
paid their money and did not grumble. Still, they had all sorts
of tricks to make their betting safe.' 'One artifice', said Mr
Ward, 'was to keep a player out of the way by a false report
that his wife was dead. Then these men would come down to
the Green Man and Still, and drink with us, and always said
that those who backed us, or "the nobs", as they called them,
sold the matches; and so, sir, as you are going the round
beating up the quarters of the old players, you will find some
to persuade you this is true. But don't believe it. That any
gentleman in my day ever put himself into the power of these
blacklegs, by selling matches, I can't credit. Still, one day, I
thought I would try how far these tales were true. So, going
down into Kent, with "one of high degree", he said to me,
"Will, if this match is won, I lose a hundred pounds!"

227

"Well," said I, "my lord, you and I *could* order that." He smiled as if nothing were meant, and talked of something else; and, as luck would have it, he and I were in together, and brought up the score between us, though every run seemed to me like "a guinea out of his lordship's pocket".'

'You see, sir,' said one fine old man, with brilliant eye and a quickness of movement which showed his right hand had not yet forgot its cunning, 'matches were bought, and matches were sold, and gentlemen who meant honestly lost large sums of money, till the rogues beat themselves at last. They overdid it; they spoilt their own trade; and, as I said to one of them, "A knave and a fool make a bad partnership; so, you and yourself will never prosper." Well, surely there was robbery enough; and not a few of the great players earned money to their own disgrace, but there was not half the selling there was said to be. Yes, I can guess, sir, much as you have been talking to all the old players over this good stuff' (pointing to the brandy-and-water I had provided), 'no doubt you have heard that B— sold as bad as the rest. I'll tell the truth; one match up the country I did sell – a match made by Mr Osbaldeston at Nottingham. I had been sold out of a match just before, and lost £10; and happening to hear it, I joined two others of our eleven to sell, and get back my money. I won £10 exactly, and of this roguery no one ever suspected me; but many was the time I have been blamed for selling when as innocent as a babe.

'In those days, when so much money was laid on matches, every man who lost his money would blame someone. Then if A missed a catch, or B made no runs – and where's the player whose hand is always in? – that man was called a rogue directly. So, when a man was doomed to lose his character, and to bear all the smart, there was the more temptation to do like others, and after "the kicks" to come in for "the halfpence". But I am an old man now, and heartily sorry I have been ever since; because but for that Nottingham match I could have said with a clear conscience to a gentleman like

228

you, that all which was said was false, and I never sold a match in my life; but now I can't. But if I had fifty sons, I would never put one of them, for all the games in the world, in the way of the roguery that I have witnessed. The temptation really was very great – too great by far for any poor man to be exposed to no richer than ten shillings a week, let alone harvest-time. I never told you, sir, the way I first was brought to London. I was a lad of eighteen at this Hampshire village, and Lord Winchilsea had seen us play, and watched the match with the Hambledon Club on Broad-halfpenny, when I scored forty-three against David Harris, and ever so many of the runs against David's bowling, and no one ever could manage David before. So, next year, in the month of March, I was down in the meadows, when a gentleman came across the fields with Farmer Hilton; and, thought I, all in a minute, now this is something about Cricket. Well, at last it was settled I was to play Hampshire against England, at London, in White Conduit Fields ground, in the month of June.

'For three months I did nothing but think about that match. Tom Walker was to travel up from this country, and I agreed to go with Tom; and found myself, at last, with a merry company of cricketers. All the men whose names I had ever heard as foremost in the game, met together, drinking, card-playing, betting, and singing, at the Green Man (that was the great cricketers' house) in Oxford Street – no man without his wine, I assure you; and such suppers as three guineas a game to lose, and five to win (that was then the sum for players), could never pay for long. To go to London by the waggon, to earn five guineas three or four times told, and come back with half the money in your pocket to the plough again, was all very well talking. You know what young folk are, sir, when they get together; mischief brews stronger in large quantities: so many spent all their earnings, and were soon glad to make more money some other way. Hundreds of pounds were bet upon all the great matches, and other wagers laid on the scores of the finest players, and that too by men who had a book for every race and every match in the sporting world – men who lived by gambling; and, as to honesty, gambling and honesty don't often go together. What was easier, then, than for such sharp gentlemen to mix with the players, to take advantage of their difficulties, and to say, "Your backers, my Lord this, and the Duke of that, sell matches and overrule all your good play, so why shouldn't you have a share of the plunder?" – that was their constant argument. "Serve them as they serve you." You have heard of Jim Bland, the turfsman, and his brother Joe – two nice boys. When "Jemmy" Dawson was hanged for poisoning the horse, the Blands never felt safe till the rope was round Dawson's neck; to keep him quiet, they persuaded him to the last hour that no one dared hang him, and that a certain nobleman had a reprieve in his pocket.

'Well, one day in April, Joe Bland traced me out in this parish and tried his game on with me. "You may make a fortune," he said, "if you will listen to me: so much for the match with Surrey, and so much more for the Kent match –" "Stop," said I: "Mr Bland, you talk too fast; I am rather too old for this trick; you never buy the same man but once: if their lordships ever sold at all, you would peach upon them if ever after they dared to win. You'll try me once, and then you'll have me in a line like our friend at the mill last year." No, sir, a man was a slave when once he sold to these folk: "fool and knave aye go together". Still, they found fools enough for their purpose ... 'But Sir, I can't help laughing when I tell you: once, there was a single-wicket match played at Lord's, and a man on each side was paid to lose – one was bowler and the other batsman – when the game came to a near point. I knew their politics, the rascals, and saw in a minute how things stood; and how I did laugh, to be sure! For seven balls together, one would not bowl straight, and the other would not hit; but at last a straight ball must come, and down went the wicket.' ...

'This practice of selling matches,' said Beldham, 'produced strange things sometimes. Once I remember, England was playing Surrey, and in my judgement, Surrey had the best side; still, I found the Legs were betting seven to four against Surrey! This time they were done; for they betted on the belief that some Surrey men had sold the match; but Surrey then played to win.

'Crockford used to be seen about Lord's, and Mr Gully also occasionally, but only for the society of sporting men; they did not understand the game, and I never saw them bet. Mr Gully was often talking to me about the game for one season; but', said the old man, as he smoothed down his smock-frock, with all the confidence in the world, 'I could never put any sense into him; he knew plenty about fighting, and afterwards of horse-racing; but a man cannot learn the odds of Cricket unless he is something of a player.'

THE REV. JAMES PYCROFT
The Cricket Field
(1851)

Dudley Nourse

Even today, in 1971, when there are more forceful batsmen in South African cricket than ever before in its history, no one has risen to top-class cricket with anything remotely resembling the remarkable background of Dudley Nourse. Surely there can never be another like him.

In modern times so much is done to teach boy cricketers, from their very first sign of promise, that it is virtually impossible for the country to produce a self-made Springbok. Nourse defied anyone to tell him how to play the game.

While others are groomed methodically through the niceties of technique, he learned the rudiments of the game as a raw lad playing barefooted in a street and public parks.

231

Despite the awesome example of his illustrious father Dave, the Grand Old Man of South African cricket who appeared in more tests than any of his countrymen, except Johnny Waite, and who was still playing at the age of sixty, he did not want to be a great cricketer.

As a young man he was far more interested in soccer. In no game did his father teach him. In fact he did not see Dudley bat until he was twenty-one years of age. Yet I wonder if a few words that the old man once spoke to his son when he was a lad did not do more than anything else in his life to shape the future of one of the country's outstanding batsmen, a giant in his era.

In that part of Durban where the Nourses lived there dwelt a score of eager young cricketers. Often they played in Lancers Road ground or Albert Park, but when the urge was irresistible a double wicket of paraffin tins was set up on the tarred road and the issue was decided with an old bat and tennis ball.

Nourse was king of the street cricket, but one day his sovereignty was challenged by a ginger-haired participant who told him bluntly that he didn't know how to hold the bat.

The argument developed heatedly. One group maintained that the back of the left wrist should face down the pitch, the other that it should face the wicket-keeper. Tempers were rising when Nourse decided that the only way to settle the dispute was to ask his father. As Dave was an idol of cricket this was a solution not to be questioned.

Fortunately it was a time when his parent was at home. So often he was away somewhere – in South Africa or overseas – playing cricket. Indeed, he was abroad when his son was born, on November 12, 1910, and had just scored 201 not out against South Australia in the opening match of South Africa's first tour of Australia in 1910–1911 when he heard the news. In deference to a wish expressed by the Earl of Dudley, then Governor-General of Australia, the boy was christened Arthur Dudley.

With hot flushed faces the little band trooped through the garden into the house to hear the judgement of the oracle.

'Dad, which is the proper way to hold the bat?' asked the indignant victim of the accusation.

His self-composed parent took him by the arm.

'Son,' he said, 'I learned to play cricket with a paling of a fence. Now you go and do the same.'

Whether or not the rebuttal was a shock to the lad's pride it must have left a lasting impression in his mind. If that was how his father felt, he would teach himself. Never again did he ask anyone's advice.

LOUIS DUFFUS
Giants of South African Cricket
(1971)

Humiliation of the Great

Vivian Richards, Joel Garner and Ian Botham will never play for Somerset again. They have given me great pleasure, as great pleasure as I have ever had from watching cricket. Their coming together in one English county side, and my own county, was astonishing good fortune.

For a few years Somerset, of all cricketing counties, has been the most exciting team to watch in the world. Last Saturday it all ended in a drafty barn near Shepton Mallet where, by more than two to one, the Somerset members voted to sack Viv Richards and Joel Garner, well knowing that Botham would also leave the side as a consequence.

Such a verdict cannot be overturned. I would like however to express the gratitude which those who voted to turn out the committee feel that the club itself ought to have shown. I believe in gratitude; I believe in loyalty; I am ashamed that the Somerset Club does not.

I have never met any of the three; my own gratitude to

them arises simply because their cricket has been so delightful to watch.

I feel grateful to Joel Garner because he combined such ability as a bowler with an obvious sweetness and simplicity of nature.

That made him the favourite of the Somerset crowds, particularly the children, who used to hang out banners at Lord's with 'Big Bird' written on them. They have fired the big bird now.

His bowling seemed even from the pavilion to be unplayable, rising up from the pitch at an acute angle corresponding to his great height, presenting the batsman with a problem in three dimensional geometry at more than motorway pace.

Viv Richards is the best batsman I have ever seen, save only for Bradman. In both men the speed of their reactions set them apart, making the fastest bowlers appear to be of medium pace, and medium pace bowlers appear to be slow. Richards never wears a helmet because he can trust himself; at Taunton he would have done well to wear a backplate.

He has a commanding personality; his visage is ancient and dignified, almost semitic, as though Haile Selassie, the Lion of Judah, had taken to cricket when he was in temporary exile in Bath. Even more than Bradman his batting is power in action – he is a stronger man than Bradman was; that combination of power, agility, intent and speed of reaction is now for Somerset only a memory.

Ian Botham is Ian Botham. I suppose he is impossible – though no more impossible than great tenors in the world of opera. I doubt whether anyone can have these surges of energy when performing without them coming from some deep and perhaps uncontrollable source in the personality. Yet on the cricket field for Somerset and even more for England he has repeatedly performed the impossible.

I did not speak at Shepton Mallet, but another member, Mr Blanchard, put what I felt, in referring to 'an extraordinary ingratitude, not only in the deed but in the way the deed was done'.

What makes a good friendly Somerset crowd support an obviously inadequate committee, who have so mishandled things that the one spell of glory in Somerset's cricket history has ended in such disunity and dark ingratitude? Why do we support people who have shamed us?

Not, I think on any cricket argument. 'Dasher' Denning, from Chewton Mendip, perhaps the one man whose cricket record could have persuaded me to support so feeble a committee, put a point which went entirely unanswered. 'Bowlers win matches – why get rid of your only strike bowler?' Crowe, the white knight from New Zealand, who describes himself as 'very ambitious', has a bad back and can no longer bowl much. Next season Somerset may well get some runs, but they are going to be hard put to bowl any other county out.

The roots of the desire to humiliate genius go very deep in human nature. Most of us have a very English preference for mediocrity. Ian Botham is, in particular, a disturbing character. He represents, in an open form, energy which is chained in every man's subconscious mind. There is in his cricket none of the repression which helps the rest of us to function as civilized beings. Yet the result of his unrepressed libido is an explosion of energy which none of the rest of us could ever have achieved.

Garner, I think, is a threat to none. He has merely been trapped by being a third in what Nigel Popplewell, a retired player, son of the Judge, called the 'Superstars'. I thought it unjust and ungenerous of Popplewell to include Garner in what was properly a criticism of Botham and Richards.

Viv Richards is a threat, which is why he is so formidable at the wicket. Botham and Richards are extraordinary men as well as extraordinary players; they have a Jungian archetypal force about them, reinforced in Richards's case by the blackness of an Othello. People project onto such figures psychic material from the sub-conscious mind, often material they cannot face in themselves. That makes such heroes exciting to watch, but also deeply threatening to men of infirm psychic confidence. The committee were also much influenced by Roebuck, the county captain, an edgy young man who was put in a position that was perhaps too difficult for him. It is never easy to lead one's betters. Roebuck is a batsman of almost painful talent who owes his success more to determination than nature. It seems likely that he thought that he was meaning well, though he does not seem to have been able to behave with complete frankness.

The gap between talent and genius is always a tormenting one, however good one's intentions. It is tempting to feel that God plays an unfair trick in giving only talent to the men of good character, but bestows genius on those apparently less worthy of it.

With such less gifted cricketers I have some sympathy; I have never found men of genius easy, and I do not suppose they did. With the committee I have no sympathy at all; they have lost the Somerset Club's honour and fouled the memory of its greatest period. No good will come to any of them, nor to Mr Crowe, from this affair. But then no good came to Salieri when he stood, grinning with grief and envy, by Mozart's open grave.

SIR WILLIAM REES-MOGG
The Independent
(11 November 1986)

236

VIOLENCE

Dream of Revolution

MOON: ... Sometimes I dream of revolution, a bloody *coup d'état* by the second rank — troupes of actors slaughtered by their understudies, magicians sawn in half by indefatigably smiling glamour girls, cricket teams wiped out by marauding bands of twelfth men.

TOM STOPPARD
The Real Inspector Hound
(1968)

Riot Stops Play

Another riot, more serious than yesterday's, ended play an hour early in the first Test match between England and Pakistan here [in Lahore] this afternoon. This time the origins of the trouble were clearly political, the supporters of Mrs Nursrat Bhutto, who had come to the ground before tea, taking the opportunity of demonstrating in a turbulent manner their support for her husband's Pakistan People's Party. England at the time were 85 for 2 in reply to Pakistan's first innings total of 407 for 9 declared.

When calm, or relative calm, had been restored, and the umpires went out to inspect the field, by now littered with bottles, sticks and stones, they were sufficiently affected by the tear gas, which had been used to disperse the trouble-makers and still hung in the air, to decide that no further play would be possible. The police, as is usually the case in these cricketing disorders, had seemed only to aggravate matters when they moved into action.

Having been diverted from the main gate to the women's stand, Mrs Bhutto's arrival there with her daughter caused pandemonium to break out. Boycott and Randall were in the process of steadying England's innings after Brearley and

Rose had been out in quick succession. There being a restriction on the size and nature of public gatherings imposed by the martial law administrators, a crowd of 30,000 at a Test match provides a rare chance of drawing attention to a cause.

What will have to be decided tomorrow, which is the rest day in the Test match, is how to ensure conditions in which it is possible to have a worthwhile game of cricket. If that cannot be done there will be little point in continuing with the tour. The people one is sorriest for are the true cricket lovers, and there are a lot of these, as well, of course, as the Pakistan team. No one could have looked more crestfallen than they did when they left the field this afternoon, with the railings in front of the popular stand being torn from their sockets. Pakistan had bowled and fielded splendidly, too, keeping Boycott at full stretch to survive.

If recent English tours to Pakistan are anything to go by, the signs are not promising. In 1968–69, after several weeks of regular disruptions, the last Test match in Karachi had to be abandoned on the third morning. Five years ago, also in the last Test match in Karachi, the players had to leave the field twice on the third afternoon, once when the shamianas, or Hessian screens, were set alight.

JOHN WOODCOCK
in *The Times*
(17 December 1977)

'Jones, Jones, What Jones?'

W.G. Grace always said Kortright was the fastest bowler he ever played when C.J. was at his very best. How much faster than other really fast bowlers he was one may judge from a remark of W.G.'s. Somebody once said to him, *à propos* of pace, 'And how fast was Jones, Doctor?' 'Jones, Jones, what

Jones?' said W.G. 'Ernest Jones, the Australian.' 'Oh, the man who bowled through my beard,' said W.G. 'Yes he was fast.' Stoddart used to tell that story. It appears that on one occasion at Lord's Jones started the bowling when there was still that 'jump' in the wicket which Lord's used to have to the real pacy bowler in the old days. Grace played forward to a ball pretty well up to him – he had to play forward at that pace – and the ball *did* go through his beard and shot away to the boundary for four byes. For the first half hour or so of the day's play the ball used to be inclined to kick at Lord's, perhaps on account of the dew.

F.B. WILSON
Sporting Pie
(1922)

The Laugh of the Year

Sir,

Now that it is officially announced that the bitter feeling already aroused by the colour of Mr Jardine's cap has been so intensified by the direction of Mr Larwood's bowling as to impair friendly relations between England and Australia, it is necessary that this new 'leg theory', as it is called, should be considered, not only without heat, but also, if possible, with whatever of a sense of humour Test Matches can leave to a cricketer.

It seems funny, then, to one who did not serve his apprenticeship as a writer by playing for Australia that a few years ago we were all agreed that cricket was being 'killed' by 'mammoth scores' and 'Marathon matches', and that as soon as a means is devised of keeping scores down to a reasonable size cricket is 'killed' again. It seems comic to such a one that, after years of outcry against overprepared wickets, a scream of horror should go up when a bowler proves that even such a wicket has no terrors for him. It is definitely the laugh of the year that, season after season, batsmen should break the hearts of bowlers by protecting their wickets with their persons, and that, when at last the bowler accepts the challenge and bowls at their persons, the outraged batsmen and ex-batsmen should shriek in chorus that he is not playing cricket.

These things seem funny: but there is, of course, a serious side to the Australian Board of Control's protest. This says that the English bowling has made 'protection of the body by the batsman the main consideration', and if this were so there would be legitimate cause of complaint. But let us not forget that Mr McCabe, in his spare moments during the first Test Match, managed to collect 180 runs, and Mr Bradman, in the second, 100; each of them scoring (even though scoring was necessarily a minor consideration) four times as quickly as Mr Jardine, whose body (up to the cap) was held as sacred. Let us not forget that, if this new form of bowling is really as startlingly new as is implied, lesser batsmen than these two should at least be given a chance of adapting themselves to it before the white flag is waved. But if modern batsmanship is really so unadventurous and unflexible that after three failures it announces itself beaten and calls for the laws to be altered, why, then, let the laws be altered; let everybody go on making runs, the artisan no less easily than the master, and let us admit frankly that the game is made for the batsmen only, and that it ceases to be cricket as soon as it can no longer be called 'a batsman's paradise'.

A.A. MILNE
Letter to *The Times*
(20 January 1933)

Bodyline and Leg Theory

James Agate, the drama critic, wrote to the *Daily Telegraph* to ask for an explanation of bodyline and leg theory. The reply excited much interest, since it came from the man who had been MCC manager during the recent bodyline series. P.F. Warner, a former England captain, was born in the West Indies.

Mr James Agate's letter in the *Daily Telegraph* of Thursday last demands a reply. I was 'sorry the West Indies had recourse to leg theory,' or 'bodyline' (Australian), because I had hoped that my countrymen would avoid a type of bowling which I believe to be against the best interests of cricket.

But I agree that its exploitation at Old Trafford will serve a useful purpose in giving Englishmen some idea of what this bowling is like, though it is well known that Constantine is at least two yards slower than Larwood, and also lacks his control of the ball.

In the Test Match at Trent Bridge in 1905, W.W. Armstrong bowled slow to medium leg-breaks wide of the leg stump, for three hours and a quarter without a rest, with eight fieldsmen on the leg side. The Australians were playing for a draw, and Armstrong's was a negative form of attack, used, not primarily with the object of obtaining wickets, but in order to keep down runs.

But long before that H. Trumble and J.T. Hearne, S. Haigh, of Yorkshire, and many others, had bowled off-breaks, generally from round the wicket, on sticky pitches with five, six, or even seven men on the on side.

That, too, was 'leg theory' – and so was the method employed by Hirst and F.R. Foster – fast, good-length left-handers, bowling round the wicket, with six or seven men on the leg side. No objection has ever been raised against such tactics.

What is objected to now by a great many cricketers is fast leg theory on hard, fast wickets. A bowler must be fast to carry out this plan of attack, but it requires not only speed, but accuracy of direction and control of length. No batsman objects to fast half volleys on his legs, however many fieldsmen may be placed on the leg side. What is objected to is when the ball is pitched short. It is the length of the ball, not so much the pace of it, to which exception has been taken.

Short-pitched very fast deliveries on hard wickets on the line of the batsman's body look – even if the bowler is acquitted of all intention to hurt the batsman – as if the bowler was 'bowling at the batsman', in the sense in which that expression has hitherto been understood by cricketers.

It is akin to intimidation. At the end of the last century, and at the beginning of this, English cricket boasted many fast bowlers – every county had at least one; Surrey two, the renowned Richardson and Lockwood. Some hard blows were received at times.

Sir Stanley Jackson, for example, had a rib broken by E. Jones, the Australian, but these bowlers did not give the impression of bowling at the batsman, and the short very fast 'bouncer', on the line of the batsman and which caused the batsman to duck, was certainly not defended, or encouraged.

At all events, fast bowling was very much in vogue at that time, and no cry was raised against it, whereas today we have practically every Australian cricketer of every generation definitely opposed to what they call bodyline bowling.

This vast mass of opinion deserves the deepest thought and consideration. To suggest that the Australians are 'squealers' is unfair to men with their record on the battlefield and on the cricket field. Rightly or wrongly they believe that such bowling is contrary to the spirit of the game.

Mr Agate hopes that 'the Australians are now raking the bush for some Hercules who can bowl faster than Kortright, in order that, without regard to length and aiming solely at the batsman's head and heart, we shall, next season, try on the English goose the sauce that has been deemed proper for the Australian gander.'

I should be sorry indeed to see 'a Red Terror' from the 'Never-Never', some Saltbush Bill of Richardsonian proportions, exploiting this bowling against England in a Test Match at Lord's, or anywhere else.

The courtesy of combat would go out of that game in ten minutes: and one of the strongest arguments against this bowling is that it has bred, and will continue to breed, anger, hatred, and malice, with their consequent reprisals.

Admitting it is within the law – there are many things in cricket which by the laws of the game are right, but which are 'not done'. Is it worth while if, as a result of bodyline, England and her greatest cricketing Dominion are to 'fight' each other?

It was not thus that cricket gained its great name, a name synonymous with all that is fair, and kindly, noble, and upright.

Some would urge that the laws should be altered. I do not agree. This is a case where one should rely on the spirit, kindliness, and good will which should be inherent in cricket. But if a change in the law there must be, why not draw a line across the pitch and no-ball any delivery pitched the bowler's side of the line? The cricket pitch might look somewhat like a tennis court, but would that matter greatly if we got back to the old happy state of affairs? For the cricket world today is most decidedly not happy.

Always have I been opposed to this bowling which has aroused so much controversy, and, right or wrong, I am only pleading for what I honestly believe is best for the great, glorious, and incomparable game of cricket. I am not the least of the lovers of cricket.

P.F. WARNER
Letter to the *Daily Telegraph*
(June 1933)

No Meat

When one looks at the fine physique of the stalwart Voce [Larwood's bowling partner in the bodyline series], it seems almost incredible that he had never even tasted meat until he joined the county staff.

SIR HOME GORDON, BT.
Background of Cricket
(1939)

Bumpers

The main reason for Australian superiority in England in 1948 was the fast bowling of Lindwall and Miller. These two men, with their persistent ability to demoralize the early English batsmen, swung the balance completely in Australia's favour.

Several times during the rubber there was a well-pronounced undercurrent of feeling against their overindulged inclination to hurl down the short, high-bouncing 'bumper'. On one occasion in particular, I thought that the umpires standing at Manchester might have been justified in exercising their right to 'call' a man who persists in delivering the 'bumper'. Since the 1932–33 season in Australia when the word 'bodyline' entered the cricket vocabulary, a rule had been instituted which allowed the umpire to 'call' a bowler who could be rightly deemed to be bowling the short stuff with the one purpose of intimidating the batsman.

The one sane way to look at this prevalency of the 'bean ball' is to consider its worth in dismissing batsmen in any of the accustomed ways. Firstly, it can never claim a 'bowled' victim unless the batsman, by some acrobatic feat, deflects the ball on to his stumps either with the aid of his bat or his head. The odds against a 'bowled' decision are of the 'write your own ticket' variety. Leg before wicket is utterly impossible; the ball is bouncing round the batsman's whiskers. That leaves only the 'caught' method of dismissal. But as the ball has no possible chance of dismissing the

246

batsman unless he hits a catch, what need is there to use the bat at all? Most batsmen realize this truth and they begin to duck beneath the high line of trajectory and the game turns from cricket as we are glad to know it to some 'Jack-in-the-box' type of athletics, wherein the batsman stakes his 'all' upon his ability to detect the 'bumper' quickly and the suppleness of the set of muscles which allow him to imitate the Arab at his orisons in the shortest time possible. What happens to cricket when the two leading exponents of the 'bumper' attack are opposed to the quickest thinking and most agile batsmen? There would arise the need to incorporate some modification of the baseball umpire's right to call 'ball one' or 'strike one' according to the altitude gained by the leather projectile.

If the batsmen are anxious to have a crack at the 'bouncer' then it behoves the fielding captain to place his field in the most advantageous formation for this type of bowling. The field set by Douglas Jardine in the Tests of the 1932–33 rubber in Australia was the best example I have seen for this bowling. But the first captain who imitates that field placing is likely to bring down a hornets' nest about him. That would be much too easily recognized as bowling which has been banned by the rule which says that intimidatory bowling is not to be countenanced. Therefore it seems to me that short bowling can go along unquestioned so long as the captain does not decide to take full advantage of his bowlers' methods by setting the field which it requires. In other words, in fact, it means that the captain must be content to be a bad captain whilst that bowling is being bowled regularly.

I detest these bowling methods. I have no quarrel with the bowler who lets one fly occasionally. It is a privilege allowed to any bowler. But I can see no merit whatever in bowling which has to be interpolated with several of these 'scalpers' each over. The Australians certainly 'let them go' in England. There were several occasions when the only difference I could see between our bowling and that of Jardine's team was the disposition of the field.

I felt certain that, had England possessed the bowlers, the Australians would have been given a course of their own medicine. Had it been given, our successes would not have been quite so regular. On returning to Australia it soon became apparent that there were very few of the members of Bradman's victorious side who could cope with this type of attack.

What will happen in 1950–51 in Australia if England can be fortunate enough in the meantime to find a couple of young, stout-hearted speed merchants who can bounce them dangerously? Will our Australian bowlers forget that Len Hutton is allergic to the high bouncer? That Compton is likely to fall into his wicket as he swings at it? That Bill Edrich's hook shot is almost invariably lofted? That Crapp takes them on the back of the neck? That Watkins swings lustily, but misses, and gets hit so painfully that he is no longer able to play his proper part in the game? That Cyril Washbrook can be so upset by them that he is likely to square cut and hook at the most inopportune moments? The answer to these questions can be supplied by a completely adequate and gloriously euphonious phrase from George Bernard Shaw's *Pygmalion*. If a bowler knows quite well that a certain ball is likely to dispose of his natural enemy, then it's 'pounds to peanuts' that he gives that particular ball a 'go' quite frequently. Therefore I am quite certain that the remedy lies, as does the responsibility for it, with the captain of the team.

Probably there are many umpires administering the rules of the game today who have no clear memory whatever of the incidents which led up to the incorporation of the word 'intimidatory' into the rule book. In Australia there is only one umpire today still officiating in first-class cricket who had anything to do with the 1932–33 season. Do umpires, preparing themselves for their duties, have any definition or interpretation of this sinister word given to them? In most cases Australian umpires have never played first-class cricket.

Their knowledge of 'bumpers' comes from observation at a very safe distance. But where is the captain who does not know immediately when this malignant growth, which defiles the bowling art, is being exploited with the one intention of rattling nerves and ribs and heads?

It has become the accustomed rule to appoint a batsman as captain. It has never been, to my knowledge, openly stated that batsmen represent the 'brains trust' of cricket, but it has often been implied. Quite often you will hear it said that a bowler cannot be a competent captain because he never knows when to take himself away from the bowling crease. This argument is unworthy of an intelligent cricketer, and is certainly not worthy of vehement denial. Australia has not had a bowler captain since the days of Hugh Trumble. England gave G.O. Allen a chance to show the bowler's aptitude for the job and he made a good job of it.

However, the fact remains that batsmen are the pampered darlings of the committees which appoint leaders, and the bowlers are classified as necessary appurtenances of the game who can be best designated as 'cricketers' labourers'. If batsmen, therefore, are given the responsibility of directing the destiny of the game on the field, surely they ought not to be slow to recognize a type of attack which promises to make buffoonery of their dignified department of the game? Or does the winning of the game allow the eyes of the skippering intelligentsia to remain closed when rules are being broken?

I have always advocated, and will continue advocating, a policy of 'play the game hard' in Test matches. There is no time for levity or gallant gestures in international cricket. Every man must be prepared to go for his life all the time that the game is in progress. But that policy is based upon a strict observance of the rules of the game – even the rule which allows for substitute fieldsmen for those who have been 'incapacitated' during the course of the game. No international cricketer expects any quarter to be given during the course of a Test match. Those doubting Thomases who declare that the result of a match is likely to be rigged so that the gate receipts will be favourably affected never have been worthy of the time wasted in listening to what they have to say. But the game is governed by a set of rules – most of them excellent ones, too – which must be obeyed, otherwise the character of the game disappears. There is a rule which deals with intimidatory bowling and that rule should be played hard, too. There is not the slightest doubt in my mind that there were several instances of intimidatory bowling by the Australians in England last summer. The time has come for us to take full stock of it. If it is allowed to continue unbridled, there is every likelihood of another momentous rubber looming ahead of us.

W.J. O'REILLY
Cricket Conquest
(1949)

Modern Fast Bowling

I couldn't wait to have a crack at 'em [the English team]. I thought: "Stuff that stiff upper lip crap. Let's see how stiff it is when it's split.'

JEFF THOMSON
Thommo Declares
(1986)

Boycott in the West Indies

Five hours and more
Stalwart Boycott batted
Against the scathing bullets
Coming fast and furious
From the most savage bowlers

In this, or any other Town:
Like the matured Gary Cooper
In 'High Noon'
He played the hand
From where he stood, solo.

The heat, dust, sullenness,
The stench of failure
Then crept in:
He stood ruthless
As the man he faced,
And played the only game
In Town

IRENE MURRELL
A Tour in the Game
(1986)

Touring in Nazi Germany

At the farewell Dinner to the tourists in the Restaurant at the
Olympic Stadium, the host, the Reichsportsführer himself,
stated that 'cricket is a very good game. I hope I may visit
England to watch cricket in 1938', and he presented Major
Jewell with a tie-pin surmounted by a Swastika which – as
the Major confided to the writer – was later presented to the
Memorial Gallery at Lord's. During the Dinner, the Reichsportsführer asked the Major how he could increase enthusiasm for the game in Germany. In reply, the Major made
several suggestions, such as that an English professional
could be engaged in Berlin as tuition and practice were
essential, and he recounted a story that the team had been
told about the Prussian-type captain, Thamer. Apparently,
during the previous season, he was one man short for a match
in the Berlin League and would not begin until he had a full
team. Eventually, a lad was recruited who had never played

before and, fitted out in flannels, he was sent to field at deep mid-off, the safest place (the captain thought) as he opened the bowling with his off-breaks. In the second over the lad dropped a skier off his bowling and repeated the performance in the captain's next over, whereupon Thamer walked across and felled him with a right hook to the chin. Major Jewell suggested that such action would not encourage the German youth to play the game, to which the Reichsportsführer replied: 'Yes, I have heard about the incident, but I understand it was a very simple catch!'

JAMES B. COLDHAM
German Cricket
(1983)

A Match in the Solomons

Mr K. Bolton, who returned recently to Sydney from a trading trip to the island of Malaita, in the Solomon group, describes a cricket match that took place between two groups of natives. An engagement was made for the men of Tai to visit Atta, another small island, for the purpose of deciding the inter-island cricket championship.

Cricket at Malaita is a peculiar game. As many as 30 or 40 men play on each side. The bat is a piece of wood, roughly shaped, and the ball a hard ivory nut. Scoring is carried out in primitive fashion by tearing off a frond from a palm leaf for every run scored.

When Tai visited Atta, the home team batted first, and scored 10 runs. Tai claimed the match, and said it was unnecessary for them to bat, as they could not possibly score less. Amid protests from Atta, they proudly paraded as the winners, and announced their intention of going home. In this they were loudly supported by their women, who were standing off the island in their canoes.

As the men of Tai waded out to their canoes their boasts proved too much for the Atta natives. Brandishing hatchets and knives they fell upon the self-styled winners. A fierce struggle ensued, and one of the Atta team had his arm chopped off at the shoulder. Many others received knife wounds.

The Government officer in Malaita, hearing of the fight, called at the scene of the struggle and held a court. After hearing evidence, while both teams stood glaring at one another and breathing threats, the officer fined the captain of each team 5s. for disturbing the peace. When the fine was paid, he assembled the teams, and in pidgin English told them that if they played British games they must observe the spirit of British fairplay.

New Zealand Herald
(10 October 1933)

Fingers Struck Off

Robert 'Long' Robinson (1765–1822) played as a professional successively for Hampshire, Surrey, Kent, and Middlesex. He experimented with spiked shoes; and he also wore angled boards on his leg for protection (i.e. pads), until he was laughed out of them.

The English common people are a sort of grown children, spoiled and sulky perhaps, but full of glee and merriment, when their attention is drawn off by some sudden and striking object. The May-pole is almost gone out of fashion among us: but May-day, besides its flowering hawthorns and its pearly dews, has still its boasted exhibition of painted chimney-sweepers and their Jack-o'-the-Green, whose tawdry finery, bedizened faces, unwonted gestures, and short-lived pleasures call forth good-humoured smiles and looks of sympathy in the spectators. There is no place where

253

trapball, fives, prison-base, foot-ball, quoits, bowls are better understood or more successfully practised; and the very names of a cricket bat and ball make English fingers tingle. What happy days must 'Long Robinson' have passed in getting ready his wickets and mending his bats, who when two of the fingers of his right-hand were struck off by the violence of a ball, had a screw fastened to it to hold the bat, and with the other hand still sent the ball thundering against the boards that bounded *Old Lord's cricket-ground*! What delightful hours must have been his in looking forward to the matches that were to come, in recounting the feats he had performed in those that were past! I have myself whiled away whole mornings in seeing him strike the ball (like a countryman mowing with a scythe) to the farthest extremity of the smooth, level, sun-burnt ground, and with long, awkward strides count the notches that made victory sure!

WILLIAM HAZLITT
'Merry England', *The New Monthly Magazine*
(1825)

Blood and Fingers

The blood of a cricketer is seldom, however, shed from any part of his body but his fingers; but the fingers of an old cricketer, so scarred, so bent, so shattered, so indented, so contorted, so venerable! are enough to bring tears of envy and emulation from any eye – *we* are acquainted with *such a pair of hands*, if hands they may be called, that shape have none.

THE REV. JOHN MITFORD
The Gentleman's Magazine
(July–September 1833)

An Infernal Machine

Thoms has communicated another instance of Mr Grimston's old Toryism in cricket, and Thoms's description, which bears the stamp of truth upon it, will speak for itself. It runs as follows:

On the day previous to one of the great matches coming off at Lord's, Mr James Dark, the ruling spirit of that ground, called on me to borrow the use of my mowing machine, a large and good one, with which we kept down the grass on the cricket ground that used to adjoin Primrose Hill. The machine was duly taken to Lord's, and we had got it to work on the wickets between nine and ten o'clock, when lo! and behold, *who* should stalk into the ground but the Hon. Robert Grimston!

After standing still and having a look, he seemed to take in the whole matter at once. Walking up past us and the machine, with his hands behind his back and his hat on back of his head as usual, and not saying a word to Mr J.H. Dark or any of us, he went straight to the top of the ground, where some navvies were at work – close to where the printing office now stands – and exclaimed, 'Do any of you fellows want to earn a sovereign?' Of course they said, 'Yes, master.' 'Well, come along,' replied he, 'and bring your pickaxes with you,' and down they came. 'Now then,' said he, 'slip into it and smash that "infernal machine" up.'

Old Jordan, the ground man, got in front of the navvies, and threatened them at their peril to touch it, whilst I and my two men sloped off with the machine and left the Hon. Mr Grimston and Mr Dark *whispering* to each other in the most frantic manner. In an after conversation with Mr Dark on the matter, I remarked that, being a huntsman, he must have scented the machine from where he lived, or what else could have brought him so early to Lord's that morning? That was the first time a mowing machine was used at Lord's, and not again for years after; for the Hon. Robert Grimston, like many others, believed in sheep grazing, but there is little doubt that if the mowing machine is used at the right time of year it is an improvement.

FREDERICK GALE
Life of the Hon. Robert Grimston
(1885)

Boardroom Brawl

It will be remembered that the team had practically been picked for the Third Test match [of 1911] when Hill [the Australian captain] sent the following telegram to McAlister: [a co-selector, and former Australian vice captain]:

'Macartney all right. Think must have left-arm bowler. Suggest Macartney and Matthews in place of Whitty and Minnett. Minnett twelfth.'

McAlister was by no means pleased with this suggestion, and he immediately telegraphed the following reply:

'My team as forwarded yesterday. Still opposed Macartney's inclusion. If Iredale agrees with you, favour yourself standing down, and not Minnett.'

That was a telegram that Hill could not forget, and when the discussion between the two men touched the question of captainship, some bitter things were said. Hill said, according to a statement that had been made, that the Australians would not have gone to England under McAlister, to which McAlister replied that he was a better captain than Hill and Trumper put together.

'You are the worst captain that I have ever seen', he added. According to Hill, he warned McAlister not to repeat his insults, and as they were reiterated he struck McAlister gently with the open hand as an indication that he had been heckled beyond endurance. McAlister, however, declares that Hill punched him hard and unawares under the left eye. Whether the blow was struck with the open or shut fist, it roused McAlister to retaliation, and he rushed round the table and grappled with Hill. They fought fiercely, and, locked in each other's arms, swayed round the room, crashing against the table and the walls. The two spectators were powerless to interfere, and, in spite of their efforts to separate the combatants, the struggle proceeded. At the end of a ten-minutes' bout McAlister was on his back on the floor, and Hill was standing over him.

McAlister jumped to his feet, and made to follow Hill, but Messrs Iredale and Smith, seizing the opportunity, closed the door and barred his egress.

Interviewed on Monday with reference to the occurrence, Hill was reluctant to refer to it, but, on being pressed, he said that as soon as McAlister entered the room argument ensued, and McAlister repeatedly insulted him. 'I told him,' went on Hill, 'that if he kept on insulting me I would pull his nose. He said that I was the worst captain he had ever seen, and, as he aggravated me beyond endurance, I gave him a gentle slap on the face. He said I had hit him when his hands were down. I said my hands were down now, as I put my hands behind my back. He rushed at me like a bull, and then I admit I fought him. Messrs Iredale and Smith held him back, and as I went out he called out that I was a coward, but as the others prevented him from leaving the room, the matter ended. I told Mr Smith I could not act as selector any longer with McAlister. He asked me to put my resignation in writing, and I did so.'

McAlister, on being interviewed, said that he preferred not to make a statement, as the matter was in the hands of the Board of Control. It was pointed out to him that the occurrence was being freely discussed in the city, and he then stated decisively that Hill had given him no warning of an attack, but had punched him heavily with the right hand on the face before he had time to put up his hands in defence. 'I would not have minded so much', he conduced, 'if he had invited me to come outside, as I would have known what to expect. You see that my face is scratched in several places; it must have been knocked against the table and walls. No doubt, the secretary of the Board, who was present at the disturbance, will report the matter officially.'

When asked to give his version of the fight between Messrs Hill and McAlister in Sydney on Saturday night, Mr Iredale was very diffident. He remarked that the desire of the Board was that nothing should be said until a report had been presented to members for consideration at an early special meeting.

'However,' he continued, 'in view of what has been printed, and of the fact that I was present, it might be just as well to say that up to the time the quarrel began no reference was made to the telegram sent by McAlister to Hill at Adelaide prior to the selection of the team for the Third Test match. When the meeting opened, Mr Hill and I sat at one side of the table; and McAlister was opposite. We were discussing bowlers' merits, and McAlister told Hill that he did not think he used his bowlers to the best advantage in the previous Tests. Hill replied, that as captain, he thought he had done his best. Then heated remarks were exchanged. McAlister said he thought that Hill was one of the worst captains he had seen. Hill replied by partially getting up, and leaned across the table and struck McAlister a severe blow on the face and side of the nose.

'After this,' said Iredale, 'they went at it hammer and tongs. Very few blows were struck; it was more like a wrestling match. Smith and I did our best to part them, but they were all over the place, and when the big table was upset I was pinned in the corner. I strained my side, and still feel the effects.'

'How long did it last?' Mr Iredale was asked.

258

'Well, about twenty minutes, I should think,' he replied. 'It all occurred as quick as lightning. They were both game and determined. We are all very sorry about the whole affair, and I don't think any one regrets it more than the participants.'

The Australasian
(1911)

Umpire Lee

Once as I read through wastes of prose,
    And wearied of the labour,
These words tremendously arose
    Like sudden flash of sabre,
'When umpire Lee
Was hit on the knee
    By a very fast ball from Faber.'

'Twas but a humble cricket match
    And but a daily's pages,
And yet it somehow seemed to catch
    A splendour from the ages
When poetry
Was apt to be
    The diction of the sages.

There stood these scintillating lines
    Mere common prose their neighbour
To cheer us as a light that shines,
    Or sound of pipe and tabor,
'When umpire Lee
Was hit on the knee
    By a very fast ball from Faber.'

LORD DUNSANY
Fifty Poems
(1929)

The Sabbath-Breakers; *or,*
Young-Man's Dreadful Warning-Piece

Being a very dismal Account of four Young-Men, who made a Match to Play at Cricket, on *Sunday* the *6th* of this Instant *July* 1712, in a Meadow near *Maiden Head Thicket*; and as they were at Play, there rose out of the Ground a Man in Black with a Cloven-Foot, which put them in a great Consternation; but as they stood in the Frighted Condition, the Devil flew up in the Air, in a Dark Cloud with Flashes of Fire, and in his Room he left a very Beautiful Woman, and *Robert Yates* and *Richard Moore* hastily stepping up to her, being Charm'd with her Beauty went to Kiss her, but in the Attempt they instantly fell down Dead.

The other two, *Simon Jackson* and *George Grantham*, seeing this Tragical Sight, ran home to *Maiden-Head*, where they now lye in a Distracted Condition.

Also the Minister of *Maiden-Head* Pray'd with them frequently his Prayer is here at Large, and likewise his Sermon which he Preach'd the *Sunday* following, the Text is *Remember the Sabbath Day, to Keep it Holy.* Exod. 20 ver. 8.

From a pamphlet of 1712

MEMORY

It Went Like Butter

I remember one shot of mine in 1938: it was the first match of the season, against a school called Hillside: the captain bowled a medium-paced full toss, outside the off stump; I hit it square off the front foot past point for four: it went like butter. I have never hit a ball better. Cricket was worth playing for that shot alone.

JOHN GALE
Clean Young Englishman
(1965)

At Lord's

It is little I repair to the matches of the Southron folk,
    Though my own red roses there may blow;
It is little I repair to the matches of the Southron folk,
    Though the red roses crest the caps, I know.
For the field is full of shades as I near the shadowy coast,
And a ghostly batsman plays to the bowling of a ghost,
And I look through my tears on a soundless-clapping host
    As the run-stealers flicker to and fro,
        To and fro: –
O my Hornby and my Barlow long ago!

It is Glo'ster coming North, the irresistible,
    The Shire of the Graces, long ago!
It is Gloucestershire up North, the irresistible,
    And new-risen Lancashire the foe!
A Shire so young that has scarce impressed its traces,
Ah, how shall it stand before all resistless Graces?
O, little red rose, their bats are as maces
    To beat thee down, this summer long ago!

This day of seventy-eight they are come up North against
      thee,
   This day of seventy-eight, long ago!
The champion of the centuries, he cometh up against thee,
   With his brethren, every one a famous foe!
The long-whiskered Doctor, that laugheth rules to scorn,
While the bowler, pitched against him, bans the day that he
      was born:
And G.F. with his science makes the fairest length forlorn;
They are come from the West to work thee woe!

It is little I repair to the matches of the Southron folk,
   Though my own red roses there may blow;
It is little I repair to the matches of the Southron folk,
   Though the red roses crest the caps, I know.
For the field is full of shades as I near the shadowy coast,
And a ghostly batsman plays to the bowling of a ghost,
And I look through my tears on a soundless-clapping host
   As the run-stealers flicker to and fro,
            To and fro: —
O my Hornby and my Barlow long ago!

FRANCIS THOMPSON
Collected Poetry
(1913)

The Bats

There is a street in London called Cranbourn Street, which
serves no particular purpose of its own, but is useful as
leading from Long Acre and Garrick Street to the frivolous
delights of the Hippodrome, and serviceable also in the
possession of a Tube station from which one may go to
districts of London as diverse as Golders Green and
Hammersmith. These to the ordinary eye are the principal
merits of Cranbourn Street. But, to the eye which more

minutely discerns, it has deeper and finer treasure: it has a shop window with a little row of cricket bats in it so discreetly chosen that they not only form a vivid sketch of the history of the greatest of games but enable anyone standing at the window and studying them to defeat for the moment the attack of the dreariest of weather and for a brief but glorious space believe in the sun again.

And what of the treasures? Well, to begin with, the oldest known bat is there – a dark lop-sided club such as you see in the early pictures in the pavilion of Lord's, that art gallery which almost justifies rain during a match, since it is only when rain falls that one examines it with any care. Of this bat there is obviously no history, or it would be written upon it, and the fancy is therefore free to place it in whatever hands one will – Tom Walker's, or Beldham's, or Lord Frederick Beauclerk's, or even Richard Nyren's himself, father of the first great eulogist of the game. Beside it is another veteran, not quite so old, though, and approaching in shape the bat of our own day – such a bat as Lambert, or that dauntless sportsman, Mr Osbaldeston ('The Squire', as he was known in the hunting-field), may have swung in one of their famous single-wicket contests.

Beside these is even more of a curiosity. Nothing less than the very bat which during his brief and not too glorious cricket career was employed to defend his wicket, if not actually to make runs, by the late King Edward VII when he was Prince of Wales. For that otherwise accomplished ruler and full man (as the old phrase has it) was never much of a C.B. Fry. He knew the world as few have known it; he commanded respect and affection; he was accustomed to give orders and have them instantly obeyed; but almost anyone could bowl him out, and it is on record that those royal hands, so capable in their grasp of orb and sceptre, had only the most rudimentary and incomplete idea of retaining a catch. Such are human limitations! Here, however, in the Cranbourn Street window, is His Majesty's bat, and even without the accompanying label one would guess that it was the property of no very efficient cricketer. For it lacks body; no one who really knew would have borne to the pitch a blade so obviously incapable of getting the ball to the ropes; while just beneath the too fanciful splice is a silver plate. Now all cricketers are aware that it is when the incoming man carries a bat with a silver plate on it that the scorers (if ever) feel entitled to dip below the table for the bottle and glass and generally relax a little.

So much for what may be called the freaks of this fascinating window. Now for the facts. A very striking fact indeed is the splintered bat with which Mr G.L. Jessop made a trifle of 168 against Lancashire. I wish the date was given; I wish even more that the length of the innings in minutes was given. Whether the splinters were lost then, or later, we should also be told. But there it is, and, after seeing it, how to get through these infernal months of February and March and April and half May, until real life begins again, one doesn't know and can hardly conjecture. And what do you think is beside it? Nothing less than 'the best bat' that Mr M.A. Noble ever played with – the leisurely, watchful Australian master, astute captain, inspired change-bowler, and the steady, remorseless compiler of scores at the right time. It is something to have in darkest February Noble's best bat beneath one's eyes.

And lastly, there is a scarred and discoloured blade which bears the brave news that with it did that old man hirsute, now on great match-days a landmark in the Lord's pavilion, surveying the turf where once he ruled – W.G. himself, no less – make over a thousand runs. Historic wood, if you like; historic window!

No wonder, then, that I scheme to get Cranbourn Street into my London peregrinations. For here is youth renewed and the dismallest of winters momentarily slain.

E.V. LUCAS
Loiterer's Harvest
(1913)

Scoring Methods

Did we say Running a Notch? *unde* Notch? What wonder ere
the days of useful knowledge, and Sir William Curtis's three R's
– or, reading, writing, and arithmetic – that natural science
should be evolved in a truly natural way; what wonder that
notches on a stick, like the notches in the milk-woman's tally in
Hogarth's picture, should supply the place of those complicated
papers of vertical columns, which subject the bowling, the
batting, and the fielding to a process severely and scrupulously
just, of analytical observation, or differential calculus! Where
now there sit on kitchen chairs, with ink-bottle tied to a stump
the worse for wear, Messrs Caldecourt and Bayley ('tis pity two
such men should ever not be umpires), with an uncomfortable
length of paper on their knees, and large tin telegraphic letters
above their heads; and where now is Lillywhite's printing press,
to hand down every hit as soon as made on twopenny cards to
future generations; there, or in a similar position, old Frame, or
young Small (young once: he died in 1834, aged eighty) might
have placed a trusty yeoman to cut notches with his bread-and-
bacon knife on an ashen stick. Oh! 'tis enough to make the
Hambledon heroes sit upright in their graves with astonishment
to think, that in the Gentlemen and Players' Match, in 1850, the
cricketers of old Sparkes' Ground, at Edinburgh, could actually
know the score of the first innings in London, before the second
had commenced!

THE REV. JAMES PYCROFT
The Cricket Field
(1851)

Subjects Which Never Tire

The Rev. John Mitford, when vicar of Benhall in Suffolk, provided a roof for
the famous old player, William Fennex.

Peep through the shutter of my snug parlour, and behold me and envy. There is the small oak table (it is now nine), with the pint of Geneva and the jug of hot water, and the snuff-box smiling on it. One cricket-bat, the practice one, lies on the small horsehair sofa, as occasionally necessary for exemplifications, and Harry Bentley's volume of the matches is open beside it. Do you see him? the master of the field. There he sits, mark his animation! his gesture! he is telling of a catch he made above fifty years since, and the ball is again in the air. He was taken instantly up to the Duchess of Richmond, of whose side he was, and she made a handicap of six guineas for him. She won hundreds by it. How my heart throbs, and my eyes glisten, and in what fearful suspense I sit, when he calls to life the ghost of a magnificent hit, fresh as the life, though half a century has intervened. I see the ball running at Moulsey Hurst, that fetched ten runs off Beldham's bat in 1787, as plainly as if it were in my own field. ...

Midnight sounds in vain. Politics, scandal, Tories, Whigs, my Lord Grey, and the Bishop of Peterborough, and the last story about the Maids of Honour, and Lady Farquhar's splendid breakfast, and the unknown tongues, all solicit attention in vain; they seem as nothing, idle all and without interest; one wonders how the world can trouble itself about such toys. We fill the tumblers anew; and for the hundredth time I ask, 'What was young *Small's* favourite hit? How did *John Wells* get his runs?' Behold the advantage, ye parents, of bringing up your sons (why not your daughters?) to the love of subjects which cannot be exhausted, which never tire.

THE REV. JOHN MITFORD
The Gentleman's Magazine
(July–September 1833)

268

The First Inter-University Match (1827)

In the newly published Life of my younger brother Christopher, the late Bishop of Lincoln, the following words are to be found, quoted from his private journal: 'Friday' (no date – but early in June 1826). 'Heard from Charles. He wishes that Oxford and Cambridge should play a match at cricket.' ... And as I have been asked to put upon paper what I can remember concerning the first Inter-University Cricket Match ... I venture to take those words for my text. Yes; I was then in my Freshman's year at Christ Church, and both my brother and I – he at Winchester, and I at Harrow – had been in our respective school elevens. But more than this, as captain of the Harrow Eleven I had enjoyed what was then a novel experience in carrying on correspondence with brother captains at other public schools – Eton, Winchester, Rugby and even Charter House; and I well remember how the last amused us at Harrow, by the pompous and, as we presumed to think, bumptious style of his letter, proposing 'to determine the superiority at cricket which has been so long undecided.' Having played against Eton for four years, from the first match in 1822 to 1825, and in the first match against Winchester in the last-named year, I had a large acquaintance among cricketers who had gone off from those schools and from Harrow to both Universities. My brother, as I have said, was one of these, but though successful in the Wykehamist Eleven at Lord's in 1825 (when he got 35 runs in his second innings, and 'caught' our friend Henry Manning – the future cardinal – of which he was wont to boast in after years), he did not keep up his cricket at Cambridge, whereas I continued to keep up mine at Oxford and was in the University Eleven during the whole time of my undergraduate course. Nothing came of my 'wish' to bring about a match between the Universities in 1826. But in 1827 the proposal was carried into effect. Though an Oxford man, my home was at Cambridge, my father being Master of Trinity; and this gave me opportunities for communicating with men of that University, many of whom remained up for the vacations, or for part of the vacations, especially at Easter. I remember calling upon Barnard of King's, who had been captain of an Eton Eleven against whom I had played, and who was now one of the foremost Cambridge cricketers, and he gave me reason to fear that no King's man would be able to play at the time proposed (early in June), though that time would be within the Cambridge vacation and not within ours, because their men, at King's, were kept up longer than at the other Colleges. And this, I believe, proved actually the case; and if so, some allowance should be made for it. But the fact is, there were similar difficulties on both sides, and I am not sure they were not as great or greater upon ours. In those ante-railway days it was necessary to get permission from the College authorities to go up to London in term time, and the permission was not readily granted. To take my own case: My conscience still rather smites me when I remember that in order to gain my end, I had to present myself to the Dean and tell him that I wished to be allowed to go to London – not to play a game of cricket (that would not have been listened to) – but to consult a dentist; a piece of Jesuitry which was understood, I believe, equally well on both sides; at all events my tutor, Longley – afterwards Archbishop of Canterbury – was privy to it.

Thus, though not without difficulties, the match came on, but unhappily, the weather presenting a fresh difficulty, it did not fully go off. We could only play a single innings ... The precise day in June on which it was played has been disputed. One report gives the 4th; another states that 'the match did not take place on the 4th as intended, but was deferred for a few days.' I can only say that I do not remember any postponement, as I think I should do had such been the case; and what is more, 'a few days' later would have brought it within our vacation, and so would have rendered my piece of

270

Jesuitism unnecessary. The players on the Cambridge side were mostly Etonians, though there was, I think, no King's man among them; and on the Oxford side, mostly Wykehamists. We scored 258 runs to our opponents' 92, but it cannot be said we were a strong eleven. The bowling was divided between Bayley and me; and the state of the ground being in my favour, I was singularly successful with my left-hand twist from the off, bringing down no less than seven wickets in the one innings for only 25 runs. Jenner, famous as a wicket-keeper, and well known afterwards as Herbert Jenner Fust, was the only batsman who made any stand against it. He had learnt by painful experience how to deal with it. We had been antagonists in the Eton and Harrow match of 1822; and I can well remember even now, though it is sixty-six years ago, his look of ineffable disgust and dismay when I had pitched a ball some four or five inches wide to the off, and he had shouldered his bat meaning to punish it as it rose by a smart cut to point, the tortuous creature shot in obliquely and took his middle stump, when he had only got two runs. Precisely the same happened again in his second innings, only then he got no runs at all. Again in Eton v. Harrow 1823 I had bowled him at 7. And yet he was considered the best bat on the Eton side next to Barnard. He now made 47 runs, while no one else on the Cambridge side scored more than 8. He was also successful as a bowler, taking five wickets, mine included (against which he had a very strong claim), though I do not remember that he had much reputation in that line; and certainly upon the whole the Cambridge bowling must have been very indifferent to allow some of our men to run up the scores which stand to their names.

Though often successful as a bowler (left-handed, under-hand), batting (righthanded) was, if I may be bold to say so, my *forte*. In 1828, the next year after this match, my average, upwards of 40, was higher than that of any other in the Oxford eleven. I mention this with the less compunction because in the second Inter-University match my name appears without a run in either innings, and I wish to state how the failure is to be accounted for. In that year, 1829, the first Inter-University boat race took place at Henley, and I was one of the eight. As boating and cricket were then carried on in the same (summer) term, and the race and the match were both to come off in the same week, I wished to resign my place in the eleven. But this was not allowed. I had therefore no alternative but to make my appearance and do my best, though I had not played once before during the season, and though I was suffering from the effects of my rowing in a way which made it almost impossible for me to hold a bat. However, though I got no runs, I was so far of use that I bowled two, and caught two of our opponents; and we won the match, not quite so triumphantly as in 1827 (if a 'drawn' match can be so described), but quite easily enough, as we had won the boat race quite 'easily' two days before, Wednesday, June 10th.

Of the players in the two elevens, who contended at Lord's more than 60 years ago, five – if not six – I believe, are still living. Who shall say how much the lengthening of their days beyond the ordinary span of our existence here is to be attributed to 'Cricket's manly toil'?

I have now done the best I could to comply with the request made to me as an old cricketer, and if I have been garrulous, and if I have been egotistical, I can fairly plead, that this is no more than was to be expected when an ultra-octogenarian was applied to for his reminiscences.

CHARLES WORDSWORTH, Bishop of St Andrews (16 May 1888)

The Badminton Library of Sports and Pastimes (1901)

Memories of Harrow

High through those elms, with hoary branches crown'd,
Fair Ida's bower adorns the landscape round;
There Science, from her favour'd seat, surveys
The vale where rural Nature claims her praise;
To her awhile resigns her youthful train,
Who move in joy, and dance along the plain;
In scatter'd groups each favour'd haunt pursue,
Repeat old pastimes, and discover new;
Flush'd with his rays beneath the noontide sun,
In rival bands, between the wickets run,
Drive o'er the sward the ball with active force,
Or chase with nimble feet its rapid course.

Friend of my heart, and foremost of the list
Of those with whom I lived supremely blest,
Oft have we drained the font of ancient lore;
Though drinking deeply, thirsting still the more.
Yet, when confinement's lingering hour was done,
Our sports, our studies, and our souls were one:
Together we impelled the flying ball;
Together waited in our tutor's hall;
Together joined in cricket's manly toil,
Or shared the produce of the river's spoil;
Or, plunging from the green declining shore,
Our pliant limbs the buoyant billows bore;
In every element, unchanged, the same,
All, all that brothers should be, but the name.

LORD BYRON
Hours of Idleness
(1807)

273

Cricketer Immortalized

Captain C.F. Buller, a Harrow and Middlesex player (1846–1906), figured frequently in I. Zingari teams in these years and made a lot of runs for them. I like to think that he is the cricketer immortalized in literature by James Joyce (Bloom's morning monologue on page 78 of the Standard Lane edition of *Ulysses*).

> Heavenly weather. If life was always like that. Cricket weather. Sit around under sunshades. Over after over. Out. They can't play it here. Still, Captain Buller broke a window in Kildare Street Club with a slog to square leg. Donnybrook Fair more in their line.

The breaking of a window in the Kildare Street Club with a square leg hit from the College Park is usually credited to W.G. Grace, but the *Evening Herald* of June 19th, 1901 (less than thirty years after W.G.'s first visit to Dublin), speaks of 'the insane belief of the tellers of that tale', and Captain Fowler, the oldest cricketer member of the Kildare Street Club, tells me that the only window he ever heard of being broken was 'when a sniper had a shot at Lord Fermoy and missed him!'

W.P. HONE
Cricket in Ireland
(1955)

A Bloody Drongo

We may be a small and callow race but there is a divinity to our cricket. There are profound social and cultural reasons for it. As late as the 1950s, the curriculum in Australian schools was identical to that of an English grammar school. Poetry cut out at Tennyson. The only history was European history. When we spoke of literary figures, we spoke of Englishmen. But when we spoke of cricket, we spoke of our own. We couldn't make it in literature because we had none of the right seasons, the plants laughed at European botany, the absurd animals had no mythology behind them. But cricket was possible! We knew why it was. We had more sunshine, we ate more protein, we washed more regularly than the Poms! In the manner in which soccer is the great way up for children from the economic sumps of Brazil, so cricket was the great way out of Australian cultural ignominy. No Australian had written *Paradise Lost*, but Bradman had made 100 before lunch at Lord's.

About the age of ten, therefore, I had my cultural aspirations irretrievably tangled with my lust to be opening batsman for Australia. At that stage I played a game which I believe was common throughout the British Empire – it was played with two hexagonal strips of metal or wood. On each face of one of the pieces was marked a number – 1, 2, 3, 4, 6 – and on the sixth face was printed *Howzat!* On the other piece the various ways you can lose your wicket were listed – bowled, lbw, caught, etc., with on the sixth side the most exalted and exalting words ever spoken, *NOT OUT.*

I spent most of the waking hours of my pre-adolescence playing this game with two imaginary cricket teams composed of the world's greatest writers and the world's greatest composers. I remember that Tolstoy went in at first wicket down for the writers. Thomas Hardy was always high in the batting order yet for one whole summer managed a batting average of only about 11. H.G. Wells was twelfth man for a long time and at one stage was even dropped back to play Sheffield Shield for New South Wales. Handel and Bach, despite their paunches and their progenitive urges, were the stars of the composers' line-up, and I remember that Borodin – though a Russian and low in the batting order – sometimes scored a century at eighth wicket down.

The realities of cricket were more painful than this delightful and private game. Thursday afternoon, we put on our creams under the brazen sky and set off in a crocodile line to some parched suburban pitch. At the head of the line strode a lanky religious brother, possibly Irish but always a fanatic for this British game. Behind him, carrying the blanched cricket bag, two of the best cricketers in the class walked, chatting to him about field placements and test innings which, already in a young life, they had seen plenty of. From the bag came a delicious smell of leather, linseed oil, sweat, padding. And they walked in the midst of it, high on it, as acolytes should be. To us butterfingers further back in the line, as to the unbeliever and unworthy at the back of the temple, only the faintest tang reached. You knew that the two bag-carriers were going to be the captains of the day's cricket and you sent messages to them up the line, begging each of them indiscriminately to pick you in his team. It was a humiliation to be picked ninth or lower. If someone had made me the right offer, I would have sold my soul to be picked fifth.

There were certain glamour field placements too. Point, cover, silly mid-on, square leg and slips were the placings of glory, and I was torn between them and the fear of that fierce six-stitcher ball with a bullet at its heart. The worst insult was to be put somewhere out of trouble, on the grounds that even if you stopped a ball, your return would be so wide and erratic that overthrows and similar disasters would result. I had a curly-headed Byronic friend who was always placed at deep fine leg, a point to which very few Australian schoolboys of that era ever walloped the ball. Sometimes he would forget to change position at the ends of overs, or when a left-hander was in. The others would forget him and he would stay out there dreaming, oblivious of all the passion at the central pitch. Occasionally a wild hook would send one his way. He would not have seen the stroke. He would not be aware that the red pellet was diving at him out of the sun.

276

Then, having shaken his head and returned to reality to see the brother, gentle *confrère* of Christ, glaring at him from the umpire's position at the bowler's end, he looked to the sky from which he knew the threat was coming and was struck in both eyes by the fierce sun. So that while the ball hung in its easy trajectory, the fielders closer in, the bearers of the aromatic bag loudest of all, would begin to mourn the inevitable dropped catch. 'Geez, ees gunna drop it. Stroik a loight, Viney, keep yer bloody eyes on it.'

A look of focused intelligence would now come to Viney's features, his hands would be raised like an Ethiopian's in prayer and the ball would bounce on his shoulder and so hit the grass. 'Geez, yor 'is mate, Keneally. Some mate 'e is. Geez, bloody drongo, that Viney.' And the wicket-keeper would be standing with gloves on his hips, shaking his head and saying, 'Geez, bloody drongo.'

From such disasters I came to understand that one watched the ball, never let it out of one's sight. There was no other way to social success in the antipodes. And in fact there was no other way to deification – even today, there are few other ways.

I am proud to say that out of some instinct I stuck to Viney – I knew that ultimately he was playing a more serious kind of cricket in his head, even as the ball lobbed on his shoulder, even as it refused to fall into the sensitive web of his fingers. But I was a more social animal than Viney. Therefore, I had to come to terms with the leather orb.

Nature is always profligate, and the rule is that when you have a few million children all under a national onus to catch, bowl, bat, then you have to produce some good 'uns. But Australian society has become more sophisticated since then. There *are* one or two writers and even a historian who are revered. We have found that it *is* possible for Australians to have literary ideas about the place, that Australia is not outside the aesthetic universe. In short Australia – which used to have one unifying rite, cricket – has now become

277

pluralist. I cannot but predict it will be a disaster for Australian cricket.

Recently I played in a game between Australian writers (and yes, all you Aussie-bashers, we were able to find eleven!) and Australian Actors' Equity. It was a brilliant Sydney day, the sun coruscating off the harbour, and we striding around inspecting a pitch on which Victor Trumper had played. The actors' team looked impressive. They were all angular Australian Adonises, stars from the Australian soapies which you see, as an alternative to the Carson show, in Californian motels at 10.30 at night. They looked like the sort of lads who in my generation would not have been permitted not to be brilliant cricketers. In truth they were frightful. We had them out before the wives, mistresses and small party of devotees had the lunch ready or the beer cold. We noticed that there were no recriminations, that they took a cavalier attitude towards their ducks and run-outs. Later, in the field, they commiserated with each other over dropped catches. There was no one there to stiffen them with the appropriate chants of 'Geez, no bloody hoper drongo!'

And because of that there was no exultation to the game. I played a stroke over mid-on which would, in the old days when cricket counted, have won me a week's social grace and a nod from the fierce Christian Brother at the stumps. Now, all the urgency and all the ecstasy were gone. Even Kerry Packer, who avenged some forgotten school cricket-team slight by buying the game for himself, must be aware of this. That despite the big money, cricket in Australia has become merely a game. And when that happens, we're in trouble.

THOMAS KENEALLY
'The Cyclical Supremacy of Australia in World Cricket' in
Summer Days
(1981)

Never Played

I never was a boy, never played at cricket; it is better to let Nature take her course.

JOHN STUART MILL
Autobiography
(1867)

Footnote on Philadelphia Cricket

Roslyn Heights
Long Island, N. Y.
March 15, 1951

Dear John:

The best I can do — and a bit feverishly, I fear: your letter reached me in the final figuring of an income tax, and the prostration of a sweep of flu — is write you a footnote why I can't possibly do a preface for your *Century of Philadelphia Cricket*. . . . I know nothing about Philadelphia cricket; all I knew was what I saw as a child at Haverford, of which *pars magna fuisti*. It was an ideality which never came to the carborundum of the mill. Yes, I have watched cricket in later years; in village games in England and in Canada; I have known such screwball players as you mention — Sir James Barrie and E.V. Lucas — and have seen good old Sir Jack Squire, after too heavy a lunch of shepherd's pie and village Treble-X, fall on his face while making his absurdly long run to deliver his first ball. . . . As I heard a Surrey spectator say, watching Sir Jack trudging over the shaggy meadow (fingers so hopefully curved and palpated on the red ball), 'Oi blieve e'd do better if 'e wouldn't go so far down 'ill.'

I remember too the notice that used to flutter on the bulletin board on Founders Porch: *The following freshmen turn out tomorrow to Roll the Crease.*

If I had the knowledge, or the impudence (dear John) I'd hurry to help roll your crease. But my cricket lore, however dear to me, is entirely private. It includes the permanent vision of old Henry Cope (class of '69, wasn't he?) for whom our immortal field is named, and who used to stand endlessly under the great elm trees watching every stroke. In those days there were still the old benches discarded from the Meeting House, whitewashed for fifty years and at last fell to pieces. When I was watching a cricket match at Haverford a year ago I suddenly realized that I, even I myself, out of college forty years and whiskered, was of the same superannuation as the old Henry I remembered.

There is certainly some psychic reason why cricket in America was born in Philadelphia, flourished, passed away, and now – in our instinctive hunger for some last remaining uncommercialized sport – shows tender signs of revival. But I can't write about such things. Cricket to me is our adored old teacher Frank Gummere, sitting on the front steps of 1 College Circle in those spring afternoons of the first decade, and knowing – as he would know the prosody of the Roman de la Rose – the snick, the click, the whack, the crack, the slock, the knock, of every batsman's stroke, how it sounded on the cunningly molded willow, and how much it was likely good for. And of all games ever invented, it is the game for Philadelphians: if you don't think you can score, you don't have to run. What a cricketer John Wanamaker might have been; but don't let me get frisky.

Your distinguished memoirists know, better than I, the things that endear the game to me: the smell of grass, the creak of straps on pads, the thud of running feet chasing a near-boundary. I have not forgotten that I was a mascot (in a very tiny scarlet-and-black blazer) in your own team of 1896 that played Cambridge University; and I still remember the lissom and darkling Prince Ranjitsinhji, delicate and devilish at the bat as any of Kipling's panthers. But, I repeat, I know cricket only as dream and poetry. For a hundred years cricket has been the only kind of poetry Philadelphia has really approved. And all your participants – Frankford, Germantown, Merion, and U. of P. and the others – were poets without knowing it. Isn't that the most delicious of all our dear old Home Town's achievements? Its greatest triumphs by accident.

Think of the different tunes and tones of the laminated willow (so severely wound with thread, so deeply and cunningly sprung with an autographed XXXX sheave, mostly from Birmingham?) and twirl the bat for chance; was it, they used to say, flat or round? I don't remember. But cricket was always to me just a notion, a love afloat. Those who actually played it, beautiful as they were (even bulging a bit in the midriff like some Scattergoods at the wicket, and how slick they were with their How's That's?) were the hardworking actors. I was, and I remain, and fade away into my pitiful silence, the unspoiled spectator.

Speaking of Barrie, I always wondered how it was possible for him to handle a ball. I'm sure that cricket was just one of his island fancies. Did you ever see his hands? Tiny little dimpled clumps, like the puds of a little girl of ten. Whereas E.V. Lucas had great corned-beef lunch-hooks. But for both of them, as for Philadelphia in her reminiscence, cricket was a fairy tale. An excuse to get out into the afternoon air, the smell of maple-pollens, the gentle choreography of white pants in pattern on the turf, the batsman thumping down some pimple of sod, the bowler waving his field into some fanciful expertise (like income tax inspectors), the umpires in their long white surplices – these are what spectators, like professors of literature, can relish and sizzle in their membranes. These are part of cricket, and part of Philadelphia.

And so, to have been born, by chance, into cricket's Golden Age at Haverford, in the 1890s, was like having been born among the dramatists of Elizabeth the Queen (in the 1590s) or among the Wordsworth–Coleridge [circle] (of the 1790s). It was being born into something beautiful and unique. In my childhood (which seems to have lasted too long) a Lester, or a Scattergood, or a Hal Furness (to mention one of my own era whose mild and wary art was perfect) made drives, or cuts, or slices, or even unforgivable slogs, that were like Elizabethan sonneteers hoisting an Amoretto clear across Maple Avenue.

I love to think of the story of Henry Pleasants, who, thrilled beyond belief to play against Sir Arthur Conan Doyle at Lord's (1904, was it?) had two chances for a catch – and dropped them both. Henry was too gentlemanly to admit the truth; he allowed Sir Arthur to think that reverence for Sherlock and Watson had unnerved him. Actually, he had a painful blood-poison in his hand. If it had been basketball of 1951, what might we have thought?

I have one tangible souvenir of what Quiller-Couch, or maybe Andrew Lang, called 'sweet hours, and the fleetest of time'. When the old batting-shed was gently collapsing – it stood deserted for years, abaft the Library, in a sort of tropic jungle of overgrown sumacs; like one of the Malayan bungalows where Mr Somerset Maugham puts his poor pukka-sahibs through such psychosomatic despairs, his District Officers with outwashed shorts and their memsahibs with such preshrunken tempers – I picked up an ancient forgotten cricket-ball; a bit sideswiped in shape, as though once smitten by a Baily or a Biddlebanks, or a Gummere or a Comfort, of ancient kindlier time. I keep it in a mug, an empty mug, on top of a bookcase. More intellectual sensualists would have plaster busts of Homer or Halitosis, the classical warnings; but that head of an Amazon victim, almost indeed like the parched walnut of poor glorious little Sir James Barrie's suffering skull, is what I sometimes look at. I keep it in the same mug with an old dusty and equally defeated battle flag of the Confederacy. My only honesty is that I was always the first to admit defeat. So here is the ball that was never hit, in the game that was never played, in the story that will never be written.

CHRISTOPHER MORLEY
included in *A Century of Philadelphia Cricket*
(1951)

The Allahakbarries

Sometimes the three of them went for long tramps in Surrey, oftenmost to lovely Shere, in which village, 'over the butcher's shop', Meredith told me he had written one of his novels. On these occasions they talked so much cricket that it began to be felt among them that they were hidden adepts at the game, and an ambition came over them to unveil. This was strengthened by the elderly appearance of the Shere team, whom they decided to challenge after letting them grow one year older. Anon [J.M. Barrie] was appointed captain (by chicanery it is said by the survivors), and he thought there would be no difficulty in getting a stout XI together, literary men being such authorities on the willow. On the eventful day, however, he found out in the railway compartment by which they advanced upon Shere that he had to coach more than one of his players in the finesse of the game: which was the side of the bat you hit with, for instance. In so far as was feasible they also practised in the train. Two of the team were African travellers of renown, Paul du Chaillu of gorilla fame and the much loved Joseph Thomson of Masailand. When a name for the team was being discussed, Anon, now grown despondent, asked these two what was the 'African' for 'Heaven help us', and they gave him 'Allahakbar'. So they decided to call themselves the Allahakbars, afterwards changed with complimentary intention to the Allahakbarries.

It is immaterial now how many runs Shere made, but the score was a goodly one ... At last, however, they were out, and the once long-looked-for time arrived for the Allahakbarries to go in. There was no longer a thirsty desire on the part of any of the team to open the innings, but in its place a passionate determination that this honour should be the captain's. I forget whether he yielded to the general wish, but at all events he ordered Marriott Watson to be No. 2, because all the time they were in the train, when others trembled, Marriott had kept saying gamely, 'Intellect always tells in the end.' For a lovely moment we thought it was to tell here, for he hit his first ball so hard that the Allahakbarries were at the beginning of a volley of cheers when they saw him coming out, caught at point by the curate. The captain amassed two. One man who partnered him was somewhat pedantic and before taking centre (as they were all instructed to do) signed to Anon that he had a secret to confide. It proved to be 'Should I strike the ball to however small an extent I shall run with considerable velocity.' He did not have to run. The top scorer (as he tells to this day) was Gilmour, who swears he made five. The total was eleven.

The next time the Allahakbarries played Shere they won because they arrived two men short. They scoured the country in a wagonette, seeking to complete their team, and took with them, despite his protests, an artist whom they found in a field painting cows. They were still more fortunate in finding a soldier sitting with two ladies outside a pub. He agreed to accompany them if they would take the ladies also, and all three were taken. This unknown was the Allahakbarrie who carried the team that day to victory, and the last they saw of him he was sitting outside another pub with another two ladies.

Soon it became clear to Anon that the more distinguished as authors his men were the worse they played. Conan Doyle was the chief exception to this depressing rule, but after all, others did occasionally have their day, as when

A.E.W. Mason, fast bowler, 'ran through' the opposing side, though one never knew in advance whether he was more likely to send the bails flying or to hit square leg in the stomach. Augustine Birrell once hit so hard that he smashed the bat of Anon, which had been kindly lent him, and instead of grieving he called out gloriously, 'Fetch me some more bats.' Maurice Hewlett could sometimes look well set just before he came out. E.V. Lucas had (unfortunately) a style. Will Meredith would have excelled in the long field but for his way of shouting 'Boundary' when a fast ball approached him. Owen Seaman knew (or so he said) how to cut. Henry Ford was, even more than Tate, an unlucky bowler. Jerome once made two fours. Charles Whibley threw in unerringly but in the wrong direction. You should have seen Charles Furze as wicket-keeper, but you would have had to be quick about it as Anon had so soon to try someone else. Gilmour could at least continue to prate about his five. The team had no tail, that is to say, they would have done just as well had they begun at the other end. Yet when strengthened in the weaker points of their armour, namely in batting and bowling, by outsiders surreptitiously introduced, they occasionally astounded the tented field, as when by mistake they challenged Esher, a club of renown, and beat them by hundreds, an Allahakbarrie (whose literary qualifications I cannot remember) notching a century. Anon never would play Esher again, though they begged him.

J.M. BARRIE
The Greenwood Hat
(1930)

Days Well Spent

I am fond of my old cricketer in spite of a certain mendacious and malign element in him. His yarns of gallant stands and unexpected turns of fortune, of memorable hits and eccentric umpiring, albeit sometimes incredibly to his glory, are full of the flavour of days well spent, of bright mornings of play, sunlit sprawling beside the score tent, warmth, the flavour of bitten grass stems and the odour of crushed turf. One seems to hear the clapping hands of village ancients, and their ululations of delight. One thinks of stone jars with cool drink swishing therein, of shouting victories and memorable defeats, of eleven men in a drag, and tuneful and altogether glorious home comings by the light of the moon. His were the Olympian days of the sport, when noble squires were its patrons, and every village a home and nursery of stalwart cricketers, before the epoch of special trains, star elevens, and the tumultuous gathering of idle cads to jabber at a game they cannot play.

H.G. WELLS
Certain Personal Matters
(1898)

'My old cricketer' was Joseph Wells (1828–1910), the father of H.G. Wells, who played for Kent in 1862–3. At Brighton, in 1862, against Sussex, he took four wickets in four consecutive balls with his fast round-armed delivery.

Recollections of Harris

David Harris was, I believe, born, at all events he lived, at Odiham, in Hampshire; he was by trade a potter. He was a muscular, bony man, standing about five feet nine and a half inches. His features were not regularly handsome, but a remarkably kind and gentle expression amply compensated the defect of mere linear beauty. The fair qualities of his heart shone through his honest face, and I can call to mind no worthier, or, in the active sense of the word, not a more '*good* man' than David Harris. He was one of the rare species that link man to man in bonds of fellowship by good works; that inspire confidence, and prevent the structure of society from becoming disjointed, and, 'as it were, a bowing wall, or a tottering fence'. He was a man of so strict a principle, and such high honour, that I believe his moral character was never impeached. I never heard even a suspicion breathed against his integrity, and I knew him long and intimately. I do not mean that he was a *canter* – Oh, no – no one thought of standing on guard and buttoning up his pockets in Harris's company. I never busied myself about his mode of faith, or the peculiarity of his creed; that was his own affair, not mine, or any other being's on earth; all I know is, that he was an '*honest man*', and the poet has assigned the rank of such a one in creation.

It would be difficult, perhaps impossible, to convey in writing an accurate idea of the grand effect of Harris's bowling; they only who have played against him can fully appreciate it. His attitude when preparing for his run previously to delivering the ball would have made a beautiful study for the sculptor. Phidias would certainly have taken him for a model. First of all, he stood erect like a soldier at drill; then, with a graceful curve of the arm, he raised the ball to his forehead, and drawing back his right foot, started off with his left. The calm look and general air of the man were uncommonly striking, and from this series of preparations he never deviated. I am sure that from this simple account of his manner, all my countrymen who were acquainted with his play will recall him to their minds. His mode of delivering the ball was very singular. He would bring it from under the arm by a twist, and nearly as high as his armpit, and with this action *push* it, as it were, from him. How it was that the balls acquired the velocity they did by this mode of delivery I never could comprehend.

When first he joined the Hambledon Club, he was quite a raw countryman at cricket, and had very little to recommend him but his noble delivery. He was also very apt to give tosses. I have seen old Nyren scratch his head, and say – 'Harris would make the best bowler in England if he did not toss.' By continual practice, however, and following the advice of the old Hambledon players, he became as steady as could be wished; and in the prime of his playing very rarely indeed gave a toss, although his balls were pitched the full length. In bowling, he never stooped in the least in his delivery, but kept himself upright all the time. His balls were very little beholden to the ground when pitched; it was but a touch, and up again; and woe be to the man who did not get in to block them, for they had such a peculiar curl, that they would grind his fingers against the bat: many a time have I seen the blood drawn in this way from a batter who was not up to the trick; old Tom Walker was the only exception – I have before classed him among the bloodless animals.

Harris's bowling was the finest of all tests for a hitter, and hence the great beauty, as I observed before, of seeing Beldham in, with this man against him; for unless a batter were of the very first class, and accustomed to the best style of stopping, he could do little or nothing with Harris. If the thing had been possible, I should have liked to have seen such a player as Budd (fine hitter as he was) standing against him. My own opinion is that he could not have stopped his balls, and this will be a criterion, by which those who have seen some of that gentleman's brilliant hits may judge of the extraordinary merit of this man's bowling. He was considerably faster than Lambert, and so superior in style and finish that I can draw no comparison between them. Lord Frederick Beauclerk has been heard to say that Harris's bowling was one of the grandest things of the kind he had ever seen; but his lordship could not have known him in his prime; he never saw him play till after he had had many fits of the gout, and had become slow and feeble.

To Harris's fine bowling I attribute the great improvement that was made in hitting, and above all in stopping; for it was utterly impossible to remain at the crease, when the ball was tossed to a fine length; you were obliged to get in, or it would be about your hands, or the handle of your bat; and every player knows where its next place would be.

Some years after Harris had played with the Hambledon Club, he became so well acquainted with the science of the game of cricket that he could take a very great advantage in pitching the wickets. And not only would he pitch a good wicket for himself, but he would also consider those who had to bowl with him. The writer of this has often walked with him up to Windmill-down at six o'clock in the morning of the day that a match was to be played, and has with pleasure noticed the pains he has taken in choosing the ground for his fellow-bowler as well as himself. The most eminent men in every walk of life have at all times been the most painstaking – slabberdash work and indifference may accompany genius, and it does so too frequently; such geniuses, however, throw away more than half their chance. There are more brilliant talents in this world than people give the world credit for; and that their lustre does not exhibit to the best advantage, commonly depends upon the owners of them. Ill luck, and the preference that frequently attends industrious mediocrity, are the only anodynes that wounded self-love or indolence can administer to misapplied or unused ability. In his walk, Harris was a man of genius, and he let slip no opportunity to maintain his pre-eminence. Although unwilling to detract from the fame of old Lumpy, I must here observe upon the difference in these two men with regard to pitching their wickets. Lumpy would uniformly select a point where the ball was likely to shoot, that is, over the brow of a little hill; and when by this forethought and contrivance the old man would prove successful in bowling his men out, he would turn round to his party with a little grin of triumph; nothing gratified him like this reward of his knowingness. Lumpy, however, thought only of himself in choosing his ground; his fellow-bowler might take his chance; this was neither wise nor liberal. Harris, on the contrary, as I have already observed, considered his partner; and, in so doing, the main chance of the game. Unlike Lumpy, too, he would choose a rising ground to pitch the ball against, and he who is well acquainted with the game of cricket will at once perceive the advantage that must arise from a wicket pitched in this way to such a tremendous bowler as Harris was. If I were urged to draw a comparison between these two great players, the greatest certainly in their department I ever saw, I could do it in no other way than the following: Lumpy's ball was always pitched to the length, but delivered lower than Harris's and never got up so high; he was also slower than Harris, and lost his advantage by the way in which he persisted in pitching his wicket; yet I think he would bowl more wickets down than the other, for the latter never pitched his wicket with this end in view; almost all his balls, therefore, rose over the wicket; consequently, more players would be caught out from Harris than Lumpy, and not half the number of runs got from his bowling. I passed a very pleasant time with Harris when he came to my father's house at Hambledon, by invitation, after an illness, and for the benefit of the change of air. Being always his companion in his walks about the neighbourhood, I had full opportunity of observing the sweetness of his disposition; this, with his manly contempt of every action that bore the character of meanness, gained him the admiration of every cricketer in Hambledon.

In concluding my recollections of Harris, I had well nigh omitted to say something of his skill in the other departments of the game. The fact is, the extraordinary merit of his bowling would have thrown any other fair accomplishments he might possess into the shade; but, indeed, as a batter, I considered him rather an indifferent hand; I never recollect his getting more than ten runs, and those very rarely. Neither was his fielding remarkable. But he was game to the backbone, and never suffered a ball to pass him without putting his body in the way of it. If I recollect, he generally played slip.

JOHN NYREN
The Young Cricketer's Tutor
(1833)

The Ashes

In affectionate remembrance of English cricket which died at the Oval, 29th August, 1882. Deeply lamented by a large circle of sorrowing friends and acquaintances. R.I.P. N.B. The body will be cremated and the Ashes taken to Australia.

REGINALD SHIRLEY BROOKS
Mock obituary in *Sporting Times*
(1882)

Pride and Prejudice

Let me record with pride that I was conceived in that great and glorious year wherein for the first time Kent won the County Championship.

E.W. SWANTON
Follow On
(1977)

Earliest Days

From the very earliest days I can recall, I have loved the feel of a cricket bat.

SIR LEONARD HUTTON
Cricket
(1961)

Beard Story is True

We all remembered a certain match at Sheffield Park in 1896. This was the first match played that year by the Australian team captained by G.H.S. Trott, and it included the redoubtable Ernest Jones, whose first appearance it was. In that match W.G. went in first with Arthur Shrewsbury. I was playing too, and I vouch to you that it is true that in the first over a ball from Ernest Jones did go through W.G.'s beard, and that W.G. did rumble out a falsetto, 'What – what – what!' and that Harry Trott did say, 'Steady, Jonah', and that Ernest Jones did say, 'Sorry, doctor, she slipped.' . . . W.G. topped the twenties, and his huge chest was black and blue.

C.B. FRY
Life Worth Living
(1939)

A Desert Island Cricket Team

The idea was the editor's. 'Alderney is not exactly deserted,' he said, 'but why not pick a desert island cricket team?' That, we decided, did not necessarily mean the strongest or the finest eleven; but the one the selector would most enjoy watching ...

The choice involved a pleasant dinner of discussion and reminiscence and the eventual team – in battle order – was Sir Jack Hobbs (Surrey and England), Wilfred Rhodes (Yorkshire and England), Vivian Richards (Antigua, Somerset, and West Indies), George Brown (Hampshire and England), Keith Miller (New South Wales and Australia), Ted Dexter (Sussex and England), Mike Brearley (Middlesex and England), Ian Botham (Somerset and England), Lord Constantine (Nelson, Trinidad, and West Indies), Jim Laker (Surrey and England), Doug Wright (Kent and England), Wesley Hall (Barbados and West Indies).

JOHN ARLOTT
Wisden Cricket Monthly
(September 1982)

Village Cricket Remembered

The 'mellowing glass' of memory may be false to detail and yet delightful; but the vanishing of all circumstances from a man's mind is a sad matter. The ancient man who had been a young visitor to the Great Exhibition, 1851, when I sat next to him evening upon evening in 1931 remembered only that he remembered it. Even that I suspect depended on someone telling him his duty. I am sorry to surmise that if my life is prolonged in the same way, I shall be in very much the same unentertaining condition. Youth will await my picturesque impression of K.S. Ranjitsinjhi and his leg-glide, or perhaps of the Fourth of August, 1914, and the end of an era, and I shall promptly mumble with grim pride, 'Yes, I saw the Prince bat -- he was an Indian gentleman, you know', 'Yes, that was the day one of the Wars broke out – I was told about it.' Indeed, even now, I can hardly offer anything like a sunlight moment when I may be tempted to mention that I saw R.H. Spooner at the Oval. He made 224 runs, Lancashire altogether 360 – that much survives; it was an innings of grace and strength – you all know that; he stood nobly tall, easy, untired in manner, all through – you would expect that. Studious also – every ball. It was the sunshine of cricket at his end of the pitch, that I feel; for the other end, the batsmen who one after another supported him (a little), are all in a shadow now.

If any benefactor offers a prize for a clear memory, there is a candidate in our parish. When I was last able to take my seat at the Flower Pot – for even now there are some in those cottages who do not count me as altogether an exile – a gentleman came in whom I recognized by degrees as one of the occasional bass singers in the long-lost heroic era of our village choir and concert. I did not quite like it at first when he discovered us, as a family circle, talking of cricket in the

293

day of battle, but he was not frowning over that; it was the small range of our recollections that troubled him. So he took up the subject, and detailed several mighty performances (his own not overlooked) on the part of our cricket teams in the past. They were so mighty, and his appearance so youthful, that I was perplexed at not having such records engraved on the tablet of my own memory. Someone asked him pensively when these local cricket masterpieces happened. 'In the Nineties', he answered simply, as though that was surely a date we all shared and had in the front of our minds, a mere matter of the calendar.

But what can I say for my own memory? It seemed to undertake a burden for life during the War of 1914–1918 – a case which must be far from unique. When I would rescue some exact instance of the cricket which was formerly so like earthly paradise to me, and of which perhaps I was an official scorer at twopence a match, the resistance is strong. There is no cure except perhaps future time. Yet I have a general remembrance of the village game, and even if some later influences have imbrowned the colouring I cannot but take my picture as something that I perceived, an aspect of the actual.

A thunderstorm is stooping over the old cricket ground in my memory. It is not a date that I can identify, and I do not know who the awaited opponents of our team are – an Estate, a Brewery, the Constabulary, some sort of Rovers, more likely just another village side. It is the forenoon, and that inky cloud is working round the hill, as black almost as the spinney of firs on the boundary, imported trees which I always suspect of being aloof in their hearts from the scene and its animations. I feel oily splashing drops and doubt if we shall have the promised encounter in the afternoon. The summer seems to have fallen into low spirits, and there is nobody about except the rooks and pigeons – we have heard all they have to say – and a crying woodpecker down under the oak at the river. The storm drifts, the cloud-edges are effaced; but the rain patters steadily on the metal roof of the mowing shed, the gutters gurgle, all the trees are grey with the shower. Past the far side of the field a figure with a sack for hood drives his cycle apace, never turning his eyes this way for a moment; and no one from the vicarage steps out to see if there is any prospect of play.

Yet the hours pass, and after all the rain has wearied, and stopped, the smoky-looking day may remain thus, neither better nor worse, and the turf is good. A bicycle is being pushed through the meadow gate by a cricketer in flannels under his mackintosh, and one by one they all assemble. An unlocking of padlocks and shifting of benches in the pavilion, a thump of bats and stumps being hauled out of the dark corners. The creases are marked, and the offer of a bowling screen rejected. Our boys put catapults back in their jackets and affect to know personally the visitors now arriving, pointing out one or two with awe — that one who hits sixes, and that one with the spectacles who never scores less than seventy. There are not many cricket caps on show, and some of the players are observed to feel safest with braces and ties on.

Sawdust wanted! The fielding side have spread themselves about the soaked ground, and all is otherwise ready — even the two batsmen have gone out to their creases, casting rather unhappy looks on their companions in the pavilion, who sit down in a row and brood. It is odd, this serious game; perhaps it is the greyness of the day that causes it to take this mood. Sawdust! A bucket is being carried forth by the groundsman, whose squat shoulders and beard look like the picture of Hudibras; he tips out his two little mounds of sawdust, and marches off to his shed, as who should say, 'That is the end of the match for me. That *is* the match.' The one-armed bowler measures his run, dips the ball into the sawdust, and with three or four sharp steps whizzes it at the opposed batsman; it passes with a wet smack into the gloves of the man behind the stumps. All the fieldsmen attend gravely. This bowler has pace. But no smile. . . .

The cricket was all rather a grave affair. I suppose it was the weather mostly that made it so, and any one from abroad who knows the prevailing summer gloom surrounding a landing at Dover may concur. But the game gave me some sense of being rather a continuation of rural labours than a sport and pastime. It was carried through as earnestly as, say, measuring the hops in a bin, or bringing a team of horses over the bridge with that queer thing a car steering along from the other direction; where there was skill, it was applied with the same attentiveness as the skill of grafting a tree. Perhaps it was the weather I say to myself again, and there must have come another day, and come many a time, when the laughing sky was reflected in the light-hearted frolics and gaieties of my old country cricketers. Not even thus can I find a way from their habit of cricket, a hard game. They were too firmly fixed within necessities of toil and shrewdness, duty and plainness, to be easily renewed in a short interlude as children of the sun. Their cricket was of another mood from that which would be played on the same ground a few days later by those whose tradition was polished entertainment, the social round, the glorious indolence of a 'modest competence' or a small fortune.

EDMUND BLUNDEN
Cricket Country
(1944)

EPISODES

Clerical Garb

E.H. Pickering, a celebrated old Etonian, was once called upon so suddenly to bat in a Gentlemen v. Players match at Lord's that he was obliged to go to the wicket in clerical garb.

F.S. ASHLEY-COOPER
Cricket Highways and Byways
(1927)

An Innocent Abroad

'Dont forget Saturday morning Charing Cross Underground Station,' ran the telegram which arrived at Royal Avenue during the week, 'at ten fifteen sharp whatever you do dont be late Hodge.'

Saturday morning was bright and sunny, and at ten minutes past ten Donald arrived at the Embankment entrance of Charing Cross Underground Station, carrying a small suitcase full of clothes suitable for outdoor sports and pastimes. He was glad that he had arrived too early, for it would have been a dreadful thing for a stranger and a foreigner to have kept such a distinguished man, and his presumably distinguished colleagues, even for an instant from their national game. Laying his bag down on the pavement and putting one foot upon it carefully – for Donald had heard stories of the surpassing dexterity of metropolitan thieves – he waited eagerly for the hands of a neighbouring clock to mark the quarter-past. At twenty minutes to eleven an effeminate-looking young man, carrying a cricketing bag and wearing a pale-blue silk jumper up to his ears, sauntered up, remarked casually, 'You playing?' and, on receiving an answer in the affirmative, dumped his bag at Donald's feet and said, 'Keep an eye on that like a good fellow. I'm going to get a shave,' and sauntered off round the corner.

At five minutes to eleven there was a respectable muster, six of the team having assembled. But at five minutes past, a disintegrating element was introduced by the arrival of Mr Harcourt with the news, which he announced with the air of a shipwrecked mariner who has, after twenty-five years of vigilance, seen a sail, that in the neighbourhood of Charing Cross the pubs opened at 11 a.m. So that when Mr Hodge himself turned up at twenty-five minutes past eleven, resplendent in flannels, a red-and-white football shirt with a lace-up collar, and a blazer of purple-and-yellow stripes, each stripe being at least two inches across, and surmounted by a purple-and-yellow cap that made him somehow reminiscent of one of the Michelin twins, if not both, he was justly indignant at the slackness of his team.

'They've no sense of time,' he told Donald repeatedly. 'We're late as it is. The match is due to begin at half-past eleven, and it's fifty miles from here. I should have been here myself two hours ago but I had my Sunday article to do. It really is too bad.'

When the team, now numbering nine men, had been extricated from the tavern and had been marshalled on the pavement, counted, recounted, and the missing pair identified, it was pointed out by the casual youth who had returned, shining and pomaded from the barber, that the charabanc had not yet arrived.

Mr Hodge's indignation became positively alarming and he covered the twenty yards to the public telephone box almost as quickly as Mr Harcourt covered the forty yards back to the door of the pub. Donald remained on the pavement to guard the heap of suitcases, cricket-bags, and stray equipment – one player had arrived with a pair of flannels rolled in a tight ball under his arm and a left-hand batting glove, while another had contributed a cardboard box which he had bought at Hamley's on the way down, and which contained six composite cricket-balls, boys' size, and a pair of bails. It was just as well that Donald did remain on guard, partly because no one else seemed to care whether the luggage was stolen or not, partly because Mr Hodge emerged in a perfect frenzy a minute or two later from the telephone box to borrow two pennies to put in the slot, and partly because by the time the telephone call was at last in full swing and Mr Hodge's command over the byways of British invective was enjoying complete freedom of action, the charabanc rolled up beside the kerb.

At 12.30 it was decided not to wait for the missing pair, and the nine cricketers started off. At 2.30, after halts at Catford, the White Hart at Sevenoaks, the Angel at Tunbridge Wells, and three smaller inns at tiny villages, the charabanc drew up triumphantly beside the cricket ground of the Kentish village of Fordenden.

Donald was enchanted at his first sight of rural England. And rural England is the real England, unspoilt by factories and financiers and tourists and hustle. He sprang out of the charabanc, in which he had been tightly wedged between a very stout publisher who had laughed all the way down and had quivered at each laugh like the needle of a seismograph during one of Japan's larger earthquakes, and a youngish and extremely learned professor of ballistics, and gazed eagerly round. The sight was worth an eager gaze or two. It was a hot summer's afternoon. There was no wind, and the smoke from the red-roofed cottages curled slowly up into the golden haze. The clock on the flint tower of the church struck the half-hour, and the vibrations spread slowly across the shimmering hedgerows, spangled with white blossom of the convolvulus, and lost themselves tremulously among the orchards. Bees lazily drifted. White butterflies flapped their aimless way among the gardens. Delphiniums, larkspur, tiger-lilies, evening primrose, monk's-hood, sweet-peas, swaggered brilliantly above the box hedges, the wooden palings, and the rickety gates. The cricket field itself was a mass of daisies and buttercups and dandelions, tall grasses and purple vetches and thistle-down, and great clumps of dark-red sorrel, except, of course, for the oblong patch in the centre – mown, rolled, watered – a smooth, shining emerald of grass, the Pride of Fordenden, the Wicket.

A.G. MACDONNELL
England, Their England
(1933)

Sport and Science

Sir Walter Vivian all on a summer's day
Gave his broad lawns until the set of sun
Up to the people ...
                    round the lake
A little clock-work steamer paddling plied
And shook the lilies: perched about the knolls
A dozen angry models jetted steam:
A petty railway ran: a fire-balloon
Rose gem-like up before the dusky groves
And dropt a fairy parachute and past:
And there thro' twenty posts of telegraph
They flash'd a saucy message to and fro
Between the mimic stations; so that sport
Went hand in hand with Science; otherwhere
Pure sport; a herd of boys with clamour bowl'd
And stump'd the wicket; babies roll'd about
Like tumbled fruit in grass ...

ALFRED LORD TENNYSON
The Princess; a Medley
(1847)

Wordsworth, Southey, and Canning

The most memorable of these few incidents of my Harrow cricketing days has been reserved for the last. It was on the

302

occasion of my first visit to the Lakes in 1822. My father had rented 'Ivy Cottage' (as it was then called, now Glen Rothay), close to Rydal Mount, and I had joined him there to spend my midsummer holidays. One afternoon, quite (I believe) unexpectedly, a carriage drove up, containing Mr Bolton of Storrs, the well-known Liverpool merchant, and Mr Canning, who had just been appointed Governor-General of India, and had come to pay a farewell visit to the friend who had been one of his chief supporters in his Liverpool elections. They had driven over from Storrs, Mr Bolton's residence on Windermere, to invite my uncle [the poet William Wordsworth] and Southey, then at Rydal Mount, and my father to return with them to dinner and stay the night. While my father went upstairs to arrange his toilette for the evening, I had the honour of showing the great orator and statesman into the garden – a beautiful spot – and he walked by my side with his arm upon my shoulder (I was then a boy of sixteen) listening in the kindest manner and with keen interest to all the particulars I had to tell respecting the grand cricket match – then a novel occurrence – between Eton and Harrow which had been played only a few days before, and in which I had taken such a prominent part, with the result of defeat to Eton and victory to Harrow; Canning's own sympathies of course being with the former, though he was too generous to disclose them. I need not say how much I was charmed with the simple grace and condescension of his manner. It was perhaps, in its small measure, the proudest moment of my young life. Only a few days later came the intelligence that Lord Castlereagh had committed suicide. The event caused Canning to give up his appointment to India, and opened the way first to his succeeding him as Foreign Secretary and eventually (1827) to his becoming Prime Minister.

CHARLES WORDSWORTH
Annals of My Early Life 1806–46
(1891)

303

More unemployment – and still I carried a cricket-ball as I trudged the streets.

I had drifted into a lower grade of cricket, though it was still of a fairly good standard, and I was told by some of my team-mates that I was capable of bowling a very dangerous ball. It didn't come up as often as it should, but it might lead to something. However, I would be well advised to lessen the spin and concentrate on length.

I was flattered that my fellow-cricketers should think that even a few of the balls I delivered had devil in them. All the same, there was a rebellious imp sitting on my shoulder that whispered: 'Take no notice, cobber. They're crazy. Millions can bowl a good length but few can really spin the ball. Keep the spin and practise, practise, practise.'

Then came a commission for a house-painting job. It was a house near Botany Bay and it belonged to my brother-in-law. Wages? A bat that had been given to my brother-in-law by a distant relative who had taken part in the 1904 English tour. But what a relative! It was Victor Trumper himself – the fantastic, legendary Trumper, my particular hero. A hundred pounds could not have given me more pleasure.

Fancy getting a bat which my hero had actually used in a Test at Lord's; a flattish bat with a springy handle and a blade curved like the bowl of a spoon. This was another link closer to the great batsman and I was more than ever determined to improve my bowling.

The 'wrong 'un', that legacy from the great Bosanquet, like Bateman's 'one-note man', seemed to be getting me somewhere, for after several seasons in Sydney lower-grade teams I found myself in first grade, a class of cricket in which inter-state and Test players participate.

At the same time, and having done my house-painting, I got another regular job. I became an A Class labourer on the

304

Water and Sewerage Board.

Things were certainly coming my way; I had never worn a collar and tie to work before. My mother had always hoped that I would get a 'white collar' job like Mr Rumble some day – and here it was.

It is difficult to realize that a relatively minor event in one's life can still remain the most important through the years. I was chosen to play for Redfern against Paddington – and Paddington was Victor Trumper's club.

This was unbelievable, fantastic. It could never happen – something was sure to go wrong. A war – an earthquake – Trumper might fall sick. A million things could crop up in the two or three days before the match.

I sat on my bed and looked at Trumper's picture still pinned on the canvas wall. It seemed to be breathing with the movement of the draught between the skirting. I glanced at his bat standing in a corner of the room, then back at the gently moving picture. I just couldn't believe that this, to me, ethereal and godlike figure could step off the wall, pick up that bat and say quietly, 'Two legs, please, umpire', in my presence.

My family, usually undemonstrative and self-possessed, found it difficult to maintain that reserve which, strange as it may seem, was characteristic of my father's Northern Irish heritage.

'H'm,' said Father, 'Playing against Trumper on Saturday. By jove, you'll cop Old Harry if you're put on to bowl at him.'

'Why should he?' protested Mother. 'You never know what you can do till you try.'

I had nothing to say. I was little concerned with what should happen to me in the match. What worried me was that something would happen to Trumper which would prevent his playing.

Although at this time I had never seen Trumper play, on occasions I trudged from Waterloo across the Sandhills to the

Sydney cricket ground and waited at the gate to watch the players coming out. Once I had climbed on a tram and actually sat opposite my hero for three stops. I would have gone further but having no money I did not want to take the chance of being kicked in the pants by the conductor. Even so I had been taken half a mile out of my way.

In my wildest dreams I never thought I would ever speak to Trumper let alone play against him. I am fairly phlegmatic by nature but between the period of my selection and the match I must have behaved like a half-wit.

Right up to my first Test match I always washed and pressed my own flannels, but before this match I pressed them not once but several times. On the Saturday I was up with the sparrows and looking anxiously at the sky. It was a lovely morning but it still might rain. Come to that, lots of things could happen in ten hours – there was still a chance that Vic could be taken ill or knocked down by a tram or twist his ankle or break his arm. ...

My thoughts were interrupted by a vigorous thumping on the back gate. I looked out of the washhouse-bathroom-woodshed-workshop window and saw that it was the milkman who was kicking up the row.

'Hey!' he roared – 'yer didn't leave the can out. I can't wait around here all day. A man should pour it in the garbage tin – that'd make yer wake up a bit!'

On that morning I wouldn't have cared whether he poured the milk in the garbage tin or all over me. I didn't belong to this world. I was playing against the great Victor Trumper. Let the milk take care of itself.

I kept looking at the clock. It might be slow – or it might have stopped! I'd better whip down to the Zetland Hotel and check up. Anyhow, I mightn't bowl at Trumper after all. He might get out before I come on. Or I mightn't get a bowl at all – after all, I can't put myself on. Wonder what Trumper's doing this very minute ... bet he's not ironing his flannels. Sends them to the laundry, I suppose. He's probably got two

306

sets of flannels, anyway. Perhaps he's at breakfast, perhaps he's eating bacon and eggs. Wonder if he knows I'm playing against him? Don't suppose he's ever heard of me. Wouldn't worry him anyhow, I shouldn't think. Gosh, what a long morning! Think I'll dig the garden. No, I won't – I want to keep fresh. Think I'll lie down for a bit ... better not, I might fall off to sleep and be late.

The morning did not pass in this way. Time just stopped. I couldn't bring myself to doing anything in particular and yet I couldn't settle to the thought of not doing anything. I was bowling to Trumper and I was not bowling to Trumper. I was early and I was late. In fact, I think I was slightly out of my mind.

I didn't get to the ground so very early after all, mainly because it would have been impossible for me to wait around so near the scene of Trumper's appearance – and yet for it to rain or news to come that something had prevented Vic from playing.

'Is he here?' I asked Harry Goddard, our captain, the moment I did arrive at the ground.

'Is who here?' he countered.

My answer was probably a scornful and disgusted look. I remember that it occurred to me to say, 'Julius Caesar, of course' but that I stopped myself being cheeky because this was one occasion when I couldn't afford to be.

Paddington won the toss and took first knock.

When Trumper walked out to bat, Harry Goddard said to me: 'I'd better keep you away from Vic. If he starts on you he'll probably knock you out of grade cricket.'

I was inclined to agree with him yet at the same time I didn't fear punishment from the master batsman. All I wanted to do was just to bowl at him. I suppose in their time other ambitious youngsters have wanted to play on the same stage with Henry Irving, or sing with Caruso or Melba, to fight with Napoleon or sail the seas with Columbus. It wasn't conquest I desired. I simply wanted to meet my hero on common ground.

307

Vic, beautifully clad in creamy, loose-fitting but well-tailored flannels, left the pavilion with his bat tucked under his left arm and in the act of donning his gloves. Although slightly pigeon-toed in the left foot he had a springy athletic walk and a tendency to shrug his shoulders every few minutes, a habit I understand he developed through trying to loosen his shirt off his shoulders when it became soaked with sweat during his innings.

Arriving at the wicket, he bent his bat handle almost to a right angle, walked up the pitch, prodded about six yards of it, returned to the batting crease and asked the umpire for 'two legs', took a quick glance in the direction of fine leg, shrugged his shoulders again and took up his stance.

I was called to bowl sooner than I had expected. I suspect now that Harry Goddard changed his mind and decided to put me out of my misery early in the piece.

Did I ever bowl that first ball? I don't remember. My head was in a whirl, I really think I fainted and the secret of the mythical first ball has been kept over all these years to save me embarrassment. If the ball *was* sent down it must have been hit for six, or at least four, because I was awakened from my trance by the thunderous booming Yabba who roared: 'O for a strong arm and walking stick!'

I do remember the next ball. It was, I imagined, a perfect leg-break. When it left my hand it was singing sweetly like a humming top. The trajectory couldn't have been more graceful if designed by a professor of ballistics. The tremendous leg-spin caused the ball to swing and curve from the off and move in line with the middle and leg stump. Had I bowled this particular ball at any other batsman I would have turned my back early in its flight and listened for the death rattle. However, consistent with my idolization of the champion, I watched his every movment.

He stood poised like a panther ready to spring. Down came his left foot to within a foot of the ball. The bat, swung from well over his shoulders, met the ball just as it fizzed off the pitch, and the next sound I heard was a rapping on the off-side fence.

It was the most beautiful shot I have ever seen.

The immortal Yabba made some attempt to say something but his voice faded away to the soft gurgle one hears at the end of a kookaburra's song. The only person on the ground who didn't watch the course of the ball was Victor Trumper. The moment he played it he turned his back, smacked down a few tufts of grass and prodded his way back to the batting crease. He knew where the ball was going.

What were my reactions?

Well, I never expected that ball or any other ball I could produce to get Trumper's wicket. But that being the best ball a bowler of my type could spin into being, I thought that at least Vic might have been forced to play a defensive shot, particularly as I was almost a stranger too and it might have been to his advantage to use discretion rather than valour.

After I had bowled one or two other reasonably good balls without success I found fresh hope in the thought that Trumper had found Bosanquet, creator of the 'wrong 'un' or 'bosie' (which I think a better name), rather puzzling. This left me with one shot in my locker, but if I didn't use it quickly I would be taken out of the firing line. I decided, therefore, to try this most undisciplined and cantankerous creation of the great B.J. Bosanquet – not, as many may think, as a compliment to the inventor but as the gallant farewell, so to speak, of a warrior who refused to surrender until all his ammunition was spent.

Again fortune was on my side in that I bowled the ball I had often dreamed of bowling. As with the leg-break, it had sufficient spin to curve in the air and break considerably after making contact with the pitch. If anything it might have had a little more top-spin, which would cause it to drop rather suddenly. The sensitivity of a spinning ball against a breeze is governed by the amount of spin imparted, and if a ball bowled at a certain pace drops on a certain spot, one bowled with identical pace but with more top-spin should drop eighteen inches or two feet shorter.

For this reason I thought the difference in the trajectory and ultimate landing of the ball might provide a measure of uncertainty in Trumper's mind. Whilst the ball was in flight this reasoning appeared to be vindicated by Trumper's initial movement. As at the beginning of my over he sprang in to attack but did not realize that the ball, being an off-break, was floating away from him and dropping a little quicker. Instead of his left foot being close to the ball it was a foot out of line.

In a split second Vic grasped this and tried to make up the deficiency with a wider swing of the bat. It was then I could see a passage-way to the stumps with our 'keeper, Con Hayes, ready to claim his victim. Vic's bat came through like a flash but the ball passed between his bat and legs, missed the leg stump by a fraction, and the bails were whipped off with the great batsman at least two yards out of his ground.

Vic had made no attempt to scramble back. He knew the ball had beaten him and was prepared to pay the penalty, and although he had little chance of regaining his crease on this occasion I think he would have acted similarly if his back foot had been only an inch from safety.

As he walked past me he smiled, patted the back of his bat and said, 'It was too good for me.'

There was no triumph in me as I watched the receding figure. I felt like a boy who had killed a dove.

ARTHUR MAILEY
10 for 66 and All That
(1958)

Second Visit

It was from some humble artisan job that he [Arthur Mailey] emerged to bowl against England and both teams were invited to a reception at Government House in Sydney. The wife of His Excellency chose to be somewhat patronizing: 'I suppose this is your first visit to Government House, Mr Mailey.' 'No, ma'am, it isn't. I was here for a while last year. I came to fix the gas.'

BEN TRAVERS
94 Declared
(1981)

Bonnor and the Umpire

When George Bonnor was batting in a county match in England they put a lob bowler on a bowl, and when George came in this chap had only two balls to finish his over. As soon as the ball left the bowler's hand, Bonnor came skipping down the pitch to meet it on the full, six feet eight high he was, and covering as much ground at every jump as a kangaroo. He was nearly down at the other wicket when he met the ball and the umpire and the bowler thought that if he hit it at them, he would kill them. So they started to run round and round each other, each trying to hide behind the other and pushing and cursing a treat. Well, George didn't hit it at them, but he hit it so hard that everybody lost sight of it for a minute. It was probably the biggest hit ever made on any cricket ground in the world and even then it was caught. Of course I wasn't there, but Charlie Bannerman was there and he told me about it and I always believed every word that Charlie Bannerman said. Charlie told me that this ball was caught by a chap fielding at deep third man in a match that was being played in another county altogether.

After that, there was another sensation. This lob bowler had to finish his over, and after his narrow escape he was badly rattled. The umpire was rattled too, and this is what happened. The lob bowler tried to pitch one wide out where

Bonnor couldn't reach it, but in his excitement he dragged over the crease and the umpire called, 'No ball'. Then, when he saw how far out the ball was going, he didn't dream that Bonnor could reach it so he called 'Wide'. But Bonnor could reach anything and the next thing the umpire said was, 'No, by heavens he's hit it.' Then a fieldsman caught the ball and the umpire said, 'Well caught! Out.' Then he pulled himself together and said, 'Not out. Over.'

So his decision ran 'No ball, wide, no by heavens he's hit it, well caught, out, not out, over', all in one breath as you might say. I see that Woodfull had some trouble with the umpires in Melbourne the other day. I don't know how he'd have got on with this umpire.

A.B. 'BANJO' PATERSON
Songs of the Pen: Collected Works 1901–41
(1983)

Mr Kipling Refers to Cricket

Shortly after Mr Rudyard Kipling wrote *The Islanders*, in which appeared the words 'flannelled fools at the wicket or the muddled oafs at the goals,' I happened to be in Cape Town, and had the good fortune to meet Mr Kipling. In the same party was the late Colonel Gordon Neilson DSO, a Scottish Rugby International, and he ventured to ask Mr Kipling whether he had not been rather hard on cricketers and footballers. He replied, 'Possibly, but if you don't exaggerate no one will take any notice,' and he added, 'You have to hit an Englishman more than once on the jaw before he will take a thing seriously. Look at the Boer War, for instance, with its "We shall be in Pretoria by Xmas."'

He also remarked that he 'imagined a cricket ground in Hell would be something like the Wanderers ground at Johannesburg,' which is now grass, but in those days was all red sand with a peacock-coloured matting wicket like an oasis in the middle of a desert. Yet many a cricketer has a very warm corner in his heart for the famous old ground where, in 1906, an ever-famous Test Match was played.

Mr Kipling refers to cricket again in his 'Kitchener's School':

> How is this reason (which is their reason) to judge a
>   scholar's worth,
> By casting a ball at three straight sticks and defending
>   the same with a fourth?
> But this they do (which is doubtless a spell) and other
>   matters more strange,
> Until, by the operation of years, the hearts of their
>   scholars change.

P.F. WARNER
in *The Cricketer*
(March 1936)

A Caravan of Bats

Neither, the Foreign Office nor the MCC has seen fit to comment on a report from Kalimpong that a large consignment of cricket bats, transported on the backs of mules, is on its way to Lhasa at the behest of the education authorities in Tibet. Accustomed as we are to being baffled by International affairs, it is difficult to recall any recent development in that sphere of which the significance was harder to evaluate. There is, of course, nothing odd in the Tibetans wanting to play cricket: the natural and salutary aspiration does them credit. The mountain torrents of their native land and her frequently frozen lakes severely limit the opportunities open to wet-bobs, and it was perhaps inevitable that a passion for our national sport, repressed for centuries, should break out sooner or later.

It is, all the same, a little surprising that King Willow should come into his own at a time when Tibet is under Communist control ... It seems all too probable that the report from Kalimpong may foreshadow the launching of a vast conspiracy throughout the New Democracies to undermine the influence of cricket by evolving a similar but ideologically sounder game. How fast or how far this threat to one of our dearest institutions may develop it is impossible to say. It depends to a certain extent on whether the people in Lhasa remembered to order any balls.

Leading article in *The Times*
(12 May 1952)

Alfred Jingle b. Quanko Samba

'Capital game – well played – some strokes admirable,' said the stranger as both sides crowded into a tent, at the conclusion of the game.

'You have played it, sir?' inquired Mr Wardle, who had been much amused by his loquacity.

'Played it! Think I have – thousands of times – not here – West Indies – exciting thing – hot work – very.'

'It must be rather a warm pursuit in such a climate,' observed Mr Pickwick.

'Warm! – red-hot – scorching – glowing – Played a match once – single wicket – friend the Colonel – Sir Thomas Blazo – who should get greatest number of runs. – Won the toss – first innings – seven o'clock, a.m. – six natives to look out – went in; kept in – heat intense – natives all fainted – taken away – fresh half-dozen ordered – fainted also – Blazo bowling – supported by two natives – couldn't bowl me out – fainted too – cleared away Colonel – wouldn't give in – faithful attendant – Quanko

Samba – last man left – sun so hot, bat in blisters, ball scorched brown – five hundred and seventy runs – rather exhausted – Quanko mustered up last remaining strength – bowled me out – had a bath, and went out to dinner.'

'And what became of what's-his-name, sir?' inquired an old gentleman.

'Blazo?'

'No – the other gentleman.'

'Quanko Samba?'

'Yes, sir.'

'Poor Quanko – never recovered it – bowled on, on my account – bowled off, on his own – died sir.' Here the stranger buried his countenance in a brown jug, but whether to hide his emotion or imbibe its contents, we cannot distinctly affirm. We only know that he paused suddenly, drew a long and deep breath, and looked anxiously on, as two of the principal members of the Dingley Dell club approached Mr Pickwick, and said –

'We are about to partake of a plain dinner at the Blue Lion, sir; we hope you and your friends will join us.'

'Of course,' said Mr Wardle, 'among our friends we include Mr – '; and he looked towards the stranger.

'Jingle,' said that versatile gentleman, taking the hint at once. 'Jingle – Alfred Jingle, Esq., of No Hall, Nowhere.'

CHARLES DICKENS
Pickwick Papers
(1837)

Joseph Conrad at Canterbury

I did not see him again until not long before he died and under very unexpected conditions, for it was in the Kent county cricket ground during the Canterbury week.

For the most part this ground is a mass-meeting of

motor-cars, but on this afternoon the placidity of the game was suddenly broken into by the notes of a guard's horn, and in rolled a coach-and-four driven by a benign gentleman in gold spectacles and a white hat who might almost have come over from Dingley Dell. Behind him, on the next seat, was a distinguished bearded foreigner, amusedly surveying the scene through a single eyeglass. When I came to look again I saw that the driver was J.B. Pinker, the literary agent, since dead, and the distinguished bearded foreigner was Joseph Conrad. After the horses had been taken out and the vehicle was transformed into a private box, I joined the party, and for an hour or so sat with Conrad and did my best to qualify him to go in first for Poland. Cricket was strange to him, but he liked the crowd, and all our excitement about such trifles as bats and balls fed his sense of irony. Again the thought struck me that there can be no defence like elaborate courtesy.

I noticed that he had become much more restful; prosperity was suiting him; and, although grey, he was handsomer than ever, and his eyes as luminous. But for his gout, he said, he would be perfectly happy.

E.V. LUCAS
Reading, Writing and Remembering
(1932)

An Editor Demonstrates

One day Scott [C.P. Scott, editor of the *Manchester Guardian* 1872–1929] revealed that he had not altogether removed me from the kaleidoscope of his memory. I had returned from Old Trafford and written my column, had dined in my club and looked in at the office on my way home. A message waited for me on my desk; he wished to see me.

'Sit down, Cardus,' he said. 'I have been reading the proof of your cricket article. Now, as you know, the first rule on my paper is accuracy. You can be as fanciful with your prose as you like, but only from the basis of strict attention to the facts.' He paused, and I waited for the thunderbolt.

'Now,' he continued, 'in your article today you write of a batsman playing with a straight bat, and you describe that his right elbow suggested an inverted V, and you compliment him in consequence. Now I agree that the inverted V metaphor is quite good. But surely you mean that it was the batsman's left not his right elbow that was so shaped?' To my horror he walked to the fireplace, picked up a long brass poker and went through the action of a right-handed batsman playing back with his left arm immaculately arched, to keep the bat straight. 'I once played cricket myself when I was a boy – years and years ago, maybe, but I remember it all. When a batsman wishes to keep his bat straight, it is his left arm, not his right, that should suggest the inverted V. You must be careful, my dear fellow. Observation must always precede and control fancy and metaphor. Don't let it happen again, please.'

Terror in my heart accumulated as he spoke; for he had walked into an awful hole, and I feared to expose his blunder to him. But for my own sake it had to be done. Swallowing apprehension, I said: 'Yes, sir – but you see I was writing about Woolley; he's a left-hander – so well known that there's no need to allude to his left-handedness ... and when a left-hander plays a straight bat it is his right arm that...'

He stopped me. I shall not forget it to my dying day. He said: 'Cardus, I'm sorry. My mistake; my ignorance. I shall never again question one of my special writers on a point involving his own knowledge and observation.' This was the most terrible of many experiences with C.P.S. in his room. I felt I had almost handed him the rope for his

317

hanging or tripping – I had let him go on with his description of how he himself had once played forward; I had let him perform before me with a poker. I never afterwards dared to refer in conversation with him to this incident, not in our most friendly moments.

NEVILLE CARDUS
Autobiography
(1947)

A Distant Report

The worst thing I ever perpetrated must now be confessed. In those days I was private secretary to my cousin in Lloyd's. He knew nothing about cricket, but liked people in The Room telling him they were interested in what I wrote. At the last moment, owing to pressure of insurance work, he cancelled his permission for me to go up North for a Test. This placed me in a predicament, for if I notified the paper, not only should I involve it in a difficulty about a tardy substitute, but also I might never again be entrusted with this work. So, with the help of every evening paper, I proceeded to describe the match in detail just as if I were looking on, and my personal knowledge of the idiosyncrasies of those taking part enabled me boldly to put in individual touches. I suffered tortures of anxiety, but not only did it all go through well, but this was the only match I ever described which any editor – in this case Sir Arthur Pearson – deemed deserving of a personal letter of appreciation.

SIR HOME GORDON, BT.
Background of Cricket
(1939)

The First English Tour of the USA (1859)

Fred Lillywhite too accompanied us as reporter, and took his printing-press and scoring-tent along with him. . . .

I recollect that Fred Lillywhite's printing-tent was a great nuisance to us on the journey. It was a most complicated arrangement, and took a lot of carting about, and he was always complaining that the railway porters did not stow it away properly, until at last George Parr lost all patience and in pretty plain language consigned both Fred and his tent to an unmentionable region. . . .

Fred Lillywhite's printing-tent had been lost on the journey, and consequently there were 'no cards' on the first day at Hamilton.

WILLIAM CAFFYN
Seventy-one Not Out
(1899)

A Bizarre Pilgrimage

Bullocky was absent 'without a satisfactory reason' on 13 June 1868, when the Australian Aborigines commenced their second innings at Lord's. Without its opening batsman, the team collapsed before the attack of the Earl of Coventry, Viscount Downe and the other officers and gentlemen representing the Marylebone Cricket Club. Although they had compiled 185 runs in their first innings, and Lieutenant-Colonel Bathurst twice failed to score against them, the Aborigines lost by 55 runs. It was a decade before the first white Australians took the field at Lord's, and fourteen years before a mythological cremation created 'the Ashes'.

Bullocky's bizarre pilgrimage to Lord's began on 16 September 1867 when with twelve Aboriginal team-mates, cook, coachman, English captain and Australian manager, he rolled out of the western Victorian hamlet of Edenhope, in 'a large American waggon drawn by four horses, supplied with tents and "tucker"'. That night their wagon bogged on the track. However, even the continuous rain during their eight-day trek to the coast at Warrnambool, under 150 miles distant, failed to dampen the team spirit for nocturnal hunting forays after possum and kangaroo. Charles Lawrence, their 'new-chum' captain and coach, cheerfully adapted himself to the conditions and joined the hunters.

The team made an auspicious entry on to the field to open its Victorian tour. At Warrnambool it scored 140, and then twice dismissed the sixteen-man European side for a total of 43 runs. Their exit from the colony was even more auspicious. They proceeded in leisurely fashion from Warrnambool to Geelong, playing cricket at Mortlake *en route*. After the second of their two Geelong matches against the Corio Club, and before supposedly resuming their Victorian tour, they drove to Queenscliff on 22 October for a fishing holiday. A brief game concluded at Queenscliff, they went fishing near the entrance to Port Phillip Bay. On the same day the coastal vessel *Rangatira*, 460 tons, sailed from Melbourne. Off Queenscliff the Aboriginal anglers boarded her and, as steerage passengers, they were spirited out of the Colony.

D.J. MULVANEY
Cricket Walkabout
(1967)

Parnell Declines

That great Irishman [C.S. Parnell] was always keen on cricket. When the Free Foresters were in New York, being one short they asked him to play in a match which the American press was erroneously entitling England v. United States. Parnell regretfully declined, his refusal being:

'It won't do. If it was in the papers that I had played for a side called England, there would be no end of a row.'

SIR HOME GORDON, BT.
Background of Cricket
(1939)

Pick, Pack, Pock, Puck

The fellows were practising long shies and bowling lobs and slow twisters. In the soft grey silence he could hear the bump of the balls: and from here and from there through the quiet air the sound of the cricket bats: pick, pack, pock, puck: like drops of water in a fountain falling softly in the brimming bowl.

JAMES JOYCE
A Portrait of the Artist as a Young Man
(1916)

Mitford Meets Fennex

One evening we had been practising so much to our own satisfaction that one of our number, doing what he pleased with the bowling, fancied that for the time, with eye well in, he could keep up his wicket against Lillywhite himself. Just then it happened that I observed a hale and hearty man of between fifty and sixty years of age, leaning on his stick, with a critical expression of countenance which induced me to say, 'I think from the interest you take in our game that you have been a player in your day.' This led

321

to a few observations about a defect in my friend's play, and eventually Fennex, for he it was, offered to bowl a few balls. Much to our surprise he rattled about our stumps in a way that showed us that in the art of cricket there was, after all, a great deal more 'than was dreamt of in our philosophy.'

THE REV. JOHN MITFORD
quoted by THE REV. JAMES PYCROFT
The Cricket Field
(1851)

H.G. Wells

I like Wells, an odd bird, though. The first time I met him, we had barely finished the initial pip-pipping when he said, apropos of nothing, 'My father was a professional cricketer.' If there's a good answer to that, you tell me.

P.G. WODEHOUSE
Letter to William Townend, August 1932
Performing Flea
(1953)

Hutton's Son

The most tedious result of being the son of a famous father is that when introduced to certain people by others, I am often introduced as 'the son of Sir Leonard Hutton', and not by my own name. This can often lead to embarrassment, when the person to whom I am introduced is not quite sure who Sir Leonard Hutton is or was. When I was in South America with the MCC, I was introduced as such to one gentleman, who said, 'Ah, delighted to meet you. Yes, I remember your father well, used to bowl fast for

Hampshire.' Which comment caused much merriment amongst my fellow players. During this same tour an elderly English gentleman, who was living out his latter days in the Hurlingham Club in Buenos Aires, insisted for a fact that my father used to open the batting with Jack Hobbs for Surrey! Indeed, he went further to say that he himself had once opened the batting for Surrey with Hobbs!

RICHARD HUTTON
in *The Cricketer*
(March 1967)

SADNESS

A Harmless Lunatic

In the neighbourhood of Loose, in Kent, there lived, I remember, many years ago, a poor harmless lunatic, remarkable for the craze of imagining himself to be a man beside himself, that is, he was two identities in one. His name was Sam Marler – Sam was one person, Marler was another. He used to hold such conversations with himself that, if he were heard and not seen, one might believe that two persons were speaking in the presence of each other. The poor fellow lived sometimes with one relative until they tired of him, then another would take him. His relatives were respectable farmers, and it seemed that every one compassionated him. However the ravings and gibberings of the insane moved our compassion and sympathy, there was something in his babblings so remarkable as often to excite surprise and even amusement. 'How are ye, Sam?' one would say when met. 'How's Marler?' 'Very well when I saw him last,' would be the answer. One of his most extraordinary caprices was his fondness for cricket. His talk was chiefly about it; his dreams, marvellous to relate, were as rational as if there were no aberrations of intellect, which was confirmed by his talk in them. All about cricket. He would go miles to see a county match, and his talk would be as sensible about the merits and demerits of the players as if one of them.

One morning he was observed with a bag containing bat, ball, and stumps for single wicket trudging along a path in a meadow. 'Hilloa, Sam, where be ye going so yearly this morn?' said one of his uncle's men. 'Going to have a match with Marler.' 'I'll come and see you both.' 'Better not.' 'Why?' 'He don't like it. We want to have it all to ourselves.'

However, the man followed, unperceived by Sam and his *alter ego*, inquisitive to see a cricket match with an eleven minus ten. He was observed to set up the wicket all right with the bail balanced at top, and after moistening his hand from his mouth he gave the ball lying on the ground a strike and then took two hearty runs. 'Score two, Marler.' 'All right, Sam.' When he fetched the ball and his poor mind saw his *alter ego* at the wicket, he bowled him out, and then, clapping his hands, gathered up the stumps, bat, and ball, and proceeded on his way. 'Beat you by six runs, Marler.' 'It's a lie, Sam.' 'That's another lie; I'll fight you for it.' He was then seen deliberately to take off his jacket, throw his cap down, remoisten his hands, and square at his vision. Many vigorous rights and lefts did he vent upon the pure air, and after two or three imaginary rounds he put on his jacket and hat and went his way with his bat-bag under his arm, muttering, 'You'll know better than call me a liar agen. Call a cricketer a liar indeed. Why, the devil knows better than that.'

He was followed once by a stranger unknown by him to a small ditch across a field. 'Bet ye sixpence, Sam, I jump over this ditch.' 'Done,' said imaginary Marler. He jumped clean to the other side. 'You owe me sixpence, Sam.' 'Yes, Marler.' He came to a broader part of the stream. 'Bet you another sixpence, Sam, I jump this.' 'Is it a bet Sam?' 'Yes.' Marler in jumping came plump up to his middle in the water of it. Wading to the other side he shook himself like a water spaniel, saying, 'We're level now, Sam.' 'Yes, Marler.'

Amongst the few serviceable things he could do or be entrusted with, he could plough with the aid of a boy as well almost as any ploughman. Only at times of full moon was he obstreperous, and then his little sister, hardly out of her babyhood, could manage him better than anyone else.

'What are you laughing at, you impudent fellow?' said the parish clergyman to one whom he was catechizing

and instructing in his duty. 'Please, sir,' said the boy, 'Sam
Marler asked me if there be any cricketers in heaven.'

'AN OLD CRICKETER' (CHARLES BOX?)

A Cricketer's Notebook

(1881)

The Sadness of Cricket
(Many facts from The Golden Age of Cricket 1890–1914 by David Frith)

The happy summer game, where fun
lies like a playful cat in golden sun –
true innocence in every ball and every run –

where all is for the best, they say,
nostalgia only when it goes away –
romantic memories that haunt the close of play –

is like that poem, 'Dover Beach',
like Arnold's lovely world it's out of reach,
and there are other lessons it might also teach.

How golden lads of Housman's sort
lose all that beauty and can end up caught –
by portliness – and far too fond of gin and port.

And how the agile cover point
slows with arthritis in each stiffened joint –
his briskest fielding now would only disappoint.

Those godlike carefree flashing blades
don't flash for ever in that field of shades
and time can trump a Trumper[1] like an ace of spades.

All right for private incomes, turn
to them they could, money they had to burn,
the amateurs, the Gentlemen! But Players earn

their living in a young man's game –
when they retire it's never quite the same.
If they despaired, would they be very much to blame?

Coaches and pros at public schools,
they taught the rudiments to flannelled fools;
like swimmers striking out in private swimming pools,

the young were trained in all the strokes.
But did *they* feel like victims of a hoax?
Famous fast bowlers, run to fat, now schoolboy jokes?

We'd one at Wellington, that A.E. Relf,
who'd bowled for England – since long on the shelf –
in 1937 stalled and shot himself.

Remembered bowling in the nets,
a little irritable (I thought – but one forgets),
doling out stumps to junior games, like doubtful debts,

from the Pavilion's mean back door.
He had this job, I wouldn't think him poor,
but losing it would put him firmly on the floor.

Professionals lose jobs? They could.
Respectful, yes, you had to be – and 'good'.
Some amateurs cut loose, but it was understood

that there was really no appeal
(although it seems to me a dodgy deal)
when Players misbehaved; witness the case of Peel[2],

a Yorkshire bowler, too content
to stay in the beer tent, his favourite tent.
A Test Match bowler too, but did Lord Hawke relent?

Peed on the pitch! A County game
was scene of his unheard-of drunken shame.
Hawke threw him out; and Peel's a long-forgotten name.

Pro with a County? Umpire? Then
that was 'retirement' for such humble men.
Cricket Schools? Sports goods? These were rare in 1910.

Though Gunn[3] made bats. The 'Autograph'
by Gunn & Moore, his sporting epitaph.
Used once by me. My batting, though, would make you
   laugh.

Strength, talent gone – then what to do?
Great Albert Trott[4], like Relf, was gunned down too
by his own hand in Willesden – very sad but true.

'His powers waned in 1904'
the record says – and just £4, no more,
was found, his wardrobe left to landlady. The score

of that fine bowler/batsman: small.
'He liked a pint'; but dropsy took it all.
In 1914 – thousands more about to fall –

Harry Graham and Johnny Briggs
died in asylums – and among the prigs
who wouldn't fancy Burns (corn rigs and barley rigs)

you might count batsman A.E. Knight[5],
'mental' perhaps, at least not over-bright,
who prayed while batting – an extraordinary sight!

And Arthur Shrewsbury[6], tipped by Grace
as runner-up in the Great Batsman Race –
he was a suicide. He couldn't stand the pace;

thousands of runs that he amassed
made Grace a generous enthusiast
but didn't help. And Aubrey Faulkner[7], too, was gassed

in London, 1930, by
his own sad hand. It makes you want to cry –
but all they wanted was some peace, simply to die.

And Arthur Woodcock[8] also went,
in 1910, by his own poison sent
to that far bourne. Each cricket season was lent

to Leicestershire. He coached the lads
at an American College; and their Dads
remembered him as fast as Kortright. Oiks and cads

such may have been. At 44
he thought it time to leave and shut the door ...
The Gentlemen had deaths as well, but in the War.

Poor Stoddart[9] was another case,
who shared great opening partnerships with Grace –
but shot himself at 52. Life's hard to face!

The blazer and the ribboned coat?
The most pathetic soul for Charon's boat
was Percy Frederick Hardy[10] – he just cut his throat

at King's Cross Station; old and mean,
the Fates attacked him, March 1916.
Ten years for Somerset, a useful pro, he'd been

scared of the Front, the shells, the mud.
A public lavatory received his blood.
The County of London Yeomanry found him a dud.

The Captains toss. It's Heads or Tails;
but Time and Death at last remove the bails,
though you weep buckets of the Bard's prophetic pails.

You can work gents into the mix.
George Lohmann[11] died (T.B.) at 36,
and Alfred Lyttelton[12] was himself hit for six –

an abscess from a cricket ball,
a Cabinet Minister when toffs walked tall.
A famous Foster[13] was most interesting of all –

one of the Worcester brothers who
made Worcester Fostershire, and rightly too.
Down in the world he went, an easy thing to do.

A tart was murdered, and police
knew that he knew her. Questions didn't cease,
frequent as cigarette burns on a mantelpiece.

He took her home (200 fags,
a bottle of Scotch whisky bought – old bags
like this) but she was young and not the kind that nags.

At 20 Nora Upchurch had
gone loose in London – also to the bad.
Strangled in Shaftesbury Avenue (that's also trad).

An empty house. A man called Field
confessed to Press, and all was then 'revealed'
that for two years had been quite well concealed.

'Not guilty' at Old Bailey (he
retracted all he'd said), in '33
he walked away, he was released, completely free.

But later tried the same trick twice.
This time the jury turned out not so nice.
You win some, lose some, it's the shaking of the dice.

Nobody gets away with much.
Even late cuts, the Ranjitsinhji[14] touch,
leg glances, don't impress the fates and gods and such.

A Gorgon married C.B. Fry[15].
Call no man lucky till he's come to die;
So said the Greeks, and they had ancient reasons why.

Notes

1. *Victor Trumper (1877–1915)* One of the greatest Australian batsmen. Like Grace and Hobbs, he could make high scores on very difficult wickets. He died at the age of 37.

2. *Bobby Peel* Yorkshire bowler (Yorkshire won the County Championship nine times between 1893 and 1912). He took 102 Test wickets against Australia; once winning a Test by ten runs (taking 6 for 67) but had to be sobered up in a cold shower beforehand by his Captain.

3. *William Gunn* A great Nottinghamshire and England batsman (George Gunn was his only slightly less famous brother). In 1896 he went on strike, refusing to play in a Test team unless he was paid £20, instead of the usual £10. He died a wealthy man – because of his partnership in Gunn & Moore.

4. *Albert Trott* An Australian bowler with several styles, and a tremendous hitter. He took 8 for 43 in his first Test against England. When the selectors ignored him, he played as a pro for Middlesex (4 wickets in 4 balls and later a hat-trick against Somerset, in his benefit match in 1907). In 1899 and 1900 made over 1,000 runs, took 200 wickets in each season. An umpire in 1910.

5. *Albert Knight* Went to Australia with P.F. Warner's team of 1903–04. He is slandered in the poem, since he was apparently 'thoughtful and well-read'. Nevertheless the Lancashire fast bowler Walter Brearley is supposed to have reported him to the MCC for praying during an innings.

6. *Arthur Shrewsbury* The greatest professional batsman of the 1880s and 1890s. His 164 on a dangerous pitch in the Lord's Test of 1886, against the bowling of Spofforth, is reckoned one of the finest innings ever played. He was an opening batsman of extraordinary patience. He captained England in seven Tests in Australia. Committed suicide in 1903, aged 47.

7. *Aubrey Faulkner* A South African Test cricketer, who also played for the Gentlemen. Very successful in the 1909–10 series against England. A DSO in the War.

8. *Arthur Woodcock* Described as 'a magnificent specimen of Midlands manhood'. Kortright was the fastest bowler of his day, and at his best Woodcock was thought to be as fast.

9. *A.E. Stoddart* Captain of England at cricket and rugby. While leading England in the 1894–95 tour, he made 173 at Melbourne – highest score by an England captain in Australia until 1975. In his last match for Middlesex in 1900 he scored 221. His opening partnerships with W.G. Grace were legendary. He shot himself in 1915, soon after his 52nd birthday.

10. *Percy Frederick Hardy* He was a Dorset-born left-hander, but played for Somerset. Top score: 91 against Kent at Taunton in 1910.

11. *George Lohmann* One of the 'strikers' of 1896, and a principal professional bowler for Surrey. Took 100 wickets, for example, in 1892 – when Surrey were champions for the third year running.

12. *Alfred Lyttelton* Brother-in-law of Arthur Balfour, Prime Minister. Wicket-keeper batsman for Eton, Cambridge, Middlesex, Worcestershire, the Gentlemen and England. In 1884, in a Test at the Oval, he

removed his wicket-keeper's pads and took 4 for 19 with underarm lobs. In 1913, when he was 56, a blow from the ball caused an internal abscess – from which he died.

13. *The Fosters* There were seven Foster brothers, sons of a Malvern clergyman. R.E. ('Tip') Foster made two centuries at Lord's in his first appearance for the Gentlemen. He was the only brother to play for England (287 in his first Test v. Australia, 1903–04). He captained England in South Africa (1907). Once hit W.G. Grace for four consecutive sixes. Died of diabetes in 1914, aged 36. For details of the Field case, see *A Reasonable Doubt* by Julian Symons. (Editor's note: The poet has apparently slipped up. F.R. Foster, who was linked to the Field case, captained Warwickshire; he was not related to the Worcestershire Fosters.)

14. *K.S. Ranjitsinhji* The famous Indian Prince who played for Cambridge, Sussex and England. A great stylist, he was the first man to score 3,000 runs in a season.

15. *C.B. Fry* The blue-eyed boy. Scholar, athlete, footballer (Association and Rugby Union), journalist, Naval officer, schoolmaster. Played for Sussex and England. Six successive first-class centuries in 1901 (still a record). Married Beatrice Sumner, a very tough lady who (after his death) took over command of a training ship for Royal Naval cadets, forbidding all masturbation, dumb insolence and answering back.

GAVIN EWART
in *Poetry Review*
(June 1986)

Eddie Gilbert

The Queensland aboriginal cricketer Eddie Gilbert, famed for his bursts of express bowling during the 1930s, had not been heard of for so long that I took it upon myself when in Brisbane to track him down.

An old-timer in the suburb of Red Hill, where Eddie was last seen, thought he had died about five years before. We checked in the general store run by a cricket fan of some sixty summers:

'I'd just about swear to it. Old Eddie went right out of circulation and we never heard nothin' of him for ages. I reckon he must've died ten years back at least. They had him in Goodna for a while.'

I drove out to the psychiatric hospital along the Ipswich Road in the hope of establishing the truth of the matter. The superintendent, barely concealing his surprise at my questions, led me through to the records office, where he produced Eddie Gilbert's hospital history card.

'Eddie was admitted on December 8th, 1949. His age was shown as 37.'

I thought he would have been slightly older than that; perhaps the paperwork was completed hastily that sad day.

'If you're writing about him,' the superintendent volunteered, 'I can tell you a few things. He took six wickets in his last game for Queensland. Terrific bowler – only ran half a dozen steps. He got the knack from boomerang throwing. Some reckoned he chucked, but I never thought so. It was just his funny wrist action. Wish we had somebody like him right now.'

Some weeks earlier Bill Hunt, the pre-war New South Wales player, had been in no doubt about it:

'Eddie threw *me* out! By cripes, yeah! And later on I deliberately did the same to him. And d'you know what he said? ... I'll tell you. He put his arm round my shoulder and said "Well bowled, Bill. That was a beauty!" So you see, the little fellah couldn't tell a bowl from a chuck anyway! Nice chap, but.'

It was Hunt's contention that Stan McCabe, whose name will live for three classic Test innings, himself considered his best hand to have been a 229 not out against Queensland at Brisbane in 1931 after Eddie Gilbert had served Don Bradman with 'the luckiest duck I ever made'.

The lithe black man that day, bowling with horrifying hostility on an underprepared pitch, had New South Wales in ribbons at 31 for three, with Alan Kippax in hospital after a dreadful blow on the temple from a mis-hook off Thurlow.

336

At that point McCabe took command. . . .

So long ago. Now here was I seeking to trace the conclusion of a life story. The superintendent glanced up from the
history card.

'He was married at the time he came here. Nobody's
visited him for ages. He used to be violent occasionally, but
he's all right now – no trouble. But he's bottled right up
within himself. You won't get him to talk. We've tried
everything. He'll never change. Just as well perhaps. If he
went out again he'd be back among the plonkies down at
the *Adelaide* in no time.'

'You're telling me he's here – alive?'

He nodded. 'As I say, he's completely withdrawn. It's
impossible to get through to him. He walks the grounds all
day – he's content in his own private world. We've tried to
interest him in some kind of recreation: his reflexes are still
sharp. But when we put a cricket ball in his hand he just
stared at it.'

It came as a shock. Eddie – still ticking after all! Even the
locals had seemed so certain. I had fallen into line with them
and quietly and briefly mourned their popular hero of long
ago, the fast bowler to whom they had bellowed encouragement to 'give Jardine a taste of his own bodyline medicine'.

In *That Barambah Mob*, David Forrest's amusing blend
of fact and fantasy, Eddie has already been immortalized:
on the top of Henry Stulpnagel's head was imprinted in
reverse '. . . nufactured in Austra . . .', a living souvenir of a
Gilbert bumper.

'When that ball hit the concrete,' he exclaimed, 'she'd
smoke!'

Mr Stulpnagel also knew why Eddie never became a Test
cricketer: 'He made an ape of Bradman, and he was black,
and he was born in Queensland, and they didn't like the
look o' that whippy wrist of his.'

I made my reverent plea to the superintendent: 'I'd like

337

to see Eddie.'

'It's no use. He won't talk.'

I pressed him. I had to see the historic cricketer.

He picked up the phone and asked the attendant at the appropriate wing to 'find Eddie'.

We walked across the sunlit lawns, past slumbering patients, small-talk lost in the insistent buzz of insects. The coolness in the outer block was a relief.

Eddie was some time in coming. Sitting in the office, I scanned the grounds through the open window. Suddenly a male nurse was standing at the door, and behind him, reluctant to advance, was a thin man in a maroon T-shirt and black shorts. His hair was white and close-cropped, his skin glistening ebony. It was unmistakably Gilbert.

He shuffled into the room, head to one side, eyes averted, impossible to meet. His physique would have been insignificant beside Tom Richardson, Miller or Trueman, yet he was not the midget legend has depicted. Five feet eight, with long arms: the devastating catapult machine he must once have been was apparent.

'Shake hands, Eddie,' his attendant urged kindly.

The hand that had propelled the ball that had smashed so many stumps was raised slowly; it was as limp as a dis-lodged bail. He was muttering huskily and incoherently, gently rocking his head side to side.

'Want a fag, Eddie?' the nurse asked softly.

Eddie grunted, watched the cigarette begin to smoulder, and puffed at it. His legs, typically of his race, were thin. He turned on them restlessly. He was an outdoor man; a room was a cage.

When I asked the nurse if Eddie could write his name for me he coaxed him to pick up the ball-point.

At the end of an agonizing minute Eddie backed away, leaving only a tortured 'E' on the paper. His squinting eyes, deep-set and bloodshot, flashed briefly across all of us.

I thought then of what Archie Jackson, Australia's batting genius, had written about Eddie Gilbert in 1933: 'The adulation he has received has not affected his mental equilibrium. Such a player is an ornament to the game; may he continue to prosper!'

Eddie walked off, still breathing his wheezy monotone; he wandered through the meal hall, and the last I saw of him was as he drifted, a desolate individual, across the parched grass.

DAVID FRITH
in *The Cricketer*
(November 1972)

A Last Game of Cricket

G.N. was a celebrated cricketer of Kent. His power over a bat and ball was of widespread fame. This power was remarkable, as his bodily frame would appear not to admit of any violent exercise. It was too handsome for a man, and all his companions refrained from making any remark in his presence respecting it. In amateur theatricals he was always solicited to take the female characters, which he would decline again and again, and either chose the hero, or the bravado, or the tyrant; but when he did consent, in spite of the false wig, beard, moustache, and whiskers, they could not disguise the feminine beauty of the face. A hectic flush under the cheek bones rivalled the most delicate harepaw rose-blush powder of the would-be-thought most fascinating belle. His unmanliness of aspect was a source of great annoyance to him, and to make it a greater, his voice, disguise it as he might, was as effeminate as his face. Any allusion to either he never forgave, and the greatest compliment you could pay him was his manly character and bearing. Poor N. otherwise was of the most generous and amiable disposition. It was remarked of him that if he could not speak kindly of his companions he

339

would at all risks hide their faults, even at the hazard of his own credit.

He was devotedly attached to the game of cricket, and was always ready with his five or ten pound note to head any subscription to help, as he said, any poor lame dog over a stile, in the crooked path of the life of a cricketer. In three years he became consumptive, and so rapid was the progress of the cruel malady that his eminent physician doubted if he would ever attain his twenty-fifth year.

A small cottage, part of his property, which had served for the convenience of cricketers, as it looked out on the heath of the cricket ground, he had furnished in the latter part of his illness. Then he left his little park and hall altogether, and had taken up his residence to be near his brother cricketers, as his rapidly failing health would no longer admit of a bat. My friend's description of his last interview with him was of the most painful yet interesting character. The little cottage was smothered in roses, honeysuckles, and the wild sweet-scented clematis. It had four rooms only, the front door being between the two latticed windows of the lower rooms. He lay in one of the two rooms upstairs, with the window wide open, that he might observe the process of the game in which, when in good health, he took so much delight. My narrator added, 'My mind was so torn with his dying, loving look that I gave not a ready consent to engage in the game, preferring to sit with him, and to give him as much consolation as in my power. His countenance, still with the tell-tale flush on each cheek, which elsewhere on his face was as white as virgin wax, was a type which the imagination of an angel painter might conceive of those who people heaven. Every time I lifted my eyes up to the little window, as his head lay on a raised cushion, struck me to the heart. I took the opportunity when not engaged to take an armful of sweet hay they were making at a little distance off in the next field, and placed it on the sill of his open window, for I knew he never omitted to give me an invitation to help making his hay with some of his brother cricketers. The look he gave me as his poor wasted handsome hand took mine, saying, "Dear good old fellow, this is kind and thoughtful of you." I hung about his neck until a reproof from his old nurse, "You are doing no good, sir," forced me, sobbing like a coward, down the little stairs, out of the front door, away from the place. He left me, at his death, his gold watch, chain, and seals, his bat and its appendages, his meerschaum, for which he gave a fabulous price, quite a recherché work of art, and which he never smoked, which held, when full, something less than a coffee cup, and £20 for the engraver to commemorate the gift. This was the inscription:

Gift of G.N. to A.N.:
The kindest of hearts, the dearest of friends, and the best of cricketers.

'After his burial I left the club, its locality, and Old England, and remained abroad in India for some time. All other relics are only seen when in my little study, and that's not often; but his watch I have close to my heart in the left waistcoat pocket. I believe this was my last of a game of cricket.'

'AN OLD CRICKETER' (CHARLES BOX?)
A Cricketer's Notebook
(1881)

W.G. on his Deathbed (1915)

Probably the last of his cricket friends to talk to him was Mr Leveson-Gower, who was stationed near by and came over to see him. He said that the air raids worried him. 'You can't be frightened of aeroplanes, old man,' said his visitor. 'You, who had Jones bowling through your beard.'

'That was different,' he answered. 'I could see that Jones, and see what he was at. I can't see the aeroplanes.'

BERNARD DARWIN
W.G. Grace
(1934)

The Presence of Ranji

It is, naturally, at Jamnagar that the presence of Ranji remains most evident. Although the princes have long since been stripped of their titles and their privy purses – within a score of years all Ranji's predictions came to be fulfilled, though whether for the general good or ill is a matter of opinion – in many princely States the trappings, if not the reality, of power survive. Nawanagar was never anything but a minnow in the large pond of princely India but Ranji, by his own prestige and his progressive management of industry and agriculture, saw that it counted for far more than its size might have warranted. Fifty years after his death Jamnagar is still recognizably his city. Cattle may wander beside the bazaars or be parked like motorcars outside the arcades of Willingdon Crescent but the job of clearing and cleansing, that was Ranji's first priority when he became ruler, has not been undone.

The four main palaces of Jamnagar still remain, externally, much as Ranji left them. They may be the habitat of birds and bats, like the enclosed and highly decorated City Palace, or of pet animals, bucks, antelopes, gazelles, like Ranji's preferred Bhavindra Vilas, or simply shuttered and empty, except for the rare cold weather visitor, like the multi-domed Pratap Vilas Palace, or used as a government guest house like Vibha Vilas Palace; but whatever uses, or disuses, they are put to, they stand within their palace walls – the locked gates attended by Arab guards – as stately and resplendent as ever they did.

The grounds, alas, are scarcely kept up and gradually their handsome outbuildings – stables, garages, badminton and racquet courts – are being disposed of or converted. It is ironic that the huge and magnificently ornate Pratap Vilas Palace, which Ranji himself had built, should have received as its first guests his own mourners.

Within, the palaces reek of desertion, though their long corridors are still swept and a residue of ancient palace servants, a dozen or so in all, emerge sleepily from compounds or pantries to preserve the illusion of occupancy.

It is in Ranji's own room in the Jam Palace – the room in which he died – that the illusion is most devotedly fostered. Nothing here has been disturbed since Ranji's body was carried from it. The bed with its silver headboard is made up, and propped against the pillow lies a portrait of the Jam Saheb in ceremonial dress. On a bedside table Sir Pelham Warner's photograph, inscribed 'To Ranji, the greatest batsman of my time, from his sincere admirer and friend "Plum", December 1912' bears witness to Ranji's farewell season in English cricket. Popsey's cage is there, and many portraits; a row of cricket bats the colour of rich tobacco; old uniforms and turbans.

The heart of the room is not the bed but the locked glass cabinet beside which, on a shelf, stands the romantic alabaster head, in the *art nouveau* style, of a beautiful young woman. The cabinet itself contains such items as a letter from George V's secretary commiserating on the King's behalf on the loss of Ranji's eye; Ranji's glasses and cigarette case; his medals and Orders; his half-hunter on its gold chain, a miniature silver bat, a lighter; rings and cuff links and pins; pieces of jewellery.

On the highest of the three shelves Ranji's passport, the photograph in Indian dress with turban and eye-glass, lies open: Caste/Rajput; Religion/Hindoo; Indian home/Na-wanagar; Profession/Ruling Prince; Place and date of birth/Sarodar 10 Sept 1872; Domicile/Nawanagar; Height 5ft 9; Colour of eyes/Dark brown; Colour of hair/Black/grey; Visible distinguishing marks/Smallpox marks on the face.

On the right of this, the six glass eyes which took their turn in Ranji's face are lodged in two satin-lined cases, marked 'G. Muller, 8 New Oxford Street'. For nearly a third of his life the socket of Ranji's eye had each night to be bathed by his doctor. During his years at Jamnagar, Dr Prosser Thomas later recalled, he had made efforts to establish a clinic in the city. Always, though, Ranji would mischievously summon him from his work to make up a four at bridge. Until the last days the ritual of replacing the eye and washing the eye-socket were the only tasks the doctor was allowed to perform.

There are still two servants alive at Jamnagar who have looked after the Jam Saheb. In their old age they carry out their shadow duties, materializing silently on bare feet, much as if His Highness were still alive. They attend and guard his room as if it were a shrine, allowing nothing to be moved.

For all that, Ranji's room is not a solemn place, simply the bedroom of a much loved and revered ruler who, in his day, happened to be a great cricketer. His trophies and personal effects are all around and though the sun streams through the shutters over the marble corridors outside and the hyenas and peacocks screech, within all is shuttered cool.

'When a person dies who does any one thing better than anyone else in the world,' wrote Hazlitt, discussing the fives player John Cavanagh in his famous essay 'Indian Jugglers', 'it leaves a gap in society.' That was certainly true of Ranji. Elsewhere in the same essay Hazlitt wrote, again about Cavanagh: 'He could not have shown himself in any ground in England, but he would have been immediately surrounded with inquisitive gazers, trying to find out in what part of his frame his unrivalled skill lay' – and that was true of Ranji too.

His effect on people was not confined to cricketers. The sculptor Eric Gill observed in his *Autobiography*, published seven years after Ranji's death:

> And while I am thus writing about the beauty and impressiveness of technical prowess I cannot, for it made an immense difference to my mind, omit the famous name of Ranjitsinhji. Even now, when I want to have a little quiet wallow in the thought of something wholly delightful and perfect, I think of Ranji on the county ground at Hove ... There were many minor stars, each with his special and beloved technique, but nothing on earth could approach the special quality of Ranji's batting or fielding ... I only place it on record that such craftsmanship and grace entered into my very soul.

ALAN ROSS
Ranji
(1983)

A Lost Cause

I cannot leave the subject of the game without expressing one great and deep-rooted regret. It applies particularly to first-class cricket and it is this. I have failed to convince the authorities in this country and overseas of the evils of the lbw law introduced in 1935. And as I retire along with others of my generation who had the experience of playing under both laws, I fear the cause is as good as lost.

I am now more than ever convinced that this change in the laws, to which in my infancy and to my everlasting shame I was in some small degree party, was the most disastrous piece of cricket legislation in my lifetime. The 1935 Law was designed to prevent batsman 'padding up' to balls pitching just outside the off stump. Well, this it has done to some extent but the administrators of the day clearly failed to examine in depth the possible by-products of their brain-child. It was argued that it would help all types of bowlers equally and increase off-side play. In the event it has done precisely the opposite, as looking back it was surely going to. As it has helped disproportionately the bowlers who bring the ball in to the batsmen, it has in fact reduced off-side play, has contributed in no small degree to the demise of the leg-spinner and orthodox left-armer and, perhaps worst of all, it has bred a race of front-foot batsmen for safety reasons.

So what have we now got as a general pattern: 'seamers' bowling endlessly at a funereal over rate, off-spinners and an occasional left-armer pushing the ball through flat, to batsmen pushing endlessly forward. Containment is the theme. Efficient it is, backed by brilliant fielding, but variety and a sense of urgency, once amongst the charms of our game, are no longer there.

G.O. ALLEN

Treasurer's Report to the MCC Annual General Meeting
(1976)

September

There is always a sense of sadness about the drawing of the stumps. Standing alone upon the Heath, filled an hour ago with a crowd of excited people, now deserted by all but the workmen taking down the tent, hearing the voices of the players departing in twos and threes dying away in the lanes as the stars come out, you feel the very air breathe a chastened melancholy. But at the end of the season it is doubly sad. To know that the last ball is bowled, the last run made – 'tears inhibit my tongue' as I think of it. Before next season a hundred changes may have happened. The goodly fellowship of our eleven may never meet again unbroken; the calls of business – or that louder call – will have taken some, at least, away. And one change is already determined on, to me as serious almost as any could be. We have played our last match on the Heath. We finished the season gloriously just now, beating the Shalford men after a close match by three wickets; and when old Martin, our umpire, drew the stumps and walked gravely to the tent, the last game upon the old Heath was ended; the scene of a thousand pleasant contests will see us no more.

I protest I feel a choky sensation as I write it, but it is true. The turf, they said, is bad; the furze grows too near; they urged a hundred trifles such as these in favour of the change. The real reason, I believe, is that the mile walk from the village across the Park deters some spectators, and even some lazy players, from coming up. And they are going instead to the new Playing Fields close to the village. The turf there may be as good, the out-fielding a little better, but to me the change is bitterness and vexation of spirit. To break the old associations; to get no more fours up to the Park palings, no more late cuts up to the window where my cousin Frank sits watching us from his invalid chair; to turn no more to look at the clouds rising over the firwoods, or to note between the overs the Peaslake mill standing clear against the August sky – this to me will be like losing an arm.

E.B.V. CHRISTIAN
At the Sign of the Wicket
(1894)

It is well known that George the Second and his son, Frederic, Prince of Wales, during several years previous to the Decease of the latter, lived on terms of complete alienation, or rather of hostility. Scarcely, indeed, were any measures observed, or was any veil drawn, before their mutual recriminations. The Prince expired suddenly, in the beginning of 1751, at Leicester House, in the arms of Desnoyèrs, the celebrated Dancing-Master; who being near his bed side, engaged in playing on the Violin for His Royal Highness's amusement, supported him in his last moments. His end was ultimately caused by an internal Abscess, that had long been forming, in consequence of a blow which he received in the side from a Cricket-Ball, while he was engaged in playing at that game, on the lawn at Cliefden House in Buckinghamshire, where he then principally resided. It did not take place, however, for several months subsequent to the accident. A collection of matter having been produced, which burst in his throat, the discharge instantly suffocated him. The King, his father, though he never went once to visit him during the whole progress of his illness, sent however constantly to make enquiries; and received accounts every two hours, of his state and condition. But he was so far from desiring Frederic's recovery, that on the contrary, he considered such an event, if it should take place, as an object of the utmost regret. He did not even conceal his sentiments on the point: for, I know from good authority, that the King being one day engaged in conversation with the Countess of Yarmouth, when the Page entered, announcing that the Prince was better, 'There now,' said His Majesty, turning to her, 'I told you that he would not die.' On the evening of his Decease, the 20th of March, George the Second had repaired, according to his usual custom, to Lady Yarmouth's Apartments, situated on the ground floor in St James's Palace, where a party of persons of distinction of both sexes, generally assembled for the purpose. His Majesty had just sat down to play, and was engaged at cards, when a Page, dispatched from Leicester House arrived, bringing information that the Prince was no more. He received the intelligence without testifying either emotion or surprise. Then rising, he crossed the room to Lady Yarmouth's table, who was likewise occupied at play; and leaning over her chair, said to her in a low tone of voice, in German, 'Fritz is dode.' Freddy is dead. Having communicated it to her, he instantly withdrew. She followed him, the company broke up, and the News became public. These particulars were related to me by the late Lord Sackville, who made one of Lady Yarmouth's party, and heard the King announce to her his son's Decease.

SIR NATHANIEL WILLIAM WRAXALL, BT.
Historical Memoirs of My Own Time, 1772–1784 Vol. 1
(1815)

Jack Hatch

I do not know, and I begin to fear that I never shall know, Jack Hatch. The first time I had occasion to hear of this worthy was on a most melancholy occurrence. We had lost – I do not like to talk about it, but I cannot tell my story without – we had lost a cricket match, been beaten, and soundly too, by the men of Beech Hill, a neighbouring parish. How this accident happened, I cannot very well tell; the melancholy fact is sufficient. The men of Beech Hill, famous players, in whose families cricket is an hereditary accomplishment, challenged and beat us. After our defeat, we began to comfort ourselves by endeavouring to discover how this misfortune could possibly have befallen. Everyone that has ever had a cold must have experienced the great consolation that is derived from puzzling out the particular act of imprudence from which it sprang; and we, on the same principle, found our affliction somewhat mitigated by the endeavour to trace it to its source. One laid the catastrophe to the wind – a very common scapegoat in the catarrhal calamity – which had, as it were, played us booty, carrying our adversaries' balls right and ours wrong; another laid it to a certain catch missed by Tom Willis, by which means Farmer Thackum, the pride and glory of the Beech Hillers, had two innings; a third to the aforesaid Thackum's remarkable manner of bowling, which is circular, so to say – that is, after taking aim, he makes a sort of chassée on one side, before he delivers his ball, which pantomimic motion had a great effect on the nerves of our eleven, unused to such quadrilling; a fourth imputed our defeat to the over-civility of our umpire, George Gosseltine, a sleek, smooth, silky, soft-spoken person, who stood with his little wand under his arm, smiling through all our disasters – the very image of peace and good-humour; whilst their umpire, Bob Coxe, a roystering, roaring, bullying blade, bounced, and hec-tored, and blustered from his wicket, with the voice of a twelve-pounder; the fifth assented to this opinion, with some extension, asserting that the universal impudence of their side took advantage of the meekness and modesty of ours (*N.B.* – It never occurred to our modesty that they might be the best players), which flattering persuasion appeared likely to prevail, in fault of a better, when all on a sudden the true reason of our defeat seemed to burst at once from half a dozen voices, re-echoed like a chorus by all the others – 'It was entirely owing to the want of Jack Hatch! How could we think of playing without Jack Hatch!'

This was the first I heard of him. My inquiries as to this great player were received with utter astonishment. 'Who is Jack?' 'Not know Jack Hatch!' There was no end of the wonder — 'not to know him, argued myself unknown.' 'Jack Hatch — the best cricketer in the parish, in the county, in the country! Jack Hatch, who had got seven notches at one hit! Jack Hatch, who had trolled and caught out a whole eleven! Jack Hatch, who, besides these marvellous gifts in cricket, was the best bowler and the best musician in the hundred, — could dance a hornpipe and a minuet, sing a whole song-book, bark like a dog, mew like a cat, crow like a cock, and go through Punch from beginning to end! Not know Jack Hatch!'

Half-ashamed of my non-acquaintance with this Admirable Crichton of rural accomplishments, I determined to find him out as soon as possible, and I have been looking for him more or less ever since.

The cricket-ground and the bowling-green were of course the first places of search; but he was always just gone, or not come, or he was there yesterday, or he is expected tomorrow — a tomorrow which, as far as I am concerned, never arrives — the stars were against me. Then I directed my attention to his other acquirements; and once followed a ballad-singer half a mile, who turned out to be a strapping woman in a man's great-coat; and another time pierced a whole mob of urchins to get at a capital Punch — when behold it was the genuine man of puppets, the true squeakery, the 'real Simon Pure', and Jack was as much to seek as ever.

At last I thought that I had actually caught him, and on his own peculiar field, the cricket-ground. We abound in rustic fun, and good humour, and of course in nicknames. A certain senior of fifty, or thereabout, for instance, of very juvenile habits and inclinations, who plays at ball, and marbles, and cricket with all the boys in the parish, and joins a kind merry buoyant heart to an aspect somewhat rough and careworn, has no other appellation that ever I heard but 'Uncle'; I don't think, if by any strange chance he were called by it, that he would know his own name. On the other hand, a little stunted pragmatical urchin, son and heir of Dick Jones, an absolute old man cut shorter, so slow, and stiff, and sturdy, and wordy, passes universally by the title of 'Grandfather' – I have not the least notion that he would answer to Dick. Also a slim, grim-looking, white-headed lad, whose hair is bleached, and his skin browned by the sun, till he is as hideous as an Indian idol, goes, good lack! by the pastoral misnomer of the 'Gentle Shepherd', Oh, manes of Allan Ramsay! the Gentle Shepherd!

Another youth, regular at cricket, but never seen except then, of unknown parish and parentage, and singular uncouthness of person, dress, and demeanour, rough as a badger, ragged as a colt, and sour as verjuice, was known, far more appropriately, by the cognomen of 'Oddity'. Him, in my secret soul, I pitched on for Jack Hatch. In the first place, as I had in the one case a man without a name, and in the other a name without a man, to have found these component parts of individuality meet in the same person, to have made the man to fit the name, and the name fit the man, would have been as pretty a way of solving two enigmas at once as hath been heard of since Œdipus his day. But besides the obvious convenience and suitability of this belief, I had divers other corroborating reasons. Oddity was young, so was Jack; Oddity came up the hill from leeward, so must Jack; Oddity was a capital cricketer, so was Jack; Oddity did not play in our unlucky Beech Hill match, neither did Jack; and last of all, Oddity's name was Jack, a fact I was fortunate enough to ascertain from a pretty damsel who walked up with him to the ground one evening, and who, on seeing him bowl out Tom Coper, could not help exclaiming in soliloquy, as she stood a few yards behind us, looking on with all her heart, 'Well done, Jack!' That moment built up all my hopes; the next knocked them down. I thought I had clutched him, but willing to make assurance doubly sure, I turned to my pretty neighbour (Jack Hatch too had a sweetheart), and said in a tone half affirmative, half interrogatory, 'That young man who plays so well is Jack Hatch?' 'No, ma'am, Jack Bolton!' and Jack Hatch remained still a sound, a name, a mockery.

Well! at last I ceased to look for him, and might possibly have forgotten my curiosity, had not every week produced some circumstance to relumine that active female passion.

I seemed beset by his name, and his presence, invisibly as it were. Will-o'-the-wisp is nothing to him; Puck, in that famous Midsummer Dream, was a quiet goblin compared to Jack Hatch. He haunts one in dark places. The fiddler, whose merry tones come ringing across the orchard in a winter's night from Farmer White's barn, setting the whole village a-dancing, is Jack Hatch. The whistler, who trudges homeward at dusk up Kibe's lane, outpiping the nightingale, in her own month of May, is Jack Hatch. And the indefatigable learner of the bassoon, whose drone, all last harvest, might be heard in the twilight, issuing from the sexton's dwelling on the Little Lea, 'making night hideous', that iniquitous practiser is Jack Hatch.

The name meets me all manner of ways. I have seen it in the newspaper for a prize of pinks; and on the back of a warrant on the charge of poaching — N.B. the constable had my luck, and could not find the culprit, otherwise I might have had some chance of seeing him on that occasion. Things the most remote and discrepant issue in Jack Hatch. He caught Dame Wheeler's squirrel; the Magpie at the Rose owes to him the half-dozen phrases with which he astounds and delights the passers-by; the very dog Tero — an animal of singular habits, who sojourns occasionally at half the houses in the village, making each his home till he is affronted — Tero himself, best and ugliest of finders — a mongrel compounded of terrier, cur, and spaniel — Tero, most remarkable of ugly dogs, inasmuch as he constantly squints, and commonly goes on three legs, holding up first one, and then the other, out of a sort of quadrupedal economy to ease those useful members – Tero himself is said to belong of right and origin to Jack Hatch.

Everywhere that name meets me. 'Twas but a few weeks ago that I heard him asked in church, and a day or two afterwards I saw the tail of the wedding procession, the little lame clerk handing the bridesmaid, and a girl from the Rose running after them with pipes, passing by our house. Nay, this very morning, some one was speaking – Dead! what dead? Jack Hatch dead? – a name, a shadow, a Jack-o'-Lantern! Can Jack Hatch die? Hath he the property of mortality? Can the bell toll for him? Yes! there is the coffin and the pall – all that I shall ever see of him is there! – There are his comrades following in decent sorrow – and the poor pretty bride, leaning on the little clerk. – My search is over – Jack Hatch is dead!

MARY RUSSELL MITFORD
Our Village
(1824)

354

Index of Authors and Sources

BEDE, CUTHBERT (1827–1899)
*The Adventures of Mr Verdant Green, An
   Oxford Freshman* (Blackwood & Co., London,
   1885)   52

BERRY, SCYLD (1954–   )
The Observer (27 November 1977)   213

BETTESWORTH, WALTER AMBROSE (1856–1929)
The Walkers of Southgate (Methuen, London,
   1900)   19
Chats on the Cricket Field (Merritt and Hatcher,
   London, 1910)   43, 210

BLUNDEN, EDMUND CHARLES (1896–1974)
Cricket Country (Collins, London, 1944)   98, 292

BOSE, MIHIR (1947–   )
A Maidan View (Allen & Unwin, London, 1986)   79

BOTHAM, IAN TERRENCE (1955–   )
Ian Botham on Cricket (Cassell, London, 1980)   20, 227

BRADMAN, SIR DONALD GEORGE (1908–   )
The Art of Cricket (Hodder and Stoughton,
   London, 1958)   25, 195

BREWER, REV. E. COBHAM (1810–1897)
A Dictionary of Phrase and Fable (Cassell,
   London, 1970)   143

BRITTENDEN, RICHARD T. (1919–   )
Barclay's World of Cricket (Collins, London,
   1980)   44

BROOKS, REGINALD SHIRLEY
Sporting Times (1882)   291

BUTLER, BRYON
The Cricketer (March 1973)   137

BYRON, GEORGE GORDON NOEL, 6TH BARON
   (1788–1824)
Hours of Idleness (S. & J. Ridge, Newark, 1807)   273

358

363

WELLS, HERBERT GEORGE (1866–1946)
Certain Personal Matters (Lawrence & Bullen,
  London, 1898)   285

WHITE, GILBERT (1720–1793)
Letter to Samuel Barker, 1 August 1786   216

WILSON, FREDERICK BONHOTE (1881–1932)
Sporting Pie (Chapman and Hall, London, 1922)   53, 139, 240

WODEHOUSE, SIR PELHAM GRENVILLE
  (1881–1975)
Psmith in the City (A. & C. Black, London, 1910)   12
Performing Flea (Herbert Jenkins, London, 1953)   322

WOODCOCK, JOHN (1926–   )
The Times (17 September 1986)   143
The Times (17 December 1977)   239
Wisden Cricketers' Almanack (1986)   66

WORDSWORTH, CHARLES (1806–1892)
Annals of my Early Life 1806–46 (Longmans
  Green, London, 1891)   302
Cricket: the Badminton Library, (Longmans
  Green, London, 1888)   269

WRAXALL, SIR NATHANIEL WILLIAM BT.
  (1751–1831)
Historical Memoirs of my Own Time 1772–1784,
  Vol. 1 (T. Cadell & W. Davies, London, 1815)   348

The publishers gratefully acknowledge permission to quote copyright material owned by authors and publishers named above. They also gratefully acknowledge the permissions granted by A. P. Watt Ltd and Jill Gale, by Secker and Warburg Ltd and the late Sonia Brownell Orwell, and by A. P. Watt Ltd on behalf of the Trustees of the Wodehouse Trust No. 3 and Century Hutchinson Ltd.